James Stephenson is a tall fifty-seven-year-old. He has been a type 1 diabetic since the age of four. So, he knows about life-long suffering and the pain this awful condition causes.

He studied accountancy at university and has worked in the public sector for most of his adult life.

He is a healthy optimist who is regularly seen riding his bicycle through the wet and windy countryside. He enjoys watching entertaining films and listening to good music.

He loves writing and gains real pleasure in creating interesting characters so they can dance across the pages.

This book is dedicated to my mum and my inspiring friends.

James Stephenson

TORTANUENCE

AUSTIN MACAULEY PUBLISHERS™

LONDON • CAMBRIDGE • NEW YORK • SHARJAH

A CIP catalogue record for this title is available from the British Library.

ISBN 9781528945806 (Paperback)
ISBN 9781528945813 (Hardback)
ISBN 9781528971492 (ePub e-book)
ISBN 9781398418431 (Audiobook)

www.austinmacauley.com

First Published (2020)
Austin Macauley Publishers Ltd
25 Canada Square
Canary Wharf
London
E14 5LQ

Chapter 1
Expensive Information

It was a July morning and it was still raining. Only light rain this time. Spits and spots of drizzle. Most of the heavy stuff had left the shoreline during the night. Sending itself away into the movement of the sea. Its departure had calmed the breeze and deposited a grim looking skyline. One, wearing a coarse greyness that was straining itself to deposit half measure coatings of water droplets.

Maxwell Oakley was laid out on a bare pavement surface. He was laying on his side and peering across a silver looking puddle. It had captured a piece of the sky in its appearance and he was looking into it for inspiration.

Although it was overcast, the clouds were not uniform. They moved like a fragmented paving spree. Chopped and chafed at the edges. If you looked closely, you could even make out their individual shapes. Each one; weaving into a corrugated line of darkness. Occasionally, cracked open, with powerful crescents of white.

All of this was moving across the surface of a puddle and Maxwell was captivated by this expressionist art. Pondering how so much of heaven could possibly fit into such a small splash of earthly water.

Maxwell Oakley was a self-employed drinker. Of course, he used to drink the finest quality wines and sometimes he partook of the odd glass, or two, of vintage champagne. He adored being at parties; the pageant of being on display to his elders and betters. He rallied in such places, met numerous, interesting and important people. Drank with some of the best and made important business connections with the rest.

He loved those events. He adored the feelings which such pleasures generated. Only, as the work pressures had grown, so did his dependency. He began as the bright boy of the show. He knew how to close deals. So, he was a valuable asset. He could easily bring the money in and sell expensive new contracts, so his behavior was tolerated. Yet, it was not static. He thought that he was enjoying his work, but as the drinking grew, his life gradually lost its girding. He ebbed away into a place where other things began to matter far more. He never lost his focus. It was just that he couldn't find it anymore. He soon started falling apart.

From being the perennial workaholic, he started to became a rowdy alcoholic. With it, the entrepreneur took a step sideways. His life skills began to fade. Something new had appeared. He had started to develop a sharp level of violence. He was always arguing. Endless, pointless arguments, with everyone he could. His relationships folded. And worst of all, he really didn't care anymore. He was happy, but only when he was full of his new love. And, this kind of happiness did not fit well, with his former existence.

His new esteemed self didn't drink quality. It simply became an issue of quantity. Since he had lost his job, he no longer had the income for fine wines. Instead, he grafted and burrowed himself into an off-licence culture. A place of unbranded whiskies, gin and the like. His need was such that he finally stabilized on the beverage of apples. It was cheap and effective and it fulfilled his needs. This was what mattered most. His decaying life had taken him on quite a journey and, this time, it had alighted him with a sharp tangy taste. Dry cider, which came gift-wrapped in a huge pale plastic bottle.

By now, he had convulsively gulped most of the contents down and proceeded to develop hiccups. Somehow, this began to amuse him. At least it did, until he had tumbled off the wooden seat and landed solidly on the ground. His head was scuffed by the fall and it began to bleed.

Unperturbed, in his new state, he was looking out again. His mind was desperately trying to assemble itself. Pulling frantically from the self-enclosed blanket of confusion. Trying to put things into a focused place of understanding. There was a constraint, though. The conflict being; that he didn't want reason or knowledge anymore. He didn't want to understand anything, any longer. He just wanted to escape. Just to escape from it all.

As he lay there, sprawled out. The sky gently dribbled on his features. In his amused state, he noticed that the world was changing shape. It wasn't round anymore. He was certain of it. He really was. It wasn't square, but he knew it wasn't round either. In a misty, mazy haze, he exhibited an awakening of the moment. What if the world was flat? He turned and leant up onto his elbows. Looking at all he could see, he realized that; by God! He was right! Everything was totally flat!

The sky was flat! The puddle was flat! And the pavement was definitely flat! He whacked his hand onto it. His knuckle instantly stung and started to drip with red blood. But, in this swirl of drunken emancipation, his thoughts were all jingling and jangling. Incoherently competing. Each one with each other. He, himself, was clearly drifting away. Like a dinghy in the richness of a mist. Drifting away; into who knows where.

But, then the tide changed, and he was coming back again. It was cool! Sometimes he was on the level and other times his thoughts came along in a great crescendo. Wave upon wave of them. All desperately trying to come to terms with his manifest discovery. The one where the world was no longer three-dimensional. He knew it. It was flat! No doubt remained at all.

He laid down again and looked up. Searching for further inspiration in this place of imaginary mirrors. As he lay by the roadside, a car drove slowly by. Its lights were dancing through his retinas. All he had to do was look and he was sure that it would become even more crystal clear.

On the soggy wet asphalt, Mr Maxwell Oakley was strewn like a semi-wrapped toffee. A toffee encased in an expensive half-open wrapper. Chest down, he was lain. His head turned on its side. Left ear to the ground. His arms were sprawled out. His weathered, navy blue Crombie was unbuttoned and openly spread around his smelly body. All of this was on show; across the wet surface. Just as though he had fluttered down from a low-lying tree branch and unfurled himself.

Surfacing again, he was still drifting through the endless remnants of an ebbing consciousness. Coming and going, he was completely entranced by a world which he no longer understood. Truly amazed by a small circle of water and its deep sense of meaning to his miserable life. He splashed the fingers, of his open hand, into the puddle. It felt good and he loved it.

Bolt upright and just beyond his eyeline, there was a stationary figure. It was holding a thick brown paper bag. He had actually been standing there for a while. Chewing on a piece of liquorice and observing the specimen who was laying on the tarmac. A tall, upstanding gentleman. But, he was soaked right through to the skin. He was also wearing a white tailored shirt. No jacket or coat. His cuffs retained two cufflinks; they were hall-marked and made of gold. Below his waist lay the deepest shade of dark blue jeans. So dark that your eyesight could fall into them. His apparel was all tailor-made. Even his jeans bore the mark of quality. They were cut to perfectly hug his body. All the way down to his ankles. Below which, appeared a line of loosely-moving toes. Barely encased at all. Just aimlessly situated inside the flimsiest of footwear. Sports sandals they were, completely immune to the effects of rain water.

Although he looked nonchalant, that was hardly the case. He was alert and very aware of what was to take place. Standing, as he was, in his expensive clothes and peering down at the disheveled Maxwell Oakley. He was enjoying the moment and discreetly weighing things up. Seeing if there was any real life remaining in the man. As a test, he moved and slightly changed position. Then, he tilted his head to see if this subject was paying attention: he wasn't.

To Wilbur, this pursuit was more intense than it first seemed. He was also aware that something was missing, and that time was moving along. Missing the flavour, he unfurled another quality sweet from the extensive paper bag. He purposely bit it in half and smiled. He was content now. This was indeed the man he needed to see.

A few more moments passed and his confidence grew. It was time to stop observing and make a constructive move. He straightened his back and stood up; straight. He was now just a few feet away and meaningfully looking at a man who lay by the side of a peaceful road. This engaged his curious nature. He understood these kinds of situations well and, in his soggy garments, he quietly came closer.

The result, saw a line of undressed toes materialize; right in front of Maxwell's forehead. They wriggled slightly, for his attention. Slowly, there followed a descent and two deeply blue knees opened wide, before him. He knew what they were and that the space higher up was taken by a man. Perched above the rim of those knees was a dark-haired figure. It came with words and spoke quietly, "I am looking for Mister Bailey."

Max looked bemused. These words meant nothing to him. They went nowhere and were instantly dismissed from his consciousness. The man didn't seem upset. He unfurled something which looked like a large cigarette. Unusually, it was wrapped in some sort of plastic which he proceeded to peel away. Max didn't understand.

Again, came the words, "I'm looking for Mr Bailey." For a moment, the man in the blue jeans didn't move, but then he 'clicked' his tongue against his teeth. Calmly, he went on, "Do you know where he is?"

Max retreated into a shabby look of bewilderment. To him, people didn't enter his world anymore. How could someone ever pretend that he understood? His confusion entrenched itself into the movement of his face. He really was so departed from this world that none of what this man was saying made any sense. None at all. Still, he knew that some sort of reply was needed. So, he garbled his teeth together and said, "I'sh been asheep."

Wilbur raised his eyebrows and waited. He lowered himself again and camped down on his knees. Stationary, still, and fully bent. For that moment, there was silence. Stillness and calm. But then, Wilbur spoke out and, this time, his pitch meaningfully rose. "Is that it? Haven't you got anything else to say?"

Max felt the words, harshly. He also tried to sit up and accommodate their meaning, but he couldn't manage himself to do it. In truth, he really didn't understand. Yet, this man was talking in such a slow and delicate way that he was beginning to pick out some of the fragments. He had to reply with something. He knew he had to. So, he shook his head and waved a dismissively shaking hand.

Wilbur breathed in, through his teeth. He looked down at this weakened creature and felt deeply hurt. He was giving this specimen every last ounce of respect that could be administered. He was trying so very hard to communicate with him; in such a way that he could understand. Being decent, being friendly, being nice. And yet, it wasn't responding. It was becoming completely hopeless. Truly hopeless.

He moved especially close, to the subject, and made deep, resonant eye-to-eye contact. He even placed his wet knees into the puddle. Leaned forward and placed the palms of his hands into the wetness of the surface. Then, he quietly asked, "Nothing… at… all?" and waited.

"Nope," said Max.

Wilbur audibly sighed and slowly nodded his head. He finally understood what he was dealing with. With that in mind, he stood up again and took a refreshing breath of air. His face filled with dismay. "Why does it have to be like this?" he quietly said.

A few seconds later, a drying hand discreetly reached deeper down into a bedraggled paper bag. In the quiet of that July morning, a tall figure leaned slightly forward and there followed a succulent sound. *Pop* it went.

Going onto his knees, for a second time, Wilbur said, "Sometimes it has to be like this." Then, he thoroughly felt inside the worn coat. He was searching for something that should be in there. He came across a tailor's label which read, 'For my Al'. That made no sense. So, he carried on. He ran his hands around the lining and finally, detected something firm near to the inner pocket. He placed his hand inside. Only to find that it couldn't be reached with his fingers. Next, he produced a naked razor blade and cut around the stiffened shape. Whatever it was, it had been roughly sewn into the lining. The stitches were tidy, but they were visible. It felt like a big credit card, and he wanted to see it. He picked away at the stitching and, from the neatest of cuts, he lifted something away from the shiny inside of the Crombie. His face became awash with what had just happened. After which, he patiently rose. Standing upright again and then looking at what he had captured. A white card was attached to a folded note. The note had been torn in two, but the card was intact and it had something written on it: a few scrawly numbers. Hand-written digits. Slanted, shanty capital-sized things. Meaningless, as they were, right now, but nonetheless, he felt their relevance.

It was now raining properly again. Re-energized, the size of the droplets had notably increased and were splattering around, in loose propensity. Wilbur quietly took breath. To him, there was an edge to this cloud. So, he paced his unprotected feet away and headed out, into the cool falling wetness. Taking himself out, in the form of a self-styled shadow. Riding under the snog of a darkened and shady July morning.

***

Chapter 2
Domestic Turbulence

Beccy had woken up first. It was six ten already. Both she and Adrian were supposed to be in town by seven. She kicked him hard in the back and he yelped. "Move your bloody arse now," she said. Next, she leapt out of the matrimonial bed and focused on the weakling who was still laid on her pillow. Out came a pointed finger. "I told you not to go out drinking! Move it now, or you will never get the chance again." She turned around and stomped off into the shower. Crying out, as she banged her elbow on the bathroom door.

Adrian tried to sit up and then immediately felt sick. So, he quickly laid back down. He was still drunk and he knew it. What the hell had got into her? He really didn't know. But, he did recall that they had promised Linda and Brian something or other. Then, it suddenly hit him. "Oh God!" he said. They were supposed to be helping them decorate their flat this morning. The one over the butchers, in the town. He looked at the clock. It was six twenty-two. That was six twenty something: on a Sunday morning. Realizing this; he looked on and started to yawn. Why had she promised this? The last thing he wanted to do was wall paper some walls. All he needed now was some sleep.

Adrian tried looking up again. He knew they were going to help out and he didn't mind. But, not this early in the day! At that moment, Beccy shouted something obscene from the bathroom. So, he attempted to climb out of the bed. But doing so, saw him catch his left leg inside the duvet cover. Although his right leg was free, his body weight was in the wrong position. This meant, he only went one step forward, when there should have been two. As a consequence, his head went straight down; into the bedroom carpet and it tasted foul.

Beccy heard the thump whilst she was spraying herself. *Good,* she thought. He was finally getting a move on.

A second or two later; the bathroom door flew open. Adrian's nose was bleeding everywhere. "Why the hell are we going there now?" he choked out.

"Because!" she replied.

Adrian sat on the closed loo seat, with his forehead in a roll of clean toilet paper and shouted, "Because what?" He pulled handfuls of the paper from the roll and covered his face.

"Because I fucking told you so. That's why!" she said. "And get out whilst I'm showering! I don't like you ogling me."

Adrian lifted his head from his hands, "Ogling you? You're stood behind a bloody red shower curtain, woman. All I can see are a bunch of moving red poppies on the go. And I can assure you, they aren't doing anything for me!"

"Sod off!" she said.

Adrian raised his hand and was about to strike back when he realized it was a waste of venom. This bitch ruled the earth and, after all, he was just playing her game. With that, he lifted her bath towel from the heated rail, wrapped it around his middle and went into the kitchen to make a drink. *That would teach her,* he thought.

The middle of town was well lit this Sunday morning and that was because several blue flashing lights were on the go. Brian didn't know what was happening, but the lights had woken both him and Linda. It looked as though something had just taken place behind one of the main buildings. He couldn't be sure, though. Nothing seemed to be taking place, at the moment and seeing that all was well, he kissed her on her cheek. Then, set off to make a cuppa. By the time he got back nothing much had changed.

He had noticed an ambulance pull away. Leaving a couple of police cars on the street. Nothing sensational. Whatever it was must have already taken place. Linda could remember an old person once passing away on the street. But, that was a few years ago, and she couldn't recall this kind of fuss happening back then.

Now, though, she was looking at Brian. He was nice. He cared about her, and she really did love him. Above all, he was hers and she was going to keep him that way. They had only been married for three months. She was really happy and sure that he was too. She snuggled up to him, which meant Brian had to put his hot cup down.

They lived in a small flat above the butcher's shop. It was a tiny place, perched above a small premises. One bedroom, one kitchen, one bathroom and one loo. A small rectangular living room came off the staircase and a ropey back door lurked below. The wind blew through it, so Linda had draped a long, thick curtain from the rail. It worked. Just, not very well.

The back door took you out into a well-kept church yard; which was as old as the town itself. It was pretty in the sunshine, and they had made this place their home. Which, today, they were going to transform with some new wall paper. The living room walls were a bit tatty. They looked weathered and uneven. So, they had spoken to the owner and got her permission to decorate. Brian had spent the previous week filling the minor holes and cracks with wall filler. They also paid a few pounds for some blown vinyl wall paper. Once it was up, then their aim was to paint it with a new tin of magnolia emulsion paint. That should brighten up their living area a little. Linda was sure that it would be really nice. They might even be able to hang a picture above the fire place? Linda was inspired. She really wanted a cozy room. Maybe Brian would hang one of her own paintings up? She hoped he would.

The rain had petered out by eight o'clock. Beccy had got the Ford Focus out of the parking space, but she had come out in reverse and in a hurry. This meant, she had to drive straight through the old gate posts and pull out onto the road. All of this and backwards too.

She was doing fine until she hit some rubble on the driveway. That caused the car to veer towards the old gate hinges. Why Adrian hadn't removed them she did not know. Nothing had swung on them for years. But, something certainly collided with them now.

Adrian finally came out, with a paint brush, a carrier bag and some paint cleaner; in his hands. He came to the car and that's when he saw it: a whopping great scratch, right down the middle of the driver's door.

He walked around to the passenger side front door and reached out for the handle. At that moment, Beccy stupidly let the clutch up and the whole car jolted forward, causing one of Adrian's fingernails to tear. He yelped out, in pain and shouted, "Will you stop!" She did and then he climbed in. The door slammed shut and not a word was spoken. Beccy just roared off; along the quiet Sunday morning road.

It took fifteen minutes to reach the dual carriageway. Brian and Linda's place was the second turning off. Today was really sultry and, without any words, the atmosphere in the car was becoming anxious. Adrian's hand was also really sore and it had started throbbing. His nail was torn right down the middle. So, he was fuming and Beccy knew it.

They had been together for a while now. She had met him at a local bar after the town rugby club had just won a big game. News about promotion, to the next division, was in the air. And she remembered a night of smiles and laughter: cheering and excess. She knew he could be charming and, that night, he had certainly been all of that. She recalled looking into his eyes and seeing a vulnerable man with lots of potential. All he needed was a little female guidance. She asked him where he worked. He told her that he was an electrician.

So, he was bright then. She also asked where he spent his time and he answered that had just bought a place on the Roughton Road. It needed some work. So, he and his mates were doing it up. Maybe, he would sell it or he could just move in.

He had his own place then! It sounded like heaven to her.

Beccy spent the night with him and over time they got to know one another well. She worked at the local builder's merchant and he started to pop in. Soon, they were living together. Even talking of marriage and children. She decided that she wanted an extension built on the back of the house. Adrian was okay with the idea and began to make plans. Everything seemed to be going well. Until one day, she heard his phone accept a message. He was in the shower at the time. So, she crept over, picked it up and read: 'It was really nice to see you again, Aidy. Don't be afraid to call round. Remember, Sam is never here in the afternoons.'

For Beccy, that was it! The bastard was going to die and she was going clean him out, in the process. He was going to be left alone and broke. Only, they weren't married and she hadn't actually been with him very long. So, she decided that she needed some time to work out a proper strategy. Basically, she knew that she wanted to keep the house. All she had to do, was get rid of the owner. That would teach him!

As they came along the road, she dropped the clutch again, selected the wrong gear and then, let the car engine scream out.

"Try fifth instead of third," said Adrian and concentrated on licking his burning finger.

The sun was fully out now and, in July, it was a powerful aid to warming you up. Wilbur had arrived back at his lodgings. By this time, he was completely dry and had no concerns about developing a chill. He opened the front door with a simple key. Before him was a steep looking staircase. It went up, one level at a time. Right up the entire height of the building. The stairs were attached to the walls. When you reached the first-floor balcony then the staircase swapped sides. It repeated this, all the way up to the fourth floor.

Each floor had its own balcony area; with a balustrade and a few rooms which were tucked in, behind some solid looking doors.

Wilbur knew where his room was. So, he climbed up the first three floors and then headed right to the top. His room was easy to use and high enough to keep any trouble makers away. The building itself was an old Victorian boarding house, the kind you used to see in well-kept areas. Especially at seaside towns.

Complete with its large landlady, his home was perfectly decent and respectable. His room allowed him a commanding view of what was taking place outside. His window faced down onto a wide two-way street. Directly across, he could see onto the distant shores of another four-floor dwelling. That one was dressed up with some glossy tangerine eves. At this height, his room was closeted, comfy and quiet. The sun's rays didn't reach here until it was late afternoon. At this hour, the pale walls just looked bland. But, in the evening sunlight, a richly orange glow completely adorned his little home. Bathing it in a magnificent warming tinge.

Although the room was secluded, if you opened the sash window; then the sound would come up from street below. It only took one car to drive by and you could hear the noise it made. The line of tall buildings made the street into an echo chamber. That meant, you could tell something was approaching, minutes before it arrived. To Wilbur, it was all a part of the spectacle. One which suited him well.

Yet, today had started in the wrong way and Wilbur was feeling disappointed. He had set himself the target of finding Mr Bailey and, for some reason, it just wasn't happening. He paused, looking outside the window of his room and breathing in the summer warmth: he was unhappy. After all this time, he still had no idea where the man could possibly be and that mattered. He pulled the torn piece of paper out of his pocket. A small fragment of something fell onto the floor. He wasn't interested. Instead, he looked at the half letter, in his hand. The words made little sense:

Dear Mr Oakley,

I am anxious to trace your whereabouts, in relation to an outstanding amount of monies which we believe are owed to your former employer: S Kingsley Enterprises.

We have been instructed to take formal recovery action against you and legal proceedings will follow, unless you quickly respond.

We are currently receiving submissions from a pre-hearing counsel and, once the sums involved have been finalized, then we shall take action.

I have undertaken to make a request of your attendance at my office on the morning of July 6th. As you know, your former employer is already aware and their representatives will be in attendance.

Please ask for Stephanie, when you arrive. She will take care of your needs and sufficiently prepare you to see us all in person.

Yours truly

Edvard Soames-Smith and Peterson

The bottom of the page was ripped off, as was a large part of the top. It was dated 6 July, but that could well have been last year. Or a decade ago. In other words, here was the gubbins of a letter. But, without the necessary garbage to make it complete.

Wilbur tentatively put the page down and let his eyes engage with a silver kettle on the dresser. He needed some time to think. He also wanted a hot drink. So, he made his way towards a container full of candlestick beverages. A line of little plastic packets; all standing in a row of attention. They offered a limited unbranded selection of coffee, tea, sugar; some sweeteners and a few tiny packs of dried milk. He chose a coffee sachet and liberated the contents by tearing at the seal. Then, he poured some hot water into a cup and inserted some powered milk. That almost turned it white. Wilbur looked into its texture. Lifting it up, he took a sip. It tasted satisfyingly vile; which is just what he wanted. He continued to carefully sample the appalling concoction and this stimulated his mind. He came alive again, his emotions rose and, then he set firmly to work on the next stage of the puzzle.

***

Chapter 3
A Variety of Combinations

Jenny was adjusting her uniform, in the lounge. She knew that she was a big girl. Her apron used to have spare capacity, but now, it was getting a bit tight. It was definitely restricting her movements. She liked to imagine that this was the result of her hot, hygienic washes. Sixty degrees was a high temperature and that could have caused it to shrink. She thought about that for a while and then delicately felt that whilst her cleanliness was certainly an important part of daily life; her ambitious size may equally be a part of the problem. After all, she did have a desire for the sweeter things in life. Frustratedly, she sighed.

Jenny had run the 'Omregana Guest House' for nearly twenty years. She was immensely proud of her business. A long, prestigious line of distinguished guests had crossed her landings. She had even had film stars staying there. Imagine that! Real-life actors and actresses. Some had even signed pictures and left lovely messages for her. She kept them in her autograph book. She could remember Fren Aims and The Lady Somantha Melder. These days, she wondered what had happened to them. After all, it didn't seem that long ago.

No one like that came here now. The TV studios had closed. These days; only a few films were made there. She couldn't see herself in a horror movie, and the new actors didn't need her facilities anymore. It was a shame. But, what was past is past, she thought and then straightened out one of her table cloths.

She was conscious that the guests would be coming down soon and she always felt better once the kitchen was up and running. Cooking, she found, always generated life. The aroma of a hot breakfast could raise the dead from their sleep. By eight thirty, she would be rushed off her feet. But, at this moment, she stopped and looked around.

Her little dining area contained a number of pictures. They were hung on one long wall. One of them caught her eye and she giggled. A young girlish giggle, which made her blush. She had just remembered something nice. Then, she twisted her apron and decided to loosen the belt by one more notch. That gave her the extra room she needed and it felt so much more comfortable. And, with that done, she went to set a new light under her cooker.

From the early morning street, there was suddenly a hefty door bang. Beccy looked down and saw Adrian struggling to carry some paint brushes, plus a heavy bag, away from the car. She knew she should have stayed with him really, as carrying all that decorating stuff meant he didn't have a free hand. The door must have swung shut in front of him. Hence the noise.

Brian and Linda were thrilled to see their friends. It was great of them to come over at this hour, and they really appreciated them giving up their Sunday, just to help out.

Brian and Linda were good fun. They worked together as a team and always seemed to enjoy sharing life's little problems. Beccy had known Linda since school. Brian was a year senior to her. And, although she could remember him being there, she couldn't recall ever speaking to him. Anyway, he was good company. Plus, Linda and her were good friends.

To begin the job, they set about clearing the room of everything they could. They placed the sofa against a spare wall. Then they set up the pasting table and began measuring things up. The paper they had chosen didn't need matching. So, there would be no waste in trying to match a complicated pattern. That also saved buying another roll. They had two packets of paste and the two girls went off to mix up the first one. The boys looked at the task in hand.

"Are you okay?" Brian spoke in a dulcet tone.

"I ain't got a clue. She's behaving like I'm king pong. Something's gone off and I don't know what it can be."

"Have you done anything to upset her?"

"I wish I had. Then, at least I'd know what it was. Every time I ask her, 'Are you all right, my love?', she says, 'Yes darling.' Then, she won't talk to me! This morning, she went into the shower and told me to stop looking at her. I mean, you can't see anything through that shower curtain. It's brick wall thick!" he sighed, "I just don't understand 'em, man. I really don't. Anyway, how's life for you two?"

"We're fine. Linda's got the chance of taking a job over at a farm. All they want is the company paperwork doing, and if she can manage that, then there will be more than enough work to pass her way. It would be brilliant for us. 'Cos then she wouldn't have to run the car and she would be able to earn more money. It's a win, win. Couldn't be better really. Is Beccy still looking to get out of 'Petersons'?"

"Yes, she is!" said Beccy. She had just come into the room with some wet paste in a bright yellow bucket. She stood, looking right at the male pair. Her hands came up to her hips. "Come on!" she said, "This is a once-in-a-lifetime opportunity for the two men in our lives to show their worth!" The way she said it made everyone laugh, even Adrian couldn't help himself this time.

By mid-morning, the cold corpse of Maxwell Oakley was laid out in the mortuary. The police had made their preliminary assessments and it was clear what had happened. A poor drunken male, possibly in his mid-forties, had been shot in the head: at point-blank range. This had been done with a small-bore firearm. The shot looked as though it had entered from under the chin. The skin, below his jaw, had visible burn marks and there wasn't much left of the upper skull. The face was largely intact, but most of the lower jawline and the top of the head, had been shot away. There was no identification on the body. The poor soul stank of stale sweat and partially digested alcohol. Neither smell being very pleasant.

The Detective Sergeant had made out her first report. She lodged it within the computerized system and was content with what had been written. But what perplexed her most, were the things she could not write: her feelings. *Why attack a man with such unnecessary force? A man so under the influence; that a summer breeze would have blown him over. Who on earth would do such a thing?* It really concerned her.

On days like these it was a pleasure to get up. The warm air inspired the masses to perform all sorts of social exploits. Dog walking, cycling and plenty of consumer shopping. Before long, it was soon heading for mid-day and business was booming. The hot spell of weather had seen all manner of summer items fly off the shelves.

Items; from freshly flowering plants to bags of commercial cement. Even air coolers and plastic swimming pools were all on a rampage to the open doors. Everything was travelling to the tills and the hardware store was totally packed out. One couple had come to 'Saps Stores' to buy some paint. The shade they wanted was a pale creamy pink. This colour had to be mixed at the counter. They had the correct bar code. So, all they had to do, was hand over a tin of white paint; and the people at the till would mix it up for them. Happy with their choice, they went to the counter, at which point, their two fair-haired teenage boys began to fall out. As they started to scream and swing punches at one another, a tall dark-haired man discreetly approached. He came to the opposite side of the retail counter and was wearing the bluest of tailored denim jackets. That, together with a very tight shirt which also had some white cuffs on the end. He was even wearing shiny cufflinks. Margery came over and asked how she could help.

Quietly, he leaned forward and asked if there were any jobs going.

Margery looked at him. She was suspicious and immediately felt that he didn't look right. She frowned for a moment, "I don't know if there are," she said. "Matt is the guy you need to speak to. I'll just put a call out and see if he's here." As she moved away, she continued speaking, "I haven't seen him today and he may not be in until Monday." She went over to a bendy microphone, grasped it harshly, and raised her vocal cords into what was the squeakiest of 'Tannoy' systems. "Matt, please call till three, please, and I mean now!... Please!" She turned around again and watched the man at the counter. She was rapidly forming an opinion. One which confided that this man was odd. She wasn't afraid of him, but he didn't look right, to her. Somehow, he was out of place. He didn't fit in. She couldn't specifically see why, but she knew there was no way he really belonged here.

Her till phone rang and she spun around. She spoke for a short time and then came back over to Wilbur, with the fingers of her hand outstretched. "Just go down there: where the cement is. Turn left, at the end of the row, and Doug will see you. You can't miss him, he's the big rotund guy in a stripy plastic apron. I think it's green and white today."

She immediately retuned her attention towards the besieged parents, who, by now, were now holding two tins of white paint; whilst separating two warring children and hitting them with a floppy colour chart.

Walking away from the desk, Wilbur started to feel at home. He really liked this place. It was magic. He glided along the wide polished floor space and down the lengthy isles. It was the size which impressed him most. The sheer scale of the place was truly vast. There was room here. You could walk around for hours, with an elephant in tow, and no one would ever know you had been here at all. He was really absorbed by the enormity of it. It was wonderful. What an experience!

He was enjoying himself. So, at that point, he stopped and focused his thoughts. Nothing wrong with a little innocent amusement. But, he was here for a purpose. So, he restrained himself and headed straight for the dusty cement bags.

Earlier on, he had sat and looked closely at the letter. [The one without a top or a bottom]. He had pondered and thought about it; on many levels. The letter was robust. It had given its information. But, it didn't really provide anything. It was just a tease. That's all.

Besides the letter and the card, there had been a folded note. He had seen it fall onto the floor, but he paid it no attention, at the time. When he finally looked; it could easily have been part of a pay-slip. At least, that's what it appeared to be. Someone called 'Doug' had signed it at the bottom. And Wilbur knew that Maxwell had a brother of that name. He also knew where he worked. In these days of Sunday trading that meant there could easily be a 50-50 chance that the man in question would be there. If he was, then he had to find him.

After he'd left the guest house, Wilbur took a stroll and visited a local supermarket. He liked populous places. They were so easy to disappear inside. Knowing his intention, he took to the cafeteria, with an aim. The hardware store was several miles out of town and he needed transport.

Whilst waiting, he repeatedly flipped the card he had discovered over and over. He knew that it had some numbers written on it. But, he hadn't given it any of his attention. So, he stopped and noticed that it had some small hand-written text: '52 Pembrokeshire St' and then, '41-26-39'. They both appeared on the reverse. The card was also from an estate agent on Lang Street, in Bedford. Bedford was miles away from here and it didn't seem relevant. Still, he pocketed it again, and remembered the image, for comfort's sake.

The cafeteria was actually modelled as a larger reflection of what a local 'café' should be. Wilbur didn't quite think of it like that. To him these were cheap and unchallenging places. Borne out of a nineteen seventies' vision of wanting to feel better about oneself. All on a strictly limited budget. Coffee came in mediocre cups. The trendy ones were marked with a logo and they appeared in a bright-red colour. Whether they were plastic or cardboard, they had no handles and he didn't like them very much.

He took a medium sized cup from the rack; made a self-vended drink, from the machine and paid the price. Then, he sat down and waited. His expression was sullen, but he was alert. It took slightly longer than he imagined. Almost an hour had elapsed, before it took place. At that point, an older man came in with a hugely rotund woman. Both were obviously overweight and bearing down on the bulk of their strong opinions with one another. Amusingly, they were avidly calling each other a variety of unpleasant names. The 'he' was furious and his main means of communicating seemed to involve repeatedly swearing. The 'her', clearly didn't like it, but she kept trying to stay calm. Yet, in their hearts, both of them were really spitting knives at one another. It was just a matter of time until it happened. At one point, he was going onto her about something stupid. Suddenly, she stood up, stared at him and then stomped off; leaving all their frozen food in a trolley. Meanwhile, his anger was rising and he let out a further tirade of unnecessary obscenities. He even, stood up, pointing with his fingers, as she walked away. In them, were a set of car keys. Wilbur patiently tapped his forefinger on the table top and watched the episode unfold.

In the fury of the moment, the keys forcefully hit the table and the oaf of a man ran after her. He went right up to the ladies' loo and stood outside; shouting foul language through the closed outer door. Everyone's eyes were now drawn to the scene.

For Wilbur: he wasn't really interested any longer. He coolly finished his drink, stood up and came over to the vacant table, where he picked up the abandoned car keys. Whilst everyone else was avidly listening to the heated conversation taking place, he casually strolled away. Moments later, a smartly dressed young man was depicted, driving a well-worn and tired-looking Toyota Avensis. Seven miles later, it reached Saps.

That was a good hour ago, by now and suddenly, here he was, approaching the presence of yet another fat man. This time; adorned in a diagonally stripy apron. At this, he began to feel satisfied. He had achieved his goal and to celebrate, he reached his sweaty hand into a clean pocket where he retrieved a relaxingly deformed liquorice chew. As he bit, he smiled. For now he knew he was going to enjoy himself.

***

Chapter 4
Destiny and Discretion

Saps had been enjoying a remarkable time. Business had never been so good. Back in March, the manager had decided to expand the range of goods on sale. He wanted to focus on some of the more lucrative items. Electrical products made far more profit than selling wooden beams. So why not promote a range of desk fans and wall lights? Maybe even clothes irons and a few TV sets? It was all profitable stuff.

This meant reorganizing the store. They needed to be more efficient in the way they used the floor space. He still had to sell the existing range of goods, but they could show smaller amounts and remove some of the bigger fixtures. He wanted more flexibility. So, he decided to dismantle one entire row of stillages and place them on top of the existing ones. These had previously been stacked three high. They largely contained cement, sand; some dry plaster sacks and an assortment of bricks. By doing his changes, he effectively squashed the three isles into two. Only, those remaining rows were now one level higher. They also jutted out further into the isles and some items had to be taken off display. However, it opened up a considerable new sales area and he hoped that this would bring in more retail trade. It was all done in a hurry; just before the big Easter weekend.

As the year marched on, the hot weather had really witnessed some blossoming sales. The area manager came over; he was very impressed. There was even talk of a managerial promotion and significant bonuses looked very likely to be on the cards. Everyone was charmed.

Doug Oakley was a physically unfit man. These days, he wore a body of vast proportions. Way too large for his frame. He had once played rugby for the county team, but then he received a nasty ligament injury. He played on for a few more games, but it soon became clear that any realistic ambition of stardom had passed him by. He finally capitulated, hung his boots up and took to the possession of a commercial environment. Which, these days, saw him adorn the cape of a store room manager.

After his earlier misfortune, he had kept some of his old acquaintances alive. He'd even helped one or two, by finding them a job at the store. Besides that, he looked after himself by taking a strict diet of too much food, too much beer and too little of everything else. He had no wife, no family and very few cares in the world. But, this life style did afford its toll, added unnecessary years to his stature and created a gargantuan figure. No one wanted to mess with him and he did know his stuff. Saps was a good employer. Though, he didn't particularly like the weekend working. To him, weekends were supposed to be fun. Lots of running around and making hay. Being here could never be seen as that. But, once you accepted the conditions, then the rest of your lifestyle took care of itself. All in all, he was content enough.

For weeks now, there had been a huge banner at the front of the store. They urgently needed some fork lift drivers. Good pay was being offered and if this guy could drive one, then the job was his.

Doug watched the figure before him. Very neat. Almost prim. He could easily have the ability to manoeuvre a fork lift, but what was that, with the sandals? He looked again, but really didn't care that much. If he could do the work, then the job was his.

He put a hand out. "My name's Doug. I understand you want a job. Can you drive fork lifts?" It all came out on a roll.

Wilbur stopped, smiled at the man and delicately placed out his right hand. When it was firmly shaken, he confided that he could. He also produced a fork lift driving licence and Doug's face gleamed in anticipation.

"That's great! Come upstairs, William." He patted him on the shoulder. "Just a few questions. Then we'll let you know…" in a lower voice, he asked, "Erm, can you start tomorrow?"

At that moment, a young man called Terry came racing over to ask Doug about a problem he'd just seen. One of the stillages was beginning to lean over, but Doug told him to see Margery. He had something far more important to deal with.

Doug was a really boisterous character and he led, what could only be called, a busy and unsheltered life. He dealt with things the way they were. Something or other was always on the boil. On that basis, he didn't like to see the real opportunities pass him by and if he could get this guy on the payroll, then that was one less worry for him to deal with tomorrow. They went in. through a dirty canvass doorway. One that took them away from the hustle and bustle of the shop floor and into an open concreted area. It was well lit and it was pleasantly cooler. This was where the deliveries and collections took place. Doug kept walking at a pace. Then, he turned off to their right. He was following some yellow floor markings, which brought them towards a prefabricated building. Inside, there was a tired, old-fashioned wooden staircase. They clattered their way up and entered what could only be described as a smelly corridor. It had a series of sealed windows; all along the right-hand side. They offered a commanding view onto the sales area beyond. To their left were several empty offices. They all had closed doors. As he walked, Wilbur caught hold of the view below. He could faintly make out the shape of Margery pointing her fingers at the couple with the paint tins. He was also aware that there was an unpleasant taint up here. The smell was awful. He thought he recognized it. *That smell is cat pee,* he thought. *Not nice*. It was uncalled for. However, Doug didn't seem to mind, in the least. He simply looked to the left and flung an office door wide open. No one was inside and he signaled for Wilbur to come in.

Wilbur followed through a doorway, which was directly opposite the corridor and its windows. Those same windows which still overlooked the retail area below. *They must have come around in a kind of semi-circle,* thought Wilbur.

Doug sat down first and asked 'William' when could he start. Wilbur looked at him, but didn't answer. He was calmly enjoying the moment, setting the scene to play his game. As a consequence, he just raised his eyebrows at Doug and smiled back.

It was one o'clock and the girls had made some hot toasted sandwiches with coffee, for the boys. They smelled great, they tasted good too and the welcome break gave them all an opportunity to see how far they had come. They were three quarters the way around the room and had just used up the first bucket of paste. Brian was annoyed because one of the walls was out of shape. As a result, it needed a lengthy triangular strip of paper. Two inches at the top, all the way down to nothing at the bottom. It didn't look good. But Linda pointed out that when they painted over it, then you'd never see a thing. Especially if they hung one of her big paintings in the middle of the wall. "Everyone's eyes will be looking at the picture. Not at the wall," she said.

Brian got the message and nodded his head.

As they worked, Beccy had shown herself to be the dame of the show. Adrian had never seen her so cheery and busy with it. He also knew, that when she wanted to be, she really was the most attractive woman on Earth. And he definitely felt something for her. He liked being with her. But even now, she wouldn't sit near him and he actually felt hurt by that. Strange really; he hadn't noticed that emotion before.

Linda spoke up, "So how long do you think it will take?" Her eyes were on him.

"An hour, maybe an hour and a half. Then we need to clean up. So maybe two hours, tops."

"So, we should be done in time for tea?"

"Yup."

"Great! How about we go to the pub for a bite to eat?" Everyone cheered and so, by consensus, it was made an official date.

Jenny was bending over her table. She'd been staring at it for ages and it was perplexing her. Something was wrong, but she just couldn't see it. One thing was for sure: every single time she leaned on the wretched thing, it moved. There was a definite wobble. She had tried several things and, even when she put a piece of furled paper under one of the legs, it still moved. But, that couldn't be. Could it?

She had just spent a small fortune on a new dining room carpet. It cost a great deal of money and the decorators had only been in the week before. All the tables had been dismantled and, when the work was completed, they were put back together again. To Jenny, the new red carpet definitely made the room. She loved it. The rich colour had introduced a sense of pernach, a warmth of character, and she appreciated that very much. Everything was so nice. The only thing was; this one particular table would not behave itself. A couple, who sat there for breakfast, had told her about it. Every time they attempted to place their food onto a fork, the table moved. It was annoying them then, and it was annoying Jenny now!

At that moment, she heard something move behind her and she turned to look around. It was 'Hermit'. He was her cat. He wore an innocently black and white expression. One which showed that he desired some of her attention and, quite honestly, after spending so much time on this thing, she was inclined to co-operate. She decided to plop herself down on a wooden chair; wearing a heart full of melancholy. She sat, clutching a glass of ice-cold milk, whilst stroking an affectionate ball of purring fur.

Like cats, thoughts make movements and she was experiencing a few right now. So, she carefully put the glass down and proceeded to absent-mindedly stroke him; under his chin. He adored the attention. But, she wasn't really concentrating on him anymore. Her eyes were still looking across the room and then it came to her. She suddenly sat upright and spoke out loud. "Those legs aren't fixed! They screw in. Don't they?" Through gritted teeth, she said, "So, that's why!" She plonked down the milk glass, put the cat on the floor and came over to peer at the brown table legs. 'Hermit' put on a scolded face of dejection. He also decided that it was time to jump up, onto another table. The same one, which just happened to have an unprotected glass of milk on the top. He sniffed at the rim and then reached a paw into the milky recess. Licking it, he stopped to see if Jenny was interested. She wasn't and so he gently lifted himself up and placed his chin on the edge of the glass. Unfortunately, his tongue couldn't reach down to the level of the milk. So, he placed the extremity of his paw back onto the rim and pulled the whole container towards himself. There followed the sound of a dull 'clunk' and then milk went everywhere. After which, came a furious un-cat like scream, attached to the word, "Hermit!"

There wasn't much going on in the room now. Doug was looking stain-shocked, but he was still breathing and definitely showing fresh emotion. Wilbur was looking at Doug's arm. It was gently bleeding and as Doug's eyes followed the pool of moving blood, he could again see the weapon in Wilbur's hand.

Wilbur spoke calmly and business like, "Put your other hand over the wound." Doug did as he was told. Wilbur then stood up, walked over and sat down on the chair next to him. Pointing the gun sideways, in Doug's general direction. "Let's try again. I told you before that I want you to know something," he said. "I have a reason for being here and you don't know what it is. Do you?"

Doug just looked at him. He couldn't believe what was happening and unless this guy changed his questioning technique, then he may well end up giving the wrong answer. One that could be fatal.

"I'm looking for someone you know." Wilbur sat firm and straightened his seating stance. "Someone who means a lot to you." He paused to let the remark resonate. Then, he stood up again and spun the steel chair around. The back of the seat was now facing Doug. Wilbur moved it closer and kneeled on it. He rested his arms on top and said, "Where is Mr Bailey?"

Doug's eyes dropped to the floor. His expression took on a worrying look. He trawled through his thought waves and turned towards Wilbur, "Al' Bailey worked here for a few weeks, but he wasn't any good. I had to let him go." Feeling uncertain, he went on, "It wasn't down to me. Honest. He just couldn't do the work. He was useless.

"He seemed to owe money to a lot of people. He borrowed from anyone he could, all the time. One minute, he would come to work in new cars. No one knew how he paid for them. Next thing, he had no money at all. He was always going out. Always into gambling. At least, I think he was. Anyway, some money went missing from one of the tills. Five or six hundred quid, I don't remember exactly, but I had to let him go. I couldn't keep him after that. Could I?" His eyes dropped again. "I don't know where he is, Mister. I honestly don't. I think he dated Cindy a couple of times. She's the one who's on the tiling section." He paused, went white and almost whispered, "She's not in today."

After all his effort, his eyes began to fade and he started rambling. As he did so, Wilbur extracted another liquorice from his pocket. Before he bit in, he asked, "I want to know, where he is?"

Doug was visibly beginning to shake. Shock was setting in. Wilbur knew that he wouldn't be conscious for much longer. He also recognized the limits for what they were and lifted himself onto his feet again. He began to look around and quickly focused on the filing cabinets. There were seven or eight of them, in a row. He went to the first one and pulled at the top drawer. It opened with a 'clunk'. The first file label he pulled out was marked 'L-O'. He peered inside and pulled out a few documents. He saw they were an assortment of old tax forms and there were some pay-slips. He also saw that they had the full names and addresses on them. He looked straight back at Doug.

Doug was almost gone now. So, Wilbur quietly went along the row of filing cabinets until he reached the files marked 'B-D'. He pulled out all of the contents and sat down at the table; where he could browse at them in comfort. Doug was still sitting and his blood was now running along the floor boards. That didn't concern Wilbur at all. He continued to do his task, with leisure and accuracy. Leafing through the paperwork, he came to one Albert M Bailey. He read the address. Then, he neatly wrapped all of the documents up and placed them into the safe custody of his jacket pocket.

As he did this, he could also hear a noise from outside. Someone was calling out for Doug and trying to enter the structure by a side door. They were not succeeding. Obviously, that entrance was still locked. Wilbur looked on. Then, he came over to Doug and fumbled through his pockets. Inside, there was a large set of keys.

Doug was now shivering. He was also watching every move that Wilbur made. Barely conscious, he was truly terrified of what this man might do next. Wilbur had found the keys he wanted. After plucking them from Doug's possession, he peacefully walked over to the open door and confidently told Doug to take his time and come over to the corridor. Doug tried to move. Only, he couldn't. His body wouldn't go. He tried again, but his shivering became more violent and he simply fell over. The pain in his arm was getting intense and, somehow, it was that which began to wake him up again. He slowly started to crawl and drag himself along the floor. But… it really wasn't easy.

In the shop, Terry was urgently trying to get Margery's attention. He had tried twice before, but she was having none of it.

"Look," she scolded him. "I'm not from health and safety, I'm not a manager of health and safety and I wouldn't rely on your own health and safety, when you're anywhere near me!" Then, she pointed her furious fingers at his face and said, "So use the bloody 'Tannoy' yourself and STOP USING ME AS YOUR FLAMING RUNAROUND!" She was livid and her face was bright scarlet red with anger. In that state, she was truly petrifying.

At that moment, across the sales floor, someone cried out. All heads simultaneously turned to see what was happening. Over to their right, the end row of stillages was clearly beginning to buckle. It creaked and groaned. The bottom one was being visibly crushed by the weight of those above it. As it bent, it was causing the upper stillages to lean further and further over. Terry suddenly realized that there was no way he could physically get around there in time. As they all watched, there came the most awful high-pitched whining sound. Screeching metal was tearing away from its buckling supports. In full public view, the entire stack of heavy steel crates majestically bowed over and lurched sideways. Miring, under their own excessive weight.

Slowly, at first, the tall structure curved away and then politely continued its journey ground-wards. Finally, gathering pace, the whole stack accelerated in the general direction of the prefabricated offices.

***

Chapter 5
Complexities Becalm You

"Look at this then!" Sondra threw the newspaper at him.

He absently read the headline and went back to tapping his hardboiled egg. "So?" he said.

"You pay good money for this?" She pointed at the paper for a response.

Hem paused for a moment and took a refreshing sip of his freshly made coffee. As usual, he was fully dressed at the breakfast table. This time it was his favourite charcoal suit. Complete with a white, double cuff shirt and an auburn-coloured tie. His right hand came up with a teaspoon; holding a piece of steaming hot boiled egg. It was venturing towards his ample chin. "You forget something…" he started to eat it, "…I pay for what I want and…" he chewed on his food and swallowed, "… he delivers it. Always, in his own individual way. It's just his style. Nothing to worry about."

His wife retorted, "At what cost? He has just killed four of our own people for God's sake!"

"Look Sondra, I love you deeply. You know that I do. So, let me explain. He is his own man. He has his own way of working and I accept that. So must you. He does what we need. If he didn't, then all of this…" he opened his arms into the room, "…would disappear.

"I have no qualms about his diligence. Someone gets in his way, then they pay the price. Ted and Aaron obviously did something they shouldn't. So, he killed them. That's it, really. It's all done with. Now he's doing another quality job for us and when it's all over, things will settle down again. I promise. Don't worry. It isn't worth it." He rearmed his egg spoon with a cooler looking morsel.

"Hem, he's a vile monstrosity. And you pay him good money. Good money to do what, exactly?"

Hem looked disapprovingly at his wife. She was clearly very upset. He could see that. So, he spoke out of a different emotion, "Think of it this way, he is expensive. Thoroughly expensive. But, the amount he saves us is far more than an even's match. When he gets his hands on that paperwork, then we can relaunch the business as our own. Mine and yours. No more unnecessary interference. Whilst he is busy spending his well-obtained earnings, we can busy ourselves making our well-earned profits. It's one virtuous circle, darling. One which works well for the compass and the sextant."

She looked at him through her middle-aged eyes and remorsefully decided to concede. She despised this side of the business, but her husband was right; in his own way. "That bathroom towel rail still isn't working properly," she said. "I called that plumber man again to fix it."

Hem mopped his chin, with a paper napkin and shrugged. "Enjoy your breakfast, sweetheart." Standing up, he carefully kissed her cheek. "I'm in town today. Maybe we can eat out this evening?"

She half smiled. "Yes, that would be nice. I'll arrange it for seven."

With no further comment, he politely ventured out through the open patio doors.

The hospital ward was busy. Lots of squeaky shoes and mixed mumbles were crossing the varnished floors. In one room lay the large frame of Douglas Oakley. His chest was rising and falling; in a steady and consistent value to retain his life. He was fast asleep and being infused with painkillers. His concerned mother was anxiously looking on at him and trying to understand why anyone had done this horrible thing to her son. What had happened? Why did it have to happen at all?

They had to operate on his left arm, from which they removed a small bullet. The bone was splintered, but fortunately not broken. An artery had been torn and that had caused a large amount of damage. He had lost at least two pints of blood and that was why he was so weak. Why anyone would do such a thing; was a mystery. The nurse checked his vital signs again and made sure that the cannula was distributing the correct level of medication. Some colour had returned to his face now and she said; she was sure he'd be coming around soon.

She continued noting some observations and then went back to her desk.

This Monday morning, there was a lot of traffic on the main Appleby Road. It had started also pelting with rain and it turned out that the roadwork traffic lights were stuck on permanent red. The roadworks went around a bend, so you couldn't see the traffic, at the other end. That meant, you could not just drive through them and, as a result, the queue of vehicles went back for miles. Brian had just taken a call on his phone. It was that Strumshell woman again. A few weeks ago, they had fitted a new bathroom suite for her, but there was always something going wrong with it. Not that he could ever really find anything.

Her last call saw him going over in the afternoon, to fix a faulty basin tap. She insisted it had come loose. So, up he went, with a spanner in hand. Only to find that the tap was in perfect working condition and needed no attention at all.

Today, he was going over first thing. So that, he could sort her out and then get onto another job, without further delay.

With the traffic lights causing such mayhem, he decided to turn back and go across country. It took three quarters of an hour to get there. By the time he arrived, he wasn't best pleased. He crunched up to her front door at nine fifteen and pressed the hefty bell button. She opened it, in her dressing gown, and took him upstairs to the bathroom. She was telling him that the towel rail was feeling cold to the touch. She went on to say that she needed her towel to be warm. Especially, when she came out of the shower. It was important to feel the warmth against her bare skin.

Brian nodded.

She led him into the bathroom and then left him touching the chrome rails. It was cold all right. It was also switched off.

"I'll just need to flick the switch down and let it warm up," he said. "Should only take five minutes or so."

He waited for her response, but there was none. She seemed to have disappeared. So, he just let his breath out and carried on. Next thing, there was a noise behind him and he turned around to see what it was.

Standing there was Sondra Strumshell; wearing only her black see-through underwear. She was absolutely stunning. Almost athletic, in build. Her firm legs went on for miles, and her pose was extremely alluring. Both hands were purposefully resting on her smooth hips and her face was giving him a desperately longing look. Brian was astounded. Her eyes were so dark. They seemed to be filled with such deep pools of naked desire.

In this long moment, there was total silence and taking firm hold of her opportunity, Mrs Strumshell reached out her hand and lead Brian away. They went into the adjacent bedroom. A soft quiet place where he and she could wait for the heat to rise; safely within the comfort of their own natural control.

Adrian was on his way to Leamington's. He was late again and as he pulled onto the drive way, Allan waved him down. "Don't get out, mate. We're going to Saps."

"What we going there for?"

"They've had some sort of accident and they need to be sure everything is safe before they can reopen." Allan made his way around the van.

Adrian looked bemused, but he didn't feel like raising a storm. He'd just come through one at home and why the hell Beccy had to keep the pressure on him, he didn't know. This morning's little tirade had started when she decided that it was his turn to cook breakfast. Fine, he didn't mind. Except, they never had a cooked breakfast. As a result, there wasn't anything in the place to cook breakfast with. The most she ever had was a bowl of milky corn flakes. He usually managed a coffee and perhaps ate a doughnut, on his way to work.

This morning though, you would have thought he had spat on her lap. She went mad, screaming at him and telling him what a useless plonker he was. Apparently, she had had enough of his behaviour. Only, when he asked which specific piece of behavior she was talking about; she went crimson and refused to say.

Something was seriously wrong with that girl and, no matter what he did, he couldn't get her to open up. That was one aspect. But, what mystified him most was the one thing he really couldn't understand. Himself! He actually thought the world of her. Even though she could be an absolute cow. He still loved her. If she would just calm down and tell him what was wrong, then he would do anything for her. Yet, every time he tried to get close or broach the subject, she flew off like an arrow. Allan climbed in and Adrian waited for it. "Why are you late, mate?"

"Just the usual. Problems at home."

Allan smiled. "We've all been there."

"Don't make it any easier, fella."

"Is she seeing someone else?"

"No."

"Are you seeing someone else?"

"No. What she's doing is screaming at me all the time. This morning, it was because I wouldn't fry two eggs and two pieces of bacon. Even though there's no bacon in the fridge and I couldn't locate a frying pan in that place without a metal detector and some extra sensory perception."

Allan chuckled. "She loves you, mate, only she won't admit it. In case you run a mile."

"I might as well run. 'cos if she finds the bloody frying pan before I do; then she'll probably use it to put a dent in my forehead."

Allan started to laugh but, as the van chugged along the windy roads, Adrian's thoughts were drifting off somewhere else. So, he decided to turn the radio on and they listened to the rough music in silence.

Hem was looking radiant. Too much so. His face was shiny as a ball bearing. It was also gleaming bright red and he was profusely sweating from every pour of his body. He hated these kinds of charades, but sometimes they had to be. So, there they all were, standing on the front steps of the new privately financed municipal building. One which he had constructed. Next to him was the mayor, accompanied by a couple of private finance executives; whose names he never picked up. In front of them all was a little prestigious gang of selected press. Some were taking photographs. To Hem, they were all pretty much the same: a jolly bunch of wasters.

The rain had conveniently stopped and, in the heat, it was instantly July hot and July dry. Yet, he was soaking wet. He smiled at the cameras and shook several dry hands. It was a publicity event and one which would take of most of the day, in one shape or another. After the photos had been taken, he retreated into the reception area and began socializing with the indifferent group of brethren. At least it was cooler in there. He was grateful for that and began to feel better about himself. It showed on his features.

Kim Sholt, from the planning department, came over and started talking his usual drivel. "I know what the completion of this means to you, Mr Strumshell."

"What say?" said the absent-minded Hem. No one called him by his surname these days. Not unless they were after his money. The remark had caught him off guard.

Sholt went on though, "I mean, you'll get a big pay cheque now that it's all over."

The resurrected Hem bit his tongue. He hated these weaving worms. They tried to tie you up in their knots. So, he firmly replied, "As you know, we are under contract, Mr Sholt. All and every payment can only be received in set stages. I can't buck that. The whole project has to be authentically signed off, by the project management and that's before we get a penny. When they sign off, then sixty days later, we get some money and I'll certainly drink to that." With that formality settled, he walked off and refilled his glass with something which smelled invitingly fruity and looked perplexingly green in colour.

Adrian Baxter from 'Chargers Ex' saw him and came over. "What do think to this then, Hem?"

"Bloody waste of tax payers' time and money. But, maybe some good publicity will come of it. Any news on that 'Cellar Estate' project yet? I'd like to get my teeth into that one. I've never refurbished a genuine sixteenth-century hall before." As he spoke, he was constantly looking around the room. Then he pointed at something and went on, "Fancy any of that grub?"

"Too early for me. Tell me, why are we holding this at ten a.m.?"

"Costs, dear boy. Costs. They start moving employees in here tomorrow and they do not want any dirty glasses or smelly plates left over. Least of all, in the reception area. Cleaning it up, overnight, could create a whiff of unpleasant expenses. A definitive no, no, old son."

Sholt pointed too. "I see Bradley's trying to get a date with that blonde over there."

"No chance, the lady in question is far too highly educated and just happens to be the chief planning officer for the county. She also knows her verbal diction very well. I give him sixty seconds, tops." He bit into a crisp sounding celery stick and licked his fingers.

They stopped speaking and watched. Moments later, she loudly told him to "Sod off!" If they were not both clasping their drinks glasses, then they would have applauded. But as it was, both Kim and Hem nodded their heads together in a show of appreciation. It was always satisfying to be proven right and Hem was finally beginning to enjoy himself. After all, this is what socializing was all about. Wasn't it?

***

Chapter 6
The Work to Repair

Adrian and Allan pulled onto the large car park outside Saps. It was very quiet and the place was practically deserted. At one end, there were a few stationary police cars. These were parked close to the front doors. There were no flashing lights on display. Adrian turned off the engine, opened the van door and picked up his tool kit. Allan just climbed out. Both men ambled towards a dark navy-blue side door, where there was a buzzer. Adrian pushed it and jumped straight back. The door had immediately swung out, towards his face. It revealed the presence of a female police officer. She looked them over and asked what they wanted.

Allan replied, "We're the electricians, Miss. We were called here to check-over some of the circuitry. I'm sorry, but that's all we were told."

"Give me a minute," she said and closed the door. They could hear her using a radio, on the other side.

Adrian put his tool box on the tarmac surface and the two men sat down on either end of its rim.

Allan said, "Looks like we're in the usual position, mate."

Adrian replied, "You guessed it."

The hot sun was beating down. Adrian thought that it must be at least thirty degrees. They were forecasting thirty-five by mid-day and he was not going to wait here that long.

About ten minutes passed, when the blue door finally reopened, and a very pale-looking face appeared. It was Samuel Jones, the shop manager. He quickly ushered them in and carefully closed the door behind them.

They were now standing in a small and sweaty passageway. It had some wooden steps which led steeply up to a corridor area. Samuel asked them to follow and clunked his way up front. They came along, behind.

At the top, they had to turn right. It was then, that they noticed, there was absolutely nothing there. Adrian imagined that there should have been an outside wall. Or at least some facia screening. But, as he peered across to his left, there was nothing but air. He was standing on an open ledge, which was meant to be a passage. Twenty or so feet below, there was the dusty shop floor. He could see that the whole exterior of the unit was lying in pieces. It was like the entire side of the building had come off and laid itself out; all over the floor. There was a massive hole in the middle of it. And, carefully peering over the edge, he could just about see that the missing section was still attached, to a lower part of the wooden frame. It was a real mess.

His eyes came back up and caught the manager's expression at full mast. "We've had an awful event here, boys," he said. "That stillage over there...," he pointed, "...managed to topple over and tear half of the building clean away. The insurers have been informed and we have a health and safety concern because some of the main power cables have pulled away from their moorings." He pointed again. "Please can you give it a good look over and make it all safe. Then, we can get someone in to repair it."

Adrian looked it over, again. All that remained were a few wooden struts, a false ceiling and a line of unused offices. He looked back at the manager and allowed him to carry on.

"You can invoice Saps Ltd with the cost, then I will clear the payment and recoup it through our insurers. I really appreciate you coming in at such short notice."

He shuffled along the open walkway and said, "There's a temporary tea room, below. Just go down the other stairs…" he waved, this time to the far end of the open landing, "…and you're very welcome to help yourself to whatever materials you need from the shop shelves. Just let me know what you've taken, so that I can take the bar codes and adjust things through our stock control system." With that, he shrugged his shoulders and cautiously walked away.

Allan said quietly, "What the hell happened here, Aidy? It's like a film set for world war three."

"Dunno. But, we'd better shape ourselves. See if you can find that fuse box and I'll check the ceiling area for the conduit strips." Looking down, he said, "I can't see any problems from up here, but I want to be sure they are okay. Then we can send a trace signal through the lines and see what doesn't add up."

Adrian unclipped his tool kit and Allan made his way towards the stairs. The fuse box was situated at the back of the building; on the ground floor. Three of the four switches had tripped out. One was for the lights, the other two were for the socket ring main. They carried a higher ampage. He came out and looked for a cable or a conduit. In one of the steel girders, he could see a strip of white plastic. Once he saw it; he whistled to catch Adrian's attention. "I'll put the tracer on here," he said and pointed at the exposed cable.

Adrian nodded and went back to get his step ladder. *There is a strange smell here,* he thought. With a torch in his hand, he had quickly checked two of the loft covers. Then, he climbed up again and shone a bright light across the leads. He couldn't see anything out of place. He was just about to come down the stairs and speak to Allan when he saw there was one more loft hatch. It was at the end of the passageway. Not far from the stairs.

As he came to it, he could see that it was a damp musty colour. Maybe some rainwater had found its way through. There could be a roof leak? But, then he caught a waft of the smell. It was both sour and sweet. A bad odour, which made him feel sick. That said, he knew he had to open it. So, he bit his lip and went up the step ladder again. Prizing the hatchway back took a lot more effort than he expected. It felt like it was stuck with some sort of glue. Either that, or something heavy was resting on the top. After a great deal of pushing, he finally managed it. Then, he heard a hoard of flies buzzing around. He switched on his torch and peered inside. That was when he saw what it was. Seconds later, he fell down the step ladders. Leaning against them, he felt that perhaps he was just seeing things. It really couldn't be true. He wondered if that nice police lady was nearby and so, he called out to her. She would know what to do. Wouldn't she?

Sergeant Hallbrook was standing away from the broken structure and was still trying to determine exactly what had taken place. She knew what had been reported. Fortunately, the victim was still alive. Intensive care, but alive. She was trying to piece together how a man of his size had been able to fall off the passageway landing, slide down a good twenty-five-foot drop and drift across the sales floor. All without breaking a bone. It really was a marvel.

As her thoughts were piecing things together, she heard that nice young man from the electrical company calling for her. She looked up, "What is it?" she hollered. Adrian called back, "I think you'd better get up here, Miss. Quickly!"

"Why?"

"Because there's a God-awful smell coming from the loft and I think you'd better see what's causing it." At that point, he stopped talking and threw up, all over the floor.

Seeing this, she sighed, picked up her notepad and walked towards the open stairs. Allan just looked on, as she went by. A few minutes later, he ran up to the walkway. So that, he could hold onto the step ladder. Meanwhile, the police officer climbed the steps. Shortly after that, the hatch-cover was lifted for a second time. Only, on this occasion, all hell broke loose.

Wilbur was feeling good. When he was feeling good, he liked to reward himself. Today, he had bought himself a vanilla ice cream. It came from a van which was parked outside the Saps store. He chose it from the brief menu, displayed on the window and gave the lady his exact change. Once in possession, he proceeded to settle himself onto a vacant wooden seat; at the edge of the car park. He had watched a tyrannical parade of flashing blue lights, police cars, ambulances and associated vehicles. They had swathed their way, to and fro, over the painted stripes and markings of the car park. To him, it was a scintillating ballet. A sunlit performance to be enjoyed by all. In fact, he was so impressed that he almost felt like clapping his hands. It certainly met with his satisfaction.

After all, with the amount of noise and action going on, it would be so easy to relax, ease up and; when you were ready, simply drive away. He'd been at the car park for a little while and made some necessary cosmetic changes to the car. Satisfied with his work, his tongue protruded around the edge of the ice cream. As he ate his conquest, he was constantly watching all of the official comings and goings. Making absolutely sure that no one approached the car he was using. Once he was confident enough, he quietly finished his meal and paced towards the pink Toyota's console. He sat in the driver's seat and turned the key a little way forward.

He adjusted the driver's seat and noticed that the petrol gauge was only one quarter full. That thoroughly disgusted him. "How can anyone buy a car like this and not keep it topped up?" He shook his head in disbelief, sighed and then twisted the ignition key again. A few seconds later, he pulled onto the main road and drove off in search of his next victim. This time, complete with a new set of number plates. Firmly secured to his car.

***

Chapter 7
A Rising Spirit of Love

Brian was watching the naked form of Sondra Strumshell's body gently rise and fall. She was lying in his arms with her head resting on his chest. The lightness of her hair was moving under his breath. He leaned forward and kissed her.

He didn't really know what had just happened, let alone why. But, she was certainly some lady and he was deeply aware of the need in her passion. No one could move like that and be callous. She had a beautiful body. One that mirrored each and every ounce of his desire. Her eyes shone like beacons. Yet, they could also be so very dark and, once she had caught you in her gaze, then you were hooked. It was remarkable.

Looking at her, he wondered why she was behaving like this. It's not as if she needed him. She had a husband and two grown-up kids. So why did she do this sort of thing? He really didn't know. Did she sleep with just anyone or was it just him? He was too discrete to ask and he felt sure that she would never tell him, anyway. Suddenly, something dawned on him and he was actually amused. She had ended up paying for five hours of his work, but only twenty minutes worth of this service could ever go on the invoice. He smiled and kissed her head again. This time she turned and looked deep into his soul. She was haunting him. How could she do that? It must be some kind of a special gift. Over which, he had completely no control. With one glance, she could see right through him. Beyond his chest and right into the middle of the man she was viewing. That meant, he had to be careful. Women like these created strong yearnings. They could be dangerous.

Brian spoke, "He's going to find out, Sondra, and I'm not rich enough to afford this kind of a place." She smiled and relaxed, rubbing her head into the hairs of his chest. "Don't worry, darling. He already knows. I haven't slept with him for years. All he does is eat and drink business these days. He doesn't care about me anymore, and after all of the heartache, I don't care about him, either."

She lifted her head and looked into him. "He won't get in the way, my love. His eyes are centered elsewhere and I have a plan to make sure he stays there forever."

She began to move. Then, artfully stood up and pulled on her transparent underwear: right in front of him. Sharing every article of herself in the vision of his sight. She also had a patterned, silk dressing gown. But, she wanted to maximize the impact of her attractiveness. She liked this man intensely and she adored the feelings which he generated in her. She did not feel ashamed. It was a pleasing thing. A female desire and she found that she was affording this particular need with more and more of her quality time. She enjoyed it. She knew these feelings well and understood where they were taking her.

Releasing her vulnerability, she eased herself back across the bed. From where, she leaned forwards, placed her arms around his neck and passionately kissed her captive audience on the lips. Simultaneously, Brian's hands came out and pulled her into another loving embrace. He ran his bare fingertips up and over her smoothness, unclipped her bra and firmly pulled on her shoulders. Sondra found herself gasping again. She adored these sensations and as the lovers renewed their emotional vows, the feelings of erotic liberation rose into a climatic response.

Downstairs, the phone began to ring. It was one of those demanding sounds. As it rang, the front door bell joined in. After a few more minutes, the phone stopped chiming, but the long shadow outside of the door remained. It bore the appearance of a huge lady who was dressed in the brightest and most exhilarating plumage. A large, clinging blouse which was coloured in a reflective lime green and blood red design. It certainly attracted attention and did little to conceal the sumptuous nature of what lay beneath. She also wore a tight knee-length black skirt and the lightest shade of suede, brown leather sandals. She was big and yet she was very attractive. Her face wore a pleasant aspect and anyone she knew always greeted her with a genuinely warming smile. You really couldn't help it. She was nice.

Petula had been standing patiently for a good ten minutes and the sunshine was beginning to make her a tad too warm for comfort. Tentatively, she decided to try the door handle, which she was pleased find turned.

As the door gingerly glided open, she swore that she could hear a moan in the distance. So, she knew that someone was in. She walked through the doorway and placed herself in the centre of the foyer; just beneath the main staircase. She cleared her throat. Then, she called out for Mrs Strumshell and patiently waited. As she did, her eyes looked at some of the large pictures which adorned the pale walls. One was a painting of a curved street. It depicted a line of tall buildings. They all had dark and glossy front doors. One looked as though it had a number on it. She peered closer, but couldn't quite make out the figures.

A few moments later, Sondra came down the stairs wearing a dazzling dressing gown. Her hair was half pinned up and she looked a little windswept.

Petula approached her and put her hand out in a welcoming fashion; calling for it to be shaken. Sondra accepted the offering. They calmly walked into the living room. Where Petula took her usual seat and waited for Mrs Strumshell to pour her regular glass of vodka and tonic. Only this time, the lady of the house abstained and took to a branded diet lemonade instead. Petula was impressed.

"What do you have to tell me, Petula?" Sondra asked.

"He's been to see him again, Mrs Strumshell."

"When?"

"As always. He goes over there, in the evening. He drives to the man's apartment. It's a stylish new-build complex, on the riverside. Parks his white Mercedes car in the public car park and then discretely wanders round to his lover's abode. He visits him like clockwork. Straight after work. He's very punctilious; your husband." She smiled.

The remark struck Sondra. Momentarily, she thought about what was being said and then raised her eyes. "Petula Vancouver, you are the most precise and sweet natured woman I have ever met. I set you on a task and off you go. You are so…" her arms floated for a moment, "…enthralling. Yes, that's the word; enthralling. I love reading your observations and I believe you have a true passion for your chosen profession. What say you?"

As she moved about, some of Sondra's hair began to fall lose from its clips. She took the opportunity to re-assemble its moorings.

As she attempted to re-pin it, Petula watched, with an intelligent eye. One that completely understood what was taking place. She smiled. Not a condemning smile, but one of appreciation. She knew what was going on and she understood exactly why Sondra Strumshell was doing it. It was not for her to judge or to get involved. "You remember our contract?" She looked at Sondra.

Mrs Strumshell loosely nodded back, "Mmm."

"Well, he is having an affair. His name is Sandy Wilbertson. He's a thirty something blond who likes to come over as an ex-military type. Always dresses immaculately. Has a fast maroon coloured sports car. I'm afraid I didn't get the make or model. But, he's not afraid to socialize. They meet up in his apartment. Sometimes they go out. I know that Hem pays for his pleasures and that Sandy is improving his living standards on such proceeds."

Sondra got up and casually walked towards the bay window. With the sunlight streaming onto her shiny hair, she asked, "How much does he pay?"

"He always takes a bundle of notes in an A5 envelope. I understand it contains around five hundred pounds per occasion. Although, the size of the bundle does seem to be expanding. Affection can grow and an enlarged purse does make it appear that he may well be getting a pay rise."

"He must enjoy it then," she said. As she spoke, Sondra's eyes glazed over and she focused on a bouncing rabbit which was playing outside, on the lawn. She thought, for a moment, lifting her glass and placing the cutting edge of its texture against her cheek.

"That much, I do not know. I am aware that he pays him in cash and I presume the recipient doesn't give any kind of formal receipt.

"Do you want me to carry on? I only ask because I don't think there's any more to this story. That said, if they continue the way they are, then news is bound to break soon and I hope you can handle it." At that point, Petula looked uncomfortable and flinched a little.

Sondra changed her angle and caught sight of it. So, she waved for her to carry on.

Petula put her notebook down, changed her tone and became more serious, "Something else has turned up."

Sondra moved away from the window and came back into the middle of the room. Twisting her head slightly, she eyed Petula with care. "Meaning…?"

"Meaning that I have found something out about your husband which is somewhat disturbing. He may actually be in serious trouble and he might be taking a substantial risk."

The love glaze was wearing off now and Sondra had begun to resume her usual style of posture. She came over to the lounge settee and delicately placed herself in prime seating position, for what was about to come. She casually crossed her legs for impact.

In the next ten minutes and to the faint background noise of a running shower, Petula Vancouver unveiled something which made Sondra Strumshell's eyes light up. If, what Petula had said were true, then all her problems would soon be over.

She curled her legs up onto the empty settee and bit down on her little finger. Longingly, she looked over to the stairs and realized that she could finally be free from this horrible husband and fall in love with the man of her dreams. A real man, this time.

Her head was now swimming with ideas. So, she deliberately swung herself around and whispered, "I want to be certain. Before I make any move; I must know that you're right." She looked her guest straight in the eye. "Are you absolutely sure, Petula? I want this to be completely clear before we begin."

"Mrs Strumshell, I assure you that he is doing this. He's after the money. That's what he wants and if he succeeds, then he will take full control of the company and wage a war on all of them."

Absent-mindedly, Sondra half-whispered, "Imagine that… we could finally nail the bastard to the mast." She came forth and spoke firmly, "Will you help me?"

"Of course."

"Then, we have little time to lose. Do you have a contact and somewhere you can stay?"

"Mrs Strumshell, a girl of my breadth and my years means I'm an old duck at this sort of thing. I know this scorecard inside and out. I can take care of myself. Even when others wish to express their own brand of alternatives. What concerns me, is that you need to get away from here and hide yourself somewhere safe. Somewhere that I can keep in touch."

Sondra abruptly responded, "Why should I hide? I haven't done anything. Have I?"

Petula went peachy, but kept her karma. "Good question, and it does depend how you want to play it. You could stay here right until the very end, but it will take guts. Or, you can hide up somewhere and let me get a little team to negotiate for you. It's not about money. It's about your feelings and how you want to handle it. Which way do want to play it?"

Sondra Strumshell put on a broad smile. She had been through several fist fights before. So, with the chance of freedom in the offing, she politely walked over to Petula and kissed her on the cheek. Then, with the line of her back looking straight, she murmured, "I'm staying right where I am. I live here and let him live with that!" A few moments later, a programmed Petula was allowed to leave from the front of the house.

By this time, it was almost four p.m. Sondra stood still and tugged away at her remaining hair clips. She didn't like them and she didn't want their restriction any longer. They were confining her thoughts. She ran her fingers carefully through the length of her silky radiance and shook her head. Then, she slowly made her way to the staircase and peacefully wandered up. As she reached the middle, a free-looking Brian appeared on the top. Hair all messy and wet. Fresh from the toweling it had just suffered. She stopped him in his tracks, put her hand out and, as he dared to come closer, she looked deeper and deeper into the young man. Finally convincing herself that all she needed now was a little more of his personal attention. And, in this mood, no matter what else was due to happen, he was definitely worth the risk.

Standing there, he casually tugged at the cord of her dressing gown. It fell open and revealed the unprotected tan of her smooth bare skin. She wriggled her shoulders and let the rest of it fall away. Then, she walked into his open arms. They passionately kissed each other on the top stair and moved away into the master bedroom once again. Where, without a word or a harsh sound, the peace was luxuriously disturbed once more…

***

Chapter 8
How to Cope in This

It was still 30 degrees Celsius outside and the two electricians were sat in their van; drinking ice cold cans of orangeade. "What a day," said an ashen-faced Adrian.

"You're right there, mate," said Allan.

They were sat with both of the van's back doors wide open; trying to get some air to flow through. The van was parked at an angle, a little way back from the newly arrived police cars. Their vehicles were arrayed in a random line, at the front of the DIY store. The two guys were trying to be as normal as possible, but it wasn't working out very well. By any measure, what they had just been through was awful and it did not make any sense. Yet, it had definitely happened and Adrian was still feeling queasy about it. Although, the sugar sweet drink was helping to calm his stomach.

The work had been going well and they had located the source of the problem. The wiring was correctly wrapped inside the sealed cable ducts. Those ran inside the steel framework of the prefabricated structure. When the facia had come away, it had also taken part of the ducting with it. That had caused some of the cable to snag on the metal framework.

As the facia had continued its slide to the ground, the outer coating of the wire had been chaffed away. This allowed exposed metal to touch the live wires. That caused the mains power to earth and then, the switches all tripped out. The remedy now was either to replace the broken cabling or just isolate the whole site and seal it off. That decision had rested with the manager and he quickly told them that he wanted everything replacing and making completely safe.

Nothing too complex, really. A couple of hours or so and it should all be sorted. But, what had held everything up was what Adrian had found in the ceiling. The police said the body must have been up there for at least two or three months. Their forensic team were called out. They quickly arrived and began their task with an atmosphere of subdued normality. Adrian wanted to clean up the mess he had made, where he had been sick, but he was told to go away. So, Allan decided that they should carry on with their work. They pulled some new cable from their van and re-wired the affected section. It wasn't that big a job and, just after four p.m., it was all done and dusted.

In the middle of it all, though, another police sergeant came over and took a brief statement from them both. She said that she would ask them to call into the station once it was all typed up.

At that stage, Adrian suddenly began to feel a chill. Then, he became unsteady on his feet. In fact, he very nearly passed out. Allan managed to prop him up and then got him a sugary orange drink. After a few sips, it soon began to work its magic. Once he was coming around, Allan said that they should head off for home. He tried to lighten the mood by saying, "These vending drinks cost a fortune. We can stop off at the local and buy a cool pint for the same price, if you like?" It didn't have to be funny nor did it have to be true. But, it lifted the atmosphere just a little bit and that seemed to help.

It was getting near to tea time at Jenny's guest house. Her dining room tables were laid out and decked with her traditional red-and-white table cloths. There were six of them and they all displayed a chequered pattern. Jenny had arranged the table cloths so that the patterns were all in a straight line; pointing towards the window. As you looked at them, each table covering was the mirror image of its neighbour. All dutifully arranged for the meal which was currently brewing; in the warmth of her pristine kitchen.

This was her time of day and she was enjoying it. She thoroughly adored running her guest house. Taking all of her responsibilities seriously. She always made sure that everything was clean and tidy. On a daily basis, she took in the guests washing, changed all the bedding and towels. Then she made sure that the laundry was collected. After that, she set about dusting and polishing the place over.

She loved the smell of fresh polish and she put a great deal of effort into making her home nice and welcoming. Even her lodgers noted how shiny her staircases were. That pleased her. It was her little reward and one that she had earned; all by herself.

Now though, it was getting close to tea time. It was gone five o'clock. Jubilantly, Jenny danced a little twirl. She was so excited at the prospect of all those wonderful paying men entering into her dining room. Coming there, to eat her cooked food and talk about their daily toils. Tales about their work, what they had been up to and what they had seen out in the big wide world. It was all such fun.

As she danced inside, her eyes paraded across the dining room. Looking at it as though it were a stage show. That was when she noticed something. So, she stopped herself, walked over to table number three and concentrated. Then, she rotated the table cloth a tiny bit, to the right. This straightened it, just a smidgen and then, she gave out an approving 'ah-ha'. Now, she knew it was ready.

Standing back, she looked it over again. She loved setting these tables and she knew how important it was. When they arrived, the men always gave her the eye and she always returned her appreciation with a giggle. The forks, the knives, the spoons and everything had to be perfect. No error was ever tolerated. Especially tonight.

That was because this evening's meal was to be her home-made favourite: shepherd's pie. It came with freshly cooked vegetables. Tonight, this would be carrots, broccoli and broad beans. She loved broad beans. Just the thought of them made her lips go all wet. All of this was on offer and afterwards came her speciality; her very own recipe of rhubarb and jam-treacle sponge pudding. It came with a sensational raspberry custard. She had spent years coming up with the mixture. Years spent mixing different jams and using every kind of sugar available. After much practice, she finally arrived at the very pinnacle of success. Everyone loved it and this was going to be her special presentation, this evening.

As her clock struck five fifteen, she became full of happiness. She could also hear approaching voices. The coming of conversations and banter. Her guests were arriving home from their hard day's work. As they began to drift into her dining room, she greeted each person by name and escorted them to the chair which she had chosen for them. Gradually, her little dining area lifted itself from a place of silence into a bubbling cauldron of people. Each one, bringing their own sense of life into this arena. Their buzzing voices created an atmosphere. One that bore a testament to its creator. And, for Jenny, that raised a total feeling of joy.

Adrian and Allan had pulled off the old Stanton Vale Road and turned into the 'Re-Viners Arms'. They sat down inside, drunk two pints of lager and were just getting into the swing when Allan suddenly remembered the van. He went visibly white and looked at his colleague. "We can't drive now, can we?"

"Not with what we've gone through. I can't really care though. Beccy will be biting at the bit and ready to kill me; whatever I do. I don't want to face her anymore. I'm sick of her endless remarks and pointless accusations. To hell with it! Let's drink the place dry."

Allan looked at him. They had been around some tight curves together. Adrian had always stuck by him and he felt for him right now. Though Adrian couldn't see it, Beccy wasn't really the issue. He was a good-looking bloke and if she wanted to lose him, then that was her stupid affair. The real issue was that Adrian had just been face-to-face with a rotting corpse. And, there really was no way of dealing with that.

Who the dead man was, no one could say. From the conversations they heard, no one could identify him. Nobody knew who he was and although everyone was very professional about it, no one did a thing for the guy who had made the terrible discovery. No comfort was offered and it was one hell of a shock to get over. As a result, he was feeling really worried about his friend. "Are you all right, mate?"

Adrian's white face stared back and he quietly replied, "Yeh, of course I am. It's just one of those things, isn't it? Pity no one knows who he is. He must have a family out there somewhere." He raised a full glass to his lips and swallowed.

"Do you think someone deliberately put him up there? I mean, if he was working, then someone would have missed him weeks ago. Wouldn't they?"

Adrian shrugged. "Maybe he was a burglar? But, then he'd have had clothes on."

"Perhaps he worked alone? That way, no one would have ever known about him being up there."

"All bit of a mess really. Weird too. If that facia hadn't torn those wires apart, then he could have been up there for an eternity. Except…" Adrian paused, "…except, that smell was really bad. Why on earth didn't somebody find out what it was. How come nobody looked?" He shivered.

Allan said, "I'm going to call Brenda [his partner] and see if she can pick us up."

He pulled out his phone and began to dial their number. The phone rang and rang, but no one answered. Then, the caller messaging service kicked in and he left a few urgent words. In the next hour; he tried four more times. By that time, they were on to their fifth pint. No one had phoned back and it was slowly dawning on Adrian that he was going to have to make a move. He did that on the basis, that if he didn't go now, then he probably wouldn't be able to. Allan went to the loo and whilst he was gone, Adrian stood up and made his way to the exit door.

They had been in the pub for the best part of three hours and, by now, it was heavily raining outside. When Adrian opened the door, he saw it for himself. He paused and looked out across the rain-darkened car park. They were a good five miles away from his home and he knew he was in no shape to walk it in these conditions. So, he just stood and watched the slewing rain drops hitting the ground. It all seemed so pointless to him. Looking out, at this scene, he realized that all of his entire life was just falling apart. Nobody cared about him. Not even himself. That thought pricked his state of mind and, as he watched the rain falling, Adrian began to cry…

It was seven fifteen a.m. when Petula Vancouver arose from her slumber. Her right eyelid raised itself to face a faint looking green number. Yup! It was definitely time to get up. She cruised herself into the upright, placed her arms on either side of her body and swung her legs over the edge of her bed. Momentarily, she was confused. Confused, because, there, on the end of her bed was a fluffy black and white kitten.

Petula couldn't see that well without her glasses. So, she tilted her head a little to try and gain some perspective. Wherein, the little fluffy creature did the self-same thing back to her. They were both looking at each other on the wonk. At which point, Petula gave in to the most hilarious laugh. It tickled her pink and to round it off, she clapped her ample hands. "Well!" she said, placing them forward and picking up the cuddly little bundle, "who on earth are you?"

In her hands, this little puzzle of warmness began to nuzzle against her. Without doubt, it was love at first sight and thereby, Miss Petula had now been chosen in the comfort of her own bedroom, by a mysteriously uninvited guest. A fact which she never questioned at all.

To Wilbur, the summertime was nice. You could get up when you wanted and wander wherever you wanted. Then come back, if you wanted. All in the glorious splendour of daylight. He liked that. It was regular and he adored predictability. Above all, it gave certainty and that allowed you to make plans.

He crunched into his red delicious apple. His first bite gave an audible 'crack'. He liked that. It was a satisfying sound; one which agreed with his belief, that all was well in the world.

Wilbur was standing on the front patio; outside a sizeable house. It was a big property with a long curvy drive. From the road, the driveway swept away to the right and took you to a prominent building that was completely out of sight. If the driveway were straight, then you would have had no problem seeing it from the roadside. As things were, the end of this particular curve portrayed your arrival to a modern facsimile of a structure. One which was pretending to be something else. This address looked like it was made out of chalk and cardboard. The outside was painted in a ghostly whiteness. Matt effect and certainly not glossy. It also looked completely fake. What made it worse was that someone had seen fit to cover the roof in some shiny dark-green tiles. They were reflective and Wilbur thought it was way too garish. It could even be described as 'tarty'. Not his choice at all, but then he had to concede, things rarely were, these days. Nonetheless, he continued his pleasurable eat and only paused when there was no more apple left to bite. At this point, he threw away the core and rang the doorbell.

It took a long, long while. Not that Wilbur was in a hurry, but it did take a great deal of time and he found that particularly irritating. It was gone six a.m. on a sunny summer morning. The world was doused in sunlight. How could you possibly fail, but to be alert?

The door made a sound and it eased open, half a whisker. There appeared a semi-bearded boy of twenty years or so. He eyed Wilbur up. "What do you want?" he said and scratched at his facial hair.

Wilbur licked his lower lip and peered at the ridiculous vision in front of him. Satisfied with what he saw, he spoke, "Where's your dada?"

The bearded youngster returned a bemused gaze and said, "What?"

Wilbur sighed and then said, "I have an appointment with Tony Filby. Is he here?" Then, he smiled politely.

Today, Wilbur was looking especially prim. He had been staying in his rented accommodation for a while and, this time, he had taken the opportunity to partake of their laundry service. Everything was neatly washed, ironed and returned; within twenty-four hours. He was pleased with the results. So, there he stood, showing them off. Before him, however, stood an unshaven cretin wearing only a knotted bathroom towel around his middle. All that, whilst exhibiting the aimless expression of a prat on his face. This behaviour was highly insulting. It annoyed Wilbur, intensely and his own facial muscles were having extreme difficulty in not betraying his thoughts.

The twenty-two-year-old Simon Filby, however, was well used to this sort of interruption. His old man had done well for himself and he was proud to give his wealth to his eldest son. Occasionally, things went sour and, to him, this was just one of those times.

Simon nodded at Wilbur and waved him through. The door duly opened a little further and Wilbur Mortanant proceeded inside. Simon immediately stopped him and made it clear that he wanted Wilbur to wait where he was. Then he disappeared up the stairs and left the new entrant, all alone, in the entrance way. Wilbur looked around and saw that the floor was incredible. The colour was so deep that you could almost fall into it. It was such a deep shade of purple that it practically showed itself as being black. Wilbur crouched down and ran his fingers across the surface. It was seamed, with a number of minute lines. A quality laminate covering of some sort. You could see the grain, through the glossy surface. It was clearly one of those more expensive and hard-wearing varieties. With this level of saturation, the colour possessed both the sheen and a richness that reflected any form of light shone onto it.

Looking away, he could make out the existence of a darkened hallway. One which led to, what appeared to be, a lounge. Further down, he assumed there to be a kitchen. It looked very nice. Just a little depressing and he wasn't sure whether there may be some pictures hanging on the walls.

Upstairs, Simon pulled on a skimpy red T-shirt. It had some obscene words written on the front. He also slapped on some stretchy white shorts and no underwear. His head had a mass of long wavy hair, which was loosely hung across a fiendishly childlike expression. Once dressed, he started to look around for his kit. Sudo had phoned to say that this dude would be turning up and that he was to waste him; without any style. So, he picked up a small hand gun, clicked a silencer onto the front and took a full clip of spare bullets; for comfort's sake.

The movements upstairs sent sounds down the stairs. Not that Wilbur minded. His own feet inadvertently tapped around on the hard floor surface. He calmly walked in, through the open lounge doors and perused the scene inside. On the carpeted floor was sprawled, a completely naked woman. She was half wrapped in a flimsy duvet cover and, when Wilbur appeared, she pulled the rest of it over herself. Wilbur obligingly raised his right hand and quietly said, "Sorry, Ma'am."

He walked backwards to leave the scene and discretely closed the door behind himself. That was when he felt something chill him. He turned. But, no one was there. With the door now shut, the hallway was even darker than before. He also noticed something moving, in the background. It was protruding, pointy and most provocative. Wilbur thought it could have been a small hand gun. He wasn't exactly sure. It wasn't light enough to see properly and thought, by itself, was never acute enough to form a reliable judgement. In response, Wilbur slid his soles sideways and moved into the empty kitchen for safety.

Simon was now wearing some kind of very tight labelled shorts and a pair of extremely expensive white trainers. He wanted the flexibility to move quickly. That, combined with the superior grip of his footwear, would allow him to abruptly twist and turn. If that tosser managed to get hold of him, then he would be ready. Except, Wilbur's dark blue clothing blended extremely well with the created darkness. He was sure that he'd just seen him down the hallway. Belinda hadn't screamed out, but she had clearly closed the door. So, where the bloody hell was he?

Simon's heart rate was rapidly climbing. He was nervous, but kept on moving. He wanted this bastard to be dead and quickly. Then, he might get another screw before she left. With taut senses, he consciously walked further down the hallway. Careful, not to make a sound. His father had placed a series of heavy old oil paintings on the walls. They dominated the passage. Their sturdy frames wore a tarnished gold finish. They contained large artistic paintings of old, long since deceased military figures. Statesmen-like salutes of solemnity. Their dead faces were gloomily looking at him, from every painted canvas. They were morbidly life-like and creepy; both at the same time. They looked like they could move at any moment and right now they were irritating Simon to hell.

He was certain that Wilbur was here, but he just couldn't see him. As he tried to make sense of it, he clipped the gun against the wall and swore under his breath. He was confused and kept asking himself: *Where is he? Where the hell could he be?* Standing outside the kitchen, he was trying to make sense of something that he didn't understand. In that final moment, his one remaining thought was savoured. A single thought, which clasped hold of his soul and flew him away.

As Simon was cursing, something new was moving like lightning in the air. Instantly, he felt the most excruciating pain. It came from nowhere and it was insatiable. Nothing had ever felt like this before. A second later, the gun hit the floor. Only, he hadn't done it. His head spun around because he knew he hadn't let go! But, the pain was truly unbelievable and he was forced to look at his left arm. He raised it up. Only, it wasn't there! He tried to make sense of it. He lifted it higher and, then he saw that below the elbow, there was nothing. Nothing at all! Nothing except blood. His blood! And, his blood was going everywhere! In those short final seconds, he began to realize what had taken place. But, a male adult body only holds seven pints and by the manual count of 'four', he was running down to six and reducing very fast. Consciousness went and his head hit the ground, with a 'crack'; where it splattered out onto the hardened dark, shiny surface.

Wilbur was now looking at him along the edge of an etched sword. He had found two of them, hanging on the kitchen wall. A plaque was placed underneath. Some kind of chivalrous display piece. Not long enough for a horse-mounted crusader. But, adequate for hand-to-hand combat. He noted that the blades had been freshly sharpened. It also had good balance and was incredibly easy to use. Someone must have cleaned them up quite recently.

Anyway, it had worked. So, he quietly reached into his pocket and located a new liquorice. In the silence, he stood there and chewed it. Gaining in reason that which no one ever dared to capture or comprehend.

In the peace, he looked at the fallen hand. It was an expensive piece of equipment. Perhaps there was more of its kind up the stairs?

After a few minutes, he quietly walked up to the first floor and made his observations. He opened a big fitted wardrobe and located a large shiny suitcase. Opening it, he wasn't at all surprised. Predictably, dirty men have dirty little habits. He knew what they were and how to deal with them. These kinds of items disgusted him: why did such men exist? This world was full of beautiful women. Women who they could love and that love would actually save them. But, these people didn't want such responsibility. They were shallow, weak human beings. Incapable of sharing or receiving the very thing they needed most.

The wardrobe had displayed its contents. It was full of guns and there was a deep green plastic bag filled with pornographic images and a heap of USB memory sticks. He spat at them.

Sad it was. But, at least the girl downstairs was alive and safe. Yet, it soon became very clear, that he had been sent on another wild goose chase. He detested that. This was nothing more than an elaborate set up. So, someone must be onto him. Still, if this was their idea of a trap, then perhaps he should repay the favour. His eye suddenly caught the image of more suitcases. He moved to open one of them. By doing so, he saw something to match with his thoughts. His prayers had indeed been answered. He smiled again and like a juggler in a show, he started to play with the instruments at his disposal.

Twenty minutes later, the lounge door began to move on its hinges. Someone was pulling at it, from the other side. Wilbur was leaning over the balcony and actively peering down the staircase. He was looking at a teenage girl, who was now encasing herself in the skimpiest of designer clothes. Waif-like; she looked so thin that, if she shivered, she may have fallen apart. Her long blonde hair was very neatly tied into a bun. "This way," he said in a soulless, dry tone and pointed toward the front door. Before she moved, she looked right at him. The blueness of her eyes came through. Their force was almost paralyzing. Piercing closely into every movement he made.

At that same moment, he couldn't care. He didn't want anything to do with her kind and he had met this situation before. Sometimes they would speak. Other times they didn't speak at all. She was nothing to him. He was concerned about something completely different. As they walked out of the house, he checked his watch. It was seven fifty-four a.m. He briefly left her by the front gate. At this distance, he stood and perused the grounds. Satisfied with the scenery, he turned to go and then there suddenly came an all mighty 'woof'!

In the background, the whole of the shiny green roof bowed out and lifted a few inches off the property. It then fell apart and erupted into a series of tiny particles, which dispatched themselves all over the freshly mown lawns. Some even made it to the swimming pool, at the back. As the fragments rained down and across the garden, Wilbur couldn't help but muse that, whatever remained in the building now, would be a far better testament to what he had seen beforehand. As that thought garnered some resonance, a free-running gas main began to hiss out loud. In that moment, it caught alight and ignited. A huge exploding mass of fire appeared. It came up like the roar of a volcano. A spectacle of war and fragments: purely for flame's sake.

On the roadside, the driver's door clicked shut. Quietly, he turned the key. At which point, the girl appeared and tapped on the passenger door. Wilbur opened it, for her, and she climbed in. Exhibiting no more a do, he drove the girl and himself safely away down the street. A sense of discretion, in compliance with professional respect, meant neither party uttered a single word.

***

Chapter 9
With Feelings Like These

Beccy was sobbing. Sobbing out loud she was and sobbing out loud, in the bathroom. Her ruddy red face was illuminated with a fountain of streaming tears. She was inconsolable. Sitting, perched on the edge of bath-tub and tightly holding onto a soggy towel for comfort. She was peering at herself in the mirror, visibly shaking and completely ridden with guilt.

In her thoughts, she must have done something terrible. She had tried everything she possibly could. But, it just wasn't working. It was going nowhere and she really didn't know what else to do.

Why were men so callous? He clearly didn't care about her. Can't! He didn't love her at all and she knew that now. No doubt! She knew it for certain! But then, here was the thing: she couldn't make herself let go of him. And, despite all of her actions, he really was a wonderful man. He looked good. He was intelligent. He could be really funny at times and he was so good humoured too. Beyond that, he was a compassionate mate. He understood her moods and her anxieties. He never pushed a raw point. That understanding was something she had never seen before, in a boy. It was something totally untouchable and so unlike a fully grown man to possess. He also listened to her. Whether she was angry or happy, he actually listened. He explained himself, so that she understood what he was doing and why. No one else was like that. Nobody she knew was as precious as him. And how had she rewarded him? As she thought about it, it became clear.

For some strange reason, she couldn't face her life without him and that frightened her. It frightened her because it meant only one thing. She absolutely hated the idea. She didn't really want to admit it. But, truth was truth and this truth was the reality. One which she couldn't escape from. The facts were obvious. They really were. The simple truth was: that she loved him.

This realization was completely new to her. She had been with other boyfriends. She had often thought that she was in love. It lasted pleasantly for a while and then went its own sweet way. But, it had never felt like this. This was intense and this time it hadn't faded. If anything, it had become stronger. Yet, it wasn't the feeling which had upset her. It was something else. An understanding. One that had just come out of nowhere and struck home with such a force. Only, that made things even worse. She wasn't prepared. She wasn't even aware about what to do. It also awoke a vulnerability. Something that she had never experienced before. Something very powerful and it was beating in her heart. She was suddenly desperate to hold him and to feel his warm arms around her. To breathe in his presence. This was new. It worried her and then she felt the anguish building again.

Suddenly, she bit into her lip. Her anger was rising. Why do I feel like this? All at once, she hated him with every sinew. Hated him for what he had done. Hated him for everything he was! Yet, as soon as she stopped that train of thought, it all opened up again. The insecurity and fear all came back. For some reason, this need just wouldn't go away. It was a jealous feeling, this time, and one which couldn't go because it was real. It was beyond all rhyme and reason.

Stopping herself, she looked up. Feeling totally inadequate, bemused and awful: all at the same time. She felt completely exposed and so very vulnerable. She needed him so much. So, why had she hit him? Why had she shouted such unnecessary abuse at him? Why couldn't she have reached out and been nice? She could have. She knew that. Thinking about it, made her feel so utterly insecure. Here she was; a fully-grown woman with the feelings and emotions of an adolescent teenager. Only, they weren't. These emotions were far stronger than a teenager could conjure up and, above all, she knew what it meant. Either, she had the confidence to walk out on him. Or she had to sit him down and tell him straight. Tell him properly; just what she felt. Tell him somehow, but where on earth could she begin? Would he even talk to her now? She really didn't know. She knew that she couldn't bear this feeling of longing. It was such a powerfully selfish emotion. She wanted him, but didn't know what to do. She didn't want to leave him. She just wanted him to love her. Only, how could she tell him that, now! He'd never believe her. The tears refreshed themselves across her face. A tirade of emotional confusions. She had to do something or this could never end and that would be truly awful.

Adrian had come in late and he'd been drinking again. He arrived and faced Beccy at the very point when last night's dinner had just turned to ash. The meal was completely burned to a crisp. Then, there he was; three quarters drunk and soaking wet. She was furious! Why hadn't he called her? Why hadn't he let her know he was going to be late? Why was he standing there, soaked to the skin and dripping water all over the place?

He never actually had the chance to give an answer, because she stomped off in a fury and left him alone. Next thing, the bedroom door slammed shut. Inside, she sat on their bed, picked up their bedside photo and threw it, with all her might, against the wall. It broke into a thousand pieces and then she started to cry.

In the pouring rain, Adrian had finally decided to leave Allan at the pub. With everything else that had been going on, he just wanted to walk and get some fresh air into his lungs. He told Allan the same and set off by himself. A short while after, Brenda pulled up and wound the window down. She offered him a ride home. But, he said he needed to walk. So, she and Allan drove on. The van was left in the pub car park. The landlord kindly said that it was okay to leave it there overnight. Adrian had the keys and he knew it would be safe enough.

By the time he got home, it was getting close to eleven o'clock. All he wanted was a quick shower and to fall sleep. But when he walked in, hurricane Beccy awoke and came at him with a force ten crescendo. It was jaw-smackingly awful. Far worse than he thought it was ever going to be. He felt so ill. All he wanted to do was fall asleep. But, she kept screaming at him and this time he couldn't muster any strength to respond. He couldn't because he was completely knackered.

If she'd been quieter, then he could have told her everything. But, she was wailing off about ruined food, missing phone calls and a lack of messages. In the middle of her tirade, he pulled the smartphone out of his pocket. Clearly, it wasn't water proof. In fact, it was soaking wet and completely dead to the world. Not that she noticed. After three or four minutes of hell, she slapped his face, then pounded off upstairs and banged the bedroom door shut. She threw something at the wall: he heard it gouge at the plasterwork. The message was strikingly clear. Half an hour later, he washed himself by hand at the kitchen sink. He did that, in case she turned on him, whilst he was in the shower. He felt really uneasy and very uncertain about her.

He finally tucked himself onto the settee, at around mid-night, and pulled an old winter coat over his shoulders. It rested on his body like a sheet. He slept, on and off, with his feet sticking out. At about five a.m. he retrieved his overalls from the warm airing cupboard and set off for work: on foot.

He marched into the town. 'Brekstars' was a local coffee shop which did a good excuse for a breakfast. At six thirty in the morning, he tucked into a freshly cooked sausage roll with some piping hot tea. He also bought a pint of ice-cold milk. It seemed a good idea. It was good to notice that he was able to eat again. That really was positive news. Then, he pulled out his phone. Leaving it in the airing cupboard overnight had yielded results. It lit up and connected to Allan's land line; they talked.

At seven forty-five, Brenda turned up with Allan in tow and he climbed into the back of their car.

They were making their way to the 'Re-Viners Arms' again. Allan spoke up, "You look rough, mate. You okay?"

"Yeh, I'm fine. Just had a few problems getting some sleep. You know how it is."

Brenda spoke, "You can get help at the doctors, Aidy? Why don't you call in sick and see someone at the surgery?"

"Thanks for the thought, Bren. Only, I'm not really sick and, if I were, a doctor wouldn't be able to help. I appreciate the advice though. Truth is; I don't really want any sleeping pills and I certainly don't want tranquilizers. I'll just have to get over it. Other people do."

"It was on the news last night, you know," said Allan.

"What was?" asked Adrian.

"What you discovered!" said Brenda. "Something about a young man found in a loft space at Saps. Did you recognize him Adrian?"

"Can't say I did. To me, he was just a bloated heap of rotting flesh. All purple and covered in flies. He wasn't wearing any clothes that I could see, either. That smell though. It was unbelievable. No one should ever go anywhere near to that sort of thing."

"Some people have to," she said.

"They're welcome to it. It's not for me. I'd be quite happy never to see such a thing again. As long as I live." Adrian suddenly remembered something. "That reminds me, the police are supposed to be wanting some sort of a statement from us. Aren't they?"

"Yeh," said Allan.

"I hope they don't call home," Adrian absently said.

"Why'd you say that?" said Allan. His eyes locked onto Adrian, just as they pulled up to the front of the pub.

Adrian didn't bother to answer.

At the pub, they found that the gate was locked tight and there in the car park was their van. Allan kissed Brenda and waved her off. Then, the two males stood still. Leaning on the gate and weighing up the limits of their options.

Brian had had a really bad night. He was still in a state of utter turmoil. He had woken up at mid-night and couldn't get back to sleep. He was anxious and it was all about that woman, Sondra. She definitely had a hold on him. He knew that, but he didn't know how to handle it. As his mind was busy, thinking these things over, he had heard Linda moan in her sleep. For one moment, that struck fear into him: he thought that she might have been awake. But, her breathing remained steady. So, it appeared he was free to process the thoughts which were occupying his mind.

He was painstakingly trying to piece things together and this was important. Because the moves he made now would set the course for the rest of his life. He calmed himself for a moment. Realizing that for the first time since he had met Linda, he was actually considering himself in the singular. He also noticed that he felt hot. In fact, his pyjamas were soaking wet, with perspiration and he was actually stuck to the bed sheets. Unashamed, his mind was wandering again. He took a breath and refocused his thoughts. He had to do something about that woman. Or did he? She was sexy as hell. No doubts there. She could easily turn you on at a hundred paces. A firm body; like a model and all of it responded so acutely to his touch. These thoughts began to arouse him, but he didn't want that. He wanted clarity instead. He knew he could have her, but did she want him? Or was he just this week's male offering? He really didn't know. So, he dared to shine a small light into his memory. He searched for the part where it all started. She had been having some problem with her boiler and, sure enough, at that stage, there was a genuine fault with it. But, whilst he was working away, he became conscious of her watching him. As time went by, this developed. She became more and more blatant.

This sort of thing happened from time to time. So, he didn't pay too much attention. At least, not until she came over and kissed him. Once she had done that, then that did it.

She had kissed him, full on the lips and pushed him onto the boiler he was working on. Then, she backed away and gave him one of her looks. God, those looks were like a supernatural force. She had the most beautiful face in the world. That: and with her hair just laying loosely over her shoulders. She knew exactly what she was doing. Satisfied with the effect, she had proceeded to remove her blouse. So, there she was; in a dark-tan see-through bra. It was clear that she was highly aroused and was showing herself off, for him to see. In that state, she reached out and he just couldn't help himself.

She led him into her bedroom and revealed the beauty of a mature, well-toned female body. All the curves and the skimpiest of clothing, which just seemed to fall away. She wore the thinnest of black knickers. The thinnest he had ever seen. Ones which precisely matched her taut stockings. Everything was on show. Right in front of him and he... touched it. She loved it. All of it. Only then, he became hers and she was demanding everything of him. She understood what she was doing. She responded to every move and every single caress. She moaned and seemed to fully adore his every appreciation. She also experienced the most powerful orgasms. He could remember her crying out and begging for more. It was a powerful passion, but was it love?

He focused on that thought, for a moment and felt deeply uncomfortable about this. But, he was certain, it wasn't love. She was enjoying herself and the attention which she had generated. She was receiving her worship. Her body looked great, covered in sweat and moving up and down on top of his own. She stimulated him until he couldn't contain himself anymore. And, then she became a kitten. She positively purred, tucking her perspiring head onto his molten chest and wrapping her loving arms around his middle. She was in heaven. But looking back at it now, was he?

No! No, he wasn't. It hurt him to reconcile these emotions, but emotions are what they were and his feelings were not hers to take. He loved his wife. Linda understood him and loved him. If she ever found out what he'd done, it would break her heart in two. She might even kill herself and he couldn't possibly cope with that. She meant everything to him. They had a house, they had plans for a family. Above all, they had a future. That woman couldn't give any of that. All she had to offer was sex. Linda loved him and that love was worth ten times more than any adulterous affair.

His chest felt heavy. His breathing was hard and he was completely ridden with uncontrollable guilt. He was still sweating, but his mouth was so acrid and dry. He paused for a moment. He wanted to analyze his thoughts further and, this time, he thought about Linda. About how she treated him and how their love-making made him feel. The way her body responded to his movements. How she felt when he was inside her. The sounds she made and the way she kissed him. The things she said, afterwards and the way they confided in one another.

As those thoughts permeated his soul, he consciously checked how he felt. Then he turned the same process back onto Sondra Strumshell. He was still highly aroused, but that wasn't it. Thinking about her exposed naked body moving under his. Remembering how she felt and the way her hands swept over his skin. She was far more touchy-feely. And then, it came to him.

They were not the same! Linda always kissed him afterwards and snuggled up for a cuddle. They would often talk and speak about the kind of future they wanted togther. But with Sondra, there was nothing. Absolutely nothing. She held onto him; like he was a bag of straw. She laid on him; like he was a park bench. She didn't love him. Couldn't! But, boy did she want his body.

Gently, he sat upright and sniffled, with his nose. It was gone one thirty a.m. and he was totally soaked through. Poor Linda was lying next to a paddling pool in pyjamas. But, at least now his anxiety was receding. He felt better. He turned to his wife and kissed her, on the side of her neck. In the darkness, she sighed, turned and moved closer to him. She never said a thing about his sweaty condition. Instead, she pulled him close and suddenly, he found the happiness which his uncertainties had been depriving them of. In those wonderful moments, he knew; Linda was the only one for him and no one else was ever going to change that again.

***

Chapter 10
Options of the Day

Since Brenda had left them, Adrian and Allan had climbed up and over the closed gate, when they encountered a problem. "How are we going to get the van out, mate?" asked Allan.

Adrian looked at him, whilst wearing a shrug. At the same moment, a brightly coloured police car was cautiously driving along. It came by the 'Re-Viners Arms' and stopped. A minute or two later, out stepped PC Fiona Mills with all her official gear on. She was stood, looking right at two men, who could be in their early twenties. They were wearing some kind of light grey and blue boiler suit apparel, with a company logo on the front. Both of them were looking straight at her, from inside the pub's car park. *Not a wimp in sight,* she thought. Then, in a hoarse voice, she called out, "What exactly are you two doing?"

It was just before eight fifty now and Allan felt that he had probably better walk over to the officer. Otherwise he'd have to shout back and that was not a good way to start a new relationship. He came closer and began to speak, "We were here last night and had too much to drink. So, we left our work van." He pointed towards the blue and crimson vehicle parked behind them. "The landlord said that we could leave it here and pick it up in the morning. So, here we are. Only, the gate's locked up and we were wondering how to get the van out."

He was holding a set of van keys in his hand and the officer could see that the logo on their tunics matched the one on the van. She pulled a face, looked him up and down; through her cautiously tired eyes. When Adrian came over, he told her about their escapades at Saps, the day before. The body they had found and whether they needed to visit the police station or not. Please could she help?

PC Mills shook her head. She had no idea. What she did know, was that this was the last thing she needed. She was due to end her shift at eight o'clock and it was now approaching eight, fifty-five; with the potential for a nine forty-five finish, at this rate. She sighed and went back to the patrol car where she called in. There was then an elongated conversation. The conclusion was: that Adrian Sormonza did indeed need to provide a formal statement. He needed to go to the police station later in the day. She gave the two men the information and then sighed again. "I suppose you'd like me to get your van out of here?" Both men's faces instantly lit up. "I thought so," she said. With method in her step, she gradually went over to the pub door and donged the bell. Five-and-a-half minutes later, it was gingerly opened by a bespectacled frowning little face. It wore a towel-style white dressing gown. One which had really seen much better days.

It was visibly frayed, at the edges, and looked like it had sampled one too many high-temperature washes. Unperturbed, the officer spoke her words and then things began to happen.

By nine forty-five, Adrian and Allan were on their way to a new housing development on Pride Road. That was off the older Summerville Lane. It was one of those new cheaply built residential developments. The kind which were popping up all over the place these days. Their company had a contract to wire up, two hundred and fifty new premises. Fifty-one had been done so far.

They were there to help their colleagues: Sam and Paul. When they met up, Sam told them to go to the site office, which they did. Ian Patterson was the day foreman and he told them to go to the house marked out as plot forty-six. So, there they were, looking at the semi-built skeleton in front of them. Totally devoid of motivation, Allan came out with the treasured words, "First one to complete their section buys lunch." Adrian thought the words were wrong. They made no sense. They already had sandwiches. Only, then he remembered he didn't. Still, that wasn't much of an inspiration, but it worked well enough to make the van doors swing open for business.

And so, it was breakfast time in Wilbur's world. He had come down the stairs in his newly laundered clothes and then entered into the dining area. He didn't much like the formality of eating to a set recipe. But, after his earlier exploits, he had developed a hunger. As he peered at the array of various delicacies on offer, his eyes landed on a small packet of muesli. Now, that would be perfect!

He took a seat; nearest the window and watched the earthly bound inhabitants performing on the street below. Moving around and wending their way about their boring business. In retrospect, his business was never like that, and today he had two new ideas which he wanted to explore. One being a must, the other being a casual idea.

With that decision made, he looked at what he was about to eat. His breakfast cereal held the appearance of something cold and damp. Little flecks of rolled oats and seeds sporadically appeared above the milky surface. He dipped his spoon into it and then looked up. There was that fat lady again. She amused him. Always overtly and overly polite. Polite to the total end of politeness itself.

Today, she was wrapped up in a black-and-white thing which, he supposed, should really be an apron. It exasperated her ample features. As usual, the buttons were constantly popping open and her under-tunic kept presenting itself into public view. She really needed to wear some thicker underclothes. He could see too much and that was unsettling his appetite. It was also affecting what was perched on his breakfast spoon.

He put it down and raised his hand, "Please, may I have a black filter coffee?"

Jenny replied with a huge smile, "Of course, Mr Wimlour."

Those words depicted the limitations of the woman. Wilbur had repeatedly tried to explain the correct spelling of his name. But, this bulging, blockade of womanhood just couldn't comprehend any measure of what he had said. The approach was simple: he gave her his name, she nodded her head and then called him something else instead. She never failed in this. He thought about it for a while and then concluded that it must be a genetic flaw. A woman of such remarkably low intelligence that she was only able only to cope, by taking on a state of complete ignorance. It mystified him.

Meanwhile, Jenny tottered over with an instant coffee in a cold cup. She gave him some hot milk in a jug. To Wilbur, it was case proven. He just looked on, in complete amazement, and saw her smile coming back; with that unmissable wink of interest. It was so unappealing. Like being turned off, in public.

Suddenly, he awoke to something of which he had almost been blind. He slowly sighed in recognition. This woman clearly fancied him and, with all the other things going on his life, that notion made him feel quite sick. Meanwhile, Jenny did a schoolgirl giggle, followed by a little curtsey and then she aimlessly tottered away. For Wilbur, this could be a worry. But, he wasn't concerned. He had just come up with a consoling thought and that was: he had bigger fish to fry.

Hem had awoken, just after seven a.m. His bedroom was awash with sunlight and he couldn't see because of it. He reached out and picked up his smudged glasses. Suddenly, it all fell into focus. He briefly looked around the room, but couldn't see her. So, he picked up the phone and asked to speak to a Mr Mortanant. The lady at the other end said that he wasn't there.

Hem sat up and sighed. "Listen, you have a guest called Wilbur Mortanant. Go and get him."

There was a penny-dropping silence at the other end of the line and then the receiver went down.

Hem was not best pleased. So, he called 'Sudo' on his smartphone and gave him the instructions instead. As he put the phone down, a piece of news caught hold of his sight. He read it and then eased the large size of his body off the bed and waltzed around to the mirrored wardrobe. He examined what was on display and patted his appreciable figure. Pleased with what he saw, he calmly moved the sliding door out of the way and extracted a stonking zig-zag green and white thing. It materialized, on him, as an over-stretched dressing gown. At that point, he supposed, it must be time for breakfast.

He pottered along the landing and heard Sondra's eager voice rising up from downstairs. Her tone was confident, but she also sounded somewhat concerned. He went down to see her and kissed her cheek. He also asked, what was going on. Sondra turned the TV off and said, "That bloody man of yours has hit another one of our friends." She scowled at him, for effect and then repeated, "Did you hear me? He's killed another friend, darling. If he goes on like this, then our entire social circle will need to recruit a whole list of new invites; don't you think?"

"Sordid, as ever, Sondra. You know full well what Tony was up to…" a hairy hand pointed her way, "…and don't say I didn't warn you. His son was always a plonker. No one will miss him. I'll bet even Tony can't say he's sorry. Simon's last little hiccup cost him over two hundred thousand. I think Simon has everything to gain. Personally."

"Personally, well, well! Simon wasn't that bad. He looked after his father's end of the stick. No one ever hurt his old man, when he was around. Did they?"

Hem stopped and looked at the warring face of his wife. "Where exactly is this going? We don't seem to get any of those casual conversations anymore."

Sondra firmed up. "Look, darling. This man you have hired is a complete and utter nutter. He's a bloody maniac and he will more than likely turn himself on you; unless you're careful. I mean, why blow a house up? I wouldn't mind, but I really liked that place. It had style. And, if I remember rightly, we've got some very passionate memories of that bedroom. Haven't we?"

Hem saw that she was in one of her irritating moods. She could be a complete bitch at times and he was not in the game for another confrontation. So, he asked, "How's the heating system now?"

"The hot water tap, dear, is fine." She used a wide table knife and scrubbed some Scottish marmalade onto a piece of sagging browned toast. The knife made a rasping sound as it reached the remaining crispy edge.

"Any more leaks likely in the near future?"

Sondra chewed on her food. "You never can tell these days. There's so much of it going on, you know. I don't want to miss out on any. Do I?" She placed her lips around another piece of dangling toast and shot a piercing dark look, straight at his exposed retinas.

"Doesn't surprise me," he said.

The phone rang. Sondra went over, picked it up and handed it to her husband. It was Sudo. He'd made contact with Wilbur. They could meet up on the golf course after eleven. Hem nodded his approval and replaced the handset into its holder.

He looked across at his wife. She was dressed in another one of those thin, wispy dressing gowns. This one was black and it tightly hugged her shape. He had to admit, she still portrayed the allure of an attractive woman. The downside was the way she solicited herself. Her behaviour could be obscene and so could her mouth. For now, it suited him that she remain, but when this was all over, he may be able to do something about that too.

He smiled at the thought, turned away and headed for the shower. A busy day lay ahead and he wanted to be on top form; to face it.

Petula Vancouver was a lonely woman. She lived a reasonably isolated life. What she knew; she also knew, she could rarely share in public. She lived in a small house, on her own. Her ex-husband had vacated her life a few years before and was merrily screwing any female who aroused his antennae. At the beginning, she was deeply hurt by his appalling behaviour. How could he do that? Why not come to his own love for that kind of passion? But, after several years of it, she realized he was not the loving type. He wanted the excitement of the moment. Not the longevity of a sustained relationship. In his world, moments came and went and he always took full advantage of each and every one. Only, actions have consequences and the consequences of this were written on the faces of every other women that he had made.

She had been treated to antibiotics on three separate occasions because of his philandering. And, finally she came too and told him to go. That was the time when she hired a mini car and followed him to a motel by the beach. She placed herself where she could see and she saw that he was enjoying the exploits of a young lady. She was years younger than him and she looked very spaced out on something or other.

That evening, she drove home and went through the house. She packed up all his necessaries into two suitcases. The rest went into a single black bin bag. Then, as he came up the stairs, she threw them at him. One after the other and told him to never set foot in her home again.

The day after, she had her brother come around and change all the locks. So that, he couldn't get in. Then, she drew the curtains, undressed herself and took a really detailed look at herself in the living room mirror. As she stood there, she thought about what she saw and realized that her days of captivating the right kind of man may just be on the wane. She wasn't emotional about it. She just looked at her blossoming figure and appreciated what it was telling her. She could slim down? Yes. She could even start exercising? Yes. All that trampolining could firm her buttocks up and then she could try bending over in some really tight short skirts. Well, perhaps!

She smiled and looked over at the table. On it, was an unattended bottle of gin and the remains of half a chocolate gateau. As she ate, she remembered thinking about all the awful things her husband had done to her over the years. She did regret; not getting pregnant. It would have been good to have had a daughter. But, those days were gone now and she felt that it was time to move on. He had kids with lots of other women. They ploughed their trough and now they were trying to get him to pay the price. It wouldn't work. He never paid for anything. Including the results of his own actions.

These days, she liked her food and she wanted a job which she could pick up and drop. As and when she wanted. So, she became a member of the Private Investigators Association and turned into a master role model for her fee-paying clientele. As things matured, she found out that humanity was pretty much the same as her life had been. No matter who you were or how you were descended, men chased women and women chased after men. Men who already had women went off with women who already had men. It was simple enough. The mess they created was catatonic to themselves and a prime exploit which kept her in her chosen profession.

To Petula, you could chase around and spend all your life trying to cover up your indiscretions. Or, you could just behave yourself and then everything would remain firmly in place. It didn't really matter. All she knew was; no one could carry off a second relationship without it impacting on the first one. That was a given fact.

Today, Petula was waiting outside the Strumshell residence. She was supposed to be following Hem Strumshell to his place of work, but something had caught her eye again. It was that plumber's van. She knew what was going on. Two sides of the same coin. She presumed that the husband knew as well. She sighed, if only people would love one another instead of seeking the quick thrills of deception. But no; people were just too carnivorous for that.

She recalled a lady called Linda Penny. A slim brunette with the kind of legs a woman would die for. Her husband got her pregnant and then slept with another woman, on the side. He liked having sex and once the baby popped out, he thought that he could just move back in and carry on as before. Only, little Linda aspired for better things in her life. She changed all of the locks and three years later found herself a good man who stuck by her through thick and thin. She was happy now. He never was. Funny old world, really.

A silver car ambled up the drive and slowed down to arrive by the front steps. Nothing moved for another ten more minutes, but then the huge figure of Hem Strumshell stepped out and into the sunny view. He was holding a phone and conducting a heated conversation. This was going to be easy. The chauffeur climbed out and swung the rear passenger door open. Still speaking, Hem dipped his head and climbed in. The chauffeur then walked around to his side of the vehicle and tucked himself away into the driving location. The car then pulled away to the end of the drive.

This morning, they decided to deviate from their usual route. Instead of veering left, the luxury vehicle took a turn for the right and set out for the motorway. Ten minutes later, it pulled off, at junction six and headed into the greenery of the summer countryside. A few miles on, it glided up in front of the 'Gamely Spires Golf Club'. Hem jumped out and paced off, up some steps. All of this whilst the swinging car door was discreetly pushed back into place for him.

Inside the clubhouse, he went to the members desk and asked if he could leave his light grey jacket there. Then, he made his way to the gaming room where he could collect his playing instruments. Golf trolley, clubs, umbrellas and all else besides.

At the fairway, there was a tall dark-haired man who was both smart and surprisingly dressed. The surprise being that he was wearing tight denim jeans. A few minutes in, and some harsh words were taking place between an official and Hem. A hand went out and Wilbur was granted consent to play in his current attire; provided that he was gone by the lunch time bell. And: that he didn't dare come to play in that outfit again.

Hem spun a coin and Wilbur found that it fell for him to pick it up. It was tails, but out of courtesy, he said it was heads and Hem teed off first.

It was very warm and the greens had been significantly impacted by the recent spell of drying weather. This was a challenge, but the course manager had kept the hoses in use overnight and it was having the desired effect. Hem was doing quite well. He was on par, at three shots. However, Wilbur managed to hit the green in one.

"Why am I here?" Wilbur asked innocently.

"Because I need a run down on what is happening. Have you acquired that wretched document yet?"

"No! I can't."

"What do you mean you can't?"

"Well, the man I am looking for has changed his name."

Hem stopped mid swing and looked at him. "What did you say?"

"I said that Albert Bailey is no more. He has become someone new."

"Who?"

"I believe he is now called something else. He changed his name at a Sudbury Solicitors. I don't know their exact address, but I can say they are a small local firm."

"How the hell did you discover that?"

Wilbur crouched down. "Isn't that what you pay me for? I have contacts and they tell me things. Things which I then approve and tell to you. That way, you know you have the truth and I can live soundly in the knowledge that I have served you well."

Hem looked at this man sideways on. To him, Wilbur was almost mystical. Confused by what he had heard, he shrugged, "And what about that do at Filby's place?"

Wilbur glared at Hem and he spoke sternly, "That was not my fault! That repulsive creature of yours: 'Sudo', told me that Bailey was residing there and he wasn't. But…" he raised his forefinger, "…there were: drugs, guns and explosives in that place. Not just that. There was a heap of repulsive pornographic stuff too.

"You know how I hate symbols of social decay. In their lounge there was even a living teenage girl. I don't believe she was anywhere near sixteen. Either way. That vomit-ridden spunk brain had obviously been screwing her." Wilbur looked upset.

Hem gazed at him; searching for inspiration.

"I mean, he just walked away and left her naked body there with absolutely no protection. It was utterly disgusting." Wilbur stopped for a moment. Then, he calmed down. "Anyway, it was clear that Bailey wasn't there. Never had been, if you ask me. I was just making my mind up to leave when that little shagging bastard decided to get creative. He wanted to kill me."

Wilbur was getting angry again; he swung a golf club at speed. It moved in his right hand. He convincingly stroked it through the air. "I heard him coming down the hall. You know, it was such a resplendent building. Completely filled with cheap nostalgic crap! Made up paintings and all kinds of false memorabilia. On the other hand, his sentimental form of nostalgia was a cocked small fire-arms weapon. Which he pointed: at me! The thing was, I saw it coming and simply chose a more historic approach. I used a handsomely made steel sword." Wilbur turned, looked right through Hem and said, "The sword won the contest: hands down!"

Hem leaned on his golf club. "And you blew the place up because...?"

"Oh that? That was just an invitation. An opportunity. One I couldn't refuse. I looked the rooms over and the place was pack full of plastic explosives. Must be part of your business, I assume?"

Hem looked shocked.

"I located two or three suitcases. One held a stash of explosives and at least three timing devices. I presume he was going to pull a job or maybe several? Or, perhaps he had planned a different celebration: once he'd dealt with me? I simply set off one caseload before the main event arrived. It seemed only fair, really. Especially, as he had taken such an individual dislike towards me." Speaking these things soured his expression.

From this, Hem had heard every word and began to sweat.

"I moved the girl away from the house. No one was hurt who shouldn't have been. But, you need to watch your information very carefully."

"Why?"

"Because he wasn't there. Was he? That said, I shall get your Mr Bailey and I will extract the documents which he is holding. It may not be pleasant, and you..." he pointed his forefinger at Hem again, "...must ensure my safety."

Wilbur then focused his words and said, "I have decided to forgive you this time. But, if this ever happens again, I shall and will lose my temper with you." At that point, Wilbur eyed his putter, leant forward, and sent the golf ball straight across fifteen feet of shady damp green. It rolled right up to the hole and stopped, with the flag still in it. He then handed the instrument back to Hem and walked off, in the general direction of the club house.

At the same time, Hem was experiencing a problem. Something new had developed. He looked down as a darkened damp patch appeared on the front of his light grey trousers. It symbolized his feelings. For the first time in his life, he felt a deep sense of fright setting in.

***

Chapter 11
Take Action

Out on a hill top, by the middle of the day, stood a lonely pink Toyota Avensis. It was deliberately placed in a dirty car park and was dangerously pointing towards the edge of a crag. Inside, the lonely occupant was busy trying something new. He was chewing at a spearmint toffee and paying particular attention to the radiance of his churning thoughts.

Sometimes, one had to think hard. None of this flighty stuff. It was this or one's actions became a completely misguided mess. He had to concentrate on this problem or he would lose his way. He understood, that there was nothing wrong with reacting by instinct, but instinct alone was not enough. Thought and process had to be firmly in control. Otherwise one lost the very means of keeping to a logical conclusion. If that happened, then you ended up in the wrong place.

Wilbur was caught between two precipices. He was duty-bound to locate Mr Bailey (whether he'd actually changed his name or not). But, he was also aware that Hem was not all of the willing employer he had first appeared to be. In fact, he may actually be seeking to terminate the existence of this particular employee. That was a concerning thought. All that he knew was that too many things were going wrong. He unraveled another trade-marked offering and placed the mint onto his tongue. At which point, he noticed that he didn't like them very much.

He had been chasing after his victim for some time now. And he always seemed to be running up to dead ends. Once again, he had located a shadow of the man. This one came from and old newspaper cutting which went on to explain about an ambitious individual. It gave a glossy description of a flourishing nineteen nineties Britain. At the end of the piece, was a black and white picture. On the left, was the man he was looking for and, on the right, was someone called Sudo Kingsley.

Wilbur knew who Sudo was. Although, they'd never actually met. He also knew that Sudo worked with Hem and that said it all, really.

Wilbur sat back in his seat. He was looking for something, but it just wasn't there. To him, it was clear that this Bailey had existed before he de-existed. Mystically, he had appeared here and there and then, he simply disappeared. But, not for good. Like a dreamer living in a dream, his spirit seemed to carry on. Wilbur found no evidence that he was dead. His name was still on everything, and everything was still running like a well-oiled machine. It was as though the man were no more, but his living essence continued unabated. It was strange.

A sound came from outside and he looked up. It wasn't much, though he did perceive some movement in the vegetation. Nothing was actually happening. But, he was suddenly conscious that something had awoken his state of mind and that had taken hold of his attention. Then, he began to wonder.

This time his focus centred on a change of scenery. He wanted to find a way out. He also realized that he needed a change of car. Or, at the very least, it was time to change the plates again. Perhaps he could even acquire a personal set? He smiled.

Then he paused. He wanted to be absolutely sure that he was doing the right thing. He did not want to screw it all up.

Usually, he was employed to do a job. He rose early in the morning, surveyed the scenery and proceeded to carry out the role. All to his personal satisfaction. Amen. By its very nature, such work was often unpleasant, yet necessary. So, he did it and got paid the appropriate fee.

Only, this time he was meeting undue resistance and this made him feel very uncomfortable. Normally, he would have found this 'Bailey' by now and obtained what was to be extracted. Yet, although he had a notion, there was nothing tangible to touch. Sudo, Hem or Bailey? There was no moss on the stonework and that deeply concerned him. Even more, that little fiasco with that kid called 'Simon', had disturbed him too. It seemed so unnecessary and that caused him to re-evaluate what he was getting into. He had been told to go to that property, and that there would be the 'Bailey'. Only, the 'Bailey' in question was clearly not available at that address. That sort of thing did happen in real life, but only for a specific reason. What perturbed him most, was the opening chasm that, perhaps, Bailey had never been there at all. As a consequence, he was never going to be there in the future. Yet, that kid seemed very primed. Even, supercharged to attack him. He let Wilbur loose in the house and permitted him to totter around. He didn't even try to stop his movements within.

He had clearly been sleeping with the girl. Who would do that and then leave her naked form on open display? It was barbaric. Worse still, it was dirty. Plain dirty. That's what it was. So, the little turd got exactly what he deserved. Not that Wilbur enjoyed being the purveyor. But, that was the job, wasn't it? You faced down what you faced up to and then you dealt with whatever you had to deal with. He couldn't exempt himself from that one.

Only, that side show was not the job which he had taken on. It was a flexible misnomer. A stupid trap. One which could have taken him from his prime source of employment; into a world of lost redemption. Someone had set him up. Usually, he knew who he was gunning for and where the bullets came from. But this time, the two were mutual colleagues. He was convinced. That meant: either someone was tipping off the enemy. Or, and this was the intriguing part; the missing Mr Bailey was communicating beyond the mystique. Running things; like the projector of a dream. That also seemed highly plausible.

He knew that Hem had no guts. Yes, he was big. But like most fat men, he had a very fashionable wife, a huge stage-show of a home and a paid entourage of scurrying employees. Everyone was constantly running around after him and he lived off the proceeds of their work. If he killed them, then he would have to slim down a lot and work considerably harder. He probably couldn't face that. After all, what was to be gained? Hem had waffled on about this guy called 'Sudo', but Wilbur hadn't been introduced. After reading the newspaper cutting again, he wondered: did Sudo know Bailey? Or was he acting on behalf of the Bailey? Or was this whole thing just one long game. A place where only the winner survives. He really didn't know. None the less, it was interesting. He thought about it, for a moment longer and then switched his mind to the present. Clearing away the debris and focusing on that which lay ahead.

He needed to generate some space between himself and themselves. Maybe it was time to break the ice and completely get away. In that case, the car definitely had to go and he could always use public transport. Although that undoubtedly restricted his freedom. He thought about that and laughed. How could he possibly cope like that? Buses and trains never turned up. So, a car had to be his container of choice. At least, for now.

Fundamentally, he didn't like cars. They were filthy, smutty things which putrefied the air. Their exhaust fumes hung with a stale stench and you could even taste the residue on your tongue. The alternative: electric vehicles, sounded nice and yet, were totally impractical for daily life.

At that point, he frowned and noticed that he'd been thinking too much. He was beginning to get caught up inside his own opinions and that state of mind was the start of a call. A desperate cry for help. The pressure of this job was showing itself again and he knew that this was not the way he wanted to live. But, as remarkable as that thought may be, this is the way it was right now and in order to get out alive, he had to make waves on both sides of the ocean.

At that point, he calmed down. His thoughts eased back a key and he realized that these spearmints were not doing their job very well. They were interfering with his natural flow and gnawing at his normal thinking processes. Being ever prepared, he reached across to the glove compartment and unveiled a new packet of top quality liquorices. Opening them, with a rustle, he took in the aroma. It gave him immediate pleasure, and delving inside, everything become crystal clear again. He retrieved his cultured hand, turned the ignition key and then repositioned his face into a smile. He knew he was on a journey. The destination was clear. Then, he selected the appropriate gear and calmly pulled away from the cliff edge.

Jenny was trying to enjoy her day. She had been awake again, during the night. Throughout her restlessness she had realized that she really needed a helper of some kind. The house was getting to be too much for her to manage by herself. She really needed someone to share the work with. Although she enjoyed her tasks, she was finding it more and more tiring, and there were days when all she wanted to do was take a nap. Only, she could never find the time. She loved doing some of the jobs. But, there were aspects which she didn't like at all. She could remember once reading a magazine article which said that the future was 'specialization'. She knew that she felt special and, at three o'clock in the morning, she had been lying there and blinking, into the darkness, considering what to do with it.

She was thinking about how she could get someone in to help her out. She could easily afford a couple of hundred a week. Surely, that would be enough to entice someone. After all, she wouldn't need a full-timer. In fact, that might be it. All she really needed was someone to work a few days each week. That would be absolutely ideal. Jenny tried to imagine what a part-timer would look like. A slim girl with white teeth and a big round smile. Such a person would be just the ticket. Would she be big or small? Firm or floppy? Kind or business- like? She mentally decided that she must be a feminine woman of her own vintage and come with the equivalent level of skills. Someone she could trust and share her values with. Except, where do you buy them? Apples grow on trees, but part-timers don't.

She was used to buying packets of coffee, tea and food ingredients. In fact, the comments she received from some of the delivery drivers were one of life's most favourite pleasures. But, purchasing people was different. Wasn't it? You couldn't pop in and buy them off a shelf. Could you? Discount warehouses didn't sell prepacked quantities of human beings. Did they?

As the night had drawn along; the clock began striking four a.m. Looking back, she remembered that her thoughts had started to go all blobby. She was really very confused. But then, she had jumped up in bed because a new idea had arrived. It had just come to her. Why not use an employment agency? They had dozens of these people just sitting around in their corridors. Stacks of them and they would all be waiting to come and see her. There was one on Mill Road. She had recently had a lady who stayed in room four. She worked at a national recruitment agency. She was very nice. Really well-dressed and she had told her that they pay all the tax and National Insurance for you. So, it would be cheaper than employing someone herself. All she would pay was the agency fees. And they couldn't strike! She knew, that if she employed someone by herself and they went on strike, then she would have to engage a counsellor. That could be expensive and she could never afford one of those. So, the agency would save her a fortune.

"That's it!" she said. "An employment agency." She could buy someone for a reasonable fee and not pay them herself. *Brilliant! What a lovely thought.*

At nine a.m. precisely, she deliberately phoned 'Oftan Miracle Workers' and spoke to Melony Melody. Melony spoke in a deeply syrup-like voice and arranged to come over before lunch time. Jenny was thrilled to bits. It was all so exciting! This was going to change her life forever and free up so much time. Her days would be lighter and it would give her so much independence. She just couldn't wait.

Petula was not innocent. She knew that this life style had taken its toll on her frame. Her resolve had proved itself in the shape of a professional persistence. Despite all the pain of adversity, she never once gave in. And these days, she had developed a strong sense of confidence. Confidence to face down what she saw and confidence to do what she believed as being right. No matter what followed.

In her life, she'd gone through a lot. Her husband had abused her. She repeatedly recalled his approach very well. It was simple. He wanted what he wanted and when he wanted it. She didn't matter, in the least. He also felt that it was his right to sleep around. She got sick of hearing, private things about him, from other people. In the end, the rumour mill had run its course. Only, this seemed to include everyone except herself. She even had the awful experience of being in a queue, at the town's supermarket. When she got to the front: there were two women, openly discussing who they had slept with. They were describing his bare attributes. They were very descriptive and their descriptions were right!

That had upset her and she felt that she really couldn't take any more. So, she divorced him and vowed only to marry a God-fearing angel in the future. That was before she discovered that there was a long waiting list. So, unperturbed, she just wrapped up her ambitions inside herself and plodded on through.

Nowadays, that survival streak rarely merited a whisper. Her clientele were generally weak people who wanted to be told only what they wanted to hear. So, she did her job, as best she could, and left them to pay the final price.

Often, her role centred on clearing up the unholy mess of a life which they, themselves, had created. If they didn't like her answers, then they would ignore her and pack it off onto someone else's shoulders. Another investigator would get involved. She felt that was strongly the case with Sondra. Whatever her sins were, Sondra didn't want to hold onto them. But, sleeping around with other men wasn't going to help very much either. Surely her life was worth more than that? She had two grown-up sons. Why didn't she see more of them? But then, Hem was the father. Chances were, they would be of pretty much the same calibre too. It wasn't looking good.

Petula, on the other hand, was a sturdy fighter and she looked out for the things she was paid to find. Only, she often found out what they did not want to know. She couldn't change that. These things were the nature of the truth. The truth didn't tend to take sides. Which meant, it was all right, providing they accepted what she told them. Sometimes that could hit a raw nerve. She had lived through numerous pointless arguments. Because the truth which she discovered, was not the kind of truth her clients wanted to hear. The faithful boyfriend may legitimately have a very attractive sister; who needed to discretely see him. Or, a long-lost father may reappear and give a large sum of money to his long-lost love child. No amount of heartache could ever capture what these poor people had gone through. But, the un-spoilt exploits of her customers' lives had often placed an appetite for something she simply could not provide. Their desires for her to prove the existence of something which was not there. That often caused unnecessary friction.

Then, came the shady ones. The ones who already knew what had taken place. All they wanted, was for her to find a lie and make it look true. She hated those jobs and this case was beginning to look and feel like one of those. There was money involved here. She could feel it. Lots and lots of it. Hidden, of course, but it existed all right. Hem was simply what all Hems are: a philandering figure who was sublime to the sufferings of everyone else around him. Blinded by his own success story and casting a deep dark shadow over every potential threat which he saw coming towards him.

***

Chapter 12
Pursue the Pursued

Petula wasn't really all that interested in computers. Although running a business meant she had had to acquire some of the necessary abilities. And, over time, she had gathered sufficient skills to get by. That said, she didn't exactly like the things. She was devotional to her cause, but not to the keyboard behind it. As a result, she kept accurate records, she could also produce formal invoices and keep her accounts up to date. She knew what had to be done; inside and out. But, the admin stuff did not appeal to her at all. It could never raise her interest like the active side did. The pleasures of investigating, the success of finding out something new. That feeling of making a final discovery. The last piece of a puzzle, which exactly matched the shape of the missing part. That one important component which allowed all the jangling components to form one solid piece. This is where Petula's heart was and, once she caught the scent, then her feelings always drove her on.

After leaving Sondra Strumshell's home, she drove into town and visited the library; where she just happened to have a card that granted her access to the library's computers. They were situated, at the side of the room, by a sunlit window. She didn't like to use the computer at home. Mostly because, it usually meant wasting the time driving all the way there and needlessly coming back again. This morning, she perched herself on a seat which looked out onto a heavily greened garden.

Petula was not a botanist and had never developed any of the tendencies. So, instead, she looked away and carried out some background research on the computer. There was much to weigh up, in what she was dealing with. She wanted to know what she had taken on and where she fitted in with things. She knew that websites could often prove an abundant resource, for this kind of work.

Her research quickly showed up where Hem had come from. His father was a Polish war pilot who won some important gallantry medals. He married an English lady named Amelda Shrumshell. The surname had obviously become his own. They proceeded to have two children. Toby Strumshell was born on a sunny Friday, 8 July 1955. The second child was one Herbert Peter Strumshell. He was born on the 9 February 1959. After attending grammar school, he studied for a design technology degree at university. In nineteen eighty-two, he left; with a first, and went to work for a big civil engineering company. Then, in nineteen ninety-two, he set out to create his own business. Presumably, using the contacts he had already established. In time, his company grew. By nineteen ninety-eight, he was married with two children. Business continued to do well. He seemed to live on a regular flow of profitable construction contracts. He initially worked as a sub-contractor to the bigger companies. Petula guessed that he had kept his old contacts and paid for a few favours. But then, he suddenly began buying up the competition and by two thousand and two, his company had more than tripled in size. It was suddenly directly bidding for large contracts. Ones which ran all over the world. He seemed to be having quite some success too.

Strumshell's business was a private 'limited' company. So, there was less public information available. Yet, snippets did appear here and there. One important one being; that along the route, he had acquired a partner whose name was one 'Albert Bailey'. He appeared in a magazine and there was a photo of them both: shaking hands.

She scoured the net and looked for further details. This time, about Bailey. There were several people, who came up. Without much information to work from, it appeared that nothing of any particular significance existed. He was wealthy. There were a few occasional pictures. He may even have owned a white-looking yacht, but from Hem's perspective, it was highly possible that he had brought significant funds to the table. Those funds could have underpinned the business expansion. Upon which, the Strumshells seemed to have blossomed. There was no mention of how much was involved or, how the finances were arranged. But, it would be reasonable to assume that Bailey must have taken some form of equity. Only, what the percentage was, she didn't know.

Petula had been reading for a while now and she was conscious that it was getting near of her time to go. Looking out towards the garden again, her eyes adjusted. Peering into the natural light made her frown and then she realized her throat was getting dry. She switched the session off, stood up and delicately made her way out of the library. She sauntered on, into the town, for a warm drink. As she walked, she continued to rummage through her thoughts. One thing had become crystal clear. The picture in her head was filled with too much detail. She had gone to the library to clarify what she was dealing with. Instead, what she had found simply opened up more new questions. The result of which being: she was now in more of a muddle than ever.

Adrian was up a ladder when his phone rang. It was someone from the office. She told him that the police wanted to see him by two p.m. He looked down at his watch, it was eleven fifty. He replied with a weak, "Okay." Then, he waved at Allan and said, "We got to go."

"Where?"

"Where do you bloody think? The police station!"

"Oh, yeh. I'd forgotten."

"Remember to bring your spare pants then. Just in case something else falls off."

Allan did not reply.

It was baking hot and they had to repack everything into their van. It was full of pricy items and they did have the latest alarm system installed. Although they worked for a local company; it was strictly on a sub-contract basis. So, they actually owned their own equipment. That allowed them the freedom to claim a tax rebate, but they had to insure everything themselves and keep it safe from prying eyes. The van was leased.

Allan placed the ladder on the roof-rack and closed the back doors. He then paced around to the driver's seat. He tended to drive the van more than Adrian. He also kept it round the back of his house, which was off the street. And, he had purposefully set up some security lighting. Last night was not going to happen again, he thought and revved up the diesel engine, before dropping into first gear. They sped around to the police station. It was one of those shiny new private finance things. It came with the all singing razzmatazz of a huge fancy frontage. But, very little behind it. Allan pulled up in a nearby cul-de-sac. As usual, the private finance was purely for appearance's sake. Apart from a few neat slots at the front, there really was no parking available. At least, not for the information givers. Someone said that there was a bus every hour, if you waited. Sometimes, it might even turn up.

Allan pulled up, on a side street. Then, they went up to the reception desk and pressed the button marked 'Press Here For Assistance'. No one appeared. So, Adrian pressed it again and someone through the glass frontage shouted out, "Just wait, will you?"

So far, it was all going perfectly well.

Three or four minutes later, an uncomfortably stiff lady arrived and asked, "What can I do for you?" She missed off the word 'please'.

Adrian spoke up, "We're here to see a police officer about the body; which I discovered over at Saps yesterday afternoon."

She looked blankly at him. Adrian began to see that this might be getting harder than it should. He went on. "Look, an officer has just called my boss and told me to come here and make a statement. You need it so that your investigation can be carried out properly."

She snuffled at him and then told them to sit, "...over there." She pointed at some empty blue seats which were placed in direct sunshine, right behind the building's main glass facia.

Allan spoke first, "She's got long arms. Hasn't she, mate?"

"And a tall attitude. I also think she needs the next size up in uniforms."

Allan chuckled. He looked around. "This is an awful building. It's light and airy, but it totally lacks charm."

"Couldn't agree more."

"Any idea how long this is going to take, mate?"

Adrian turned his head towards Allan. "Not a clue. Why?"

"I need to go somewhere."

"What, now?"

"Yup, right now, in fact." With that, Allan darted off. He headed towards a light blue door which was displaying a silver-grey toilet symbol. As it closed, Adrian looked at it, with concern. It was stuck to the door, on the slant: like a children's slide. He turned his head, in appreciation. He thought that if the loo was dangling, at that sort of an angle, then they'd need more than gravity to flush the souse away.

"Mr Sormonza?"

Adrian looked straight round. "Err, hello," he said and put his hand out to a lady officer. "I'm PC Clarke," she said. She explained what he was there for and proceeded to escort Adrian past the glaring receptionist. They went up a rising spiral staircase. Covered in deep blue carpet. At the top, they went to a private room, where she asked if he would like a drink. He asked for a white coffee. She phoned someone and the coffee duly arrived, inside a cardboard container. Adrian found that it tasted surprisingly good.

"I need to ask you some questions about what happened yesterday. I'd just like you to explain, in your own words exactly what you did and what you saw. I will be recording this and then a typed statement will be issued for you to read, amend and sign. We will change any errors, so don't be afraid to point out any mistakes that you see. It's important for us that everything is correct." She gave a lovely wide smile.

Adrian began by explaining that Allan and himself had been called to the super store. Their job was to make the electrical wiring safe; following the collapse of a structural wall. Sure enough, when they got there, it looked like a day trip to

Armageddon. The whole site was total mess. Huge sections of plasterboard were absolutely everywhere. But, they were there to check the wiring and not sweep it up. This meant that they had to send tracer signals through the remaining cable; to check that everything was okay. Allan had come across a break in the main wiring and after a while, they were pretty sure that all the remaining cable was still sound and secure. At this point, Adrian was upstairs in the broken complex and he noticed that there was a damp outline in the ceiling. So, he pulled out his small steps and stuck his head through the hatchway. That was when he puked all over the floor.

The external roof was a simple construction. It was made from thin metal sheeting and that allowed heat to build up inside the loft area. The body had actually been cooking. It was ripe and stunk like crazy. What made it worse were the hordes of flies which took off. They flew everywhere, when he stuck his head into the loft space.

The body itself was so bloated that it looked like one of those performance balloons; at a children's show. The ones you can twist and tie knots in. But, this particular one was all wet and slimy. On top of that was the most horrible smell. Dear God, it was awful.

"Are you all right, Mr Sormonza?"

Adrian had gone completely white again. The colour had drained from the top of his head and all the way down his face. His brow was running with perspiration.

"I'll get you another drink," she said. But, he lifted his hand up, as an indication that he wanted to carry on. And, after a few moments, they did just that.

***

Chapter 13
Is It a Bite or a Sting?

Wilbur drove off the dirt car park and onto an empty looking road surface. For some reason, the air had begun to feel really humid. At this height, some cloud cover had drifted in and that created patches of light drizzle. Just enough to wet the ground. As he drove, he wound the window down to get some air. This meant that he could hear the tyres hissing on the wet road surface. He cruised along, at a steady forty miles per hour. There was no need to rush. He knew what had to be done. With that mindset, it took all of thirty minutes to get back into the town. He pulled onto a side street, stopped and casually came out of the vehicle. Then, he rested his bum against the boot of the car.

With his arms folded, he perused the street layout. He was in need to go to his room, but that meant the fat woman would see him. He kept looking around for some kind of inspiration and then he finally noticed something. Out of nowhere, an even fatter woman had appeared and she went right up to the front door. Wilbur smiled: this was looking good!

Petula was getting to know Hem. His routines were patently regular, like a mouse dancing through the same doors of a maze. Although he was in charge of a large construction company, he remained resolute to his principles. He always wore a suit and a tie, which made him very easy to see and very difficult to hide. That made her work much simpler to execute. That was, until today. For some reason, he was running off-piste. As a result, she had been sitting in her nineteen nineties Peugeot 206; which she had parked up, outside the clubhouse of the 'Gamely Spires Golf Club'. *Strange name that,* she noted. Surely, golf courses have holes, not spires? Anyway, as she sat there, an elderly man in an untidy wide hat approached her car and sternly knocked on the glazing. She lowered her driver's window and stared at the over-dressed piece of arrogance. "Yes?" she said.

He replied, "Excuse me, madam, I take it that you are not a club member. Nor, I surmise, are you a guest of a paying club member. So please, just waft yourself away from these exclusive premises. Will you!?" He flicked his hand, at her face and then pointed to the open driveway.

Petula tried. She really did try, but the disgust she felt completely overrode her ability to make any sensible speech. Her lips moved, but for the first time in her life, no words came forth. He had actually stunned her! Realizing the importance of her predicament, she used her eyes: glared at him and wound her window up. The engine started. Then, she put the car into first gear and poodled along, at the customary five miles per hour. Gradually, the rising dust vaporized his image out of her rear-view mirror. The only thing which remained, was her anger.

As she drove down the long drive way, she began to notice that her car was making a strange noise. She was not in the mind for dealing with this and so, she had to dismiss it. At the road entrance, she turned a sharp left and drove slowly, until she saw a break in the hedgerow. Seeing what she had been looking for, she pulled the car up and onto the empty verge. Then, she climbed out of the driver's seat and opened up her hatchback.

Petula's car was far from new. She could vaguely remember polishing it, once. That was when she was married. So, it might have been ten years ago. Anyhow, these days, her boot was just a functional jumble of essential constituents. Her line of work meant she often found herself in some strange and isolated places. Places, where she could be looking out onto any number of extremely weird people. To compensate for this, she had acquired a suitable range of investigating utensils. Useful pieces of equipment, specifically there to help her in this line of duty. They were all in her car boot: somewhere. So, she did the customary untidy search. This time, for some binoculars. She knew they were inside a hard case and that they were hot property. She had paid a lot of money for them, at the time. This was because they were good quality and she needed all of their goodness right now.

Once she had found them, she turned around and looked at what faced her. Seeing it, made her groan. In front, was a steep grass-covered bankside; with a mixture of protruding bracken and prickly thorns. She was only wearing a short skirt and some black leggings. She knew that she needed to see what was going on, over the other side. That meant, she had to go up there. So, for emotional reassurance, she raised up the sleeves of her patterned cardigan. This exposed all of her lower forearms. Then, she slung the binocular's strap over her shoulder, and trudged into the knee-high undergrowth.

For about ten minutes, she puffed and panted her way up. She knew that she wasn't wearing the right footwear for this kind of a job. She was only a size seven and wearing a pair of those cheap flat-soled pumps. The ones you can buy in any discount outlet. They were great indoors and on concrete footpaths, but they were not really meant for clambering over an overgrown hillside. As fast as she went up; her feet kept slipping back down. But, she was absolutely determined.

Finally, she arrived as a wheezing sweaty heap at the top. From the ridge, she stood and twirled around; to get a good view. She was about to put her binoculars on, when her slippery feet went completely from under her. On top of that, her leggings snagged against a really prickly bramble bush. So, there was a loud ripping sound, combined with a yelp, and then she slid down the entire inside of the hill. She ended up on her bottom at the bottom and that was located in a secluded wooded area. She looked a complete wreck, but she was already smiling because she had just spotted something. This wood was directly overlooking the play area of the golf course and the view was a good one.

With holey leggings, she kneeled up, focused the lenses and watched the proceedings taking place; half a mile away on the golf course. In the distance were three people and two arguing figures. One was a blue denim man, who was tall, dark and slim. The other was fat man Hem. But, who was the denim guy? He was standing upright and was certainly animating his cause. She actually thought that he might swing a golf club at Hem. But, he seemed to calm down a little and then he just stomped off; leaving Hem and a grey-suited guy staring at each other.

Who was the tall man? She thought about that for a moment and then realized that if he was leaving the golf course then she had better get back into her car and follow him. "I wonder who he is?" she said. At that point, two passing squirrels heard the question. They stopped scurrying around and looked at her for an encore.

Petula knew that she was overweight. It didn't please her. She had relentlessly tried to get slim before, but it never really worked, and so here she was. She stood upright and looked at the hillside from a whole new perspective and sighed.

There was no easy route up this thing and she didn't have the services of a Sherpa. Nonetheless, she had to get over it and quickly. So, she ran full pelt, slipped over and went head-first into the bracken. Unperturbed, she stood up again, thumped her feet onto the ground and proceeded to grasp at every piece of vegetation she could. Eventually, she reached the ridge top again. Still breathing heavily, she tightened her skirt around her middle, plonked her bottom onto the grass, lifted her feet up and cried, "Yippee!"

With that, she slid down the hill and towards her waiting car. On arrival, she now had holes all over her leggings and a musty green bum. Her hands were tainted dark green and she had exclusive white marks on the front of her skirt. But, she was still intact and raring to go.

As she stumbled around to the driver's side, she noticed a pink car approaching and there, in the driver's seat, was the very man she wanted to follow. She opened her door and flung the binoculars onto the back seat, started the engine and set off in pursuit. As she drove, her adrenalin was pumping and she was beginning to feel super human. A super heroin, in laddered leggings. That thought tickled her fancy and she started to howl with laughter.

Petula followed the pink car as best she could, but on the last roundabout, she lost it behind a large waste lorry. She knew it must have gone down one of the back roads. So, she perused the streets and looked for a convenient parking space to pull into. Finally, she saw one. But, it had a parking meter. She took the space and got out, with her purse in hand. Fortunately, it did take money, but only pound coins and it gave no change. So, she fed it and sat back in her car. She sat there for nearly an hour and then the curiosity bug started to bite. She'd seen this street somewhere before, but couldn't remember where. Was it in a newspaper? *No*. She shook her head. Could it have been on a website? She mellowed into disapproval again and then it struck her. The building across the way was featured on a street painting in Sondra Strumshell's hallway. It looked different there. The blue door of today was a deeper shade of green, on her picture. But, something told her that there must be a connection. So, she opened her car door and stepped out into the sunlight.

Cautiously, she wandered over the wide street and ventured towards the closed door. Someone had stuck a small note on the knocker and she peered at it. It read, 'Applicants, please ding the bell'. She reached forward and pressed the little white button. Then, she waited for a response.

Above her head, she heard a sliding window close and then it took a couple of minutes for a sweaty little face to appear at the doorway. In that moment, what her eyes saw simply took her breath away.

Time was running along and he'd been sitting there for a few minutes; watching what was taking place. From experience, he knew that someone was following him and he wanted to be sure that he was all right to make a move. If he couldn't, then the whole show was off and he would simply go to ground. He was watching the lady Jenny. She was waving a duster, flimsy style, out of an upstairs window. She shook it in the wind as she cleaned. It amused him, but this also meant that all was well. Except, the other lady in a little hatchback car, got out and started walking towards the guest house. Wilbur couldn't help but think; *what a size she is*. He also couldn't avoid to notice, that her underwear was almost fully on display. Her skirt was clearly far too short for its purpose. Some ample shade of yellow and musty green knickery was freely available for the viewing. All of that through some torn black leggings. Ones that also had huge white patches on the outside. *Honest, some people,* he thought.

Anyway, she proceeded to the front door and rang the bell. Jenny then appeared and the two women rapidly disappeared inside. He gave them five minutes together and then quietly walked to the self-same door himself, inserted his key and went up to his room. As he passed the dining area, he could hear an excited conversation taking place. Jenny was saying how she had been looking for someone like this all of her life. Not meaning to intrude, he calmly walked by and quietly moved away to his room.

Wilbur was after his lock-picking kit and some pocket-sized metal files. The ones which fitted inside a breast pocket of his blue pilot's shirt. He also collected his blond wig: an essential tool, when being followed. Then, he turned his attention to the outside world again and that was because, this time, he was ready to take it on.

Earlier on, Jenny had seen her woman. Melony had come over first thing and said that she could help. All that Jenny had to do was sign some forms which Melony had brought along. Then, it would all be taken care of. That sounded good. Except, the price had gone up: quite a bit actually. They were looking to start at three hundred and fifty pounds a week and possibly a little more. Those words had deflated Jenny. She was suddenly filled with sorrow and felt very sad. So, she made a cup of tea and opened a new packet of milk chocolate digestives. That recipe always helped ease her stress. She also decided to put a note on the door, in an attempt to attract some entrants for her job. Maybe she could pay someone herself. That way they'd get more beef and she'd pay less money. She used a small piece of paper because, strictly speaking, the planning regulations prohibited anything at all from being stuck to her front door. "Rules," she sighed.

After that, she had just restarted her cleaning regime when the front door bell chimed. She was giving her duster a really good wave, when it went 'ding'. For the second time that day, she found herself parading down the steep flights of stairs. As things stood, she had no rooms available, at the moment. But, she must be pleasant, she thought. As she reached the last flight of stairs, she also noticed that some of the stair carpet tensioners were coming away from the edges. She made a quick mental note to contact her repairs man. So that, he could come and give them some of his special treatment. She didn't want any accidents. Like employment agencies, they could be very expensive.

With the comfort of long summer days, the sun had been moving around in the sky. And, as she came to the front of the house, the hallway was now falling into shadow. But, when she opened the door, there stood a glistening vision from heaven, and her heart leapt into her mouth.

Right in front of her was the most beautiful woman she had ever seen. Her eyes opened wide and a huge smile spread across her face. Without a single word, she instinctively reached out and took Petula by the hand. She was instantly lit up with joy. At last someone had come to share her lonely life and this woman was clearly so incredibly sexy.

From Petula's point of view, she was just standing there and waiting for the door to open when: suddenly, the most fantastic-looking beauty she had ever seen materialized. This woman instantly twinkled her heartstrings; with the glorious warmth of a rounding big smile. Petula was so taken in by her appearance that all she could do was look. It was remarkable. All she wanted to do was reach out and touch her, to see if she was real. Only, Jenny got there first.

The two of them went straight upstairs to the dining room, where Petula couldn't hold it in any longer. She took hold of Jenny and gave her a wonderful kiss on the lips. Jenny then swooned and landed on the floor. Petula didn't quite know what to do, at first. But, after a moment, Jenny recovered enough to sit up.

She was smiling all the time. Finally, she stood up and plopped herself back onto a dining room chair. Then, they started to giggle. They were so wrapped up in each other that they didn't even notice the slim figure of a passing man go by the open doorway. They only had eyes for each other and their unexpected passions quickly ran very high.

As Wilbur was delicately closing the front door, Jenny and Petula were wrapped in a loving embrace. An embrace which grew with intensely. It was an intensity that required full use of the venetian blinds. Behind which, were unleashed the firm windblown passion of several former years. So strong were their feelings, for each other, that even Hermit stayed away.

***

Chapter 14
Split-Second Timing

PC Clarke was going over the statement which Adrian had given. She had managed to type it up and, as she was reading it back, he was dutifully nodding his head. She now had a clear view of what had happened on that day. On the other hand; Adrian was still unsure. He knew what he'd seen all right. But, he had no idea how a fully grown man could possibly get himself up there, into the ceiling space of a busy shop. Then, fall down dead; without anyone noticing. It was also obvious that his body had been there for quite a while. Adrian spoke up, "So, why did no one miss him, Miss?"

PC Clarke looked up. "I don't really know, Mr Sormonza. I really don't. But, with these kinds of cases, we cannot draw conclusions. At least, not without some sound measure of the facts."

Adrian and the police constable signed the statement. With that done, she thanked him for his diligence and said that she would escort him back to the reception area. However, just as she was opening the office door, there was an almighty 'bang!'.

A few minutes earlier, Wilbur had made his retreat from the guest house and was certain that no one was following. Which was good enough for him. He started the car up and drove off into the moving traffic. Some of which was coming from the bypass. He felt quite secure in this scenery and he slowly came up to a set of red crossing lights. In the seconds which followed, he checked and rechecked his seat belt for tightness. Then, he pulled another liquorice from his pocket. On his head was a thick, shoulder-length blond wig. One that he had acquired some time ago. He looked like an ancient rock star and his flailing locks were actively blowing out through the open window. Despite his best intentions, he knew he was hardly a secret agent. Everywhere he went, people noticed him. This time he did not want to be seen as himself. So, the best way was not always the most obvious. Yet, this particular job did require publicity and publicity helped most; when it threw the opposition off, in the wrong direction. All things in balance, he knew what he was doing and now he was ready to throw a spanner in the works.

Brian was having a hell of a day. He couldn't seem to concentrate on anything. His mind kept fusing images across his thoughts. Strong vibrant images of a naked Sondra Strumshell kept coming up. Sometimes she was wearing a see-through night dress, but mostly she appeared as a pertly ripe female; ready to explore her indulgencies with him. By mid- morning, his state of mind was driving him insane and he just had to get out of the place. He told his boss that he needed the afternoon off and went over to the canal tow path. He took off his uniform and just walked around in the pleasant afternoon air. There were one or two dog walkers down there, and in the strong sunlight, he could feel its burning sensation on the back of his bare neck.

He didn't care. He just needed some time to reflect on what had been happening and sort himself out. He knew that he wanted to stay married to Linda. So, now he started to make plans. Tim Benyard had been on the phone a few times. He'd always wanted Brian to work for him and he was prepared to pay some good money. That would mean working away from home; for most of the time. But, the extra income could get them a mortgage. Maybe, even a place of their own. He knew that Linda would like that. After all, she was the home builder. She was the one who had the visions. The ideas to change things and make them better. He liked that and he loved her for it.

As he was walking on the tow path, he saw some maniac cycling towards him. He was travelling like a lightning rod. He nearly hit one person and then that man cried out, the cyclist had just nicked his wallet. As the guy on the bike approached, Brian took a breath. When he came close enough, Brian turned to catch him with his shoulder. The rider; plus the bike, went into the canal. A few minutes later, the person who had lost their wallet caught up and they both lifted the drenched youngster out of the mud. The case was settled there and then. The only harm being that the cyclist's pride felt an old-fashioned freehand style of justice.

Down the stairs of the police headquarters, things had been going all neat and calm. But, comfort was desperately thin on the ground. The blue seats, which Allan had been indicated to use, were hard as rock. He couldn't sit comfortably. No matter what he did. Plus; they were positioned in the direct sunlight. It was hot July sunlight, which was being magnified through the vast glass frontage. Allan was stretching himself up to look at it. It must be at least thirty metres high and it was angled to meet up, at the top. From the outside, it portrayed some arty kind of blue-tinged sculpture. On the inside, it generated heat. To him, it didn't work. Art was one thing. A functional building was another. Either way, it was way too warm and he was tempted to go and sit outside in the van. He took his keys out and sat looking at them. The thing was; the police might want a word with him too. So, going outside would only double his discomfort. Especially, if he had to come back inside again. However you looked at it, this was a lose-lose situation.

It was getting on for two fifteen p.m. when Wilbur drove on to the trading estate. The layout was built in a kind of symmetry. This was a long straight road. Other roads branched off, at various points, on the left and to the right. Down them, were a number of small business units. Some were available for lease. Wilbur was not in the least bit interested.

At the end of this estate was the new grand-standing police headquarters. It was a PFI-built thing. As Wilbur drove, that's all he could think to call it: 'a thing'. It certainly wasn't pleasant to look at and it wasn't appealing either. So, what use did it serve?

The Toyota Avensis was an older model, but it still had a lively petrol engine. Wilbur was cruising at forty miles per hour and all seemed perfectly okay. Some guy in a loaded truck was about to pull out, but then he saw the pink car approaching and thought better of it. For Wilbur, that was good to see. He liked respect. He was also doing forty-seven miles-per-hour and gaining. He kept the car in fourth gear. Gaining more speed, he came down the road like a missile and he didn't stop. He hit the kerbstones first: making a nasty clang. Wilbur knew that the car would require new front wheels now. Next, the car collided with the limited vegetation and then mowed straight through the glass frontage and into the police station, beyond. Large pieces of glass and metal flew everywhere. It tore down most of the building's front structure. Cascading much of the immediate interior onto the ground. All of this, before, neatly imbedding itself into the reception desk.

For a few seconds, there was a strange air of silence, and a mild, singe-like burning smell arose. It was like the pause after the show had ended, but before the applause commenced. Wilbur liked these moments. The essence of surprise. It confounded the innocent and brought out the true charisma of its creator. Satisfied, with what was done, a side door of the wreck opened and out strode 'blondie'; into the disheveled remains of the foyer. He was looking for something which he had just seen bounce off the windscreen wiper, and sure enough, there it was. On the floor in front of him were a large set of car keys. He picked them up and walked peacefully out of the opening: into the sunshine.

Moments after he had gone, the police radios erupted and officers began to appear. Upstairs, Adrian and PC Clarke had just come out of the office and were set to go down; to re-unite themselves with Allan. But, that wasn't to be. The stairs had gone! Looking over the barrier, Adrian could see Allan lying on the floor. He shouted down and a shocked Allan looked straight up. "I'm all right, mate," he said. He looked fine. The only annoying thing was, he couldn't seem to find the van keys.

Wilbur calmly walked out onto the roadside and began patiently pressing the key fob. He did that until he heard some doors unlock. Looking around; it turned out to be a two-tone, grey and blue looking van. He came over and placed the keys into the ignition slot. They fitted. So, he removed the tool box set which had been indiscreetly left on the driver's seat and set off on part two of the journey.

Blonde Wilbur was finally making headway. The van was a nice piece of craftwork. Not one he would have chosen, of course. But, it was easy to drive and it handled itself really well. It had ample power to overtake other vehicles and it held itself to the uneven road surfaces remarkably well. He was impressed.

He travelled for three to four pleasant hours, before pulling into a service area. Where he took refuge in a café-cum-restaurant. He needed topping up. He was still wearing the blonde wig and that made him feel more confident.

He walked in, chose and then he sat down to eat. As he did so, he was aware of a pair of eyes. Like an extra sensory perception, he was conscious of something interrupting him. Children and adults were running and chasing each other, all over the place. Yet, he could feel an intensity resting upon him. There was no sunlight in here. But, his neck was glowing warm. He felt it and he was certain that he was being watched, but not by a thug and he didn't feel under any sort of threat. He looked around and around. He knew somebody was looking at him. He could tell and he felt it. Someone was actively peering into the living matrix of that which made the Wilbur real. It was highly confusing. He felt insecure and that made him blush.

He was sat in the centre of a turbulent performance. People were prancing everywhere. All around were plates and drinks and children and voices. All of which were constantly flying, on the move. Yet, in all this noise and hustle; he was aware that someone was disturbing his solitude. He had been trying to read one of those free newspapers. Checking over some local events and seeing the usual array of meaningless adverts. But now, this new presence was interrupting him. He couldn't concentrate anymore. It disturbed him. Made him look up and turn over his shoulder. And then there she was, sitting and smiling at him. Despite all of the rabble, she was sat at a completely empty table, one which was situated slightly behind and to the left of his own. She was a mature lady. Not petite, but then not overweight either. Perhaps she was in her fifties? Maybe, her late forties? She was wearing the blackest of facial makeup. The darkest he had ever seen on a woman. The contrast, with that and her light hair, dominated her features and made reading her facial expressions that little bit more intriguing. Her eyes though. It was they which made the difference. The brightness of them. They shone with a focus of car beams and they were clearly heading his way. She was truly striking and she was looking right at him, straight through him and all in the same dictation of time. At once and in one. All in the same process of existence.

He duly turned around to directly eye her up, and she raised her forefinger. Moving it back and forth in such a way as to beckon him into her realm. His meal finished, he habitually came over. Still clutching a half-consumed cup of cooling liquid, blonde wig still in situ and looking more closely into her face than ever before.

"I'm Surely," she said and waited for her man to respond.

There was no need to rush things, so he carefully indulged his senses before saying a word. This saw his head move sweetly from side to side and then slowly realign itself back and into the upright. "I'm Wilbur Mortanant. But, some people use my professional name and refer to me as 'T'," he said. He immediately protruded a warm hand which was richly received and shaken.

"What does the 'T' stand for?"

"It's a professional thing: bit of a joke, actually."

"And?"

"Oh…it stands for 'Thorough' and that's because, I always am."

She laughed.

"Why are you here?" he said.

"I was sent to find you," she replied.

He looked shocked, "By whom?" The words hung in the cacophony for a moment, where they were effortlessly consumed. All around them was a rivalry of sounds and a realm of uncoordinated activity. From juggernaut hauliers; eating reservoirs of freshly fried food, to the returning entourage of loose firing holiday makers. Whose screaming children roared around and around. It was all frantically happening and drawing away at every style of attention. Yet, like a side show in an action scene, neither of the two players were distracted at all.

"You're on a journey, my man," she said.

Without any hesitation, Wilbur said, "Yes."

"You're after someone."

"I am?"

She leaned forward. "But darling…" she reached out and touched his hand. He instantly felt something. It was something in her touch. Somehow, it betrayed her emotions. She felt remarkably loving and warm, "…you're really in need of some solace."

"I know."

She laughed and the darkness of her eyes briefly chinked with fragments of a sparkling personality. "Why aren't you questioning me?"

"Because, so far, I can find no error in your diagnosis. But, you are something quite remarkable."

Her hands came back up and paused themselves under her narrowly pale chin. She was glowing with smiles. Brim full with confidence, she said, "What strange words you use. You're a man, but you don't come across as being vexatious. May I ask; have you suffered?"

"Of course. My life is one continual line of torture, abuse and conflict. And you?" Her lips opened. She wanted to reply, but something stopped her. Even as her nostrils filled with air, she didn't speak. Instead, she retrieved herself, bit her lower lip and then pointed her finger at him. Following this, she restarted by affectionately saying, "I've come to give you a word, my love. And you, my darling, must hear me very well." She paused again, as though to regain a confidence. She also moved her head. Then, simultaneously, her expression warmed again. "You are looking for someone called Bailey?"

"Indeed, but like me, he may possess another name. Do you?"

"Perhaps and maybe, you are looking for the illusion to me?" She abruptly shook her head. "But, this is not good. Look, you will find him. Only, he's not what you perceive him to be." She grinned. "Somehow, things have distilled the forces of emotions and fermented the course of what ifs into the what has. Then, refracted the small remaining measures into that which you do not recognize any longer. This, being one of them."

Her expression changed again. She now looked much older. Maybe sixty-five? "You desperately need to be loved, my love, and despite myself, I am not the one to do it. But, soon you will find the someeone who is. She will love you at first sight and with your abilities, you will sense it straight away." Her left hand came up with an exposed finger to catch ahold of his attention. "Her name, incidentally, is Bailey."

Wilbur audibly gasped.

"As you already know, the man you are after is dead. How could it be any other way? But, you will not find her unless you continue to seek and locate him. So, you must do that. Can you do that for me, darling?" There was that radiant smile again.

Surely reached over and removed a long, draping blonde hair from his forehead.

Now, he could clearly see her again. "Am I chasing an illusion?"

"Hardly. The job you have started is real enough. Keep on it. It will reward you immensely. That I promise." She went on, "In a few hours, as things must, it will fall dark. So dark, in fact, that you will lose your way. You must stay sure of yourself, in that time. Or you will not be able to see properly."

He looked gaunt.

"Don't be concerned, my kitten, I am with you. If you were to be harmed, then I would tell you so. In the darkness, someone will cry out and you will oblige. 'tis then that the mystery will begin to unravel. Before your searching soul."

Wilbur looked at her and she was quiet. She now looked all of thirty years old. Her face was fresh and alert. Her eyes were judging everything and moving all over him. He could feel her vision penetrating his soul.

In this state, he was blinded and as such, he never saw it coming. On his right-hand side, a mouthing child was carrying far too much on a heavy tray. The wordy little boy caught his foot on something. Then, he simply toppled over and the entirety of his contents flew themselves all over the table top. There were loose peas, pieces of beef burger, wet tomato sauce and a collage of rice and chips; everywhere. Out of nowhere, two uniformed cleaners appeared. With instant speed, they discretely swept all of the waste away. Seconds was all it took and finally, they were gone. It was only then that Wilbur retrieved his soul again and looked up to search into those remarkable dark eyes. But, like the wisp of a ghost she had vanished out of sight.

***

Chapter 15
Challenge to the Fore

The new police station was in complete meltdown. The pink car had not only collided with the glass display at the entrance, it had also mangled some of the metalwork. Somehow, it had shorted-out the main power line. The spark had temporarily taken down their entire telephone system. The emergency generator had kicked in, but because the power was fed straight to earth, it simply tripped all of the fuses out and then everything went onto emergency lighting.

A short while after, the phones came back, but no one had access to the computers. The call centre staff were all sitting in a semi-gloom with no air conditioning. And, the control team were urgently trying to re-route the calls away to their secondary site. Once that was done, they could get started on the next job. Namely; sorting out the mess and seeing about getting things properly up and running again. Meanwhile, officers were running around and trying to get to grips with what had just taken place.

The staircase, on which Adrian and PC Clarke were standing, was out of use. The car had struck it and pushed the frame towards the bulky reception desk. As a result, the stairway was now curled up under itself. Twisted and completely unusable by any pair of human feet.

Adrian was still calling down to Allan. Surprisingly, he was perfectly okay. He also said that he had lost the van keys. But, then he remarked, "They could be under the car."

As he was saying that, a police officer tapped him on the shoulder. "I think we'd better clear this area, sir. This structure isn't safe and that car may be full of fuel." His words made sense. So, reluctantly, Allan nodded his head and then the two men retreated outside; into a row of gathering reporters.

PC Clarke took Adrian along the gantry and then around the rear of the call centre. At the back of the police station, there was a descending pedestrian walkway. It led out to a police vehicle car park. They both calmly walked down the slope.

Outside, everyone was meeting up on the tarmac and several roll calls were taking place. Adrian noted that from the back; the building looked absolutely fine. From the front though, Allan's eye line noted that it had been pulverized. With the mainstay of the building in between them, neither of the two men could see one another. And, at this stage, it began to rain. With big, splattering rounds of transparent water droplets.

Wilbur came out of the eatery with a clarity of mind that he had searched for most of his adult life. Whilst he'd been inside, the atmosphere outside had heavily clouded up and it was beginning to spit with rain. It was only four thirteen p.m., but it felt more like nine thirty in the evening. Either way, he didn't care. He knew that what he was doing was right, and so he climbed back into the van. Turning the key, he watched the dashboard light up. He looked around for the stereo system and found it. It looked like a good one too. So, he eagerly turned it on. "Thump, thump, thump, bang, bang, bang, diddly, diddly doo…" He turned it off. "Why, can't anyone write proper songs anymore?" he said.

Unperturbed, the engine came alive under his footwear. By now, the rain was just steady enough to warrant switching on the windscreen wipers. He also felt it appropriate to turn on the lights. After which, he pulled off the car park and went back onto the motorway. There was a lot more traffic now and, in the greyness, the huge lorries seemed to magnify their presence with a reddening line of tail lights. They also kept pulling out in front of him, so he had to keep his attention riveted to the road conditions.

He drove for another couple of hours and as he made his way south, the heavens opened up. There was loose rain splashing around absolutely everywhere and those heavy goods vehicles now became spray generators. Torrents of misty, wet spray was abundantly being thrown around. The wipers could hardly clear the screen quick enough to see. By seven thirty, it was practically dark and the traffic had proceeded to slow down, to a crawl. He was heading for Trowbridge. Quite why, he didn't know. He just knew that, that was where he had to go and after his previous conversation, he knew that his instinct was right. He'd seen a Trowbridge address, in a previous life. It may just be a fool's errand, but he wanted to explore and check it out. After all, it could lead him to the right answer. Who knows?

All was proceeding to plan when suddenly, the traffic halted and Wilbur found himself immediately behind the butt end of a huge grey lorry. It was covered in road muck. There was some writing on the back. But, most of the lettered words couldn't even be read. Sitting about six feet from the back end of this thing, he could just make out the gold tinted words 'Carriage guar…'. They didn't make any sense. But then, neither did what happened next.

Jenny and Petula had spent the most wonderful day together. They were in love and full of its remarkable joy. There was no doubt about it. By two thirty p.m., Petula asked if she could take a shower and Jenny showed her where to go. As Petula washed herself, Jenny started to get all nervous. She was filling up with doubt. What worried her most, was that perhaps she had taken things too far: too quickly. But, then she started to realize that maybe she couldn't help it.

This woman was so fantastically attractive. How on earth could Petula possibly be alone? It was totally beyond her. She couldn't understand why every man on the planet wasn't gravitating towards this beautiful female. She was terrific and maybe, just maybe, all hers.

Petula was busy washing herself. The water was hard hereabouts and she was unaccustomed to using a bar of soap. As she soaked her bits, she thought about moving in. If she did that, then there were going to be some changes. First of all, Jenny was going to have to have a water softener fitted. Otherwise, Petula's hair would go all heavy on her head. She distinctly liked it to be frizzy, not flat. Especially, on the top. She also wanted Jenny to wear a different style of clothing. Something to bring out her attractiveness. One thing she had noticed, as she'd looked around Jenny's wardrobe; there wasn't a single pair of leggings. That disappointed Petula. She really wanted to see her new love in something tight and revealing. Just that thought alone warmed her up inside and that was when she had to turn the shower control from warm to cool.

By six p.m., it appeared that reporters had been flown in from every part of Christendom. Even though it was light, the rain was draining away the remaining colour. Camera lights were required and they were illuminating everything they could aim at. Camera flashes were also being primed and the slide show was all set to roll out. Meanwhile, the front of the savaged police station was now guard-railed off and some temporary lights were finally switched on. A few minutes after that, the chief constable appeared and stood outside to face the assembled crowd. She took a breath and then started with thanking everyone for "...being here in this awful weather."

As her words began, the veracious noise of the gathering evaporated. Everyone became quiet and all the lenses focused on her. Then, she cleared her throat and spoke out loud, "Earlier, this afternoon, a male driver purposefully drove a car and mounted the pavement, over there..." she pointed at the obvious scuff marks, "...Then, he continued driving straight into the front of our new police station.

"This violent act has caused extensive damage to the building behind us. But, I am very grateful to say that no injuries have taken place. Neither police nor civilian."

A reporter shouted, "How much damage is done?"

"We have no specific details as yet."

"Why?"

The Chief Constable looked annoyed and said, "Please allow me to make this statement, then you may ask your questions: afterwards.

"As you know, we are at the early stages of our investigation. All that we do know is that a male driver came down this road..." she pointed over their shoulders, "...at speed, mounted the pavement and proceeded to collide with the police station.

"Fortunately, there have been no casualties. Everyone is safe and we have a number of witness statements concerning what happened.

"From the point of impact, the vehicle careered through the glass frontage and settled in the reception area. Where it currently sits. The air bags went off and the driver was able to escape capture by walking away.

"The point of impact also housed some of the power connections for the building. So, it severed much of the electricity supply. When the backup supply kicked in, it shorted some of the circuits and that tripped the fuses. Hence, we have had to switch all emergency service calls to our sister site.

"I want you to know: everything is now working. All nine, nine, nine calls are being answered in accordance with normal service standards. So, there is absolutely no need for anyone to worry about what has happened here." She nodded her head for the questions and raised her hand towards an individual. "Yes!"

A member of the press asked her, "What are you doing about the driver?"

"We are currently working on several leads. A further statement will then be issued. Next."

"What does this mad driver look like?"

"We do not know that he is mad, as yet. We have a brief description, but officers are presently compiling an accurate image for you to see. It will be released to you in due course. Next!"

"Tom Sanksby of the *Murrel Times*."

"Yes, Mr Sanksby."

"Is this part of a terrorist strike at the British establishment?"

The chief constable never flinched a muscle, "We have absolutely no evidence to suggest that this event marks any resemblance to any organized terrorist activity at all. If that's all you have to say?"

Another voice came up, "Who's going to fix it, Ma'am?"

The chief constable turned and gave a long look. "That's a good question, Miss Walters…the damage behind me is currently being dealt with by our private finance partners. Agents are already on site and I am anxiously awaiting their response.

"One thing I do wish to make very clear is, that apart from the shock of what has taken place, everyone is perfectly safe. No one has been injured, and given a little time, then everything be up and running, and back to normal once again. Let me emphasize, this will be done as soon as practicably possible. Thank you all and good evening."

With that, she walked over to her chauffeur-driven car, tucked herself inside and was taken away from the disturbing wreckage, of the scene.

The press was still hungry though. A couple of TV reporters had heard that Adrian and Allan had been there when it happened. The two lads had just appeared and they were caught high and dry.

Adrian also found that someone had nicked their van and all their kit was inside it. They were both making phone calls; trying to let work know what had happened and sort out some kind of insurance assistance. The insurance company told them that they had to let the police know what had taken place. So, Adrian set off, back to the rear of the station. He was completely soaked and not in the best of moods.

The press saw him and asked him what he had seen. So, just to get rid of them, he told them his story. But, instead of retreating, his comments simply livened things up. Next thing, a TV camera arrived and then a stream of further questions were aired; alongside a tirade of numerous flashing lights.

Back at home, Beccy was totally glued to the screen. There was her man, live on TV, telling the whole world about the most extraordinary tale she had ever heard. How he was standing on top of the stairs, when the whole glass front had exploded before him. And, how he had courageously rescued his friend Allan. By abseiling down, from the balcony, and landing straight in front of the demon driver. She was completely transfixed about his story and wondered how on earth he had ever survived. She wanted to know how he must be feeling and what was going through his mind. Most of all, she wanted him there with her. In fact, this may be the very opportunity she had been praying for. A chance to get him back. *Heaven must be a strange place,* she thought, but sometimes things happen for a good reason. With that in mind, she pulled on her raincoat and went out to get the car. Her man was safe and well. So now, she was going to bring him home.

***

Chapter 16
Take Him Away

Wilbur was getting frustrated. He'd been sat in a line of stationary traffic for almost three quarters of an hour. They had moved little more than a quarter of a mile since the hold-up began and that had only allowed him to muscle into the left-hand lane. He could also see, a few yards ahead, that a camper van had pulled up. Maybe it had a puncture? The people from inside were standing out in the pouring rain. As the traffic began to crawl again, he wound down the passenger window and offered to give them a lift to the next service station. At this, all three piled in.

There wasn't much conversation. Just stodgy silence. They kept eying one another. But, nothing was really said until the traffic picked up and the vehicle began to gain speed. As they cruised to fifty miles per hour, the guy to his left told him to pull off at the next junction. Wilbur looked around and viewed the barrel of a hand-gun pointing at him. Something occurred to him and he spoke, "If you shoot me at this speed, then you will die."

His guests put things in a different light. "If you miss that turning, I'll blow your brains all over that nice white shirt and take the rest, as it comes."

So, that was it. Wilbur put the indicator on and duly turned off. He came onto a small roundabout which then led off to a country lane. At which point, Mr Pointy tapped the dashboard for him to stop and they quickly did. Wilbur saw little merit in arguing. So, when the master of the gang told him to get his hands behind his back, he complied. It just so happened that they were carrying a fresh reel of duct-tape; which they liberally spruced onto his wrists and over his eyes and head. They took his keys and threw him in the back, where they also taped up his legs at the knee. It wasn't very nice.

Time was getting on now and although he could hear their voices, he couldn't quite decipher what was being said. They were clearly a bunch of rabble, because all they appeared to be doing was arguing with each other. In Wilbur's mind, if they couldn't work together, then they were finished. He knew of such weaknesses before.

The van suddenly started up, lurched into gear and then stalled.

Not a good driver, Wilbur thought. The engine suddenly revved up again and this time, they tore down a road which seemed to have a very tight right-hand bend on it. The contents of the van jingled as the brakes were heavily applied and some sort of dangling cables struck his bare arm. There was no comfort in the rear of the van and their driving worsened as they kept clipping the kerbstones and hitting numerous pot holes in the road surface. It really was very unpleasant. After a while, the heated conversation died a death and all he could hear was the retching of the engine. They were clearly driving in the wrong gear. From the movement in the back of the van, he guessed they were doing something like fifty or maybe sixty miles per hour, but only in third gear. This told him that they had to be morons. A few minutes later, there was a cry. Then the whole vehicle lurched sideways. This time to the left and it went onto some seriously uneven ground: still doing a noticeable speed. Wilbur bounced around with a rain storm of electrical components hitting him.

Gradually, the van slowed down and eventually it stopped with a thump. *That must be the driver's door,* he thought. Then, there was silence. He couldn't see a thing in that state, but his mind fully compensated. He wanted to locate a blade and free his hands, but that wasn't to be. Because, at that same moment, the back doors swung wide open and two burley men grabbed a hold and lifted him straight out.

They threw him onto a wheel barrow, of sorts, and took him over to an open garage in which stood Trudy.

Trudy was a bitch. She was forty-seven years old. She did what she wanted, with whosoever she wanted and she was very proud to say that she had never done an honest day's work in the entirety of her adult life. She knew that she was idle. Some even dared to say 'lazy', but she was also mean, lean, and very, very attractive. She didn't mesh her words either. Without removing the tape, she hollered, "Who the hell are you?"

Wilbur grimaced. The vibes were indeed that bad. "I'm Wilbur. Who are you?"

She instantly didn't like that. He had spirit. She looked straight at one of her assistants who duly belted Wilbur right across the forehead. Now there was blood.

"I tell you. Is who I am and you don't ask me a fucking thing. Got it!" Her tone rose and Wilbur got the message in one go.

"I want your van and I'm going to do a job with it."

"Why?" he was daring her again.

"'Cos I can and you can't do sod all about it. Tit head!"

She gave an instruction to someone, "Move his arse hole out of here." Her pitch changed and she said, "Merv, have you still got those handcuffs?"

He replied, "Sure have, boss."

"Then put them on the clown and hang him up to dry."

Next, she came over to Wilbur, bent down and uttered the lazy words, "Cozy little fucker," loudly, into his ear.

It was some sort of a taunt. Wilbur knew that and he wasn't fazed. They weren't killing him yet. So, they clearly had a need of some kind. However, that notion didn't really ease his situation. Except; he had now made his mind up. He was going to kill them all, and that meant, he was quite prepared to let them have their five minutes of fun.

Merv and some guy called Mory lifted him cleanly off the floor, cut and ripped the tape off his wrists and then applied some metal handcuffs. Feeling safe, they placed his hands around the front and cuffed them. They were easier to fit, that way and that was good enough. Then, they lifted his body up and hung him upside down, on some sort of a metal pole. The pole was at an angle to the floor, so it wedged partly between his thighs and was really uncomfortable.

He was actually hanging upside down from the pivot of a large meat hook. It was attached somewhere at the top of the pole. It had been speared through the tape which was wrapped around his knees. He could feel other smaller hooks digging into his back. But, they didn't matter. Wilbur just hoped that the tape around his knees was strong enough to take his weight. He had heard their feet clicking on the paving, when they brought him in. That suggested he was hanging well off the floor and the last thing he needed was to fall head first onto solid concrete. Least of all, without his hands being available for protection.

Once they had hung him up, they celebrated and slapped each other's hands in joviality. Then, they closed the door. Suddenly, it was quiet again. That was: until he heard the electric motor start up. At which point, the refrigerator began to kick in. It was then that he realized time was not being coaxed very friendly on his side.

Petula was in her own spacious garage when she heard the news. She was sat in her car and heard something, on the radio; about a blond man driving a pink car into a police station. Hearing this, she ran inside and turned on the television set. Looking up, her jaw dropped. On the screen, the back end of a Toyota Avensis was clearly on display. Seeing it: the first thought, which entered her mind was, *What the hell has happened?*

Hem was in a furious state. He was angry at himself and for a while, he felt that he was losing his grip. What annoyed him most was that Wilbur had frightened him. He'd never faced that situation before. When he paid the man, he did what he was told. No questions asked. Why in hell had he turned on him; he truly didn't know. But, it was disgusting. That's what it was: disgusting. He felt so bad that he had actually chatted to Sudo about his concerns. They had sat, staring at one another in the clubhouse. It was getting well on, into the evening. So, he decided to book a room for the night.

He also chose to take a meal. The club had an excellent menu and all manner of services were provided for their clientele. During this pampering spree, he decided to open up to Sudo again. "What exactly is wrong with the man?"

"He's not used to us, Hem. He is an independent player. Our rules do not confine his judgement. He chooses his own route. When things happen, he has no one to ask. He just does."

"You might have a point." Hem shrugged, he still felt like sulking.

"He is reliable and I think he will deliver the goods we want. He has never let us down before. Stay calm and keep the spirit up, old friend."

"What does that mean?" Hem looked suspicious.

"It means that we give our little man all the help that he requires to do the job. We can even raise the stakes and pay him a bonus. That should reassure him. And then, when it's all done, when everything is nice and tidy: he will come for his final pay cheque and that's when we remove him."

Hem whispered, "You mean kill him?"

"Precisely! Don't be ashamed, Hem. He is merely the barber of barbarism. Once he's done his deeds, we can deal him a deed of fair value."

Hem was annoyed yet again. "Do you have any idea what you are dealing with here? I've seen this man walk into a warehouse with eight hardened criminals. All wielding guns. It took him forty-five minutes. But, when the last shot rang out, it was a fresh-faced Wilbur who reappeared. Not a nick in his skin. No marks. Nothing. Nor were there any one of the other eight left alive. This man is amazing. If you think that you can take him out, then bloody good luck because once he's on your arse, then the devil himself takes second place. I can assure you of that."

Sudo smiled. He was a funny little man. Dressed in a grey, three-piece suit and wearing a neat evening bow tie. He may have been all of five feet three inches in height. Certainly, no taller. But, he was always immaculately dressed and explicitly loyal to his principles. He carried a small fire arm. It popped more than it hurt. But, in this business, prestige counted for everything.

"I will take care of it," he said.

"On your own head, Sudo. If it goes wrong, then I can't help you. I used to be able to handle things like this myself. But, this business has driven the compulsion away." His eyes narrowed and he said, "You do what you feel is right. I just hope that you can get rid of this bloody maniac; for good."

Sudo nodded with a sense of approval. "Nothing more to say then?"

Hem didn't reply.

"I have a commitment down in Trowbridge and I need to get going. If it all works out, then I shall see you on Friday." They shook hands and Sudo serenely departed the scene.

At this point, Hem needed a drink. A good one too, and moments later, he found himself sitting at the bar. He began his drinking with a small vodka and tonic. A few more followed on. Perhaps too many. Anyway, across the room, he saw his new flame. He screwed his eyes up and, yes, he was sure he recognized him. So, he picked himself up and carefully walked over.

As a stage show performance; it went very well. They affectionately shook hands and his associate loudly said, "Well, well, if it isn't Herbert Strumshell, as I live and breathe. How the devil are you, my dear friend?"

"I didn't know that you were a member?"

"No reason to spill such beans. How are you, old boy and what brings you into my neck of the woods?"

To anyone else, it all seemed like a casual conversation: between two old friends. A conversation which naturally led onto informal drinks and quietly carried them on. Until, they quietly retired upstairs. Going to Hem's chosen room, where they could share a few of life's special needs together. Safely, on the suite's authentic leather upholstery.

Sudo existed in fast cars. He had three thoroughbreds in his garage. They were the adulation of his adult pride and joy. This evening, he was liberating his Jaguar XJ220 and it was going at some pace. He knew the roads around here like the back of his hand, and with a car like that, ninety miles per hour was a mere gallop. He hit the motorway at seventy miles per hour and opened the car up further. It was soon doing a hundred and five. As he drove, at this speed, he was not paying much attention. His mind was preoccupied with something else.

He knew that he hated Hem. He really couldn't stand the man. He saw him as nothing less than a complete and utter liability. He had ideas, but they were often wrong and he had one serious flaw; he was totally incapable of seeing anything through. In the long run, he had to go. But, right now, he had another idea, and this time, he had the means to achieve it.

Wilbur had been hanging upside down for quite a few minutes before he dared himself to make a move. He knew, that what he intended to do, would take time and he mustn't be interrupted in the middle of it. Hence the wait. It was starting to get cold. Initially, he thought he was in a refrigerator, but as the temperature continued to fall away, he realized that it was some kind of industrial freezer. Maybe a cold store? Although his eyes were covered with duct-tape, he was still conscious of the metallic smell and that it was pretty dark inside. His left eye was running a little and that had caused the tape to slightly lift from his eyelid. With it, he could just make out something akin to a small red glow. Certainly, a weak light was coming from somewhere. Perhaps, from the back of the room? He couldn't see or focus on anything properly, but at least he could gauge the glow and use it as some form of a reference.

Wilbur was grateful that the two hulks had left his hands around the front. One of those was now feeling inside his breast pocket. He was going for the lock picks. He finally got the one he was after and placed the edge of the box (holding the remainder) firmly between his front teeth. That way, if he dropped one, he could reach out for another. As he worked, the cold was beginning to buy itself into his finger ends. They kept losing grip. At one point, he almost lost the pick and the box. But, one muted swear word later; he was back on track. The handcuffs seemed good quality. The locks were positioned behind and away from the hand which was holding the pick. Although taped up, he had to mentally close his eyes and feel for every movement which they gave. As he went on, his wrists started to ache. It quickly became a savage battle; whose intensity solemnly grew. That was when he knew, he couldn't give in, and by the time the first lock gave way, he was almost crying in agony.

He hung his hands down again and rested for a moment. The ache did not relent though. So, he confronted it and refocused his mind. It was then that he remembered he had the files in his other breast pocket. He reached straight in. Moments later, the tape around his knees was off and he carefully swung himself down.

Sitting on the floor with both legs placed straight out in front of him, he was hurting all over. In this state, he decided to keep his mind alert by thinking. Firstly, he removed the tape from his eyes and scrunched it up, so that it rested on his forehead. Then he sat and meticulously picked off the second cuff lock. They weighed quite a bit and he was tempted to throw them across the floor. Only, at that precise time, the door started to open.

Now, it always takes the human mind a moment to establish itself with an unexpected adjustment. Mory was holding a fully lit torch in one hand and a machete in the other. He'd just spoken to Trudy: said he was hungry and wanted some fresh meat. She'd asked if a chilled joint was okay or did it have to be wild and fresh? He took the weapon and waltzed over to the freezer unit. It had been an hour or so since he closed it and he expected things to be tenderizing nicely by now. He pulled the latch back and swung the door wide open. Only then, he had to stop because Wilbur wasn't hanging there. So, what was going on? During the thinking process, the silver second hand, on his wristwatch, notched one more movement and then it happened.

There was an horrendous howl, like the whine from a devil, and out of nowhere, a bright piece of precision-made shining steel smashed straight through his unprotected front teeth. You could hear them crack as they broke apart.

The pain was immediate. Mory instantly dropped his torch and blade. Both hands went straight up to his agonizing mouth. At which point, Wilbur picked up the machete with focus. Seeing what was coming; Mory had no means to make amends. He didn't even attempt to run. He just watched as the blade mesmerized him. It travelled at a supernatural speed and severed his head completely away from his shoulders. Thus, Wilbur was back!

Taking his breath, he walked out into the warmth of the sultry night air and removed the wig. He ran his hand, through his hair. His head was soaking wet. He looked around for any movement and saw none. There was no one here. This was not going to be easy. So, he changed gear and went on the lookout. This time, he was searching out for number one and the second prize he was seeking was a loaded gun. The prat on the floor didn't have one, but he was sure that there would be one laying around elsewhere. The freezer unit was built inside a large wooden barn. What it was used for he did not know, but the barn did have a light switch. He flicked it on, looked around and turned it off again. For a brief moment, there was a muted whimper of glee which released itself from his vocal cords. Then, his mind took over, silence returned and so did his ultimate sense of optimism.

Trudy wasn't amused. She had told Sudo that she had his man. All he had said was to keep him there.

"Why?" she asked.

"Because I want to ask him something, that's why. I'll bring you the money and you can keep the van as a present. Maybe we can do a deal about a new job. I've just discovered a good one."

She didn't like the Chinese cupid. Though, he did do things to her which she was prepared to allow. But, only up to a degree. Right now, he was annoying her profusely. That said, he had come up with some good raids in the past, and doing them did turn her on. Which he certainly seemed to enjoy. So, maybe he wasn't that bad after all.

She had told Mory to check on their subject. Not to harm him, but just to see that everything was okay. "Maintain the temperature a little. If it is getting too cold in there, then you should up it a tad. No good having a frozen chicken when you want fresh meat."

She looked at her watch. Mory had been gone a little while and although she'd heard him giving a late-night howl, he should really be back by now. She stood up in her tight jeans and posed herself in front of the un-curtained window. Merv came back into the room and said he needed a pee. But, just as he turned towards the wooden door, the window broke apart and an arrow struck him in his right shoulder. He swung sideways with the force, and the first thing he noticed was that his arm wouldn't move anymore. He staggered about and, a second later, another one fired straight into his throat. As he stood by the shelving, the door opened and there fired a third projectile into his beating heart. He dropped dead, on the spot.

Looking around, Trudy saw the stained white shirt first. With all the strength she had, she ran forward and kicked the wooden door into Wilbur's arm. Wilbur had seen it coming and aligned his forearm with the rotation of the door. It hit him hard, but the force was distributed equally along the full length of his limb. No damage was done, and he simply swept forward, into the room.

Trudy backed away. She was leaning sideways and frantically feeling into the air for something: anything, to hit him with. She briefly turned her head and saw a gun on the table. Only, it was too far away for her to reach! All she had left was her flick knife. At this point, she realized that Wilbur wasn't moving.

He was standing perfectly still like a toxophilite on heat. The bow was at full tension and the arrowhead was both drawn and pointing straight at her breasts. Yet, he didn't fire.

"What do you want, Dumbo?" she said.

Then came the words, "Al' Bailey." Wilbur paused. He slowly swallowed and then said, "Where exactly is Albert Bailey?"

Trudy lifted her lip into a curl from which it mediated into the full richness of a snarl. "You think I'm going to tell you that, fuck breath?"

Wilbur saw her hand moving and picking up speed. So, he gave her the necessary time and measured his response accordingly. "WRONG ANSWER, SWEET TART." And then, he let the arrow go.

The first one went straight through her flimsy blouse, chest and back. It pinned her into a wooden beam which ran down the wall. The next one hit her stomach with such force that she couldn't move at all. She was still alive though, and Wilbur came over. He put the bow down on the table and picked up the gun. He checked the chamber; it was clean although the clip was holding several new bullets. He reloaded the weapon, primed it and pointed it her way. "You really are the vilest specimen of the female species. All you had to do was talk to me, but you wouldn't lower yourself enough to do that. So, here's your choice! Now could be the last decision you ever get to make. You tell me where Bailey is and I leave you here. I know help is already on its way and jealousy always keeps its appointments. It's that, or I kill you. In other words; shout it out or die."

In her mind, Trudy was as repugnant inside as her features displayed on the outside. For the first time in all of her miserable life, this bastard had actually got one over on her and she knew it. No pretence was required. Buckled by the events, she spoke quietly, almost softly. It was quite unbecoming, "I don't know a lot. He was something to do with Sudo. Not that he ever says much. Likes to keep his hand on the tiller, our little man does." She licked her lips because, in the stale humidity, they were starting to dry up. "He took him to his place, which is some sort of old sandpit near Oxford. I don't know exactly where, but one thing's for sure. No one will ever hear from him again."

She blinked and her eyes reopened within her deepness. She was taking on the mirage of a crest fallen angel.

"Why?"

"Sudo said that he had to be number one. Bailey wanted a compromise, but Sudo doesn't like those. He likes to dominate people. He's good at it. So, he picked up an axe and broke his back in." Her pain was beginning to rise and she jolted as she spoke with splinters of words. "He cried out you know... Men do that when it hurts..." She grinned. "You can't take pain; like a woman."

Wilbur wasn't concerned

Trudy went on. "Sudo is a real bastard. Like me, he doesn't have a living soul... He just wants you dead." She looked at him again.

"I know."

With tears running down her face, she said, "Will you please take me down off this wall?"

"If I do that, he will see it as an act of submission. Do you want to face that?" She gave him a sick smile and shook her head.

"Then, I will leave you as you are. It reduces the blood loss. When he arrives, he will take care of you. You're all he has left." Wilbur began to move away.

Trudy looked at him, in shock.

"Or I can call an ambulance?"

She shook her head again, "He'll come for me. Wherever I am. Even in a hospital. He will... He'll also come for you and he isn't as soft as me." She blinked at him again.

He slowly turned and surveyed the peacefulness of the room; looked across at the vestiges on the table and then picked up the lonely set of van keys. Quietly, he closed the living room door, stepped outside and noticed that the rain had finally stopped.

***

Chapter 17
Attitudes of Anger and Love

Sudo was in one hell of a mood. He had been repeatedly calling Trudy's number. Only to find that her phone was turned off. What the hell was she playing at! He needed to know what was happening. Boy, was he going to make her pay for this. The Jaguar was doing over ninety miles per hour when it left the motorway and, for a moment, Sudo had to think exactly where he was heading to. This car was fast, but it predated sat-navs and he never had the nerve to have one fitted; in case it damaged the aesthetic beauty of his pride and joy.

He came onto the small roundabout at breakneck speed. Banged on the brakes and then saw the familiar little off shoot of a road. It was jutting away to the left. He spun the steering wheel around and opened the car up again. As he was nearing the farm, he began to slow down and then a van sprung out of nowhere. It came right down the middle of the road. It was going at such a speed that he couldn't move out of its way. It glanced off his front wing and that sent his vehicle straight into the hedge row. He was furious! He climbed out. Ran straight onto the black road surface and began shouting and screaming into the night. He ranted and swore at the fading set of red tail lights. Then, he pulled his shirt cuffs down over his wrists, calmed down, straightened his tie and went back to retrieve his car. He carefully reversed away from the bankside and placed it back onto the tarmac surface. Ten minutes later, he arrived at the shack and got out.

Like his other addresses, there were three wooden buildings on this site. One was effectively a living quarter for his employees. The other two were to hide vehicles and process the necessary meat of the business. No best-before dates required for this little enterprise. If his employees decided to do some private work of their own, he didn't mind. Provided they were there when he needed them, and he needed them right now.

He stood in the still of the night and listened with his senses. He could see that the light was on in the main structure. So, he headed there first. With a total sense of recklessness and an overlay of ambition, he burst straight in through the door frame and saw the dead remains of Merv pinned below the shelving. Turning left, he saw the limp figurine of Trudy. She was hanging off the wall and was still moving, but he was not pleased with her. "Where is he?" he shouted.

Trudy didn't answer.

He came closer and slapped her across the face, "Where the hell is he?" he screamed.

In a spin, Trudy blinked and tried to regain some measure of consciousness, but her body just wouldn't comply. She couldn't muster enough of the strength. So, she passed out, with fresh blood pouring from her lips.

Sudo lifted her head up by the hair. She was out for the count and he could see it. "Bloody woman," he muttered.

He walked back out of the doorway and went over to the freezer unit. The temperature had been set on full for some time now and when Sudo opened the door, the internal light illuminated the part-remains of Mory. Pieces of him seemed to have gone everywhere. The metal floor was covered with his blood. Annoyed at what he saw, he said, "Cleaning this up is going to cost a bomb," and immediately slammed the door shut again.

At three forty-two in the morning, Sudo faced a real business dilemma. He couldn't use this site any more. He couldn't leave it like this, either. At the very least, it needed a thorough clean up. Merv and Mory were okay for now. But, what about Trudy? He was absolutely furious with her, but he had to act quickly and that meant doing something now. He romped over to the shuttered barn and swung the large door wide open. Inside were some green plastic sheets. They were meant for use on straw bales. He carved a large section off and placed it in his car boot. Then, he stomped into the main room, where he ripped Trudy off the wall. He threw her onto the plastic sheeting and then thumped the lid down; on her breathing body. After this, he set off for the town.

Beccy had kept her word. She repeatedly told herself to stop being a wimp and 'grow up'. She wanted Adrian and he was hers to love. She was going to make certain of that. The image on the TV screen had brought her out of her doubtful bubble and revealed all of her true emotions. She suddenly wanted him. She wanted to hold his hand and feel him holding her. It was strong. Strong enough to get her into her car and drive her through the pouring rain to the police station. Only, when she arrived, the whole area was fenced off. She drove around and found a parking space behind a black saloon car. Inside, some guy was reading notes out loud into a hand-held device. As she walked by, she could see that he also had a printer on his knee. So, he was speaking and it was printing his words. *Strange world,* she thought and dipped her head into the falling rain.

Meanwhile, Adrian and Allan were back inside the police station. This time, the back of it. PC Clarke had flown the coup and now they were both giving new statements to two new officers. Adrian was actually getting a bit fed up with it all. How many times could you say and resay the same thing. He'd only come here to speak about what he'd seen the day before and suddenly there he was, playing a central role in a world war three.

Allan, on the other hand, was reliving every single detail of what had taken place. He relished each opportunity to make as full a use of his vocabulary, as he could. Although, he had originally told Adrian that he needed to go to the loo. This time it became the 'lavatory'. He seemed to 'swing' the door rather than open it and he spoke deeply about the 'drama' of the moment. He elaborated about how he had seen the car headlights cascade their opulent glow across the wide expanse of the unprotected glazing. All that, just before it penetrated the first pane of glass.

In fact, the police officer already knew that the car lights were switched off. Even so, she was required to drudgingly take the information down. She kept saying, "We only need the facts, Mr Sinders. Tell me what you actually saw and we will do just fine with that." She restarted the recording device and the talented Mr Sinders recommenced with renewed exuberance. The PC audibly sighed through her teeth.

Outside, Beccy was within touching distance of the police station's cordon. That was when a torch suddenly lit her up. "You can't go there, Miss," said a male voice.

"I'm looking for my boyfriend," she said.

The officer replied, "And why would he be here exactly?"

"Because he was supposed to be making a statement here earlier today and I saw him on TV tonight. But, he hasn't come home." Her voice began to break up.

The officer came over, obtained Adrian's full name and spoke into his radio. He then put his arm around her shoulder and took her round the back of the building. They walked along a dimly lit footpath and across the edge of the car park, up to a set of normal-sized glass doors. These ones were propped open.

There was another officer inside. He was sat on a seat, and the two policemen acknowledged each other. Once inside, they finally reached the dry. The officer who had brought her around explained what he had heard Beccy say. The second officer asked for the name of her boyfriend. "Adrian," she said again.

"Err… Adrian who, Miss?"

"Adrian Sormonza," she replied.

"Okay…" he said, "take a seat here and I'll get one of my colleagues onto it straight away," which he did.

Five minutes later, a lady officer appeared and asked her to come through. They walked into a sparsely lit corridor. Everything seemed gloomy and semi-dark. The tone of the carpet didn't help; it was all in the deep shade of police blue. With the dim lights, it made it feel really eerie. The lady officer was talking away to her, saying things like, "Are you all right?" and "Do you have any friends you can talk to?" All kinds of friendly nonsense, really. Then, they turned the corner and straight away she saw him. He was holding a cardboard cup of coffee in his hand and looking at his reflection in a window.

She called his name and he instantly looked around. His eyes opened wide, his eyebrows went up and a look of total surprise appeared on his face. The empty coffee cup hit the floor. With loose arms, he looked like he didn't know quite what to do. In fact, he didn't. So, she ran to him and put her arms around his shoulders. There followed lots and lots of silly words, which Adrian fully understood. He held her tightly and then the tears began falling down his cheeks; because finally, he had his Beccy back and this time he was going to keep her. Come what may!

***

91

Chapter 18
Advantage Wilbur

Seasons can even change within seasons and this one was avidly on the move. This Wednesday was the first day of August. The sun had just risen and it rapidly set to work on making the temperature climb.

On the ridge tiles of Jenny's guest house, there was a feature performance taking place. It was the battle commensurate for two warring sea gulls. They were clearing their throats and raising their ambitions for world domination. This came in the form of them pecking and screeching at one another. This indelicate sound was echoing down to the top-floor bedroom below. One which was occupied by the householder and her new love.

Jenny was lying next to Petula. She had bought a double bed years ago and maintained it: in anticipation of what she dreamed must follow. Only, it never did. She had spent her entire adult life being turned down by men and in the end, she had completely given up. To console herself, she resorted to cooking and eating plenty of food. The aim was to keep herself happy: it didn't work. She also wrapped herself up, in running her guest house and that definitely excluded anything sexual. At least, it did, until now.

After the rooftop birds had quietened down, she found herself wide awake and listening to Petula's breathing. A regular in and out. It was a peaceful and satisfying sound. One which she relished with all of her being. This was the comfort of companionship and from that, she also knew there would be problems. She was aware that Petula didn't like the hard water. So, they had discussed getting a water softener installed. It would cost money, but Jenny thought Petula was worth it. It would also be a good marketing tool.

Petula didn't like animals. Yet, she had brought an adorable little kitten with her. Jenny fell in love straight away and volunteered to look after it. Jenny also wanted her to move in, but Petula said she was a private investigator and that she sometimes kept very busy and unsociable hours. Jenny didn't mind. As long as she came back home; safe and sound, then that was good enough for her. Jenny thought about that and then decided; perhaps she needed to work on her a bit more and see what took root.

To Jenny, this PI thing seemed like a funny business. They had been talking about that nice Mr Wilmur man. He hadn't come home last night and she hoped that he was all right. He'd never missed a meal or a payment before and that did concern her a little bit. But, Petula said that he may be a terrorist. Jenny didn't really believe that. After all, he ate jam and bread. Terrorists didn't do that sort of thing. Did they?

As she was thinking, Petula had started to snore. Jenny could feel the heat and the vibration through the covers. So, in the warmth, she decided to snuggle up to her new found love. At which point, the snoring eased away and something completely new began to develop instead.

Wilbur had had a rough night and as a result, the morning had arrived a few hours earlier than normal. When he drove away from the wooden hell hole, he misjudged the road width and managed to clip someone's car with the front of the van. To be honest, he didn't care. But, usually he would have stopped and sorted something out, even if that meant giving the other guy a few pounds to cover the costs. Not so this time. He didn't want to and that meant he must be changing. As a result, he simply carried on and, after nearly passing out at the wheel, he had decided to turn off the road. He ended up going down the muddy entrance to a field. Where he switched off the engine and instantly fell asleep.

It was somewhere around eight thirty now. Wilbur lifted his head off the steering wheel to see where he was. He sat upright and felt the strain of this movement on his neck muscles. That told him he would have to be careful and let them loosen up, before he started careering around. He cautiously undid the saggy seat belt and swung the driver's door open. Then, he dropped his feet into a vegie pie of wet mud and rainwater. Unperturbed, he walked around the van and smoothly ran his hand over the wing. It hardly had a scratch on it. Remarkable, really. He was sure he was doing somewhere around eighty miles per hour, when he hit the other vehicle. Still, at least there was no damage to identify him.

As he looked around, he noticed that his eyes were aching and he knew that he was thirsty. The air was really humid. Out here, it felt like it was twenty something degrees and he had a really dry throat, which desperately needed some fluid. He also felt weak and that meant he needed some food too. In the distance, he could hear the faint sound of moving road traffic. So, he couldn't be far from the motorway. Best bet was to get back on there and pull into another service station, which was precisely what he did.

By nine o'clock, he was sat eating some breakfast cereal; with a freshly dispensed cola drink and a very white looking coffee. It was working. His mind was coming back on line. On the way in, he had picked up some road maps. He liked the printed versions. Like works of art; they rested better in his mind. Pictures always did. He could always recall images far better than using bundles of the written words. Real maps showing the topography and featuring contours, were one of his favourites. Much better than those wispy digital displays. The maps he had, were hardly in the top league. But, as humble offerings, they were adequate.

So, he sat there and acclimatized himself with what had taken place the night before. He knew now that it was this guy 'Sudo' who was running things. That accounted for the deception and most of the unnecessary events, which he had been facing. It also meant that Hem was almost certainly superfluous to requirements. Only, in all probability, he could be the last one to find that out. Either way, Wilbur was weaving in and around the inside workings of a trap. One which could snap shut, at any moment.

It was also clear, that Hem had employed him and it was highly likely that only Hem would ever be in a position to actually deliver the pay. That was one issue. The second was equally annoying; this 'Sudo' must be a nutter with a mission and Wilbur was flying right along the sights of his gun barrel. To him, that was not the place to be. So, what was he to do?

It was then that a little 'ding' went off in his memory. That woman appeared again. What was it that Surely had said? Something about, keep following the route to Bailey and you will be all right. That didn't make much sense either. He shrugged and lifted his half-empty coffee cup. As he sipped at the contents, he thought about her. She was some lady, that one. Thinking back made him feel something. Affection of some sort? He liked her, yes, but this feeling was strangely non-sexual. Like, she was a friendly kind of cartoon figure. Penciled in by someone else. He did believe in heaven and hell. He also believed in God and Christ and he knew that when God decided to talk to you, then you heard what was coming. That's just the way it was.

As these thoughts permeated his readings, a printed card dropped out of a pocket and fluttered onto the floor. He bent down and picked it up. He began, absentmindedly, spinning it through his fingers. Then, placing it on the table top, he read what it said: 'Formative Premiums Paid for all genuine oakwood furniture.' There was an address and a phone number. It was over in Hereford and, somehow, he knew exactly what kind buildings that kind of business would be situated in.

At nine thirty a.m., a whiskery-looking, dark-haired man was seen, buying a pair of pink, mirrored sun glasses and filling up his works van with premium fuel. Moments later, he manually washed the vehicle down and then put a newly purchased Beatles CD into the stereo unit. With the sounds, of 'Rubber Soul' playing out, our Wilbur was singing his heart away. All of that and happily on the way to Hereford.

Sudo was seriously looking at him.

"It's gonna be a big job, Mr S," he said. "The whole wing will need knocking-out and respraying. We're talking about at least three or four days' worth of work. And it will be pricy. Five, six hundred at least."

Sudo wasn't bothered about the cost. It was more his inability to get back here and collect it. He looked at the man and said, "I need a car, Spike."

"No problem, Mr S. I don't have a Jag, but you can use that Peugeot over there." He pointed and Sudo sighed. On that basis, the deal was done.

When Sudo got into the car, he was actually pleasantly surprised. It had power steering, a two-litre engine and was fully automatic. It also held the road really well. So, it would do, and that's what mattered. During the night, Sudo had slung Trudy on a sheet of plastic and placed her inside his car boot. He drove over to the accident and emergency unit, where he gripped the plastic and pulled her out onto the grass verge. He felt really good about that. He knew that someone would soon see her wailing around. Then, they'd take care of her. Perhaps, he could even buy her a drink; next time they met up.

As he was driving the car, he noticed a minor problem. So, he drove the Peugeot into a petrol station; where he placed the nozzle into the tank and put some fuel in. He also bought two extra-large petrol cans and filled them both up. The price came to over a hundred pounds, in total. He paid cash and didn't offer a smile. Then, he drove back to the barns and spent time rearranging things. By this time, Mory's body had stopped oozing blood all over the place. It was frozen solid. But, there was still one hell of a mess in there and the fact that it was all sat inside a freezing cold metal container didn't make it any the nicer.

Sudo was still wearing his three-piece suit. Together with a heavy white shirt, bearing two large silver cufflinks. They showed his personalized emblem 'SK'. As did his shirt pocket. All of this on a hot August day.

So, there he was, pulling Mory's frozen remains into the cabin where Merv was still pinned to the wall. To say he was hot was an understatement. But, what he lacked in suitable attire he more than made up for with sheer determination. By ten minutes past ten, both bodies were in the front cabin and roughly seated into the wooden chairs. He decided to put Mory's amputated head onto the deceased's knees. There was a butane gas bottle by the window, and he cautiously opened the valve, then retreated outside.

He had already left an open can of petrol. It was pouring its contents into the first shed: the one that contained the freezer. Now, he was about to uncork the second petrol container, into the other shed, when he heard a new sound. He laid the opened can down, on its side, and the petrol began to pour out.

Turning around, he saw a slow-moving police car approaching. *That sod Wilbur must have tipped them off,* he thought and instantly ran off. He went out, through the rear doors, and into the undergrowth.

The police car cautiously pulled up outside the complex. To their left were two rectangular wooden buildings, like two wooden blocks. They were standing side by side and, next to them, were some old oil drums. The main cabin was placed across their vision; straight in front and the entrance door was open.

The leading officer got out of the vehicle. Following the overnight rain, there was a lot of mud on the ground. Making it easy to slip over. It looked sparse and uninviting. The PC proceeded to radio in. He said it was obvious that nothing was going on. But, he was firmly told to check the site over. At which point, the patrol car's boot went up and out came two pairs of clean khaki green wellington boots.

Seeing his final opportunity disappearing like this was too much for Sudo to take. He had perched himself in some prickly bushes, which were next to a harvested field of straw and just a stone's throw away from the open shed doors. He was out of the police officers' line of sight. The thing was, if he threw a light in there, then there would be an almighty explosion. With the doors open and facing towards himself, he guessed that most of the flame would head in this direction. So, the gauze bush he was sitting by, and the rest of the hedging, may well go up in smoke. He didn't like that idea at all. But, time was tight and he simply didn't have a choice. The police had probably already seen his car and the number plates would give its owner away. So, he bit his lip and lit a cigarette. He hated these things, but this was not the moment to get all puritan. He had a functional need and began to pick up a handful of loose-lying straw.

With the two police men still assembling themselves, around the back of their car; projectile Sudo flew. He came out of the bushes and ran straight towards the open barn. He went in, through the first set of doors. Ran along a line of deliberately placed packages and past the emptying can; with its smelly pool of petrol on the floor. As he came towards the exit doorway, he threw the lit cigarette behind himself. The police saw him come out. Upon which, he immediately veered off and sprinted into the main building: the one that contained the dead men and the leaking gas container. Inside, he crouched down, and nervously lit the ball of straw. He hurled it, at the table and ran away from the wooden structure: straight towards his waiting vehicle.

It only took a second. The policeman, in his wellies, felt it first. Then, the second one heard it. The whole site just blew up into a total mass of flames. Lighted pieces of wood flew absolutely everywhere and the heat was tremendous. Both police officers hit the soggy ground. Meanwhile, all around them was the sprinkling of red glowing embers. Each one a lighted splinter. Some of it hit them whilst others landed in the nearby harvested field. Very soon, in the warm humid air, a hungry little fire began to spring forth. Thus; it gently crackled into life.

Hem came down the wide stairs where he met David, who escorted the guest to his allotted breakfast table. Hem made a variety of menu choices and, by the time Sandy arrived, he was tucking into some pale looking Canadian clover honey. It smelled very appetizing and been abundantly spread over the heaviest piece of toast Sandy had ever seen.

Hem smiled warmly and waved at Sandy. As he came closer and sat down, Sandy unfurled the morning menu. He ordered two lightly boiled eggs with two pieces of fresh white toast. The waiter scurried off to the kitchen.

"It's been wonderful seeing you again, Herbert." Sandy affectionately put his hand out and stroked Hem's wrist.

Hem looked unsure of himself, but said, "Yes, it was nice."

"Hem, we really should try and make it more of a sustained thing. I mean, we could move in together. Couldn't we?" He gave Hem a lover's look; seeking a measure of reassurance.

"We'll see," said Hem. "What have you got on for today?"

Sandy was taken aback. "Well, I've got a meeting at the bank in a little while, but then I'm free." He looked up again with a sense of distain.

Hem replied, "I'm supposed to be at the office by nine thirty. But, that's out of the question now. I suspect that Ruth will want to commit my day to some meaningless stream of meetings. I don't really care though. I just want to be with you."

This delighted Sandy. He perked up on that last comment and firmly held Hem's hand. That was when he saw the man's expression change and he looked concerned.

Sandy asked, "What is it?"

Hem pointed at the screen. "David, David!" he shouted. "Please turn the sound up on the TV."

David abruptly obliged and the whole room then filled with the sound. Hem had loosely been keeping his senses on the go. When he looked at the screen and saw his own face peering back, it alarmed him. *What on earth has happened now?* He thought.

The TV spoke, "So, Mr Strumshell seems to be peering into a pot of trouble and not just with the town council."

A news reader then said, "And that report was from Mirriam Carter."

"Next; the pound has fallen further against the dollar and here's Dominic Herald to explain…" Hem came level with the TV set and turned it off. He turned around again to see the assembled breakfasting crowd. With this information out there, he had to move fast. "Damn!" he said, under his breath.

He went straight up stairs and collected his things. He gave Sandy his card and said they should meet up this evening. He would try to keep him posted on events. Then he shot off.

His blue BMW estate car was sat outside and he climbed straight in. He switched his hands-free phone on and called his secretary. "Oh, sir…" she said, in a patronizing voice.

"What is going on, Ruth?" he asked, and she told him the news. Someone had driven a car into the police headquarters. The one they had just built. Which would normally be fine. Fine; that was, if the police station was already owned outright by the police authority. In that case, they would bear the costs associated with its reconstruction. Except, the building had still to be formerly signed over and as an incomplete PFI contract it was up to Hem to have the insurance. Only, there wasn't any. Hem's car screeched to an immediate halt. "What!" he screamed.

"Well it seems that Walter was trying to get a good deal with a new insurance company. Everything was in place. It's just; the paperwork hasn't been signed off." At that last comment, Hem thumped the handset down and the line went completely dead.

Hem drove as fast as the speed limits would allow and arrived at the headquarters by mid-morning. He flew up the stairs and landed in his office. He called in, every single member of staff he could muster, to shout at. He had turned the colour of beetroot before finally starting to calm down.

It turned out that temporary insurance was actually in place. All new builds had to be signed off, before a standard policy could take over. In the meantime, a temporary policy ruled the roost. This, being a new build, meant that it was still subject to such a measure. But, to all intents and purposes, everything was actually in place. Only, the cover was not as comprehensive as a full policy. So, some additional costs may arise. "But…" as their insurance agent put it, "…nothing material would be involved. A few nuts and bolts might be missing here and there. The rest, you are covered for."

In a state of annoyance, Hem dismissed them all and came out to get some air. As he appeared, he was surprised to see that, in the waiting area, his wife was sitting. She was trying to look appealing, in the sunlight.

"What do you want?" he mockingly said.

"Just to see you, darling," to which she uncrossed her tanned legs, arose and walked straight into his office. For the second time that day, the chief executive's door banged firmly shut.

***

Chapter 19
Can This Be Right?

Brian was sweating buckets. He was halfway up a ladder and locking off a dripping water pipe. The ladder he was standing on was inside the remains of the new police station. The power had been isolated and some general essential maintenance was now being done. Every effort was being made to make it safe. So that the proper repairs could begin. The pink car was still firmly placed in the reception area, but soon after the accident, a ceiling water pipe had started to leak. It was that which had sprayed everything underneath with a deluge of cold water. He had cut the water supply at the main valve, but that took all of the loos and basin taps out as well. So, here he was, trying to seal the end of the pipework and get everything else up and running again. One more turn of the spanner should see it done.

It did and when he'd finished, he looked down. He was standing on a lengthy ladder, which perched him a good thirty feet up in the air. Below him, the place was void of life and, apart from the residual sound of some loose dripping water, there wasn't a single soul in his presence.

Petula was hot. It must have been all of twenty-five degrees outside and that was only at eight thirty in the morning. Jenny had got up around six o'clock because she had to take care of her paying customers. Petula pulled on her wears and went down to sample some of the breakfast delights. She noticed that Jenny's portion sizes definitely fulfilled any practical needs you may have. That, plus most of the imagined ones too. Serving plate loads like these went beyond extreme. They must cost her a fortune too. But, at the end of the day, Jenny knew her own business. So, Petula kept her nose out of it.

Filled to the brim, Ms Vancouver then went outside and sat in her car. She removed her pale green cardigan before getting in and gave herself a stern talking to. This romantic stuff was fine and she hoped it would flourish, but it didn't pay the bills. So, after her filling breakfast, she had kissed Jenny on the cheek and then went straight back to being a PI. She had seen the news about the police station incident. It looked bad, but that was because the damage was so graphic. Good pictures for the press. Wouldn't have been the same if he'd run into a sweet shop. She was sure of that.

Anyway, she had a feeling in her gut. A feeling that Wilbur must be the main man. The Strumshell lady wanted to know what she knew. And, what she knew was: that she didn't know anything like enough to understand it. So, Petula started the engine and drove off to the site of the deranged driver. She pulled out her smartphone and took some casual photographs. Then, she went home and looked through some of the online reporting.

Her big old computer sat on a table of its own. It was in her bedroom and it could best be described as a tired old-fashioned thing. You couldn't buy them these days, but at least it still worked.

It was cooler in her bedroom. That was, because the sun could never quite shine in, through the window. It also felt nice and private, in there and Petula was comfortable with that.

Looking at the material online was draining. Everyone was chirping on about the price of the damage instead of who had actually caused it. There were pages and pages about the PFI implications and Hem's face was sprawled just about everywhere possible. She actually began to feel sorry for him. Finally, she was just about to give up when she saw something and honed onto it. Some electrical guy called Adrian had had his van stolen. Someone called Allan had lost the keys, when the car had come through the glass front. Shortly after that, the van disappeared. Something about a fair-haired man was mentioned? But, there were no further details. Petula frowned.

She visited a few more websites and contacted the electrician's company. Finally, after using up a few expensive favours, she got hold of the plate number. Now she was getting somewhere.

"Exciting, isn't it."

Petula spun around to see Sondra Strumshell looking at her. She had a black shiny hand bag with her and she looked incredibly deflated.

"What's exciting, Mrs Strumshell?"

"Why, this little job I've given you." She sat down on Petula's wide bed and crossed her tanned legs in a furtive show of strength.

It didn't work. "Exactly why are you here, Mrs Strumshell?"

The question came out the way it always did with Petula, and Sondra acknowledged her. "Do you believe in spirits, Miss Vancouver?"

The question seemed odd, but Petula felt inclined to indulge, "Yes. I've known a few. I usually meet the nasty ones."

Sondra's hands came across to rest on her knees. "Oh no, not that kind. The real ones. The ones who come at you and shout out obscenities."

Petula was beginning to waver. "What do you mean, Mrs Strumshell?"

Looking down, she spoke, "Well, to be honest, I'm not entirely sure. As you probably know, Hem is all over the news and he is well and truly annoyed with that. Which doesn't worry me at all. He's also, just had a screaming fit with me. Apparently, he wants you off the pay roll. So, I know he's up to something and I feel that you need to find out what that is. Only, it may be bad."

"That's hardly spiritual. Is it?"

"Not quite." She paused for a moment and lifted her head. She was clearly weighing up something. But, then she started to speak again. "I've been having dreams, Pet, and these dreams have been really odd. In fact, I've never had such dreams before. Not, in my entire life."

"Go on…"

"Well, the first one saw me in a rowing boat with no oars and no one in sight. Everywhere was black dark, but I could see a bankside. I was shivering cold and the water wasn't water. It was a moving pool; inside a slithering cauldron. All black and moving. Like a writhing syrupy tide.

"As if that wasn't enough, I then dreamed about being on a sea shore where the waves came over the land and wiped everything out. Trees, buildings, sea walls. In fact, everything except me and a small piece of sandy beach which rose up. Out of the water.

"Then we get to last night: and this is the really creepy one. Last night, an old woman came to me and spoke. She appeared, in my dream, as a glowing head placed on the flame of a candle. She rotated inside the flame. Through her glowing face, she told me that Hem must die or he would kill me.

"She told me that he was involved in some kind of a criminal syndicate and that they were manipulating things to see if he had the guts to see it through." She was visibly perspiring now.

Petula stood up. She poured her a drink and said, "Carry on."

"So here was this woman, who I have never met, telling me things I knew nothing about. She was so real and she looked awful – really ill. Then, she tells me that the love of my life is coming to save me." She gave a confused giggle. "I couldn't be hearing these words through my ears. But, I might just as well. Because, when she said who he was, my heart leapt up inside me. As I thought about him, he even started to turn me on. Then, I realized that somehow, I know him. I must have met him somewhere before. Only, how could I?"

Petula looked deeply into this slim figure of a woman. She seemed sound enough. Her language was articulate. So, she was certainly aware. She was also steadily holding the glass, which had been placed in her hand, and she was responsibly drinking the contents. "I think someone is looking after you, Mrs Strumshell. Whether they are from beyond the grave or have been sent by God Almighty himself, I don't know. But, if she comes again, then you listen, real good, to every word she says. Because this thing is staring to blow up like a balloon. And my experience tells me that, when that happens, it will only get worse."

Sudo was driving the Peugeot for all it was worth. He was desperate to reach the main road before any more police arrived. Moments later, he got there and turned abruptly left; where he headed down a slip road, towards the motorway. As he went down the feeder lane, he faintly heard some sirens in the background. He had to move carefully from now on. There was no point in returning the car. Spike wasn't the brightest spark on the planet and he knew that the garage mechanic would blab. Especially, if any policeman showed up. That left him with little choice. Either, he hid up somewhere or he smashed the car up and disappeared off the face of the earth. Neither plan appealed very much.

As he was driving, he reminisced about what had taken place. He had turned up to cleanse the scene, meticulously poured out two large cans of petrol and laid out some explosives. The petrol went onto the floor space of both buildings: the ones that held the evidence. He also opened the gas bottle tap and, by moving a frozen Mory into the shack; he effectively assembled all the bodies in one place. Only, the police car stopped him in his tracks. Alongside the detonated explosives, he seriously hoped that the flames had done enough damage.

The reason for that being; once he had started to drive away, through all the falling fragments, he saw the second building go up in flames. He never heard a bang, but it definitely caught alight. He just hoped the fire got going quickly enough. Because, in his previous state of mind, he never thought to cover his hands. That meant his finger prints would be on everything he'd touched. That, and a large helping of his DNA too.

At that point, he stopped his conscious drivel and looked at his watch. It was two minutes to twelve. He switched on the radio, tuned it to FM and went for a local station. "Welcome to 'BD Ave', I'm Ralph Bitterme and this is yer mid-day news. The top story we have, right now, is that there is a huge fire over by the 'Realms farming estate'. Four tenders are at the scene and it appears that more may be required. Our reporter, Jill Jackson was talking to Brendene Simons: the chief fire officer."

"Mrs Simons, how big is this fire?"

"It's currently covering an area of about half a square mile square. The amount of stubble and straw laid around here, means that there has been plenty of fuel to get the fire going. But, we are on the scene. All of the necessary resources are on site and we expect to bring it fully under control within the hour." Suddenly, Sudo was feeling a great deal better about his prospects and meekly eased back on the accelerator.

On the ground however, there were some thick grey clouds of turning smoke. The breeze was twisting it all ways and sides. The two male police officers were still there. Once the field had caught alight, the wind pulled the flames down the rows of freshly cut straw and away from the scene. There was only one fragment of a building remaining. The last one to go up was nothing but a pile of cinders, now. The first one had a sizable metal container inside. It had some kind of heavy-duty clasped door, on the front. Other than that, the wooden structure had been completely blown apart and the rest simply burned away.

They were hoping that that was all they were going to find. But then, the inevitable happened. In the midst of the ashes they came across the torso of a man. Surprisingly intact, considering what had just taken place. That observation meant just one thing; another late shift, a row with the wife and, if you were lucky, a lukewarm microwaved tea, for afters.

Somebody, on TV, was talking about a helicopter: it was flying over the presenter's head. Brenda could hear it, but she wasn't interested. Instead, she turned the tv-set off. It was coming up to the time of day when she went to pick Susan up, from summer school. Only, that was not as straight forward as usual.

Allan had come over all keen. He still wanted to go to work and show his face. As he didn't have the van, he had taken her car. He was certainly full of himself, at the moment. She also knew that Adrian had been given the day off. So, why on earth her husband had to tear his heart and soul out; just so he could show up at work, was completely beyond her. But, one thing was for sure: men were definitely an acquired taste. She phoned her mum. But, Penny was not going to be around today. Still, the sun was out and the sky was blue. So, she called for a taxi: there wasn't one. That left her facing one final option. And so, she decided to walk.

Although warm, it was actually quite pleasant in the sunshine. She came by lots of pretty roadside flowers with butterflies on them. There were a lot of poppies and they looked disproportionately bright. Some were covered in bees whilst others were standing all alone.

She picked Susan up at ten past three and decided to treat her to a small 'ninety-nine' ice cream. Then they set off together on their way back to normality. Susan was so full of herself and all wrapped up in what had been happening at play school. She never once asked where the car was and, conveniently, Brenda never mentioned it either.

Sondra had just said something to Petula and it took a moment for it to sink in. At first, it made little in the way of sense and then, after thinking about it harder, it made absolutely no sense at all. Petula said as much. "Listen Sondra, we have to make a concrete plan and then hatch a way out of this. A way which sees you with the man of your dreams and me; free to live my life the way I want to. We do not need a spiritual spectator, from outside, entering our fold and turning everything upside down. Do you get that?

"I also refuse to sit in a circle, on the floor, wearing see-through underwear. Just so some spiritual dude can ingratiate himself by gazing at my assets." She paused and looked down, at her chest. Then, she went on, "Anyway, I'm too big for those kind of displays, these days and I'll probably smother him to death, if he gets too close."

Sondra burst out laughing. "And what on earth does all that mean?" She was still rolling around.

Petula looked at her and casually shook her head. "Girl, some things are best left alone. 'Cos if you don't understand things now, then dabbling into the realms of a spiritual world will not make it any the clearer. They have their own ways. Just like we have ours. That much I'm confident of. We need to think it out properly. Plan it out correctly and see it through, with all the resolve we can muster.

"If your lady God-send happens to provide some helpful information on route, then by all means feel free to contribute. But, I point-blank refuse to get up at dawn, strip naked and start dancing around in someone else's nightmare."

After saying that, she calmed herself down and then supplemented, "When I'm naked, my legs get clammy cold and then my underwear sticks to me. It's hell, when I try to pull my knickers on. So, there you have it, my dear. No, is the answer!"

In response and spoken with a gently shaking head came the words, "I do like you, Petula. You are such a golden tonic to humanity." That said, Sondra let go and burst into uncontrollable laughter. And, this time, both parties joined in.

Brian was gradually washing the feelings out of his hair. Working on the police station had been a gem. It required him to focus all of his active mind and, this time, it was holding water. He got the job done and left the place by ten thirty. The office called him, on the phone. They wanted to see how things were going. This time he said everything was in place and then he scooted off to his next job. It was somewhere in the housing estate on Pride Road. They'd managed to get a handle on a big contract and, if he did a good job, there was the prospect of getting paid a bonus.

***

Chapter 20
Is It Meant to Be?

By late evening, time was getting on and Wilbur needed a change. He pulled the van into a pub car park. It was pretty full at this time of day and he managed to pull alongside a white open-topped car, which proceeded to start up and drive away. Seconds later, a flashier-looking thing turned up next to him. The fancy dude inside banged the green door shut and went inside. He was accompanied with what must have been his girlfriend. Even from that distance, Wilbur could make out the appearance of her pink knickers; as they walked side by side, over the rough ground. He shook his head and then got out of the van with a screw driver.

Wilbur loosened the number plates of the earthly coloured car. He had just removed the back one when the proud owner returned. He wore a white face and started shouting abusive language at him.

Wilbur didn't like people who shouted. Even less, those who dared to shout at him. Just like everyone else, he had a professional job to do. There was no need to be unpleasant about it. You were always welcome to stop and ask a question. Wilbur would always give a courteous response. But, blatant extreme shouting only managed to irritate his intellect. When that happened, then nothing remained, except for the simplicity of instinct. With one punch: he floored the man. Stone cold, flat panned and out for the count.

Problem was, the pub windows were now twitching and that gave him little choice. He plucked up the car keys, from the unconscious man and then drove off. He also began to tell himself off. *Why not take the van and leave the car?* This reaction didn't make any sense. Unless it was some deep-seated need for speed, which he admitted, he did desire. He didn't know what model of car this was but he knew it was fast and then his worst thought came to be realized. Behind him, he saw an approaching blue flashing light. Odds were on, that it was him they were after. Yet, that was extraordinarily quick. So, what could he do?

The lights were still coming up from behind. He could see them in his mirror. That meant, this was going to be tricky. He was doing about seventy and he knew the car could easily go a whole lot faster. In front, he was rapidly eating up the miles and approaching what looked like an old-fashioned steel bridge. It wasn't stationary, though. Things were beginning to move and some red looking ground lights were flashing across the concourse. They looked like those tall kind of traffic cones with some bright lights on the top. By now, he estimated that he was around two hundred yards from the bridge and the ramp was just starting to go up. The angle of ascent was probably five or six degrees and rising.

Wilbur was usually the most amicable of gentlemen. Given the choice; he could be quite charming, but a flashing blue light in his rear and a series flashing red lights in his face, gave him only one chance. He took it: dropped a gear and pinned the accelerator right down to the floor.

The little car was some kind of sports thing. It actually had six gears, but Wilbur had deliberately dropped it into fourth. When he pushed the accelerator down, it went into warp drive. He must have been doing over ninety miles per hour; when he struck the cones. Then, he flew, along the rising bridge and over the water beneath. As he flew, through the air, he looked left and saw the crew of a vessel watching him go by. It was nice to be appreciated. He also instinctively eased off the pedal during the flight, but then re-engaged normal conditions before landing. On touch down, the front wheels gave a small screech. Then, they regained their traction with the road surface. More flashing cones lay ahead and the front wheel drive pulled him straight through them. Now he was moving.

Two miles up the road, he saw a secluded wooden area. Where he slowed down and discreetly tucked the vehicle into a shaded line of trees. He turned off the engine. Made sure there were no lights showing and sat there reliving what had just taken place. A few minutes later, a police car flew by. By this time, it was getting dusky and the car's earthy green paint blended perfectly into the wooded scenery. Wilbur smiled and thought the words, *You can't see what isn't visible.* Then, he instantly fell asleep.

It was somewhere in the early hours, when Wilbur eased out from his slumber and came into a higher level of consciousness. He became pinpoint alert and, in this state, his senses could instantly pick out every single thing. The air was still and there was absolutely no sound, of any kind. Sitting there, he suddenly recognized a feeling and, in his own tempo, he turned. There she was again. "Hello Surely. How are you?" She looked different this time. Stunningly attractive. She was also radiantly youthful; more or less aglow. Both and neither; at the same time and she was smiling at her choice of subject. "Why didn't you jump, my love?" Her voice sounded different. He gathered she was speaking of her sudden appearance.

"Because I feel your presence; more than I see you." He opened his eyes wider. "You're not real, are you?"

She giggled. "Of course I'm real! The thing is, you can't imagine such a thing because you're so primitive."

These words interested Wilbur. Here he was, sat in a metallic green sports car, in total darkness, with a remarkably beautiful woman, of about twenty-five and she was positively glowing; like the beams of a crescent moon. He replied, "Okay, so why have you shone into my life again?"

"I've come to save you, my darling. I have thought a lot about you…" her eyes settled onto his, "…I have decided that you are the man of my dreams. That means, I can do something with you and you can live a far better life with me. It's much better that way. Don't you think?"

Wilbur was getting confused. "Are we getting personal?"

Her face lit up. "I want to. But, not like this. You need to see me as I am. I'm different in the flesh, you know."

"Why the sudden change? Last time we spoke, you were not for me. Now, I hear that you are?"

She frowned. "I don't understand, either," she said. "Sometimes we are told what to do. But this time, I can choose. We've never actually met before. Have we?"

It went quiet for a moment and then Wilbur reached out to touch her. As he expected, his hand waved through thin air. There was no physical warmth. Nothing to take hold of. But, that didn't change anything. She didn't change either. Although, her smile did become brighter and her eyes appeared all the more intense. She had very deep eyes and such shining dark hair. Somehow, he almost recognized her, but the words were taken, before he could muster the strength to compose them.

"I love you," she said and tilted up her head. She was really enjoying the scene. He felt strangely captivated and utterly helpless. Then, he wondered: he had noticed something and so he spoke again, "What is your name?"

She giggled again and then she went quite serious. "My name is Sondra. What's yours?"

He rapidly thought: *Sondra? Sondra?* That name meant something. He felt he should know, but in his befuddled state, he just couldn't recall what it was. "I'm Wilbur."

Her hand came out and with it came all of the warmth and feeling he was seeking, "Well Wilbur, I'm looking out for you and when I arrive, I will take care of you. I really feel very passionate about you." She laughed and then said, "Perhaps, we should marry and have children?" Her eyes glinted again. "What say you, darling?"

Wilbur went completely blank.

And with that, she was gone.

Hem was wide awake. He had left Sandy sound asleep in the bed. He was now sitting, in a dismal looking dressing gown, at the kitchen table. Sondra was out of town somewhere, so he knew he was safe to bring his lover home. He also knew there was no hope of carrying on with this decrepit mirage of a marriage. So, the next time he saw her, he was going to tell her to get some lawyers and sort out a divorce. By this stage, it seemed the right thing to do. He couldn't go on like this and yet he couldn't help but be like this. He recalled his mother telling him as a teenager, "Men marry women and then they make babies. That's what you were born for. Don't try to squabble your way around the facts of life, my son. Girls produce babies, but women can't do that alone." So, he had taken her word in hand and married a woman whom he didn't really care about. They had two children, but there was never any romance in their lives, let alone any real love. He couldn't give it because all his love was always for other people. Not for her. He couldn't ever remember really wanting her at all. In truth, she fulfilled a function. So, he used her like a broach. She could be nice at times. She was useful at office parties and other social events. But, he stopped screwing her as soon as he could. The quid pro quo was that she actually loved being screwed. In every way and from all sides. So, she sought that kind of attention elsewhere. That didn't bother him. He'd never wanted her in the first place. So, why had he listened to his mother?

Their kids had long since gone. Sam and Brian had made a good life for themselves. They didn't have any needs.

Sam was in Dubai, of all places, making a pile of money with the aviation industry. Brian went to California, where he branched off into some sort of medical research technology.

Hem had spent a fortune on them. They had both been privately educated and they were doing well. But, something was desperately amiss. He never heard a thing from them and, in truth, he didn't care much, either.

Romantically, he'd always liked men. He could recall, as a teenager, watching sports events. Especially, those rowers. The ones who tucked their sturdy frames into those streamlined tunics. He really fancied the sporty types. Sandy was built like that. All muscular. Skin and bone, but wrapped up, inside a lovely firm body. One, that exhibited a perfectly masculine texture. Sondra never came anywhere near that. In fact, she never came at all and neither did he anymore. He'd truly had enough of her.

And now, as if that wasn't bad enough, his life was turning into a propaganda spree. Later today, he was being shown off to the press, at yet another pointless conference. This time he was expected to reassure the markets, by saying that everything was fine. He had to say that he was on top of the situation. All contracts would be honoured and that he was open for business, as usual.

Looking across the shiny table, he noticed that the deep gloss was reflecting some light from upstairs. It was only then that he noticed he was smoking again. He'd given that up years ago. Yet, here he was. He couldn't even remember where it had come from, let alone lighting the thing up. "I'm going mad," he said.

Out of the darkness came the softest of compassionate voices, "Darling, will you please come back to bed. I'm feeling lonely."

Hem looked up, stumped out the cigarette and casually headed back to the wedded bedroom. The one which, until now, he had always seen to be such a complete waste of time.

In the hush of the morning air, everything seemed so logical. After all; there he was, hard and fast asleep. Only to be woken up, by a beautiful vision of a woman. A woman whom he'd never actually met. She appeared in one form and then changed into another. She wasn't real and she wasn't physically there. She wasn't Surely. But, she said she loved him, and he did feel something powerful: *was that her love running into him?* She certainly didn't look like Surely, but her sense of presence was just as intense.

He shook himself to. Sondra, he had remembered, was Hem's wife. So, it couldn't be her. Then, he stopped himself, sat upright and said, "Okay!"

Wilbur had to reconcile himself to the fact that the world was a truly mad and depressing place. He had played his part in creating that, but maybe someone else was playing with an Ouija board and he was getting superimposed into the centre. All of that and inside the maelstrom of someone else's mindset. Weird it was. But, so was what he was going through.

He sat back in the car seat and wondered who he was likely to meet next. He hoped it wasn't a deceased politician. They could probably drone on for hours. But, then out of the corner of his eye, he noticed that a whole load of cars had materialized. He hadn't heard them, but they were all around him. He turned to see. It was getting light and someone was calling to him, "…get a move on, son, 'cos we're up and going!"

Wilbur leapt out of the car and ran over to the adjacent field. There, in front of him, were six massive balloons. Five were laid pan flat, but the one in the foreground was just rearing itself into shape, and the pilot had just turned off the fans and lit an enormous yellow flame. He watched as the lazy balloon slowly up-righted itself into his vision. The flame shone to a good twenty feet in height. It was an exhilarating sight and one which he welcomed with open arms. "Here mate, can you hold this for a minute." He was handed a strap of some kind. He didn't really understand, but this was filling him up with emotion. All and because, this was truly fantastic and so completely unbelievable to comprehend. As the club members made noises and raced around and around, tears quietly tricked down his face. For the first time in his life, Wilbur Timothy Mortanant was truly happy

***

Chapter 21
New Adventures

Mrs Sondra Strumshell had decided to team up with the lady Petula. They had exchanged their words and it was agreed that the best option was to crack this case wide open: together. Sondra had left Petula's home feeling much better about herself and what was happening. She needed to focus much more and drink far less. She had plans and was really pleased, that she had finally met someone she could work with; to see them through.

After they had shared their words, Sondra decided to stay the night in a local hotel. She knew that her marriage was over. Facing up to that simple fact helped clear her mind. She saw absolutely no point in going home. Where she could easily find her husband in bed with yet another floosy; be that male or female. Instead, she booked herself into an air-conditioned suite which had a balcony view over a canal. She heard the comments which were made at the front desk. But, was it really their concern that she wanted a room with a view; in the pitch dark? They seemed very negative about it. But, she thought that their comments were their own affair and, as negative comments often do, it all worked out in her favour. She purchased the room she wanted and got a discount. She also asked for some food. The receptionist said that the restaurant closed at eleven and it was ten forty-three. So, he asked her to leave her bags at the front desk and he would get them taken upstairs. That way she could go straight into the restaurant: which she did. When the receptionist looked down, he also saw that there was no baggage.

The meal was all right and she came out at twenty past eleven. She asked if they did overnight laundry. The concierge said they did; if she would be kind enough to 'pop her items' in a laundry bag and leave it outside her room. That way, her attire would be fully laundered and placed on her door handle by seven a.m. "Thank you," she said and discreetly went upstairs.

It was a dreadfully humid night and once she entered the room, she had two powerful emotions. One was to fling all the windows wide open and feel the cooling air on her body. The other was to switch on the climate control and get some sleep. She opened the wardrobe and located the laundry bag. She ticked the express service and striped off. Placing everything she wore inside. Next, she found a thick cotton dressing gown and wrapped that around herself. Finally, she hung the bag on the outside door knob and retreated back within.

She came into the room, set the air conditioner to twenty-two degrees Celsius. Then, went to clean her teeth and shower herself. She liked this kind of experience. These hotels were not cheap, but they did provide for your every need. By her bed was a slimline refrigerator. She opened it and saw a neat row of temptingly chilled beverages. Normally, she would relieve one of its contents. But, she verbally heard herself saying, "Not tonight, Josephine." Content with her new approach, she unwrapped her naked body and fell into the chill surfaces of those lovely white cotton sheets. The coolness made her take in a sharp tuck of air. But, that didn't stop her.

For, soon she was carried away on a dreamy night's excursion to paradise.

Sudo was in Hemel Hempstead. He had driven there because the sat-nav, in the Peugeot, was so old it 'buggered up the route'. It kept voicing the words, 'You are out of time'. Over and over again. It wouldn't shut up and, no matter what he did, he couldn't get it to work properly. So, in the end, he smashed it with his fist. Even then, it feebly croaked about a 'compliance upgrade'. So, he had the pleasure of hitting it a second time. In the silence which followed, he drove on until the red fuel light came on. That was when he had to pull in and buy some more petrol. This time, he filled it brim-full. At the pay desk he asked a question, and the guy told him there was hotel down the street. It actually was just behind where they were standing. But, you had to come off at the first exit and then turn back on yourself. When Sudo arrived there, the hotel receptionist said, the cheapest price was a hundred and five quid for the night. "It's two a.m. in the morning. I don't want to buy the place." He told the sour-faced woman.

"Look, do you want a room or not? If you don't like it, then go elsewhere," came the friendly reply. Her features looked like the stern end of an alabaster doll. Then, she proceeded to grin and revealed a ragged row of decaying yellow teeth, which had come from the same geological formation. He paid and got to have some sleep.

It was ten thirty a.m. when he finally surfaced. He went down, in the lift. There wasn't anyone in the entrance area, at that time and it was clear that breakfast was never going to be available. So, he marched outside and got into the car. It had been locked up for a while and, in the morning heat, it smelled of wellies and chemical farts. Maybe it had been used to smuggle rubber condoms? He really didn't care, but it honked to hell with a sweaty latex like stink. So, he had to open the windows, wide and drove off into the steamy sweat of the day.

Sondra had been amusing herself in front of a long sensual mirror. She was looking at her naked reflection and making several mental notes. She was eying the form of her body and searching out for any imperfections she could detect. In her undressed state, she was a beautiful woman. Tall, slim and highly attractive. Her brunette covering elongated her appearance. It came down and draped loosely over her shoulders. If she turned, then it exaggerated her movement. It flew out and then resettled itself around the top of her body. Satisfied with that, she carried on and looked over every part of the woman which she was. As she did so, she questioned herself: with all of this, why didn't she have the man that she wanted? It perplexed her.

She began to play with her hair, swishing it about and watching it fall back into place. For a moment, she recalled a stance, from when she was a teenager. The first time she had seen herself properly as a woman and not just a girl. It mattered a lot, at the time and she recalled those early days of new boyfriends and late night experiences. Of liaisons and affairs and then marriage to a man who really didn't love her at all. That realization hurt. Because she knew she needed to be loved. Only, in her youth, she had completely overlooked that little responsibility. She just thought that they would all want her. She had never seen it any other way. Hem had plenty of money. That meant, he could easily provide all of the security she wanted. So, beyond that, she assumed everything would work itself out. Eventually.

She looked down and a reflection of her laundered clothes caught her eye. They were laid out, on her bed. Looking at the unwrapped garments; she turned her face forwards and made moves into the day ahead. At least she could confidently pull her knickers on: without them sticking to 'her' legs. That thought made her laugh again.

Half-dressed, she sat down on the bed, trying to console an ache which just wouldn't go away. Being still, she careered through her thoughts and formed a doubt. For, of all the men she had ever slept with, Hem included, she had never really loved any of them at all. This made her feel sad. It also raised a strong yearning.

She looked at an imaginary crimson carpet. She had some very affectionate memories of lying down there and being fulfilled. But, that kind of pleasure never lasted. It wasn't love. She knew that now.

She was standing upright, at the age of forty-two and it suddenly struck her that she had never actually been loved at all. Quietly, she muttered, "I wonder what it's like?" The intensity of the question brought a tear to her eye. With that touch, she snagged herself on an emotional strand and started to cry. The tears trickled down her face and she knew that stopping them would make her eyes ache again. Unhappy with this, she firmly raised her head and sternly spoke out loud, "Time to get dressed, girl!" With that, she twisted round and walked into the bathroom, wearing nothing but her underwear. She cleaned her teeth, at the wash basin, and then purveyed some new make-up from her hand bag. Content with its effects, she came out as the glowing beauty that she was. In a few moments, she was fully dressed and on her way to the reception, where she paid the bill. Then, she calmly walked out into the heat of the day and saw Petula waiting for her; in what could haphazardly be called a car.

Wilbur was leaning out on the edge of a basket. At this height, it was perfectly silent. The other people were gawping and gossiping away at the scene. Below them, two people were having a private conversation over a garden fence. They were talking about some thunder storms which were due later that day. They were easily three hundred feet below him, but every single word was clearly legible. He felt like a child, sitting on a tree branch, and eavesdropping, as the adults spoke underneath.

Wilbur had actually climbed into the third balloon, which meant that two more were now in front and he could just make out the two which were following behind. They set off in a line, but were now spreading out and travelling in a widening span. Not quite straight anymore, yet still generally moving in the same direction. The sense of freedom was wonderful and although some of the clientele were more interested in their smart phones, Wilbur was enjoying every piece of the sensation. There wasn't a sound. No engines, no propellers and no one was required to make any effort. They just drifted in peace.

After a few minutes, the pilot turned the burner on. When she did that, you had to lean out of the basket. Otherwise, the heat came straight down on your shoulders and that was uncomfortable.

Once you looked out, then the whole world opened up beneath you. In the naked sunlight, bales of straw took on the image of golden bars. Bars that were all placed upon a spikey carpet. It was a wonderful scene and it hooked Wilbur for sure.

As the air girded them on, Wilbur could see a lake coming up. The pilot said she would just give the balloon another boost to get them over the water surface. Apparently, water did not give off any thermals and that could cause them to sink low in the sky. She flicked the burner back on and, sure enough, they rode high over the pool. But, their following compatriot took a different approach and Wilbur watched helplessly as that balloon descended towards the water. Wilbur's pilot said that they should be okay, if they turned the burner on. But, that it would take more propane than she had used. As they came off the lake, the balloon noticeably began to lift again. It was like being inside a rising yoyo and Wilbur could feel it lifting up his soul.

The trailing balloon did actually touch the water surface, but then it began to ascend. It left a big dishy ripple on the water surface. Just as though an angel had come down from heaven and stroked the shining surface. To Wilbur, it was beautiful.

The balloons finally landed in a farmer's field and the passengers were all collected together and taken away for a monster breakfast. The breakfast table was alive with chatter. A group of people, who had never met one another before, began to make friends. Shirley was married to Arthur. He had been a gas fitter all of his life. They had four grown-up kids. Two were now at university and one was a doctor. She asked Wilbur what he did. Wilbur told her that he was an architect. He had qualified years ago and now worked for a property developer; who sent him out on special jobs. Shirley seemed to like that. Apparently, they knew an architect too. "Isn't it such a small world?" she said.

They had some pictures taken, but Wilbur declined the invite. He wanted to be left out and no one pressurized him. As they all went their separate ways, he thumbed a lift. Leaving the others to climb into the van, which was taking them back to their parked cars.

His lift dropped him off in the town. He thanked the driver and took the opportunity to peruse some new attire. He also noticed that he was beginning to smell a bit. He detested that. So, he visited a chemist shop for some soapy things. Thereafter, he entered the local swimming baths which, on summer holidays, were very quiet. He went in as a denim clad short cut, brunette and re-emerged as long-haired auburn man, in a solidly striped shirt and dark black jeans. The message was clear: it was time to get back to work again.

Sondra and Petula had been talking for a while. They guessed that this character called 'Wilbur' was their man. That was easy. Sondra had never actually met him. Hem had hired the man to get at Bailey and they had to get to Bailey before Wilbur did. Though, that was easier said than done. Not least because the trial had gone cold. They assumed that Wilbur was the one who had driven the pink Toyota into the police station. Why? They didn't know. But, Petula seemed to have it in her head that he was being threatened by someone. "I mean, why take a car that you are driving, straight into a solid sheet of glass. It doesn't make any sense!" She hit the steering wheel, out of frustration and the car swerved in response.

"I think he's our guy though, chuck," said Sondra. "He must know where this man Bailey is. And what's all that about someone driving over an open bridge; somewhere in Oxfordshire?"

Petula looked round, "That's it, girl! That's where he's going." She checked her wrist watch; it was getting on for ten thirty. "I think we'd better get going. Could be the journey of a life time, this one."

Sondra started to laugh. Not that it was funny. It was the sheer corniness of the comment.

Hem was sat in front of a pivoted studio camera. He was also inside some formal TV studio surroundings and an appallingly dressed business correspondent was sussing out his microphone equipment. He also had a note pad, with nothing written on it. *Stage prop,* thought Hem.

The youngster spoke in a broad northern accent which Hem didn't like.

"So, this will be a recorded interview and it may be broadcast on the lunch time slot. Okay?"

A lowly Hem said, "That's fine."

The toxins of this place were irritating him and he was sweating like a belly dancer, under his collar. But, at least Sudo had been in touch and this time he had spoken some sense. So, here he was and on full form.

"So, we say a big welcome to Hem Strumshell, the CEO of the building firm which constructed the police station, which was hit on Tuesday evening."

"Mr Hem…" He stopped.

Someone had said, "Cut!" Next, the same voice went on. "Brian, his last name please. Use his last name and there were one too many which's… Okay, let's start again from where you left off."

"Today, we say hello to Mr 'Stroomshell' of semi-destroyed police station fame."

Hem never moved a muscle. That was because, suddenly, everything was going precisely the way he had expected.

A quarter of an hour later and Hem left the building. "What a bloody farce that was," he muttered, as a business car pulled up for him. He climbed into the back seat and asked to go to his office. The chauffer nodded and drove away.

They pulled away and headed off towards the bypass. "Do we have any drinks on board?" Hem asked.

"Yes sir, there's some in the compartment to the left of your arm. Some diet cola and one or two other little beverages."

Hem removed the cola drink's lid and took it straight down. He burped a big one and then felt better. That was, until he started to sweat again. In the confines of the car, he started to look around. Maybe, there was an air con switch somewhere?

Sudo had called Hem at ten thirty from a road side café. He said that he would meet him at two thirty and then climbed into his mothball of a motor. The smell was less polythene now and more vintage fart. He looked left and right, then he pulled straight out into a lane of fast-moving traffic. The basis was a simple one. If his nerves gave out and he shit himself, then at least the smell in the car would markedly improve.

Sondra and Petula were flying along. The traffic was light and they were motoring at a fair rate of knots. Petula was driving. It turned out that Sondra could drive, but rarely did. So, she was happy for the female company and the chance to share some of her words. With both side windows fully down, they talked about the case. They figured that Hem had hired Wilbur. Sondra repeated that she had never actually met him. To her, he was a bit like a wisp in the forest. Neither here nor there. Although, he did keep popping up in the press. So, he couldn't be that smart.

Petula wasn't so sure and said, "If he wasn't any good, then they'd have caught him by now. But, they haven't. Have they?"

"Nope."

"He's clearly onto Bailey. Otherwise, why drive all this way and say nothing to his boss." She turned her head and asked, "Hem is his boss, isn't he?"

"I think so. I mean, I believe he is" Sondra pulled a face. "You know, now you come to mention it, I'm not entirely sure. Hem can never actually find him and whenever he asks him to do something, then it all goes completely wrong." She sat back and crossed her arms.

Then, it went quiet for a while until Sondra felt the need again. "Pet?" she said. "Yup."

"Can I say something unusual to you?"

"Can't see why not. After all, it's not as if we're doing anything important, is it?"

Sondra kept a straight face. She was wanting to be serious, for a moment and Petula knew it. "I've had another one of those funny dreams and this one was really personal."

"Go on, I'm listening."

"Well, I haven't really been sleeping all that well recently. I was putting it down to the humidity and such. So, last night, I turned on the air conditioning and slept naked, in the hotel bed. I slept really heavy too. So heavy, that I dreamt some really strange dreams and one of them is still alive with me."

"Which is…?"

"I woke up in the moonlight, inside a really expensive looking car."

Petula laughed.

Sondra scowled back and said, "Ssh." Then, she went on, "So there I was, in this neat looking motor car." She stopped herself and raised a hand. "Incidentally, before you ask, I did have some clothes on."

Petula winked and Sondra continued, "Anyway, I was sitting on the passenger seat, and there, fast asleep, in the driving position, was the most beautiful man I have ever seen."

"Handsome?"

"Definitely, in fact just thinking about him makes me go all tingly." They laughed again. "Well, so there I was and there he was. Only, I was dreaming it and he wasn't."

The car swerved. "Whoa, beg pardon!" Petula had just missed another passing vehicle and then she straightened up. "Could we go over that last bit again, please?"

"Stop being a spoil sport. I know you're only jealous! Anyhow, there we were. Me, in a lose flowing night dressy thing and him, well… fully clothed, I suppose."

Sondra was beginning to doubt herself. So, Petula prompted her, "Don't worry about what it sounds like, just say it the way it is and then you can live with the consequences later on. Come on, I'm all interested now…!"

"Well, I was there on the passenger seat and he was in the driver's seat. But, the car wasn't moving. It was stationary. It looked like we were under some sort of tree branch. Anyway, he reached out and touched me. Only, I was a dream so his hand went straight through me. He was startled, but he heard what I was saying all right. I know he did."

"How do you know that?"

"Because he asked me things which no one has ever asked me before and I said things which I've never spoken of before. You know, I've just remembered, he called me 'Surely'. Ever heard that name?"

Petula said nothing.

"I really fancy him."

"Did you get his name?"

Sondra blushed. "He said something, but I wasn't paying much attention."

"Must be love?"

"I hope so. I'd be ready and willing to try him out."

"Amen then… How about some grub and a drink or two?"

"You're on sis."

With that, they chatted and drove on to capture their choice of prey.

***

Chapter 22
Measures Apparent

Sudo was late, but he still made his appointment. The door was closed behind them and they sat together around a turquoise coloured glass table. Hem had put the air con on, and Sudo disrobed himself. He threw his jacket onto an empty chair back. This revealed a soaking wet shirt and a shoulder holster; for a hand gun. He took that off too.

They sat down and Sudo took a cool drink. Then he reached out for a writing pad and commenced the discussion with the words. "What exactly did you tell him to do?"

"I wanted him to retrieve the paperwork. That's all."

"Nothing else? Only, I know all about that and whilst I started out by supporting this approach, he's proceeded to go off the reservation. I can't trace him: anywhere. So, on the basis that something has gone on, which I do not know, I have now come back to you. What exactly did you tell him to do?"

Hem sat still and thought about it for a while. He ran his naked fingers over his bald head. The same one, in which his mind churned over the tributaries of numerous previous conversations. Hem knew that Wilbur had always been highly dependable. Never missed his calling. Not once: not until now. "Something must have happened."

"Something has, he's killed three of my people and taken a piece of kit with him that belongs to me. He's driven a car over a bridge and another one into a police station. We've got to do something Hem, and quickly!"

Hem looked around and said, "Why?"

"What do you mean, why?"

"Well, why? He's not doing us any harm. Is he? We both know he can't dig up old man Bailey and if he falls down a hole, then it's totally of his own making. If that happens, then we can pile the crap on top of him. After all, we're not obliged to pander to his needs. He can go rot in hell, for all I care."

Sudo was suddenly impressed and began to feel appreciably better about the situation.

Hem carried on, "Nobody's beyond redemption. He may just be doing things his own way. He's always been like that. The reason we are panicking is because of all the other flack that's suddenly kicking around.

"Give him space and I think he will come up with the goods. Then, he will call in to collect his money and we can serve him with his deserved reward. That way, we can wrap this whole thing up and deny it ever existed."

Sudo sat back and applauded. "Just one thing, old man. Who shoots the final bolt?"

"I think I know the very person. We've been seeing a lot of each other recently. He's very nimble, light-fingered and highly precise. I think he's far better than Wilbur and I'm sure he'd relish the opportunity to prove himself to us."

Sudo nodded. The words came out all right, but they were a bit deep for him and he was beginning to feel that recognizable urge of uneasiness again.

Jeoffrey Pitman was at the epoch of obese vileness. His yellowing teeth and body odour stank. He weighed in at over twenty-five stones, stood tall; at five feet and four inches and spent most days drinking the cheapest kind of canned beer available. The principle to his life was: if you drank cheap beer, then the alcohol content was never enough to impede your abilities. Save for the odd burst of heavy peeing, he was just as fit as the next man.

He was also forty-eight next month and relished the thought of inviting a long-list of distant family members to celebrate the occasion. He was nice like that. All heart and passion.

He wheezed and coughed up some phlegm. Then, he spat it onto the ground. His mongrel dog obediently looked up and then instantly lay its head straight back down. It didn't pay to annoy the mad boss. Especially, with beer on his lips. He could beat the hell out of you and forget he ever did it.

Old Jeff lived in a shed which was placed in the centre of an old quarry. Right in the middle it was. The old quarry workings had left a forsaken moat all around the outer edges. The old workings were still there and this was his home turf. He was, in effect, sat inside his own sunken castle. There was water all around his home and he was surrounded by a sandy cliff face of at least one hundred feet in height. That's where the sand used to be taken from and its regular appearance made him feel very safe.

He liked feeling safe. No one came here, unless he wanted them to and he could pretty much do whatever he wanted there. Anything at all and with absolutely no consequences. These days, he drank a lot. But then, he didn't drive much anymore. So, he wasn't much of a threat to anybody. And if you needed some building sand for a job: he was your man. Like his brand of beer: sand was cheap.

Only, he did get lonely. That kind of loneliness which fat drunkards are eligible to acquire. So, a few years ago, he acquired a pet crocodile. He obtained it as down payment, on a high stakes gambling bet. To begin with, it was a sprat and he kept it in a shed. He fed it from the exploits of his work. Dead pigeons, rodents and such. But, as the summers rolled along, he met with a new friend and that developed a new kind of business. As a reward, he felt the need to give it its own residence. He spoke to a couple of drinking partners and between them, they constructed a heated greenhouse, over a section of the moat. It was constantly steamy in there. They also threw a few tropical plants in for good measure and then cleared off to leave him with the prize.

Over the years it had grown and he was now placing much larger pieces of raw meat into the confine. Respect was also now due and he began to leave half carcasses of road kill inside. That was when he met Sudo and then a whole new line of work opened up. One, which paid for his beer and kept him in his life of luxury. It all formed into a seamless working speciality. His work meant that he could exploit every situation to the full and he did like being full.

When he was supplied, he fed cold corpses to his crocodile enclosure and burned their clothes in a sand pit. Money was given and he drank the proceeds thereof. He also had some firearms deals and practiced shooting at the old quarry walls. No one really cared and neither did he.

In the sultry weather of an early August morning, the temperatures could scale well over thirty degrees Celsius. When it was like this; the air could hang really heavy over this sand-pit of a home. That meant, he could open the confine and allow the croc to wander around the place. Sometimes she would dive into the moat and come up with something. That didn't bother him. He just drank his beer and kept an eye on his prize. Knowing what he knew. He also had a registered shot gun and that was always by his side… just in case.

Today, Wilbur was a new man. He had adorned a new wig. This, being less itchy than the previous one and it gave his hair a crisper appearance than before. It also went really well with his new shirt and jeans. They definitely hit it off together. He knew that because he kept acquiring smiles from women, as he walked around. The only downside was, that he seemed to be sticking out. This was a nuisance. Still, such was the price of fame.

He now knew where he was heading. He had been to the library and, sometime back in June, he had acquired one of their membership cards. This, allowed him the use of their computers. It was time limited, but really useful, when you wanted to do some general research. So, he checked in with the librarian and seated himself in a place where he could begin. This time he found what he wanted.

It appears that Al' Bailey had few friends and they didn't seem to be missing him very much. Social media had numerous messages about a variety of Baileys but none seemed relevant to his enquiries. It was apparent: he was getting nowhere and fast. Then, he remembered that pay-slip and the address on the top. How on earth could he have forgotten that one!

He reached into his new garments and, yes, he still had the crumpled remnants with him. He unfurled the tatty relic in front of the keyboard and read the address. Then, he went onto a search engine and looked it up.

It turned out that it was quite a nice residence: 54 Surrey Street, Bedford. It had a nice driveway too. In fact, it had two driveways and it stood in its own grounds. It wasn't up for sale, but it had previously been rented out. The agents were 'Ellery Halemasters' of Uxminster Road. That was enough. All he needed now was some transport. Wilbur stood up and left the library. Only to find that it was raining again.

He ambled along the footpath until he came to a newsagent's, where he bought a folding umbrella. It was a flamboyant one; covered with a merry pattern of pink and purple flowers. He felt that the colours matched his mood and then went straight back out into the forceful pour down. It took him a little while to find the address he was looking for. A white whiskered old man opened the door to him and let him straight in. Wilbur stood there and said what he needed. The grey soul reached out with a peach-coloured plug-in device. "Hundred quid, now!" he said. His hand was sticking out and shaking.

Wilbur pulled it out, paid and left. The self-same way he had come in.

The rain was coming down with force as Wilbur made his way onto the trading estate. He knew that all car sale-rooms were out of town these days. He just looked out for a forecourt display and, in time he saw one. 'Alberts Motors' reined high above a line of shiny new, rain pelted models. Besides these, was a tree covered footpath. Probably some sort of an old historic right of way. Wilbur took to it. No one was about. It was just too unpleasant.

The semi-circled front, of the garage, had a tarmac driveway. It ran around to the workshops, at the rear. This was the same tree covered path that Wilbur had taken. Where the driveway stopped; then the footpath carried straight on. It went into the muddy ploughed fields beyond. As Wilbur came along, he saw the workshops where the cars were being serviced and there, in the service forecourt, was a lone petrol car. It was standing idle, with the engine running.

Wilbur eased down his umbrella, climbed in and drove away. He came down the driveway, turned left, so that no one could see him from the showroom and went on his way. A couple of miles later, he pulled over. Then, he took hold of the little peach-coloured device, he had just paid for. He slipped in into the USB port, knowing then that the cars internal tracking systems would be effectively deactivated. To him; it was a hundred quid well spent. Satisfied with his achievement, he then turned the car onto the main road and set off for a leisurely drive to Bedford. That and something interesting in the way of lunch.

When the service manager came off the phone, he smiled. He was pleased that the new panels would be coming in today. That meant they could start work on that new repair job, before lunch. He then pulled on his company jacket and went back outside. He was going to reverse the black car into the workshop. Only, as he stood still, in the sheeting rain, he noticed that the car wasn't there anymore.

Adrian and Beccy had decided to take some time off work. They were enjoying one another's company and finally, Adrian was managing to get over the Saps ordeal. He and Allan had given a second statement to the police. This one was about their van being stolen and, before it went any further, the police called back to say that it had turned up. Apart from a few tiny scratch marks on the front, it was perfectly okay. Nothing appeared to be missing. Allan had volunteered to go and collect it. So, there were no worries there. The company then gave Adrian the rest of the week off to recover, which he really appreciated.

Beccy had changed. She was her old self again, plus some more. Adrian had apologized to her about his behaviour and that seemed to light the love bulb. She was literally all over him. It was nice and he appreciated the warmth and comfort of her affection. The main thing was, that she was talking to him again. He could easily cope with things when she did that. He finally asked her what had started the whole thing off and she coughed. Her eyes dropped and she blushed. She said, "You know that time when you were away?"

"When? Oh, you mean when I had that Palmer's job on the go?"

"Yeh, that's the one. When you got back, I looked at your phone and saw a message from some woman. She said that 'Sam' wasn't there in the afternoons and that you should call around."

She lifted her face up and eyed him for a response.

"And that's what this has all been about?" Adrian looked bemused. "I don't believe this… You know that clot 'Aidy'. I can't stand the prat. Anyway, he works in their local office and I…" he pointed at his bare chest "…had to go over and get him out of a pickle. AGAIN! This time he'd only wired an historic property without using the correct type of fittings. So, yours truly had to go. I was supposed to supervise him and sort things out. One spark could have burned the whole place down. As I said, he is a prat. He also told me that he had forgotten his mobile, which wouldn't have surprised me at all. He asked if he could make a couple of calls on mine and I said okay.

"Next thing I notice is these suggestive messages are coming in from someone called Simone. Some were more explicit than others. As were the photos. I just deleted them and told him to get her off my incoming mailing list.

"A day or two later, the texts stopped coming in and I left it at that. I've never met her. I don't know who she is and I don't want to. All I want is you."

Those words struck home. She went very quiet and looked at him again. What he said did make sense. Everything tied up and no one she knew called Adrian 'Aidy'. Not even her. So, she was happy with the explanation. She wrapped her arms around him and held him so tight that she nearly broke his bones.

At that point, Adrian pulled away. "Just one thing, my love," he struggled to say. "If anything ever happens between us again, then talk to me first! Don't do all that funny moody business because I don't understand and I just don't know how to handle it. Then, I get all mixed up, because I really can't cope without you."

She nodded her head and then held him, all the more tightly.

Brian didn't need an interview. Phil knew the standard of his work and offered him a job there and then. The money was remarkable. He could earn the best part of two thousand pounds a week. He would be based on one of their sites in Saudi Arabia; where they were building a stylish hotel and some residential complexes. His skills were needed. He would work one month on and one month off. All on full pay and he would live in a secluded staff apartment. Flights and everything were included. All he had to say was, "Yes."

Brian wanted to, there and then, but he held off and asked if he could talk it over with his wife first. Phil's eyebrows went up. But, he still seemed okay about it. "Just give me a call in the morning. We'd be looking at starting you some time in the next fortnight. Is your passport up to date?"

"Sure is. It's only new."

"You may need to upgrade it soon. It's surprising how many pages get stamped, when you fly around the world. Hope to hear from you soon, Brian. We would certainly like you onboard." He shook his hand.

That was when his self-doubt fired up again. He began to feel really insecure inside. How would Linda take it? How would he take it? What the hell would it be like working in forty-degree heat and in a foreign country?

He was getting emotional and he didn't understand it. At the back of his confusion lay the thought that all of this was because of that woman. Thinking about her saw him beginning to physically shake. He was fed up with feeling like this. He really should say something to her and end it properly. Yes, a new start meant killing off a few old mistakes. He was certain that he wanted to say something firm to her and clear his mind. That way, he could focus himself on what lay ahead.

***

Chapter 23
Means Within a Means

Jenny was dusting her dining room mantel piece again. She had done it a thousand times before, but it was never done to her personal level of perfection. For some reason, the right-hand corner didn't shine up like the rest. It irritated her. She had even tried using a solid tin of wax polish and, then spent ages buffing it off. But, little difference was made. It always looked dull. Some guests had told her that it was the angle of the surface. Something about the way the light reflected off it, rather than how shiny it was. Once they'd said that, she daren't ask any further questions in case it got her into trouble. So, today, she had reverted to her old aerosol can. One quick spray and she was done. None of that applying wax, waiting for it to dry and then buffing. After all, it was far too hot for all that!

She was also wondering how Petula and Sondra were getting on. What they were doing didn't make a lot of sense to her. All this PI stuff looked very glamourous from the outside, but Petula had explained that it often meant running around all over the place. Working long hours. Acting on the flimsiest pieces of information; which often led you straight up a one-way path to nowhere. It didn't seem that great, after hearing those words. So, why was she driving off to the other side of the country? Petula said that this was, 'Because she had to.' That was why.

Never mind, at least she would be safer with a companion and that appeased some of Jenny's concerns.

Petula had asked for her mobile number and that was when Jenny had given her a strange look. It didn't take Petula long to deduce that Jenny didn't have one. Only, it was worse than that. Our Jenny didn't even know how to use one. She'd heard people talking about 'smartphones'. But, she just thought they were some kind of a kid's thing. Something you got over, once you grew up. Apparently, that was not the case at all and Petula said that she would sort one out for her. She didn't really understand what that meant, but she did like her Petula.

At that point, someone rang the doorbell and she slowly made her way down the steep flight of stairs. When she arrived, two children popped out from the garden and went, "BOO!" right in her face. Then, they ran off. Jenny knew their mothers. But, fortunately for them, she also recalled being a youngster and decided that it may be time to take advantage of the situation. She fluttered her duster, where she stood, and then closed the door.

Hem was definitively back on form. He told his secretary to call a special board meeting on Monday week. He wanted the chance to air his grievances. He was specifically concerned about where all this false publicity had come from. The company was not going under. In fact, the business was going exceptionally well. Everything he had promised was going ahead on time, on schedule and on budget.

Minutes after he had arrived, he got Ruth to come in to his office and go through the basics of the forth coming itinerary. She always wore one of those neat short skirts, which attracted your eye. And, although it didn't do anything for Hem, he did appreciate the opportunity to indulge his view a little.

When she had gone, he poured himself a small malt whiskey and savoured the taste, in the peace and quiet of his own room. He looked out of his window and suddenly felt more secure. As he sat there, his mind wandered. An iconic brain cell clicked into motion and he made a call home. The phone just rung. She clearly wasn't there, so he hung up. Then, he called his solicitor's and made an appointment for Tuesday at eleven. After which, he stood up, reached over and picked up a hard hat. It was time to do a site visit. That police station fiasco meant that the insurers were there today and it seemed good practice to be seen with them. It also gave him a good chance to show who was who, and that could do no harm at all.

Wilbur was driving at a steady pace. It had taken a couple of hours to get to Bedford and then he found he had made a couple of wrong turns. So, he was heading out again on the same route he had just taken to come in. It took another hour for him to park up the car and locate 'Ellery Halemasters' on foot. He recalled thinking, as he walked in; what a stupid name that was. Just changing the name to 'Hem the lot of them' would add so much quality to their prospective business. He came in through a clumsy rotating door. It squeaked and gave an irritating creak: both at the same time. He walked over the rich, floppy carpet and sat on a swivel chair which proceeded to rotate. He started to grin. This place was so stupidly funny. Then a young lady, in a dark-blue business suit appeared and asked how she could help. "That's a good question," he said, in a light-hearted tone. Then, he caught hold of her expression and stopped himself in mid-flight.

"Excuse me?" she responded.

Wilbur picked up her remark, straight away. He knew this routine to a tee. That was why it didn't take long for the acclaimed 'Richard Londe, Esquire' to obtain the information he needed. You see, he just happened to be in the market for some property and he was particularly interested in any period listings which she may have. Apparently, he was looking to invest some of his oil money. The young girl politely smiled.

Yes, the property had been rented and yes, it had been purchased by a private company, whose name she could not disclose. With the file on the table, Wilbur engaged her in another conversation about some more promising properties. Ones he had seen in the window. As she hurriedly rushed around to get the details, he brazenly managed to lift a copy of the former tenants, out of a file. The list he precured was for 54 Surrey Street. Staying in his place, he looked at the new offerings she had brought. He seemed very interested in one and said he would call back tomorrow. Once he had spoken to his wife. He left the estate agents at four p.m. sharp.

By the time that charade was completed, Wilbur was feeling a bit peckish. He walked down the high street and tucked himself into a fancy bar called the 'Forsaken Sailor'. He went in, ordered a grill steak with croutons, combined with some kind of a salad-like dressing. Then, he took a window seat and watched the world go by, as he sipped at a charmingly dry lemonade.

Looking out, he could see people moving up and down the street. He pondered at his frame of mind. They were only people being people. Then, his thoughts came alight again with that brunette beauty. The one he had never met and yet, almost slept with: both at the same time. It was still so strange. He was old enough now, to see the fact from the fiction. Yet, he'd never known such a thing to happen before.

He had been sitting (sleeping) in a car (a stationary car) and then she awoke him. He didn't wake himself. He was certain of that. It was more like coming out of a mist. As though someone had called his name, rather than opening one's eye lids. And there was no physical contact. Couldn't be. Not least, because his hand went straight through her: garments and body. Both, at the same time. And that was something else. When she woke him up, she did it like a breeze. He didn't jump. If someone was actually next to him, then he would have expected himself to have some kind of a physical reaction. But how could he? She wasn't there. Was she?

His tea arrived, courtesy of a slim lad with a squeaky left foot. Job done, he applied reverse gear, swerved and screeched away, leaving Wilbur with the steamy contents on a tray. The food was bland, but it filled a hole. Whereas, the dark-haired wonder girl had created a whole new one: inside him.

He came out of the pub, put on some heavy pink sun glasses and, via the courtesy of a local cash point, made his way back to the car. He drove around for a little while and then settled into an overnight hotel. One of those functional places. They were cheap enough, but the essentials were a little bare. Nonetheless, needs must and he came up to a suspicious-looking lady on the reception counter.

"You fill out one of these." She handed him a card and said, "There's no evening meals. If you want breakfast, then tick here." She pointed, with a thick pen nib. "If you don't, then don't bother."

Charmed as he was, Wilbur asked, "How much?"

"Sixty-five for one night. A hundred and twenty for two. I can come down, if you stay for longer."

That was one invite Wilbur did not wish to partake. "Two nights will be fine. Thank you."

She looked at him, with razor-sharp eyes. "You're very hairy, aren't you?"

Wilbur picked up his room fob and replied, "It's all down to the vitamins I chew, Miss. I'm afraid, it has to come out somewhere. Don't you think?" With that, he walked off and left her chewing at his bit.

Petula and Sondra had found the bascule bridge – the one which Wilbur had driven over. It was on the Hemmel Road and it was one of those strange metal bridges that rose up above the water. Tide permitting, boats went underneath and, when one was too tall to get through, up it went. It had two single carriage ways. One on each side. A raised paving section separated them, in the middle. On one side, Petula could see a welded railway line. It was bedded onto the edge of the footpath. So, originally, one lane must have been for cars. The other, must have been for trains. It was clear to see who had won that battle.

At that moment, one side was closed off and someone had placed traffic lights to control the vehicle flow. Everything had to move on the one remaining side. Petula walked up to the cones and tape, where an angry looking man shouted for her to "…bugger off. NOW!" She gave a non-verbal response and then came back to the car. Sondra was running her hands through her hair and letting the summer breeze play with the ends. "What say the big man?" she asked her friend.

"I think he's very lonely and failing miserably to hide his sexual emotions." Then, she turned herself and faced Mrs Strumshell. "I'm going to be honest, Sondra. I'm a bit lost at the moment. I've looked this place over and I really can't see anything. So, I think I may have taken us on a wild goose chase."

"How come?"

"Because, I don't have anything else to offer. That's why."

"I think the answer lies over there," Sondra pointed over the bridge. "It would still lie over there, even if we were back home. But fortunately, we're not, so let's go, Queen Bee." She pointed again.

Then, Petula turned to face Sondra and said, "Right on girl! I like your style and I'm with you all the way."

Petula's car had long since seen better days. Despite its age, she tried her best to look after it. As a result, it complained very little. Like most things, it appreciated being the way it was; because it did away with all that uncomfortable process of being something else instead. Recycling would mean being reheated, reformed and then springing up as something new. Then, the whole deterioration process would start up again. So, now it had settled into its current shape and condition, there seemed little point in complaining.

Five miles out, from the bridge, the engine popped and it began to smoke: badly. Seven miles from the bridge, the engine began to slow down and the temperature gauge went up. Eight miles from the bridge, it unceremoniously pulled into a lay-by and quietly passed away. Leaving the two girls and the remaining journey unattended. This was not looking good.

Sondra got out of the passenger seat and lifted the bonnet. There was hot, wet oil all over the top of the engine. "That's not right," she said.

Petula looked lost. "Any ideas?"

"I think your cylinder head gasket has gone. Which, if I'm right, is quite a big job." She was looking around. It was still light enough to see and it was quite clear that there was nothing on this road, but road. "I can't see a service station," she said.

"Can you look one up?"

Sondra pulled out her smartphone and the dreaded words 'no signal' appeared. "Nope," she said.

"Great!" Petula was frantically looking around.

"Do you have any spare oil?"

"Oil? How do I know? I suppose there could be. Why?"

"Because, if we keep topping the oil up, then perhaps we'll get another ten or twenty miles out of her. We can drive until the water evaporates and then we're truly buggered. Up 'til then, it should chug along.

"Best not to push it too hard though."

One minor investigation later, Petula emerged, clutching a half-full bottle of oil. She also raised the question, "And where did you get all of that expertise from?"

"A long distance love affair with a dirty old mechanic," she said.

Petula replied, "I'll believe anything if it works, sweetheart." And the thing was, it did.

Hem was outside his home. He was sat on the sunlit veranda. Next to him was Sandy. They were both looking serious. Sandy had heard the proposition and was digesting what this would mean for their relationship. In essence, Hem was opening up his heart to this man. He even wanted Sandy to move in. But, he had been asked to prove his devotion by carrying out a very unpleasant manoeuvre. And: on someone he had never even met. Someone called Wilbur, who may or may not be called by that name.

They were drinking neat scotch and his tote-filled hand came down. "I don't know, Hem. It all seems a little peculiar. I mean, if this guy is doing what you want him to, then why see him off? Unlike you, this all seems so imprecise. Don't you think?"

Hem was instantly angry. "Yes, I bloody well do think! I think about it all the sodding time. Every day, every part of every day and then every fucking night." He drew breath. "The thing is, I don't really see Wilbur as being the cause. He is a loose cannon, though.

"He's swung for me once, with a fucking golf club and I felt that very deeply. He scared me to death and made me piss my pants. It was embarrassing. I did it right in front of other people. I mean, I pissed myself in public. For God's sake!"

"That is bad."

"On the golf course, at my club. It was bloody humiliating. I can tell you!"

"Don't worry, darling, I'll do it for you." Sandy put his hand out and played with the back of Hems fingers. The motion seemed to reduce the tension a little.

"I don't know where he is at the moment. But, I do know where he's heading."

"Tell me?"

As Hem opened up, his words drifted out into the summer evening's air. Over the garden wall, they went and into the pool area beyond. Where a stony-faced Brian was sitting. He'd gone home to talk over his new job offer with Linda, but she had left a note to say that her mum was unwell. She'd also gone over to help her dad cope with things. That meant, she might be away for a few days. If he had any problems, then he was to call her. In effect, she'd left him alone with his own thoughts and nowhere to vent them.

After that, he turned tail and came over to have it out with Sondra. But, no one answered the doorbell. He heard some voices drifting over from the back garden. So, he began to walk around and was about to shout his mouth off, when he noticed that they were both men. At that moment, he stopped himself and sat down on a lounger, by the swimming pool. The water was glistening in the evening sunlight. He listened to every word that was spoken. It was as fascinating to hear as it was frightening to digest. Sondra, it appeared, was about to be divorced and her current husband was out to kill someone called Wilbur. In the course of their discussion, Hem knew where Sondra was and that relit his fuse. That spark gave him food for thought. With his anger alight, he quietly made his way back to the car and set out on a new course.

Earlier on, the girls had used their bottled water to top up the coolant. They refilled the engine with oil. Strapped themselves in, and then Petula and Sondra came down the main road like a 'Puffing Billy' on heat. Petula finally curved the old steamer into a local garage, just as it was closing. The owner came out and looked at the contraption. He instantly gave one of those pricy sighs. Which; combined with the regulated frown and sullen twisting of the head, showed that he had all of the approved characteristics to practice as a mechanic in the repairs business. He looked the car over. Then, the owner said it was definitely worth repairing. In fact, it had a lot of miles left in it. But he said, it would be at least two hundred and fifty pounds plus any unforeseen extras. He bent over her again. This caused the waist line of his saggy jeans to drop down. The rosy red tip of his elasticated underpants came crisply into view. And, from the front of his oily black denims came the pristine words that, "…it may need some new timing belts… So, we're looking at about five hundred pounds. Or thereabouts, all in all."

He was saying this on a one-horse road in the middle of nowhere. "Oh, and it will take three days. I have to get the parts in first and then strip her down and then rebuild it…" He rubbed his crumpled chin a bit more. He seemed to be expecting an answer. "Maybe, ready by Thursday. Could be Friday, give or take." His hand wavered as he spoke.

Petula liked her car, but not as an antique in someone else's collection. She needed it now and for the job in hand. Sondra said they could hire one, she'd happily pay. Hem would never notice. Petula took the bait. "Do you have a car we can use while you fix mine?"

That threw him for a moment. Then he said, "I have a car coming in tomorrow. You can borrow it then. Let's say six hundred quid and I'll throw it in for free." He held out his hand. Petula shook it whilst still trying to comprehend what exactly she had agreed to.

At least, there was no charge for leaving her car where it stood overnight and Petula agreed to the work being done. She gave Sondra's mobile number to him and the two of them called a taxi from the garage's office. They went to a local hotel with the aim of re-planning their adventure. After their evening meal, Sondra seemed to get all excited. "Why don't I buy you a new car?" she said.

Petula looked unsure. "They cost a fortune and they all play up. Add to that; two unattached ladies. Garages love a gullible customer. God knows what they would do with us two. They can fleece you naked and still wave away, as you freeze your tits off."

Sondra leaned forward. "Look, darling, this is serious stuff. I have the funds. So, either we buy a car of our own; which we can sell later on. Or, we have to go back to the prince of primates and use something which we haven't even seen the look of. What say you, ducky?"

Petula smiled again. No matter what was going on, Sondra had an infectious sense of humour. It purveyed through every situation they had faced and now, it was rubbing off again. "Okay, let's buy a replacement car: second hand, of course."

Sondra looked up with a grin and simply said, "Agreed!"

***

Chapter 24
An Errand or Two

Brian had been getting himself into a real state. Three days ago, he had been making love to an erotic woman who desired every ounce of his body. That woman was not his wife. He liked it and that had shaken him up big time. Since then, he'd come away from her and his mind was aimlessly floating around everywhere, in a constant state of turmoil. It was seriously racking his brains. It had affected his judgement. He didn't really know what to do next. Every time he tried to find a way out, then a door slammed shut in his face. He really felt something for her. She seemed really needy, but he had needs too and Sondra Strumshell did not fit into any of those at all.

Gradually, the more he thought about what that woman had done, the more angry he felt. She knew what she was doing with him and their relationship was certainly servant and mistress. He actually felt obliged to kiss her and he was certainly under her spell, when she caressed him. It wasn't him at all. It was her.

As the thoughts kept flowing, he started to feel an increasing anger building up inside. He had been sitting in the half light, near someone else's swimming pool. All because of a woman who thought no more of him than an insect. He was furious with her and he wanted to sort it out, tonight.

So, an hour after hearing the swimming pool conversation; Brian was going, foot down, to Bedford. He knew where she was now and he wanted to have it out with her. No matter what. His feelings belonged to him and she had no right to interfere with them. She had to be told: once and for all.

Somehow, he knew that his life was falling apart and he thought that she was the reason. That wretched woman had deliberately woven her spell upon him and he couldn't shake her off. He turned from the motorway at midnight and went straight down the Hemmel Road to Barnbridge. Recalling the conversation he had heard, he knew she was staying at the Rift Hotel and he was heading straight there.

He was belting along the road, when something unexpectedly appeared in front of him. It was a stray deer and a big one at that. He was going too fast to stop. So, he hit the brakes and swerved the car out of the way. It spun onto some sort of a dirt track. The car was still doing around fifty miles per hour and it a took a second or two for him to realize what he was doing. He made himself take his foot off the accelerator. He needed to stop and turn around. Which was fine except, as he slowed down, someone shot his front tyre. It made one hell of bang and then the steering wouldn't work. So, he ground to a halt: turned off everything he could. Then, sat perfectly still, in complete terror and wrapped in total darkness.

He sat there for a while and listened. Figuring, that if he opened a door, he would be a really easy target. So, he stayed rigid and upped his antennae, for anything he could hear.

Meanwhile, on top of the bankside, Jeff was sat with his back to the events going on below. He was happy now. He'd taken aim and hit something. That's what mattered. It proved something: he could cope and he knew that for certain. They could come for him anytime they liked. He was all right. Just, completely drunk. That meant, there was no way he could possibly stand up. So, he gave in, laid his head down, on the sand and fell asleep.

Twenty minutes after the shot had rung out, Brian slowly opened the driver's door and stepped out into nothingness. *It must be somewhere around two a.m.,* he thought. The half-moon was just coming up and he could hear a faint sound. It threw him, for a moment. It sounded like someone was snoring and they weren't that far away either. Somewhere, up near the rising moon, on the hillside. Hearing it, he took his breath and carefully walked in that direction.

Under foot, the ground was powdery and his trainers did not grip very well. With every step, he kept listening. Suddenly, a happy dog appeared, with a wagging tail. It scared him half to death, but then, it ran off to his left. Finally, he made it. There were no more dogs about. So, he felt better. Then, he looked at the snoring man. He stank of stale beer and sweat. To his right was a rifle and Brian picked it up. It was lighter to lift than he expected. He couldn't see any shells laying about, so he set off back towards the car.

In the semi-darkness he proceeded to carefully change the front wheel. Even with all the sound he made, whenever he stopped, the stinky man was still snoring away. When he had finished, he threw the gun over a hedge and got back into his car. Then, he put it in gear, started it up and carefully reversed back until he hit the road. At which point, he turned for home and drove, hell for leather. After an hour, he came back to his senses and slowed down. He carried on, until he could pull off the road and have a doze. He had to be back to work by nine. With that thought, he lay down on the back seat and, in total defeat, fell soundly asleep.

Wilbur was on form. He had spent the early part of the night asleep in his room. Once it got properly dark though, he woke up, came down the back passage and went outside to do some work. He re-located 54 Surrey Street and broke in through the back window. As he suspected, the place was dead to the world. It was also unnaturally warm. Even sweaty. There were some really old-fashioned furnishings in here and it was clearly being regularly dusted. He saw that, because all the surfaces were clean in his torchlight.

Now, Hem had told him what he was looking for. But, it still took over an hour to find it. By that time, eye strain was becoming a bugger.

He knew which room it was in. The only problem was finding where it was situated. He painstakingly looked the place over. He moved and looked behind each and every picture. All to no avail. Finally, he shone his light beam at the wall itself and saw a seam. Some kind of a join was visible on the surface. Then, he moved closer and forced the seal apart. This revealed a safe which had been recessed into the wall. It was painted in a light tone of blue and was already unlocked. Inside was a plethora of papers, ranging from bank statements to copies of legal documents.

Why it was open troubled Wilbur, but he had found what he was looking for. He also saw a 'Post it' note attached. It was saying that the originals were at 'Halmer and Coes Bery' Solicitors. They were on Berwick Street. He immediately thought that was going to be a problem. Not least, because Solicitors often used other companies to store their records off site. Especially, if they were archived and this one was dated before twenty twelve.

No matter, Wilbur looked around the room again. He thought he had seen something move. Only, that couldn't be. There was no sound. So, no one could be here. Could they? He turned towards the entrance door and then felt something land on his neck. It stung; like some sort of insect, which he crushed in his glove. Then, he quickly made his way outside.

By the time he was back near the car, he was having considerable difficulty keeping his eyes in focus. His left eye was worst of all. He knew it must be drugs because his sense of balance was almost gone for a burton. At that stage, he made a few more staggered paces. Then, he came upon a low-lying hedge and, accepting the invitation, he fell: head-first, upside down and feet dangling. In that position, he passed out and slept like a new-born baby.

Adrian and Beccy were sat in silence. In the warmth of the morning sun's rays, Adrian had just asked her something and those words were just taking a little time to sink in. Then, her expression changed, her whole face lit up and she said, "Yes!"

Sondra woke up with an ache in her side. When Petula came down to breakfast, she saw her employer lying on the restaurant floor with her left leg above the table. "Will you behave yourself, Miss. Otherwise, people will talk."

A pain-easing reply came back along the lines of "Go screw yourself."

Petula looked closer. "If it's not a rude question, what exactly are you doing down there?"

"I slept funny. These cheap mattresses are crap and I've pulled a back muscle. We need to stop and get something warm to rub on it."

"Aren't you supposed to cool it down?"

Sondra was annoyed. "Look, I know what I need and it isn't you telling me what I don't."

Petula looked at her again and was about to speak a word of wisdom, when she thought the better of it and walked off. She went to pick up something which resembled a recognizable kind of breakfast cereal. That was when she noticed she was feeling a bit slimmer.

When she came back, she asked Sondra, "Have I lost some weight?"

Sondra looked up from her floor-like perspective, "Maybe," she said.

Petula took her remark on the chin. She didn't feel like tempting her for any further comment.

At that moment, someone's head popped up. "So, where are we going today?" asked Sondra.

"Before we do anything, we need a car and I think we should go back to that garage and pick up the one we were promised. Then, we can set off, in search of our friend Wilbur. What say?"

Sondra was back on the floor again. "I'm okay with that." Her eyes then re-appeared just above the table line. "But, we do need to call into a chemist or I shall simply die with agony and you don't want to suffer all those screams, do you?"

"Heaven forfend," said Petula and tepidly sipped her cup of mellow coffee.

Wiry Audrey was sitting at the breakfast table with a stern cup of strong tea in her left hand. Bald-headed Ted had just come down the stairs. He plonked his belly in front of himself and sat it at the square breakfast table. He remorsefully stared down

128

at a piece of crisp brown toast and then looked at his wife. "How are you?" he asked.

She looked at him. "There's a man lying in the garden."

"Front or back?" He scraped something creamy on top of his meal and then crunched into the hardened bread.

"Front. I think he's had too much to drink."

"Usually is. Has he damaged anything?"

"Can't see, 'til he goes. Can I?"

He shrugged his shoulders. "Suppose not." Another chunk of toast went in through his widening lips.

"Well are you gonna move him?"

"Why?"

"Well, it's not nice, is it?"

"Is he naked?"

"I don't know. I didn't dare look."

"Then, why don't you?"

Audrey was petrified. Her pitch went up a key. "Ted! He could be dangerous!"

"What difference would looking at a dangerous man through a thick pane of glass make?"

"He might want to harm me."

"Can't see why he'd bother. I never have and I've had plenty of opportunities."

She went quiet, turned her head away and he reached out to pick up a cup of hot tea. The classic positions in a stalemate were clearly taking form.

Outside, it was cool and Wilbur was slowly coming too. He had managed to sit himself upright and he looked to see where he was. He was perched on the edge of a neatly cut lawn. It was growing in an organized oval shape and, in the middle, was a pale looking stone font. No water was spurting. Perhaps it was just for show? To his right was a cement footpath and adjacent to that was a black-painted steel gate. He slowly pulled himself upright. Straightened his loose shirt and then levelled his jacket. All of this, just in time to see the water come on, at the font. It drew his attention. It was a terribly weak affair which made an irritating dribbling noise. If it had a purpose, then it was completely beyond him.

With a thick head, he was trying to coordinate his movements and that was proving more difficult than he first imagined. His left hand was now uncontrollably shaking. It was a nuisance. Added to that, he couldn't help but notice the appearance of a brick-nosed woman, at the living room window. She was frantically pointing for him to go. With his style intact, he cordially waved back and made a careful retreat through the dew-laden gate.

The sun was now up and the street was very bright on his sensitive eyes. Everything appeared far too brilliant for comfort. He couldn't see properly and he felt truly dreadful. That didn't stop his will power though. He knew the effects would wear off. In the meantime, he just had to bear with it. So, on that basis, he forced himself to walk.

To regain his composure, he raised his pace up a notch and began to recall just what had brought him to this state. Someone had definitely fired some kind of a drug into him. Probably diamorphine. He didn't know for sure, but he recognized some of the effects. One thing was for certain; boy was he thirsty. As he walked, he saw a newsagent's shop. So, he went in and bought a can of sugary cola, together with a machine-made coffee; which was both warm and bubbly. As soon as he drank the sweet drink, he knew he'd been drugged because it tasted metallic. He knew that these kinds of drinks were always reliably the same and that meant something was interfering with his senses. He went to sit on someone's garden wall and then he sipped from the coffee cup. That tasted better. But, then he was interrupted again. A massive 'THUMP, THUMP' came from behind. He looked around and focused on another individual's bedeviled eyes. This time, there was a bully of a man attached. He was standing there, bare-chested and tattoo-infested: showing two fingers, which were both pointing in his direction.

Why were people so inhospitable? And, in full sight of everyone on the street. He threw the empty can into the man's garden and then, gingerly, walked away. In those moments, he was starting to feel better again and he really appreciated the sensation.

They arrived at Hambelton Motors shortly after ten thirty. Mr Hambelton was full of himself. He sat the two ladies down and offered them some hot coffee in two dirty brown mugs. He confirmed that the parts were on their way. He expected to start the job once they arrived. Petula asked about the hire car. At that point, he stood up and went off for a few minutes. The two women looked on at another and then took the opportunity to stand outside. Where, they disposed of their carnal beverages.

It's funny how things look different in the broad stare of daily light. The frontage now appeared tired and worn. At the very least, the signage needed a significant lick of paint. Petula also counted three dead plants; in some decrepit looking plant-pots. As she was paying attention, Mr Hambelton suddenly reappeared. Complete with a set of worn car keys; perched on a thick rubber band. "It's over there," he said and pointed at a large pale green estate car.

Sondra went and looked it over. "It has the words 'Vauxhall Victor' on it?" She looked mysteriously confused.

Petula shrugged, "As long as it goes, that's all I care about!" And so, in they got and away it went. Petula had no idea what the engine size was, but it certainly had some punch. Hambelton had said that if they needed to fill it up, then they must put some special additive into the petrol tank or the engine would burn out. He had explained what to do. Petula still wasn't sure, but she promised to take good care of it. She put the little red bottle of fluid inside the driver's door and pulled away.

This dream machine was actually a nineteen seventy-two Vauxhall Victor SL estate car. It had light blue metallic paint, a huge amount of rust and a three-litre engine. It came complete with a manual four speed gear box. Petula was fine with it and soon they were on their way to Bedford. Along the route, they passed three police cars. They were all parked near some trees on their left. The police were looking at something, but at this speed, Sondra couldn't quite make out what it was. She thought it was a dark-coloured car, but that was all she could say. Once they were in the town, Petula drove around, for a bit, looking for somewhere convenient to park.

As they came around the streets, Sondra began to feel something. And it was her recently acquired perceptions that were coming alive again. Nothing physical. More like a presence. Only, it wasn't quite that either. It was probably better to describe it as a realization. Whatever term you used and however you put it; she knew her new lover was nearby. She could feel him and that thought was actually quite a nice sensation. She didn't say anything to Petula. She felt that it would probably be silly. Eventually, they pulled into a supermarket car park, where they poised themselves for action.

Petula then said that she had to run a private errand. Something about meeting up with an old friend, from her school days. That meant she could get some information about what was going on. Unfortunately, Sondra would not be conducive to her success. "So, can we meet up again in a couple of hours?"

Sondra took the hint, casually said, "Okay," and wandered off.

Petula shrugged and set out for her meeting with Lily Wise Owl. She was someone very special. A person who knew everything about everybody. Including Petula Vancouver herself.

***

Chapter 25
Weighing Up to Gage

Lily Vancouver lived in a well-worn semi-detached house; just around from the old Portway Park meadow. In the nineteenth century, Mr Portway had been a wealthy merchant. He believed in civic responsibility and the rights of the common man. So, he left some properties to the council. Under the strict instruction that they were, 'for the good of the local people'.

The council effectively owned them now. They had repeatedly tried to sell them off. But, old man Portway had a term on the deeds which prevented it. Despite their best efforts; legally, they couldn't and so, begrudgingly, they didn't.

Petula knocked on the door-glazing three times and tried twisting the door handle twice. Finally, it came off in her hand. With the knob between her fingers, she blushed bright red and didn't know what on earth to do with it. Next thing, a creaky old door swung open and there stood Lily. She gazed down and over her reading glasses at her prodigy. To whom, she sniffed her nose and walked away: back inside her home.

"I got what you wanted, Penny," she said, as she retreated down the passageway.

"My name's Petula?"

"Are we arguing this early on?"

"Only when I'm right."

"Being right ain't got nothing to do with it and mind your feet on the wet floor!"

They sat down, around and old-fashioned laminate table top, with faded yellow flowers and several burnish marks, on the surface. Places where repeated elbows and dinner eating cutlery had done their share of scratching.

The old lady leaned forwards and said, "The address you want is 54 Surrey Street. But, he's not there anymore. He left one night and never came back. He used to work with some guy called 'Herbert'. Odd name that, 'Hem'. Anyhow, he's not there now, either. I checked that too."

"So, who is there?" asked Petula, still holding onto the door knob.

"No one that I can see. I'd stay away girl. That place is dead as a strangled duck." Her chin suddenly came up, "What you holdin' that for?" She pointed at the door knob.

Petula didn't know what to say.

"Why didn't you tell me you got a girlfriend?"

Petula put the door knob down and breathed in. "Look Mother, I have my own life and I don't need your permission to get into involvements. Do I?"

"Of course not! But, it would be nice to be informed from time to time."

"I only met her two days ago!"

"Like I said, you need to keep in touch more. Anyway, something else came through: have you got another woman crusading around with you?"

"What?"

She pointed at Petula. "You've got a brunette chick with you. I seen her in my dreams."

"You mean Sondra."

"Is that her name?" She said it like she had just read an ingredient off a packet of stew. "Well, if she loves him and he loves her, then don't you dare come between them. Is what I say." Her hands came down and she shouted, "Will you!"

"No, I won't!" Petula retorted and looked at where she'd placed the door knob.

"Look girl, this thing ain't about money. It's about life." Her hands started to fly off in varying directions. "I mean, if people kill people, then they quickly run out of things to kill." She swiveled herself about and touched her daughter's forearm. "Keep your eyes on the living, girl. That's the only way.

"Now, I know this man's got huge ambitions. He wanted to rule the world, but he has a frailty. He's been misinformed. Someone gave him a rum pole and he ain't got nowhere to stick it. So, he's going home." Lily banged her hand down, "Won't get there, though. But, that's where he heading. Home!" She banged the table top again. Then, her tone completely changed. "How's Mark these days?"

Petula delicately laid the door knob back down. "We divorced ten years ago. He ran off with Bethany, if you remember. I think she has four children now and one of them is his."

"I know that, that's why I asked how he is. If you don't know, say so. Otherwise lighten up. Is this new woman all right?"

"Jenny or Sondra?"

"Don't you try that one on me, girl! You know exactly who I'm talking about. Is she all right or not?"

"Yes, she's wonderful and I've got to say that I've never felt like this about anyone before. She's all I ever wanted."

Lily nodded. "Good, then there you go. When this is all over, move in together and let her look after you. You could do with some tenderness and affection, at your time of life. A real good pampering is what you need. Then, see about getting married. I want you to be secure before I go, you know."

The conversation was getting a bit deep for Petula. Her mother could fire off in any direction at any time, and if she touched enough nerves at once, then you couldn't adequately defend yourself, either. "I'll do my best, Mum."

Petula was still sitting down when her mother stood up and said, "Good. Pity you have to go right now. I had so much to tell you. Anyway, do come back soon. I really want to see your new lover. So, bring her over as well and I'll kiss her cheeks."

Next thing, Petula was walking down the road and still trying to captivate what had just taken place. That aside, there was no way poor Jenny could cope with that experience. But then, she kicked herself, because Jenny wouldn't have to. That would be down to her. How on earth she would broach that subject was anybody's guess. "What a joy," she said to herself, as she walked past a dog owner peeing into a hedge.

Wilbur had an easy morning. He treated himself to some delicate cafeteria promotions. A piece of lemon fudge cake and sweet tea arrived, as a late breakfast. Then, he retreated back to the hotel. Where he took the opportunity to look at himself in the long bathroom mirror. He was satisfied with what he saw. Although, there were one or two bruise marks and a nasty red nick on his neck. It was sore, to the touch and felt like a nettle sting. He was sure it had come from some sort of an air dart. Somebody had clearly been in that room. If he'd put up a struggle, then he would have fallen unconscious in that place and may never have woken up. Walking out was the best thing he could have done. Still, who was tipping them off? He really didn't have a clue and that seriously worried him.

He picked up the phone and asked to speak to Hem. He wasn't there. So, he left a message and coldly replaced the receiver. Then, he set off to retrieve his stolen car.

Sudo was sat in his office, opposite him was Hem, and they were talking over recent events. Hem was explaining that they had to put more cash into the business. Otherwise they couldn't generate the returns. He wanted to buy another company. But, Sudo wasn't convinced. He'd seen what happened the last time they had used that technique. They paid top dollar for a construction company and it hadn't been worth the money. "I mean, we spent four million pounds replacing all the crappy digging equipment they had. There were hidden loans all over the place. Added to that, the stuff that did work was so cheap it kept breaking down. It was worthless. No wonder they sold out. And then, there was that electricity contract, where the suppliers refused credit terms because the company we bought had such a bad payment record. That hit cash flows hard. For eighteen months, if I remember rightly. I'm just not happy with that approach and I'm not having any more of it, Hem!

"It's got be organic growth from here on in. We'll do it ourselves. Just takes a little bit longer to nurture the business. That's all."

Hem was smiling, "Okay, Sudo. Have it your way. Slow growth's better than no growth, I suppose."

"How's that Wilbur thing?"

"Nothing to report. He was supposed to be checking out that Surrey Street address in Bedford. He'll be in touch, no doubt. Then, we can wrap this all up around his neck and get on with real life; making lots of money." Hem stood up, took an unprotected chocolate éclair from a tray, on the table, and walked out.

As the door closed, there was a ringing sound. Sudo sat back and lifted up his receiver. The lady said, "It's Jeffrey on the phone, sir."

He calmly said, "Oh, put him through, Simone." The line connected. "What is, Jeff?"

"I spotted someone last night."

"And…?"

"And I dealt with it."

"So, why call me?"

"I'm calling you because some moron happens to come flying down my driveway at mid-night. On the same day that I am about to receive two hundred items of merchandise. That's why."

Sudo knew who he was dealing with. He took note and responded accordingly, "Did he see anything?"

"Of course not. I'm just telling you. The extent I have to go to, to keep your precious little business going, is a lot."

"Our business, Jeff. Our business." Sudo was getting concerned. "Are you all right?"

"Of course, I am. If I wasn't then I'd take care of it. Wouldn't I?"

This was going nowhere. "Why have you called me, Jeff?"

"I've called you because someone tried to get into the main house last night. Bee told me that he took a precaution, but he was a big muscly fella and he had to retreat."

Sudo jumped up. "You didn't harm him, did you?"

"How could I? I'm not Bee. He fired one of his things into the guy, but apparently, he just trotted out as if nothing had happened. How about that?"

Sudo was getting confused and anxious at the same time. "Look Jeff, I told Pete to let that man get in and to leave the safe door wide open. I did that for a reason. So, why in hell's name was Bee firing knockout darts at him?"

"He can't help it. It's in his nature. Like a bird with a song. He's got to sting it the way it is! Oh, and he feels that Sadie should be allowed back into the secure pool."

This was a perplexing conversation. The more he learned, the less he knew. He looked at his wrist watch. "Okay. Do it. Look, I'll come over, later on and check that everything's all right. Is tonight still on?"

Jeff ignored the question. "Got any more of that sweet stuff?"

"I'll bring a case over."

"Good enough."

The line went dead. Sudo looked up to see Hem standing in the open office door. "Trouble at mill?"

"A minor trade dispute." Sudo stood up. "I'll be in Bedford if you want me. A little issue has taken place at Bailey's house and I think Bee has put a fucking croc in my swimming pool. I need to look into it."

Hem smiled and said, "I leave it all in your capable hands." Then, he came forward, picked up another chocolate éclair and walked off again; leaving the door wide open. He knew, doing that, would really annoy Sudo.

Wilbur was stood, looking at the car. Someone had daubed something unpleasant all over the windscreen. It looked like some kind of blood. As he came closer, he confirmed that it was. Some of it had dried overnight. It had also been splashed over the other car windows. It was a rich and deep red. Probably from some sort of animal. Either way, it was highly unpleasant and completely unnecessary. Getting closer, he saw the remains of the poor creature it had come from. A deceased ginger cat had deliberately been placed on the bonnet. Somebody had actually cut its throat and forcibly wiped its open body over the vehicle. Wilbur looked at it, in total dismay. This was truly disgusting.

He looked around, but no curtains twitched and he did need to use the car. So, he climbed in and started playing with the windscreen washers. That was when a big man came up to him. With the engine running, Wilbur wound the window down.

"You don't live 'ere an' I do. This is my space and not yours. If you park here again, I'll smash your face in." Then, he turned around and walked straight back where he had come from. Wilbur thought he must be the cat murderer. Then, he calmly looked over his shoulder and drove off.

The first thing he did was pull into a car wash. It was one of those hand-held things. Three spritely people leapt up from nowhere. He decided to leave it in their capable hands and asked for a cheap and cheerful clean-up. It cost ten pounds. Once done, he headed off for the office. He had read through the paperwork which he had lifted. To him, it was obviously a set up. Someone had tried to kill him. Added to that; the documentation was clearly a copy. He wasn't sure whether that would be good enough. He also felt that the 'Post It' note was meant to draw him into the trap.

The more he drove; the more he thought about it. And, the more he thought about it; the greater his needs grew. Something was clearly wrong. Then, as he was driving along, his eye caught hold of something. He did a sudden swerve and abruptly stopped outside a newsagent's. He left the engine running and tore straight inside. A few minutes later, he rematerialized holding a new packet of stodgy liquorice. This particular one was his favourite kind and a prime choice in times of such emotional distress.

Sondra was having the time of her life. For some reason, being set free meant she had acquired a deep maternal desire to shop. She suddenly wanted to buy everything she could. That didn't disturb her too much. At least, not until she started to analyze what form her compulsions were taking. There seemed to be a trend developing. More of that sexy, black underwear. She also bought some dark-tan stockings and she was currently knee-deep in female scents. Some of which were very nice and addictively expensive. She spent around three hundred pounds and then remembered that she really needed a thick jumper.

The weather had changed and with it, the wind had shifted direction. North Westerlies meant it was getting too cool for wearing just a short sleeve summer blouse. The lady in the shop was most helpful and she really liked their array of formal and informal skirts. So, she bought one of each. Plus, two blouses and settled the bill before looking at her watch. It was eleven thirty. She made strides to the café where she was meeting Petula.

Petula duly arrived to sit alongside a single girl who was surrounded by a mass of varying packages, parcels and enough fruit scones to sink a ship.

"What have you been up to?" she asked.

"Look, you abandoned me and I had to cope," came the cordial response.

Petula shook her head. "Where I've been, no human being would want to follow. Believe me!"

"So…" between the chewing and scattering of fruit scone crumbs, came the words, "…where have you been?"

"I went to see my mum."

"Your mum?" Sondra stopped chewing.

"Yes, my mum."

"I know silly, why didn't you take me?"

"Look, if I had, she'd have devoured you. Then, you'd need heart to heart resuscitation; just to bring you around and I can't do that single-handedly. Can I?"

"That bad, eh?"

"Worse, she's going on about my new relationship and she wants to see Jenny."

"So?"

"So, no. That's how so."

"What?"

"Look, my mum can love you or eat you alive in seconds. Only, you don't know which applies until it's already happened and I don't think Jenny will survive it. At least, not without a four-week prep course first. Delivered by yours truly." She pointed at herself. Then, she said, "Any plans yet?" and gave Sondra a solemn look.

Amongst the continued fruit scone chewing, Sondra suddenly picked up the sentiment of the question. "Would you like a bite to eat, dear?"

Petula nodded and Sondra purposefully leant her a folded a cardboard menu.

***

Chapter 26
Is It All a Setup?

Wilbur finally sat in the parked car. That was when two police officers walked by. Once they'd gone, he played with the sim-free mobile phone he had just bought. He inserted the pay as you go sim card and got straight through to Hem. He explained that the documents were in his possession but, "…they have the words certified copy embossed on them. Are these what you were looking for?"

Hem sounded deflated, "Not really. What's that note say?"

"It says, 'Original with Jeffrey Sibbs Holdings, care of Hamler & Coes Bery Solicitors'. Does that mean anything to you?"

For a moment, nothing came back. No conversation flowed and Wilbur was about to terminate the call when Hem spoke up again, "It's that sod Sudo."

"Who?"

"Without saying too much, Sudo has always had his own businesses. Not linked to mine. Anyway, one of them was sponsored by his friend Jeff Sibbs.

"He's a bit of a hiccup on legs. Drinks beer like it's water and is frequently seen three sheets to the wind. Normally, you would say he has no business skills at all. I do know he deals in explosives and has an arsenal of guns. I could never work out how he gets them or where they go. But, I do know there's heaps of money involved.

"He's not wise, but he can smell a rat a mile off and I've had two runs-ins with that bastard before. He's not pleasant, but he is loyal." Hem then spoke in a lower tone, "Loyal to Sudo, I mean."

"Is this a set up?"

"Well, let me put it this way. Sudo is on his way to see Mr Sibbs right now and you are unofficially invited. If the original documents are there, then I want them. But, I haven't set you up: honest. Your money's safely here. All I want is the paperwork."

Wilbur reached for another liquorice. He chewed on it more slowly than usual and said these words, "I don't trust you anymore. I can't and that's a fact. But, I will get your precious papers and present them to you. Remember this, though. If I ever see your handywork on anything which endangers my survival, then, I will come and get my money. And take you away with it."

Hem was feeling that strike of anxiety again as he said, "Understood."

After which, the line was neatly curtailed at both ends.

Old man Jeff had been running his business for years. His father had started it off in the nineteen eighties. They used to do odd jobs for unfriendly people. But, there wasn't much money in that. So, they looked for something more lucrative and started to import weapons. To begin with, it was only the ones which fired blanks. Then, they got some interesting offers. It meant reorganizing things a little. But, the offers were good and so they set up a small workshop. The idea was to clean out the barrels and place a rifling profile into each weapon. That way, they fired live ammo. Only, they needed their own calibre of bullets. Soon, they found that bullets could be manufactured on site and it made business sense to keep a regular clientele. So, they developed a carriage of loyal customers who were discreetly reliable and also very useful people to know. One big and happy circle. Happy, that is, until one law abiding guy called Bailey found out and set about going to report them to the police. Jeff wasn't having any of that and he told the man so. Only, he would not listen. He seemed to think that everyone should be good. As if that would change the world.

Jeff had sat him in a swivel chair for two whole days. Doused numerous amounts of ice-cold water on his covered face and ardently explained every minute detail of what was going to happen to him. All he had to do was keep quiet. But, he wouldn't. He had principles. So, Jeff put a long knife, slowly through his back and then fed his remains to 'Sadie', his crocodile. That way, he dealt with it. Only the problem was, he wasn't happy anymore. Somehow, that particular experience had developed a moral streak in him. One which could best be controlled through a full glass. Wine, Cider, whiskey. He didn't care which. After all, why did moral mortals exist? The particular morals in question needed to remain on the deceased's side. Not on his.

Underneath it all, he still deeply felt that they could have come to a satisfactory conclusion. If only Bailey had listened. Learned to turn a blind eye and, then everything would have been okay.

After he had killed him, Jeff found it difficult to carry on. His father gave him support, but his social relationships fell apart and finally he resorted to drink. It became his full time means of coping. It worked too. It lifted the guilt complex. Except, it needed regular and irregular top ups.

He knew that he couldn't say anything because if he did, then everyone went down with him. And in recent times, business had picked up. Trade was increasing. How did Sudo put it? "Exponentially." That was it: 'exponentially'. Sounded good didn't it? Especially, when you'd had a drink or two, down your throat. It could even make you laugh: on occasion. Only, there was not too much laughter right now. Not in the cool air of a late summer's morning.

He stumbled around for a bottle. There were plenty of them. Except, all the ones he found were cold and empty. As he continued; rummaging around a thought entered into his head. One which inspired him to consider something new.

He knew that this wasn't a pretty way to live. He realized that all too well. He also knew that everyone thought he was a total prat. Far from the truth, but he couldn't stand up for himself, in this state. He gradually made his way back to the shed and then he opened the fridge. There was some stale cheese and some goats milk in there. Who the hell had bought that? He thought.

He sprayed his hands through the cupboards, until he found an old jar of nondescript coffee. He lifted the lid and smelled it, deeply. The powdery fumes instantly hit his nostrils and, with a hard pang, he sneezed. Coffee powder blew everywhere. It dusted the work surfaces and descended onto the unswept floor. After which, a tiny amount managed to remain in the bottom of the jar. So, the new day for Jeffrey Sibbs began with a cup of hot and strong coffee. The top of the liquid was bearing congealed lumps of stale goats' milk. As he drank his new delight, fresh thoughts began to emerge. Some of which effused themselves into triumph. He had made a decision and with that came an image. An image that things just had to improve: somehow and soon. It was that, or he was going to end it all and leave the whole bloody mess for someone else to clean up.

Brian had, had one hell of a time. Since he had set off to sort his life out, everything around him had gone wrong! He got the car away all right, but half way back home he ran out of petrol. So, he had to walk, two miles to find a garage. Then, he had to buy an appropriate container, fill it up and pay for the petrol. Walk back to the stationary car. Pour the petrol in. Then, drive back to the petrol station and fill it up; properly.

He was knackered when he got home. The time was ten fifteen in the morning and he still had to go to work. He also had to let Phil know, today. if he was coming to work for him. At that point the phone rang and it was Linda, "Now listen…" he said, "…I've got something very important to say to you. So, don't interrupt."

Wilbur was troubled. His mind was clearing up nicely now only, he could see a number of obstacles on the horizon. He didn't mind that so much. It was par for the course these days and they would be good for camouflage. What annoyed him, though, was how utterly gullible he had been. Fancy, believing Hem. Fancy, not working out that it was Sudo who was behind it all. Fancy, not working out that Jeff Sibbs was also fancied as being an underworld arms player.

Wilbur knew the name and did something which he should have done a while ago. He asked some of his friends for their thoughts. Texts and phone conversations ensued. He had a variety of responses, but one seemed the most aligned with his own. A friend called Raymond could remember that Jeff was involved in an arms shipment which was delivered to the wrong the address. He couldn't recall where, but he could remember the stink it created. Some innocent guy got murdered and ever since then, Jeff had never been sober.

After Raymond had gone, Wilbur remembered the address. He recalled seeing the place, in the papers. Only, he wasn't sure about the exact details. He did know that it had been a stylish residence, somewhere in Bedford. It may even have had a swimming pool. But, he couldn't be certain because he still couldn't recall the precise street details. That said, he felt sure that he'd probably been in one of its rooms with an open safe, the other evening. Suddenly, things were taking shape and all the time his motivation was growing. He was being swiftly taken up with the sole aim of plotting a safe route out.

Hem was holding Sandy's hand at the breakfast table. "Are you sure you can do this sort of thing? Safely, I mean?"

Sandy said he was; he had already purchased a suitable weapon from a close friend. Once the job was done, then all he had to do was return the gun to him and it would be disposed of. He saw no problem there. All they needed to do was lure Wilbur into a location where he could hit him.

Hem was giving this point some serious thought when the phone rang.

It was Wilbur, "I've located Jeff. He lives at on old quarry off the Hemmel Road."

"What time are you going?"

"Does it really matter?"

"I wouldn't go there, if he can see you coming."

"Point noted, I'll go after dark then. Say, around ten to mid-night."

"All right and get that paperwork! I need it as soon as possible."

"If it all goes to plan, then you'll have everything you want by Saturday morning."

With that, the line went quiet.

Hem turned around, "He's going to Jeff's tonight."

"Who's Jeff?"

"Jeff's a drunken old sod who imports bent guns. Err, no pun intended. He drills out the core of blank firing weapons and turns them into real guns."

"Is he armed?"

"Yes: he's a dealer. What more can I say?"

"You said he's a drunk."

"He is, he's never been sober since his old man died. That must be nigh on ten years ago, by now."

"How did his old man die?"

"He fell into the jaws of a pet crocodile. At least, that's what I heard. May not be true. Who knows? You can't tell with him."

"I'll need a car."

"Take Sondra's 'Range Rover.' She's not about, so you may as well have her play thing. Only, make sure it's clean, when it comes back or boy will she moan. And that's the last thing I need right now."

"Understood."

"When are you setting off?"

"I may as well go around mid-day. I need time to read up on the topography before I go in."

"Can you do that in the bedroom?"

Sandy looked unsure. "Well… I suppose we can…?"

With that said, they left the dining table together and walked off, towards the stairs.

Jeff didn't house any business weaponry at the quarry. It wasn't secure enough and it certainly wasn't safe. But, he did allow the occasional display. Providing everything was cleared neatly out of the way, afterwards. Today, was a presentation day. An event where prospective customers could come over and view the items for sale. A case was delivered by Bee Thomas. A strange guy who lived at 54 Surrey Street. He was in his thirties. Stood about five foot nine inches high and was as thin as a rake. If he stood side ways on, then you could easily miss him. But eat! Boy could he eat! Only, where it all went was beyond comprehension. He was always svelte like, no matter what he did.

Bee dropped the case off at ten o'clock in the morning. It had eight rifles and plenty of ammunition. Jeff offered him a coffee. Bee looked at him strangely and said, "No." Then, he got back into the truck, wound the window down and asked if he needed anything. Jeff had lost his licence years ago. He was always over the limit and finally received his three-year ban. Bee and Pete dropped off grocery items, whenever they were passing and he seemed able to survive off the land for the rest.

Jeff asked him for some coffee, "Some of that powdery mellow stuff and I'd better have some milk to go with it. Otherwise, all of the usual, please." Bee scrunched up his face and nodded. Then, he drove off into a tail wind of sand and dust.

Wilbur always liked to be prepared. Especially, if you were going onto someone else's territory. The quarry was definitely someone else's. So, he carefully and slowly drove the car over to, and just beyond, the entrance. Stopped for a while and

141

peered discreetly around. Nothing startling stood out. Then, he cautiously reversed down a rough farmers track: which ran in the opposite direction. He tucked it behind some kind of tall shrubbery. One that grew by the side of a harvested barley field. He sat there, for a while, in the peace and quiet of the afternoon. During which, he pulled out some micro binoculars and proceeded to peer and watch at everything going on.

Sandy and Hem had been together for most of the morning. By eleven thirty, it was time to clean up. So, they affectionately washed one another, in the shower and then got dressed. With his hair freshly moistened from the shower water, Sandy looked the epitome of a fictional special agent. Content with himself, he sat down and went through the route again, with Hem.

It was agreed that they should eat something small and then set about their respective duties. Sandy wanted a picture of Wilbur. Unfortunately, Hem could not provide one. Though, he did give an exact description, "A tall, slim man; wearing dark blue denim jeans and a white shirt. Dark hair and always clean shaven. Big ears."

"This should be easy," said Sandy. They laughed.

"Just wait for him at the entrance. I don't know what car he's driving now, but you can bet it will be a sporty looking thing." Hem then paused and spoke affectionately again, "Do take care, Sandy, I don't want any harm to come to you. I feel for you." They exchanged brief kisses and then the duty of the day simply broke them apart.

***

Chapter 27
A New Gala Event

Given time, the warmth of the summer sunshine and sitting still, in a stationary car, is not sufficient to engage a functioning mind. Wilbur's thoughts began to wander again. He knew where he was, but he still actually needed a good plan.

From Wilbur's perspective there were three points at issue. He placed them in order and mentally tagged each one. Some he knew better than others. Some were more certain than others and others he knew more about than they knew of him.

It mattered not. His idea was to take the lead from this set of mental objectives. Therefore, the one which had been pressing him hardest would come first. Beyond that, the order didn't really matter except, it gave him some kind of formal approach to relate to. So, his order of preference was to be:

1. Jeff
2. Sudo & 54 Surrey Street
3. Hem

He could deal with Jeff now and that was the aim of today. Sudo was not so definite. He moved around. A bit like a rabbit on a runway. He even had an uncanny habit of appearing like a ghoul in the mist. Wilbur's next mist being 54 Surrey Street. If Sudo did turn up there, then he would deal with him accordingly. Which would leave the fat Hem firmly in last place and centrally in his sights.

As he sat there, he created an image of everything that had gone wrong in his life. From his first days at a bullying senior school to his last formal beating, by his aggressive father. Thinking about it made him realize something. If any one of these vile people had actually sat down and talked to him, then they would have changed the entire path of his life. At that age, he hadn't really done anything wrong. But, his actions had tarnished their pride and they beat him hard for it. They thought they were better than him and, unfortunately, he wasn't able to fight them off. To him, these were not pleasant thoughts. But, they were relevant because that is what this life had cast upon him.

As he was sitting there, he got that sense again. He knew she was somewhere nearby. Not Surely: that other woman. He could feel her presence and it was still as strange as ever. Where it came from; he did not know. It didn't worry him anymore; it actually felt quite pleasant. Like a wrapped present, awaiting the opening event. Somehow, she was awakening in him an aspiration.

He sat upright again and twisted his neck. With determination he resolved that he was not opening that can of worms right now. So, he compartmentalized the feelings and looked at his wrist watch. It was approaching seven fifty p.m. and now was not the time for any distractions.

A metallic light-blue sports car had just driven onto the quarry road. It went at an unnecessary speed. Dust was flying everywhere. He caught the plate number and calmly reached out, for a quick rustle. All of this, for the sake of another soft and chewy liquorice.

Bee had got back to the quarry around two p.m. He had Pete with him, this time and they dropped of the stuff for Jeff. He appreciated their help and was grateful for the food supplies. In addition to his usual shopping list, there was more than enough food for the night show.

They also set up the targets, which were placed around the edge of the quarry. They covered them with some old bed sheets. When they'd done, it looked like six nervous statues had arrived and they were all under cover. The guardians now had everything in place for a forthcoming evening of fun.

At five p.m., Bee and Pete shook hands with Jeff. Then, the two men drove off.

Sudo took to his large BMW. He did that, on the basis that he wasn't going directly to Jeff's show. If he was, then he would have acquired a less obvious vehicle. Maybe Hem's 'Range Rover'? Funny thing was, he hadn't seen much of it recently. Hem had come over in that little white Mercedes he owned. Perhaps Sondra had it?

He drove over to the Bedford address and arrived late in the afternoon. He came in the back way. The place stunk, as usual. He knew they had to keep the heat and humidity up in the pool area. He didn't really like that thing being in there. But, as long as it stayed out the back, then things should be okay. He just wished that people would shut the doors properly. It reduced the smell and, if that creature escaped into the house, then the whole show would be up.

He walked through to the kitchen. When he came in, Bee was frying some chips and waved at him. "I need a word," said Sudo, but he gave him the time to finish cooking and a few minutes to eat his modest attempt of a meal.

"So, what happened last night?"

"He came in and I nicked him."

Sudo sighed, "Why, did you do that?"

"Not sure who it was."

"What do you mean?"

"Well this dude wasn't wearing what you said."

"What?"

"He had some stripy shirt top. Not jeans."

"You wear jeans on your legs."

"I know where jeans belong. But, this guy wasn't wearing any. Anywhere! May have been chinos. Not sure really. Anyway, I took the precaution. If it was him, then I could let him go. Couldn't I?"

Sudo looked on in total disbelief. This is what life had brought him, a dollop on legs. "Forget it. Did he take the papers?"

"Yeh, there're gone."

"And did they have Jeff's details attached?"

"Sure."

"Good. Well done Bee. Here's a few quid. Have this evening off, on me."

Bee's face lit up, "This mean I can go to Jeff's shoot out?"

"Indeed, it does. Send him my best wishes." But, as Sudo was saying this, the slim shadow of a man had already escaped from the room.

Bee ran out, from the back of the property. Then, across the neatly cut lawn and up to the white garages. These were in a retreat, just off main the driveway. He opened the left-facing door and swung it up with a forceful bang. He then unlocked a vehicle and climbed into an old style, olive green, Land Rover. He loved this vehicle. It fitted like a custom-made shoe. It was rugged, fully prepared and raring to be abused. It fired up, first time and he swerved it out, on a tight bend and headed for the main road, at speed.

Upstairs, Sudo was consoling himself by trying to make sense of it all. He sat in a cushioned chair which he had purposefully positioned in front of the, still open, safe. He was curious. More or less aware of something which he shouldn't be. It had all been so well planned and it really should have gone absolutely fine. The fact that it hadn't meant it wasn't quite adding up anymore. He didn't like it. Slowly, he stood up and raised a hand to his lips. He wondered just what he was seeing? Then, he approached the safe and began to look closely, at what was inside. Again, he had his doubts and then he gave a sigh. In his palm, there was the contract. Only, it shouldn't be here? In fact, what the hell was it doing there? He turned around. This didn't make any sense at all. Wasn't Wilbur supposed to break in and take this? Wasn't he supposed to be going back to Hem, right now, with this very thing? And then, wasn't he supposed to get Jeff's little crew to finish the two of them off?

Yes; was the answer to all of the above. Only, the very document at the centre of it all was sitting right here in his own hand. Why? He suddenly felt the sickening need to see Jeff. One thing was for sure, party or not, he had to know something. And that something was called, the truth.

Outside 54 Surry Street, Petula and Sondra were sat in a car; whose windows were rapidly steaming up. It wasn't their fault. There wasn't any air conditioning in this clumpy thing. And, at the rate this car drank petrol, Petula was cautiously afraid of twisting any more knobs than she had to. Especially, if that increased its thirst.

Sondra wasn't happy either. It was too stuffy and she was getting wind. "I've been sat still for too long," she said.

"I'm with you on that one," Petula said.

"So, what's going on in there, Pet?"

"I really don't know, honey. When I was following Hem. I had to do some preliminary work. I found this address on a letter head in one of your husband's files. I think it was from someone called 'Bailey', but the ink had been soaked in water and I guess it had outlived its purpose by now."

"Well there's a lot going on in there. How many cars have we seen come and go, in the last hour?"

"Too many. Problem is, we don't know who they are. Maybe we should just follow one and see where it goes?"

"Sounds good to me. At least we can get some fresh air, when we're moving."

It was gradually getting dark and, over the past hour, Wilbur had watched several hefty vehicles lazily mount the kerbstone and turn onto the quarry road. He was just watching another: a dark blue 'Range Rover', do the self-same manoeuvre. Although, this one veered off slightly, before it pulled out of sight.

Wilbur sensed something unusual. It didn't behave the same as the others and, somehow, he seemed to recognize it.

For Wilbur, the afternoon had been long and trying. But, equally fruitful. He had been ruminating. Going over and over things and making sure the dirt math all added up to zero.

Wilbur had surmised that Maxwell Oakley must have been close to Bailey. Maybe even a friend. He had to be. Only, Wilbur hadn't realized how close they really were. Bailey must have had his suspicions, for a long time, about what he was getting into. Because he set some firm milestones firmly in the ground.

When he lifted the sheet of paper from the estate agent's folder, he clasped his eyes on a note concerning 52 Pembrokeshire Place, Bedford. It even had the post code. Bailey had owned it and, once he was inside, it also had a safe. As expected, this one was tight shut. On the front was a digital combination lock. One which required a six-digit entry code. So, with a little mental dexterity, Wilbur recalled a certain six figure sequence which was still in his pocket. The code was written on the card he had obtained from Mr Oakley. He punched '41-26-39'. That opened it up, to reveal some original documents and other paraphernalia. Ones which shone a whole new light on events. He no longer needed the fake paperwork from 54 Surrey Street. Although, he did have to play along. Otherwise, the gamesters would twig that he was holding an ace card. Oakley must have been Bailey's confidant. He must also have known what had taken place. But, when he went to ground, then no one else could find him. In that respect, he was safe. At least, he was, until Wilbur found him.

He suddenly felt very sad about that. Bailey must have given Oakley the coat. Not least, because the card was professionally stitched into the fabric. Lucky, he found it. Even he wouldn't have noticed that, unless the new owner was laid out on the wet carpet of tarmac. Wilbur mentally ticked himself off and then thought: *Circumstances just circumstances.* Yet, it still felt very strange, how such small insignificant coincidences had assisted the thief.

Why had Oakley turned to drink? Travelling that way, meant you ended up being firmly sucked into demon territory. Warped inside your own delusions and totally unreachable by anyone sane. No matter how hard they are trying to help. They can't reach in and pull you out. Simply because you just aren't there anymore.

Wilbur certainly had more questions than answers and time was beginning to impinge on his musing space. He would have to make a move soon. That said, he was really annoyed with Hem. How could that ape have got him to shoot a totally innocent man? The animal was quite repulsive. At that point, he deliberately stopped the next thought; before it arrived. He had to stay focused and with that thought, Wilbur's right leg appeared outside of the driver's door. This time the jeans were new. They were branded and also completely jet black.

Petula was following a blue BMW, whilst trying to keep her distance. She also knew, that this car was not that easy to drive. It was heavy, there was no power steering and it constantly pulled to the middle of the road. Still, she kept her eyes firmly on the car in front and manually manipulated hers, discretely, from behind.

Sondra had been quiet, but her feelings were on the rise again and she finally couldn't keep it in anymore. "We need to look out Petula."

The concentrating lady didn't respond. She was too distracted. She was also developing a whole range of new aches and pains. This thing was like driving a tank. Only, with a steering wheel instead of levers. She could feel the development of new arm muscles rapidly taking place. So, in this fighting spirit, she sternly replied, "Why?"

"Because that man's a killer."

"Who is?"

"The man in that car." She pointed at the BMW.

"So, spill the beans."

"I only know him from Hem. He's Hem's work partner. They call him, 'Sudo'."

"Sue what?"

"Look, I don't know where he got the name from. He's just called 'Sudo'. Okay?"

"Okay, I suppose. So, why are we not to follow him?"

"Because he kills people. I know that Hem gets him to do the dirty work. That's how he employed Wilbur and look what happened there!"

"Point taken. But, look sis. We can stop right now and then that's it. He'll sail off into oblivion and we ain't got no more leads. That way, we hang around for a couple of days, pick up the repaired car and go home. Feeling low.

"Or, we keep our chin up, twist our sleeves around our elbows and follow this motherfucker to see where the gold is. Choice is all yours, sweetheart."

Sondra gave a laugh, "How do you do it, woman? You are so bloody funny. I try to sow a seed doubt in there and you immediately spin it right around in my face."

"Try having a mother called Lily," said Petula. All whilst keeping her pursuit at eye level and bang on target.

The quarry was now alive with invited guests and numerous drinks were on display. All of them strictly non-alcoholic. Jeff knew how important it was to keep good control. If they wanted drink, then they went to the local drinkery down the road. No free samples here.

He had arranged a small set of powerful flood lights and taken the covers off the hardboard targets. The ones which Bee and Pete had set out, across the old quarry site. It looked quite imposing. Certainly, the scene was good enough for the purpose in hand and he wanted it to go well.

There were about eight people expected. Four cars arrived and he kept them entertained with some promotional videos and conversations about what sort of guns they were looking for. He didn't sell high powered weapons. That sort of stuff, he left to the professionals. His guns were re-bored imports. They required special ammunition: which he made. It wasn't expensive, but it kept him in moccasins and allowed them to do whatever it was they needed to. All outside the eyes of the law.

Jeff saw no fault in the free the market premise. He made his money and he enjoyed the comfort of their banter. Two of them seemed very interested. Perhaps he could make a big sale tonight. If that happened, then he could cancel next month's show and concentrate on sorting his life out. That was a pleasant thought.

Over, on the ridge, a discreet figure had just popped up. He kept his head low to the ground, but was avidly watching the events taking place below. Sandy had just appeared and he was holding a high-powered rifle with authentic laser sights. The kind of weapon which Jeff could never provide. It had come, courtesy of a good-looking guy called Ian.

Sandy was familiar with these weapons. He had already filled the clip with the statutory three o three rounds and was calmly waiting for his target to materialize. Which he did, but not from where he was expected.

Wilbur had, had his eye on the blue 'Range Rover'; as soon as it pulled off the main road. The reason being, it looked so familiar. As he approached, it turned out that it was very familiar indeed. He noticed the number plate; it was Sondra Strumshell's little monster. Only, it certainly wasn't Sondra who had driven it here. He eased around to the rear of the vehicle and looked closely at the lie of the land. The driver was clearly wearing walking shoes. He was a medium weight male and the foot size was probably a size nine or ten. The steps went off, towards the quarry and then veered away up a bankside. That meant, he had gone somewhere near the open edge of the pit. Probably, to a point which was overlooking the area below.

It was getting on for eleven thirty now and a slow rising moon had just reared up, onto the clear skyline. It was very warm and the insects were purring with their eagerness to bite. Wilbur, lifted his micro binoculars and surveyed the scenery. It took a few minutes for his eyes to adjust but then, his senses tweaked themselves into life and he made out the figure he was looking for. From this distance, he appeared as a young-looking man. Lean, fit and he was dressed in some expensive kind of khaki outfit. It hugged his figure a little too well and, in his hand, was a professional killing weapon. A telescopic rifle, which perfectly matched the ego of the beholder. Wilbur couldn't make out what it was (it was just too dark). But, he could see that it was a Kosher piece of kit and perfectly attuned to kill him. He suspected that was its purpose.

Meanwhile, down in the quarry. Things were beginning to lighten up. In fact, a whole series of main beam floodlights had just come on and they revealed a small number of black and white target boards. On a shabby and bowed wooden table, were some loaded guns. They had been purposefully laid out to invite participation. The assembled group was busily eying the items on display. As this was going on, Wilbur crawled silently to gain a good line of sight on his prey.

Jeff was the first to fire a gun. His voice had been noisily echoing out. He had been talking away to someone called Mic, from Aberdeen. Mic had been going on about the beautiful scenery which Scotland had to offer. Next thing, Jeff lifted the rifle and fired an accurate shot straight through the heart of a cardboard man. One who happened to be wearing a target as a vest. The other gentleman then took to the bait. Someone fired and hit the shoulder of the same target man. Soon after that, a small number of shots pinged out across the range and, with every hit, a series of cheery voices began to rise up.

During the display, Sandy had kept his shaven chin close to the ground and his eyes were acutely focused on the events taking place below. His field of vision was wide and he was pretty much able to see anything that went on. He was looking out for Wilbur. Hem had specifically told him that Wilbur always wore a blue denim suit, with a white shirt and that he constantly chewed liquorice. At the time, it had amused him. Now though, he was paying particular attention to every word he had heard and every movement on display.

To Sandy, Wilbur sounded like a duff. A wimp of a man. Someone who would never find love because his intelligence was too low to secure the possession of it. Even if love passed right in front of his face, he would never get it, because he was simply too stupid.

Looking around, his head was deeply involved in such thoughts. To gain some relief, he checked down to see that the safety clip was off. It was. He wanted the ability to use this thing rapidly and that was when he heard something, off to his left.

148

As he turned to see what it was, there was a sudden wisp of air and a loss of breath. Then, he slumped over and stopped moving, for posterity.

Wilbur carefully wiped his knife blade along the whiteness of a kerchief. Then, he threw it away into the darkness.

And so it was, that out of the moon-lit sky, Wilbur had acquired the use of quite a potent weapon. He knew that Sandy wouldn't mind him borrowing it. He didn't need it anymore. Wilbur understood that fact all too well.

Being careful and looking down the sight of the gun, Wilbur knew that this seating angle was wrong. You could hit someone who was approaching via the road entrance, but there was too much distance for striking into the assembled crowd. A small error, at this end of the gun, would make a big difference at the receiving end. The accurate arrival of the bullet was paramount. That meant, he needed to shift position. So, he picked up the loaded rifle, collected some spare ammo, and then disappeared sideways into the night.

Jeff had already secured several hard sales. Fifteen rifles and two hand guns. Things were going well. Half way through the sales pitch, Bee turned up. He arrived in an old Land Rover which his dad had given to him, years ago. They slapped hands.

"You look great," Bee said.

"I'm going sober, son. My days of drinking are over."

"Sounds good to me boss."

"Any news on the bigger boss?"

"Oh, you know him! He's going on about why I hit that stealer the other night. I told him straight and he went quiet after that."

Bee was full of life. He loved this place and, when the guns were on parade, it filled him with a special kind of pride. They had all come together to make this happen and he had played his part.

Jeff understood his mood and patted him on the back, "Have go, son. See how many you can hit." Bee's face lit up and he went over to the table. He took up one of the rifles, loaded it and began firing at the closest target. He hit the head, a couple of times and then shot at the chest. He was enjoying himself and Jeff liked to see that. He loved that boy.

A few moments later, a big fella called 'Green Dave' turned up. He asked Jeff if there was anything to eat.

Jeff pointed. "There's plenty of food in there. Just help yourself and have a pop with a shot or two."

Dave laughed out loud. He turned around and was about to make a comment when something hard hit him square in the back. The force took him down and he went straight into the dust with a thud.

Jeff saw it and threw himself to the ground. He quickly judged that he was about twelve feet from the light switches and thirty or so feet from the nearest gun. At that moment, no one else seemed aware of what had just happened and no other shots rang out.

Dave was still breathing. Jeff saw no point in speaking. So, he crawled towards the power cables and the light switches. That was when the second bullet hit home. His shoulder took the full impact. Most of it was blown clean off and his right arm was instantly useless.

The second shot was also picked up by the assembled crowd. They all turned around. They had heard it because the sound was far more powerful than their own weapons. The menacing pitch reverberated around the walls of the old quarry. They looked at one another and then started to return fire. Bee looked at Jeff and ran straight over to the injured man.

Shots were being made in Wilbur's general direction, but they quickly ran out of bullets. They reloaded, but it was a feeble affair. Their weapons were not built for the task in hand. Looking down at them, Wilbur was full of disgust. He detested having to do this sort of thing. But now, he really had no choice. As they laid down, in the sand and recommenced their anxious tirade of shots, he simply tuned his own sights and calmly fired at will. The first two were the men who were going to buy that large consignment of weapons. Wilbur hit their heads with pinpoint accuracy. He caught two more as they ran towards their cars and then he fired at the remaining ones, who were scattered around the table: the one which had displayed the rifles.

Someone did try to return fire again. But, Wilbur was so very far out of their range that they had no chance. He simply hit the assailant right through his chest. When it all quietened down, he then looked back at Jeff. He was still writhing around and getting progressively closer to the light switches. Wilbur, half felt like giving the old goat a chance. But, then he remembered the sordid details of this business and the awful things that had been done to Bailey. No one deserved that. Decent or not. So, he raised the rifle and hit him in the rear of the head.

At that point, Wilbur knew that he had to act fast. It had been a while since he had used such a weapon, but he took the straw into his teeth. With six further precision shots, he took out the standing flood lights and then he sat back to listen. Listened: to see if anything moved. To begin with, it didn't, and so he did.

***

Chapter 28
Summing Is Wrong

Sudo had quickly become aware that someone was following him. In the beginning, he didn't mind, because he knew what he was going to do. They casually crossed Bedford together, like a groom tugging at his prospective bride. But then, Sudo wised up and decided to open the distance a little. His car could easily cruise at a hundred miles per hour. And, by the time he was approaching the quarry entrance, he had confidently out run his pursuer.

For the girls, the lights were not very good on the old car. It was a stiff thing to drive and although it had the acceleration under the bonnet, Petula couldn't see well enough to keep up. So, they lost him.

Feeling more secure, Sudo came burrowing down the quarry lane like something possessed. He pulled into the open arena and skidded rapidly to a halt. Swinging the driver's door open, he trudged out into the empty expanse. The air smelled of burned cordite, but nothing was going on. Something was wrong and he knew it straight away. It was sultry. There wasn't a breath of air and everything was deathly quiet. Not even a grass hopper stirred. It was really odd.

He opened the car's passenger door and pulled out a torch. He switched it on, but the glow instantly faded away. The batteries were dead. So, he threw it away, in disgust. It landed in the dust. Then, he turned towards the hut. Those lights were still glowing and from them he could see a shape outside. It was laying on the ground. As he walked over, his heart sank. It was a body. He crouched down and came over to see who it was. Then, he hawked. It was Jeff. There was blood everywhere and his own foot prints were now pointing into the face of a murder victim.

In a state of fright, he stood back, rubbed his hands down his trousers and made efforts to get back to the car.

As he did so, Bee slowly turned over and tried to see exactly what was going on behind him.

Wilbur had seen him arrive. But, without adequate lighting he couldn't be confident of accurately hitting him. So, he desisted the urge to try. The gun was of no further use now. So, he threw it over the edge; where it fell into the water. Then, he pursued his way back to the car. After that, he waited for, 'our man' to appear. Which, he did. He also drove like a maniac and shot off down the straight, at lightning speed.

Wilbur watched him go. Casually plucked a new liquorice from his depleted supply and started the engine. Then, he spoke the words, "54 Surry Street, here we come."

Petula and Sondra had been out gunned and they knew it. "I think we have to realize defeat, my love," said Petula.

"Should we go back to the Surrey Street address?"

"Na. Thanks for the offer. Me thinks we've had enough, for tonight. Don't you?" She slapped Sondra's knee.

"I think so."

As they journeyed back, Sondra drifted off to sleep. She slept the rest of the way to the hotel. Once there, they simply went up to their rooms. Where, they fell fast asleep in the luxury of their well-made beds.

Sudo screeched his car onto the driveway and parked it sideways, across the entrance of the house. That way, if anyone came around, he'd see them and it would provide cover for him to return fire.

He immediately ran inside the front door and sat down on an upright chair; which he borrowed from the kitchen. In his hand was a small automatic hand weapon and he was shaking badly.

He thought that, by sitting in the entranceway and having the stairs directly behind him, then no one could approach without him knowing. It seemed a good idea and one he was prepared to take.

Wilbur had already thought this one out. As a result, he wasn't in a hurry. He knew what the welcoming party had arranged and he looked forward to the applause. It was one forty a.m. when he parked on the roadside. He felt primed and fully alert. Before it stopped, he turned the ignition off and let the car casually glide into the empty space. He didn't want to arouse anyone. He gently clicked the driver's door shut and checked his hand weapon for comfort. Then, he came to nineteen Simpsons Way and confidently walked straight across their neatly mown green garden.

Simpsons Way had been built two years before Surrey Street. As a consequence, one set of properties often backed onto another. In this case, nineteen Simpsons Way backed onto fifty-four Surrey Street. A convenient coincidence. Especially, if you were expected to make a discrete call onto the other side.

Wilbur made his way across what seemed like an unduly large lawn. Then, he realized that it was actually a well-maintained bowling green. In a perfect world, he should have de-robed his shoes. But, this was true life and there was no time for such pleasantries.

In the pinkish moonlight, Wilbur walked up to the hedge and forced his way through. In the back of the targeted house, there was a huge swimming pool. It was completely enclosed and the panes of glass were all fully misted up. So, it must be warm inside. This pool was not currently for swimming and he knew why.

Carefully, he came around the enclosure and made his way over to the broken window. Gently, he eased himself in and listened intently. There was no sound at all. So, he stopped and waited. Forty minutes wended by. In that time, his muscles were beginning to tighten. He was just about to ease his stance when he heard it.

A small scrape on the hard floor. It was a steel chair of some sort and it was resting on the hallway's laminate floor tiling. Wilbur was wearing trainers. Expensive ones, at that. The kind which grip like glue and make absolutely no noise. He crept up to the hallway and peered out beyond his boundary.

His eyes were fully adjusted to the dimness and, there in front of him was Sudo. He was sitting on a tall wooden chair with metal legs. *Stylish.* His attempt to stay awake, no doubt. Except, every few minutes, his head kept falling down and that was a clear sign of exhaustion.

From this angle, Wilbur could easily hit him. But again, a hand gun could not be relied on for accuracy. He also wanted some answers before he blew this monster away.

Sudo was sweating like crazy. He was also feeling icy cold. Added to that, he was so desperate just to fall asleep. He was still wearing his business suit and it was soaked right through to the skin. He smelled awful and he was shivering in absolute terror. He wanted to put the light on. But, that would be an open invitation and he didn't want to deal with that.

Why had Wilbur killed them? All those people! Why was that maniac on the lose? What the hell had Hem done in hiring him? More importantly, how was he going to get out of this?

Despite a lack of drink, his forehead was noisily dripping sweat onto the hardened floor. You could hear the drips striking the laminated surface. He didn't care though. He was saturated with fear and all he wanted was a way out. Any way out would do. He would never do this again. That was for sure.

It was then that he heard a squeak. It came from behind. He was so tensed up that, as he tried to turn, he simply couldn't move fast enough. All he heard was a faint 'pop'. Then, his arm went numb and he dropped the gun. It clattered onto the wooden floor and noisily scraped away from him. He was still shaking. It was almost uncontrollable now and he pleadingly asked, "Who are you? What do you want?"

Wilbur turned the hall light on and gently glided around. He turned the occupied seat, by clasping at the chair back. Then, he sat down, on the staircase and placed himself in front of Sudo. His eyes drew brightly, as he glared at the man. Then, he slowly spoke, "Why did you do all this? And why did YOU involve ME in doing ALL OF THIS?"

Sudo began to wet himself. It dribbled down his leg and onto the dry floor. He was visibly shaking. Like a leaf in a storm. At first, nothing else came out, but Wilbur didn't mind the wait. "I want your answers," he said.

Sudo threw up and then started to gibber.

"Oh dear," said Wilbur. "You're not really helping, Mr Sudo. Are you?"

Wilbur stood up and came around the mess on the floor, "In fact, I don't think you've really helped anyone except yourself. Probably, for a very, very long time?"

"It was Hem," he said. "It was all Hem's idea. He wanted you to be the fall guy so that we could wrap it all up under your name. He wanted to blame you for everything. That's what it was."

Wilbur breathed in, "I don't believe you. Hem isn't smart enough or clever enough to create these shenanigans. He just wants to grow his business. Be that legitimately or otherwise. If he gets that and a rewarding good screw, all the better. That's what Hem is.

"He doesn't mind people being killed, but he has to have a reason. He's not capable of thinking outside of the here and now. He doesn't work that way. That approach takes someone else."

Wilbur came around and faced his target. "And so, we come to you, Mr Sudo. And, I really do ask myself, what exactly do we do with you?"

Sudo choked on his remaining spittle. He was noticeably shivering.

Wilbur shook his head and breathed deeply again. He looked very hard for a sign of contrition. But, there was none. Not even a glimmer. So, he shot Sudo straight through the heart. In such a way that Sudo simply stopped moving.

Wilbur sighed, he was aware that time was getting on, but he still had so much to do. Quietly, he made his journey to the back of the house. On the way, he closed several stray doors. Barring those which led directly to the swimming pool. Once there, he cautiously opened the double-glazed doorway and turned on all the lights. The place was like a steam bath, but he did not venture a whisker within.

Wilbur knew this place. Sudo must have lived here for a while. It had belonged to Bailey. But, somehow Hem's business interests had acquired it and the new showman had arrived with a pet. This particular pet needed warmth, and water. Not the chlorinated variety. And with teeth like those, you didn't go dipping your toe in, to see if the temperature was right.

Understanding these things better now, he left the pool door wide open and retreated back to the broken window. On the way, he lifted the thermostat setting to 'high'. Then, he carefully tread out, into the safety of the gardens beyond. That done; he drove away and finally pulled into his hotel at five a.m. By that time, he was truly exhausted and yet, he simply showered himself and sat up to watch the splendorous sun rise. Only then, did he relent to the inevitable and fall fast asleep.

***

Chapter 29
Surely You Knew That

A few days passed quietly by. Quietly; in the sense that nothing new appeared on the scene. News wise, the headlines were full of calamity. 'Killer On The Loose' read one. 'Lonely Pet Dog survives Quarry Mass Murder' read another. 'Crocodile Tears for Victim' was also a definitive hit.

It wasn't nice reading and Sondra was pleased, when they finally got out of it all. Once, safely home: Petula embraced her and then went to see her new romance.

Hem was his usual obliging self. He grunted when she turned up and showed absolutely no interest in her or her new purchases. He was a complete stone in the wall.

For Petula, Jenny couldn't have been more welcoming. She threw her arms around her and wrapped in her in such warm affection, that she could have lived on thin air for eternity. She also found that she had lost half a stone in weight. The past few days had been real calorie burners and, with such a head start, she made the commitment to keep it up. Jenny said she could go to a local slimming club. But, Petula said that, like riding a bike, she could slim; without being given instructions. Even if she fell off, every now and then.

With the coming of autumn, things seemed to settle down. The nights drew in and thoughts moved towards the shallow time before the season finally closed. All this and the thoughts of Christmas loomed up.

Adrian and Beccy had now set a date for their marriage. It was going to be in the spring and they booked it, at the registry office, for 22nd April. Adrian had bought Beccy a silver engagement ring and everyone on earth got to see it. They were so full of joy and that helped to ease the awful stress from the summer. Allan was going to be his best man and Brenda couldn't wait for it all to happen. Mainly, so she could see the photos.

For Brian, he accepted the new job, but then they withdrew the offer. He didn't know why. So, he ended up staying with the firm. His boss was pleased to keep him and he got a small pay rise, which helped at home. He and Linda kept the flat. Though, their rent review was due in November and their earnings had not gone up enough to cover much in the way of an increase.

Suddenly, it was a bright November morning. Sondra woke up to the news of another philandering tale, involving her husband and how he had been sleeping around with a variety of men. Petula had disclosed the merits of this before. But, when it hit the newsstands, then it cut deeper than she had anticipated. This time, it really upset her. She knew that their marriage had been a sham for a long time. Yet, for some reason she had never crossed the board with enough strength to get out of it. Instead, she had sort of accepted that she was married to a fat slob of a man; who cared more for his long player records, than he did for his sex starved wife. She felt his attitude coming through everything. He was a barbarian. She had felt that for a long, long time. But, never questioned it. She had always gone on, with her own things and lived life the way it came to her. Never standing up for what she actually wanted. Never argued with her husband. These were the things which she knew about herself.

Similarly, he had never questioned her acquisitions. He knew she was sleeping with other men. But, if he came out with anything then, she would bite his head off. He knew that, so everything was politely brushed under the carpet. She thought about that for a moment and realized, it must be getting mighty dusty under there.

All had been well until her heart had started to awaken. Those powerful dreams, in the summer, had really stirred something in her. She had been living in this Hem constructed universe, for years. Sublime to her own fears. There was no love here. Everything felt and smelled like a science lab and there was never any affection. What had happened in the summer, had awoken something which she perceived to be a real need.

She was in her forties and yet, she felt like a teenager. Like loose strands; her emotions had unwound and come free. They were new, fresh and untainted by this venomous life. Despite all the horrors of the past few weeks, she was unperturbed. Confused maybe, but not concerned. At the bottom of it all and, for a reason she could not understand, she had fallen in love with a dream of a man. Maybe, the fact that he wasn't quite real made him all the more alluring. Perhaps, the sense of peace which came, when she thought about him, made it all the more special. Possibly, more than he could ever truly be? But, emotions do not resolve problems. Like a bird in flight, they feel the air flowing under their wings. They are there and are then gone. They only stay when they are fed and nourished and there was absolutely no nourishment here.

Attraction is such an all-consuming passion. You can look at a hundred thousand men, but only see the one you want. Why it had to be him, she did not know. But, life is like that: a strange place to exist. And all she could compromise was: if she saw him once, then, she would not let him go. At least, not until she has tried every conceivable thing to keep him. If it is love, then he will talk to her. If it is love, then she will know it straight away. And: he will know it too.

With that last thought done, she shook the blossom out of her hair and looked at the clock. It was time to put on her makeup. Although, even that wasn't enough to cushion her, these days. This time it was Hem. She knew he hadn't stopped his nocturnal activities and now, she supposed he never would. He had his desires and she had hers. Never the twain to meet.

She quietly went down the stairs and knocked on the living room door. It was already open. So, he turned and waved his fingers, for her to come in. She was formally dressed and quite business like about it. She calmly explained her feelings and what she thought of him. Then, she asked for a divorce and he again refused.

For some reason, she had expected that. A homosexual man keeping power over his heterosexual wife. Only, this particular woman was not going to be his pet. So, she told him it was going to go to her solicitors. She explained again, "How can I love you, when you only love men, instead?"

Her words hit home and Hem became angry. He shouted, "You're mine! And I'm not letting you go! So, you can fuck off with whoever you want, drop your knickers in front of whoever you like, but you're not getting rid of me." He threw an empty whiskey glass at her. It missed, but the malice struck home. She casually stood up, placed her coat across her arm and walked away as 'Sondra Strumshell'. Leaving the title of 'Mrs' behind her for good.

She took a walk into the grounds of the house and thought on for a while. Hem had lately become increasingly bitter. She knew that he had lost a lover in that quarry tussle. But, she couldn't understand his hardness towards her. She knew that he had never loved her: not even from beginning. If he had then she would feel it. Especially now.

Whenever she saw him, his face was always into business or food or both. And then men. He had even started to leave some ghastly looking magazines around the place. The pictures, in them, were obscene. Even, as a female, they did nothing for her. In fact, none of it made sense and she couldn't understand why everything on earth had to turn into such a battle. But, if that's what he wanted, then he would pay the bill.

She came back to the house around eleven a.m. By that time, Hem's car was gone. So, she was able to wander around. It was Wednesday, and just after lunch, she decided to visit Petula and Jenny. At this time of year, Jenny's boarding house was quietening down. This meant that they could sit in the warm dining room, around a table, and share a laugh. Play a few games and talk things over. They were fun, those two.

When she arrived, Jenny was all excited. Petula had finally proposed to her and they were both full of enthusiasm. When it died down, Jenny made them a hot drink and they sat talking in excited terms. Trying to work out how things were going to be. Was Petula going to live here full time? Should they rent her property out? Could they advertise her PI status on the guesthouse staircases?

Suddenly, it was knocking on for four p.m. and the street lights were glowing in the distance. There were only two guests staying at the moment and both of them were going out this evening. So, the girls decided to treat themselves. They could eat out in town and that meant Jenny had no cooking or washing up to do.

Five minutes after the clock chimes, it was four twenty and the front doorbell rang. Jenny went down to see who it was. She was gone for quite a little while and then she came back with a very tall and thin looking woman called Surely, who proceeded to comfortably sit herself right by the window. She was wearing a gold blouse. Whose collar dared to peek out from behind a gorgeously rich woven coat. Below this, was a long dark skirt.

For some reason, the previous conversation had come to an end and the atmosphere seemed to have changed. Almost as though everyone was waiting for an arrival.

Unusually, it was Jenny who broke the ice. But, not with words. She was silent. The other two girls gazed at her with a questioning expression. The unspoken message being; 'Who on earth is this and why she was here'?

Surely sensed their repression and she began. She said that she had been contacted by an event and that this happening was yet to take place. Petula's eyes widened.

Surely faced sideways and said, "You must be Sondra?"

"I am she," she said.

"There, I knew you were."

"Who are you?" Sondra asked.

"Does it really matter?" she replied.

The comment threw Sondra, for a moment. Yet, she quickly recovered. "I suppose not. But, you are very intense."

"Only in this life, my dear. In all other things I am neither here nor there. Don't you know." She paused and then said, "He's here."

"Who's here?"

"Why, your man, of course."

Sondra looked shocked. She had no idea who this woman was. Yet, those words had meaning and she knew exactly who was being spoken about. Somehow, something inside her felt it. So, she threw herself onto the defensive, "I've lived that dream half a dozen times before. There's no one for me."

"Every performance is worthy of its thespians. That, and a thoroughly happy ending. Yours has only to begin and you will instantly recognize it for what it is."

"And how do you know that?"

"I came of age before you were born and I will be here long after you pass away. It's simply the way things are.

"I spoke to him and he was far more congruent than you. He listened. He didn't question the wisdom of the giver."

"What are you blithering on about?"

Surely seemed to breathe in and smiled. The measure was precise. As she moved, so all their lungs filled with life and each of their faces reddened out. Everyone felt this presence, and they looked at her with questioning eyes.

"Now, do you understand?"

In the peace, no-one spoke a word.

"I came because I was sent. I'm not an illusion from which you can repent. I am present with you so that, you can relate to me." She leaned forward. "Listen and understand."

She turned her head and faced Sondra again. "Your husband is an evil man. He is constantly scheming for something to happen to you. Then, he can claim everything for himself."

"I don't have anything." Sondra frowned.

"Ssh… and listen," said Petula.

Surely went on, "You do. Your father was annoyed when you married Hem. So, he invested something for you."

"But, that's just a small trust and I can't access it unless I divorce Hem or I die." As soon as she said it, she began to realize what was at play.

Surely put it into words. "If you are dead, then the trust ceases to be and that money will allow Hem to expand his business. That is why he won't divorce you."

In a hushed tone, Sondra asked, "And you're saying this because…?"

"Because it's time you knew."

"Knew what?"

Surely did not reply.

Sondra looked up again. Something had struck her. She looked at this woman, with such intensity, that she began to see through her. Surely visibly waned in the power of her sight and became almost transparent. Her appearance dimmed and then returned from the darkness to become a halo of light. The room electrified itself.

"I came here to find you because I am sent by another. This is no fraud, so be very clear to hear my words."

Sondra's jaw unconsciously dropped open. She wanted to say something, but nothing would move. Nothing had prepared her for this. As a result, her body would not respond.

"That man in your dreams is real. I spoke to him, in your form. You know of this; because you were there. So, you have shared yourself in some of it. He only came because I beckoned him. He didn't want to. But, I have a way with some men." She smiled again. "Quite why they think they are so clever? Perhaps, one day I will meet one who truly is?"

"What do you mean?"

With gusto she retorted, "The events of the summer are not yet completed and the time is; for a season of change. It must be fulfilled. Otherwise things can't move on." Calmer now, "I know these words seem strange and I assure you that you will all be quite safe. But, you will need to face your adversary."

"Adversaries?"

"I have said the word which I came to provide. So, now you know. You are no longer ignorant. Do not be afraid, when it happens. In fact, enjoy every single moment. For it belongs to you. Indeed, all of this is all of yours."

That said, the room consciously dimmed. A strange wind suddenly tugged at the table cloth and everyone's hands reached out to hold it down. A piece of paper flew and the curtains swayed. Everyone turned to see what was happening. When they looked back, nothing was there. And, looking again, they could see that nothing remained. She had simply gone.

In the following moments, Sondra looked at Jenny, who looked at Petula, who looked completely at ease with things being as they were. She just stood up. "Cup of tea anyone?" Then, she flicked the light switch on and went into the kitchen to warm up some water.

***

Chapter 30
A Time of Finesse

It seemed that there had been a great deal of activity and, after the shooting spree, Wilbur felt it appropriate to go to ground. He dropped the car off, near a dealership and retreated into a windswept wilderness of his own. He stayed a few nights at a variety of hotels and apartments. Off season was cheaper by the coast. The air was also chillingly fresh. It gave him the reassurance and time he needed to reflect. Time to think and get things sorted.

For the moment, Hem was off limits. He would be holed up to the degree that a nuclear bomb wouldn't rouse him. Which was a shame, because he was the one who had started it all. Wilbur still had the answer in his pocket and he was fast catching up on events.

Everyone expected a someone and it wasn't very easy living life as a nobody. He had developed his own ways of coping. But, at this time of year, he was feeling increasingly shattered. He was still having those dreams about the brunette. It concerned him that she was so real and so persistent. How can anyone conjure up someone with looks like those? He was convinced she must be real. Had to be. But then, all he knew was her name. He had no idea where she lived. Not that any of it mattered. What interested him was how she was getting into his soul. Did he have a leaky spirit? If so, who had given her the key to his cupboard? They were hardly on talking terms. It's not as if they'd met at a bar. The truth was; he didn't know her. He also thought: *all the women he knew were physical creatures*? *Weren't men too*? It was all utterly perplexing.

The more he thought about it, the more confusing it became. In the end, he reasoned, that she wasn't here: whilst he was. That meant, he had to deal with today and plan for a tomorrow, with a hotly romantic blond. Hopefully, that should end it, for good.

It was cooler now and darker too. Although, Hem didn't really feel it. He never did. Namely, because he didn't have such feelings. He either wanted something or he didn't. Nothing more complex than that. You either accepted him or you didn't. If you didn't, then he would wipe the floor with your face. That was his business model in a nut shell and yet? Hem had taken things badly to heart. The police were materializing everywhere. They had deduced that Sudo was administering some kind of illegal drug and munitions trade. That was his forte. They had seized most of his funds. They had also found numerous bodies at the quarry. The accuracy of the shooting was beyond doubt. Hem wondered whether Sandy had been the killer or whether it was Wilbur who had pulled the trigger. Either way, Sandy was one of the victims and there was no Sudo to explain things. Hem had fully expected him to reappear at any moment; with another one of his threats or ultimatums. It would certainly be his style. Except, he never did.

The authorities sat tight for some time and finally, when some power company got the necessary court order: their employees entered 54 Surrey Street. That was where they found his jacket. It was tied onto a turned over chair, in the hallway. Blood stains were strewn on the floor. The place stank and it was way too hot. Thirty or forty degrees? There was water dripping off everything electrical and it was full of humid warm air. They also found a twelve-foot crocodile romping around in the swimming pool area and that created all kinds of a raucous. Plus a few more headlines.

Hem knew who had done it and he knew what was coming. He was convinced that it was just a matter of time. So, life became a series of nervous and jerkily wrapped exploits. He hired two body guards and tried to stay out of public sight. This proved harder than he first thought. Everyone was constantly onto him for a comment or were taxing him to speak about his thoughts. Specifically, on what had taken place. The thing was, he didn't have anything more to tell. So, keeping his head down was all he could do. At some point, it had to blow over. When it did, then he would be able to raise his head again. But, his intension now, was to focus on doing things right. It seemed the only path available and that would help feed his Karma.

The truth was, Sandy had gone. He felt that deeply. Far more than he could ever express and there was another low hanging doubt; casting a shadow over his soul. The measure that it was all his fault. If only he'd taken care of Sandy, the way he should have. Looked after him, the way he should have and taken the blows himself. That way, Sandy would be here now to support him. Instead, he was covered in so much despair that he was aimlessly sailing into unchartered waters. He hated it.

Facing up to himself, in the mirror, he could just about cope. That was providing nothing else went wrong. What drove him now was that he couldn't allow Sondra to get off scot free and leave him with a guilt complex the size of a Mediterranean harbour. She was not getting a divorce. He was definite about that. The best she could do was suffer, like him; until their relationship was formally ended. He knew, without a no-fault agreement, it could take years and that would serve the bitch right!

Sondra had asked him for a divorce, a few days earlier. He said, "No," and he was determined to keep it that way. His reasoning being; that now wasn't the time. Though, to be in honest, he had to concede that the marriage was over. He felt nothing for her and he told her the same. He did try to say that she could screw whoever she liked. Just, no divorce. He did know about the trust money. But, that wasn't the reason. She could continue to spend his money. He did not want any of hers. On that basis, she seemed to believe him. Not that it consoled him any. But, at least it was the truth. All he needed now was some well-earned peace and quiet.

Like an overexcited light bulb, the actions of the summer couldn't dim the flame. Brian was getting worse. The old character of Mister Dependable was firing off in unscheduled and anxious misfits. Linda had sensed it, a while ago and it wasn't getting any better. Since the job promise had collapsed, he was becoming more and more of a grump. And less and less of a husband. He was also working longer and longer hours. Which meant they had more money, but he was turning into an emotional recluse.

They hadn't had sex in weeks and, when she tried to snuggle up to him, he kept pushing her away. Things were not good and he refused to open up and say why.

He had told her about the Strumshell woman. Apparently, she had taken a shine to her man. The thoughts of that liaison had actually turned her on but no, Brian couldn't see it. At this rate, something had to give. Christmas was coming up soon. So, she decided to put some effort into brightening their lives up a little. With the extra money he was earning, maybe they could go away on holiday, next year.

She really had to do something. Because this couldn't carry on. It was like living with a brother rather than a husband and, like her, he must have needs. So, where were they going?

She thought about the Strumshell woman again. But, he hadn't been up there in months and she knew he was working because of the money he was earning. So, what on earth was wrong with him? Could it be her? Somehow, she had to find out. Only how?

Sondra was sat with Petula. They were in her old home. Business had temporarily dried up and this was always a good time of year to have a good a tidy around. The two lovers were going to marry in January and Sondra was invited to the celebrations. But, that wasn't at the centre of the conversation, which was taking place right now.

"So, who is your father?" asked Petula. "I mean, is it the same Bailey that we have all been chasing after?"

"Yes and no," said Sondra. "To be honest, I'm not really sure. But, I can't see him placing money in a trust for me and then going into business with Hem. Can you?"

"What if it happened, the other way around?"

"Hardly possible. Hem's only five years older than me."

"Still not impossible?"

"I don't know. Anyway, Hem said he doesn't want the money."

"He's hardly going to confess the truth to you. Is he?"

"Hmm."

"What is it?"

"I was just thinking about my childhood."

"Any notable points?"

"A few…"

"Such as?"

"You know something; I really wanted to be a ballet dancer," she chuckled.

"Actually, I could see you in that role," said Petula.

Sondra looked shocked. "You must be joking! My legs would never go high enough. Can you imagine the creaks and groans. I could even get thigh lock!"

They laughed.

***

Chapter 31
Thoughtful Movements

The coincidence of coincidental coincidences. You know the way it works? Just when you think you've turned the last corner. The way ahead becomes straight and what's passed firmly resides in the past. That is precisely the point when everything begins to change.

By now ,Wilbur was done with the most of it and he found himself desiring to let go of the rest. Except, some small fragmental pangs kept niggling him. One morning, he was innocently walking down the street, when a grumpy old sod started to shout abuse at him. Something about damaging a water fountain in his garden. As if. But, that incident began to bring it all back again.

By acumen, he still possessed the original documents. For as long as he held onto them, then Hem wouldn't be any trouble. Even if Wilbur lived next door, Hem would still treat him with respect. But, only because he was holding the ace of diamonds. Then, there were his mix of emotions. Something had definitely happened back then. He couldn't ever recall feeling like this before. At the bottom of it all, he was still seriously troubled with that woman. She popped up like a cavity in a tooth. No matter where he hid, or where he laid his head; there she was. Could be two a.m. in the morning and here she comes, large as life. It was a strangeness to him because, this is what he believed love should be like. You should meet someone and fall head over heels. Both parties should love one another, equally. Or it just wouldn't work. Except, this time, it was like being taken over by a leading figure from a budget feature film. He couldn't reach out, but boy could she reach in. It was unfamiliar territory. One thing was for certain, she was stunning and, he was sure, that counted for a lot of it.

That aside, he had to turn her off and turn himself onto his other rational problem. He liked closure and achieving that element of finality. It was fulfilling and it may be easy. If Hem was willing, then he should get his money and Hem would get his documents. Alternatively, if Hem wanted the documents and a dead Wilbur then, he felt that some sort of a trap may well bound up into existence. Question was: was it worth the risk?

He knew himself better than most. In that sense, he had a talent. So, he could easily get himself another job. He could move on. But, something was tethering him. Something emotional and that was unusual. He simply couldn't let go and he couldn't reason out why. Perhaps, it was something which sat inside the realms of an unfinished piece of work. One thing was for sure, in this kind of employment you had to have a clear mind and that meant, he had to complete what had been begun. It was that; or it buggered up the rest of your life. On top of that, he had to keep his senses at full flow and he didn't want thoughts of this woman interfering with those. Even though it may be difficult: it had to be concluded. So, Wilbur phoned Hem to see if he still wanted the original documents.

"Yes," he replied.

"Good. Then, I shall supply them. But, on the basis that the original terms of payment are also met."

"Yes," came the monotone response.

"You used to be a good employer and I have kept to the arrangement we made…" Wilbur deliberately paused, to see if Hem would open up a little. He didn't, "…I feel that we should meet up on neutral ground. I will bring the authentic papers in a brown A4 envelope and I want all my money in a carry-all bag."

"Anything else?"

"Would you like the address?"

"What address?"

"The neutral address is: Room 4, The Meldross Chalet park. Just off the Ribbonside Road."

"Not far from the beach, then?"

"My schooner is just off the shore."

"Doesn't surprise me, in the least. What time?"

"Seven p.m. I will leave the front room curtains open and the room light will be switched on. It should make it easy to see me. And, Hem?"

"Yes."

"Once, I'm done. Then, I'm done with you. You and I are permanently finished. That means that you'll never see me again. Understood?"

"Understood."

With that, Wilbur quietly returned the receiver to its resting place and frowned. He knew what he'd started and, now he'd set it in motion, that meant the fuse was firmly alight.

Jenny was so excited. Petula and her really had a good friend. She was overcome with it all. It seemed like, all of her life, all she had ever done was wash, clean and cook. She never went out and she was constantly counting every bean. Her accountant was always very impressed with her book keeping skills. That was because she stayed in and spent untold hours; making sure every single transaction was correct.

But, suddenly she had friends and she had found love. A whole new world was opening up and what a wonderful life this was turning out to be. Right now, Petula and Sondra were upstairs talking. She didn't really understand it all, so she had come down to the kitchen to make some fresh coffee. She stood, a little while, as the filter machine gurgled and worked hard at its wonders. Then, she reached down for a small plate and delicately arranged some pink wafer biscuits into a circle. They were laid, edge upon edge, all around the patterned rim. She also placed a small marzipan flower in the middle. Then she loaded the tray with the hot drinks and went back upstairs.

"So, you've seen your solicitor?" Petula asked.

"Yes. He said that I have a good case. But, only if Hem accepts responsibility."

"And will he?"

"I don't know."

"Well, morally, he hasn't got a leg to stand on. He is sleeping with other men. And he certainly isn't married to them. His affairs have been broadcast all over the papers. So, I think the marriage must be irretrievably broken down. Don't you?"

"It's not that simple, Pet. He spent a pot of my money on his business. So, the last thing he wants, is to give half of it to me."

Petula began to wave a pointed finger, "Excuse me Sondra, if you're his wife, then half of it is yours anyway.

164

"He could give you shares. It's that or the money. His choice Sondra and he hasn't any right to say otherwise."

"He isn't nice, Pet. He's often foul mouthed and he's so damn manipulative. He will probably say that he'll divorce me, but then ask for some time to fully reconsider things. That could take years."

"Don't let him. You have the papers. All he has to do is sign them. You're only taking what's yours. After all; he hasn't really been your husband for years. So, why do you keep treating him as though he is?"

"That's a good question. Maybe, I still think of him as the man that I married, all those years ago."

"Well stop it! He's relying on that, whilst he's sleeping around with someone else."

"But, he's killed people Petula. I mean, that man who he's employed is doing his dirty work. I'm sure Hem's killed people before. He always uses some kind of agent and there have been others.

"They deal with his problems for him and he just goes on. As if nothing has happened. If I say I want a divorce, will he kill me?"

"We can't allow that. Do you actually know that he has had people killed? I mean, do you have any actual names and backgrounds?"

Sondra looked doubtful. "I don't really know, for sure, Pet."

Adrian had been awake in the early hours and was still coming to terms with his new life. A few weeks ago, he had been living with a wretch of a woman and tied into a job which seemed never endingly dull. But, as that crescendo had ebbed away, he suddenly found himself wrapped up in a warm and loving relationship; with the best-looking woman he had ever met. On top of that, following the recent publicity, his boss had promoted him. He was now based in the office and only hit the road, when someone was sick or when they were short staffed. He was now a boss!

When that happened, it meant he had to visit more sites. That saw him doing more miles and then there were the stop overs. But, the money was good and so was Beccy. He had honestly never seen such a transformation and, as he looked at her; laying beside him, he realized that she would be the best wife he could ever have wished for.

It was now a new phase. Merely a new phase. That was all. Yet, whilst he had been away, he had also been secluded and in absolutely no danger. Move on a tad and this new act had exchanged all of that. Suddenly he was out in the open again. A deer on the road.

But, after all the years of personal hell and misery, he was suddenly reforming. For some reason, his ambitions were changing. He decided he had seen enough of death and the look of the dying. Some, undoubtably deserved it. They had reddened their mawkish hands on the innocent blood of others. Some enjoyed the fever of the kill themselves. Whilst others took to it, with anonymity. Directing the show from behind the facsimile of those they employed. Hem was one of those.

He hated Hem. Not because of what he did, but because he denied himself the glory. He employed the assassins and they only did what he wanted them to. Even then, he would blatantly deny his own involvement. The truth was, he was a liar and you can't trust one of those; in any circumstances.

He took another malleable liquorice from the neatly opened packet. As he did so, he mused that those thoughts hadn't changed the way he felt. He knew that he'd seen enough of guns, enough of blood and enough of bad guys. Plenty, to last a whole life time. He wanted an end to it and that placed him in a strange situation. As the initiator, this meant new options were unveiling themselves. The old weapons, he could exclude: life without a gun! Although, the un-spilt blood would rejoice, that didn't change the nature of the bad guys. They tended to carry on with their usual arsenal of wares. They were a type. Generally, a principled type. Which meant, they would be fully armed and so they still had to be dealt with.

Wilbur coalesced his thinking. He was well rested now and clear thoughts were radiating far easier than they had done for some considerable time. He made a conscious commitment to use no more guns. Unless, that was, he had to. Yet, he needed an edge. He had to have an edge. That was essential and it would take planning. If nothing else, even in this emotional madras, he adored the simple choices. And they only came from good planning. After all, with a good plan, nothing obscured an exceptional performance. Nothing, that was, but death.

Hem heard the phone go dead and his expression took on a jeweled level of seriousness. One that Sondra dared not interfere with. She knew full well what it meant. Anyway, she was supposed to be going over to Jenny and Petula's. She was also wearing a new evening dress and some really nice-looking shoes. They were supposed to be going to a theatre show. That meant, she needed to make an exit, without arousing his suspicions. Conveniently, the downstairs doorbell rang and so she quietly left the chilled air of the big room.

Hem was absorbed in anticipation. This was just the opportunity he needed. At last, he could clear away all of the past. But, he was anxious that he had to deal with it on his own terms. That meant killing Wilbur Mortanant stone dead. Initially, that thought had exited him. But, then came a fear; of equal proportion. The truth was, that he dreaded that man, with every fibre of his soul.

He picked up the phone and recklessly raked his fingers over the number bearing nodules. Dennis picked up by saying, "Hi."

"Hi, Den, its Hem. That little job we spoke about? It's come up. Are you still interested?"

An eager tone said, "Of course, sir."

"Meet me at the town cross roads, near Beverley's lodge. Shall we say six thirty? I'll pick you up in the white Merc. You'll need all your tools."

"Okay boss."

With that, the conversation ended.

***

Chapter 32
A Time of Action

As Sondra was coming down the stairs, she was also busy, wrapping herself up in her new coat. It was cold outside and, when she paced on to the bottom stair, she could see someone standing under the light of the front door. Where Ian was, she didn't know, so she went to open it. Her new high heeled shoes confidently clicked on the hard surface of the floor. She pulled the windowed door inwards and the external light showed no one. She looked bemused. Was it an apparition? She looked again, but there was definitely no presence on the steps.

With a feigned heart, she double checked and then stepped firmly outside. There was still no one to be seen. So, standing on the front steps, she leafed her gloved fingers inside her new handbag and found the keys she wanted. Then, she shrugged her shoulders and went over to Ian's shiny vehicle. Lifting the boot, she removed a chunky patterned bag, which was both long and thick. It had a silver zip running down one side and a carrying strap, on the other. It could easily have contained an instrument. Only, not the musical kind.

Cautiously, she wondered over to her car. Where she put the item across the rear passenger seats. Looking again, she paused, to pop on her new driving shoes. Content with their subtle feel, she then climbed in and set off to meet up with her friends.

Meanwhile, as her car pulled away, a little figure nudged sideways against the illuminated front door and then quietly disappeared inside.

Hem was visibly nervous and, when he was nervous, he needed a drink. He poured out a large scotch and devoured it neat. He also noticed that he had been drinking rather a lot recently. It was one of the few pleasures a prospective divorcee could indulge in; whilst making plans to kill an uncontrollable employee. All that, and keeping his business firmly on the road. He knew what he was facing and the gamble gave him a sudden flair. What if it all went off on target? What if he came through to the finish; with a rose in his teeth? What if he blew Wilbur away and kept his business on track? Three what ifs and no stone-cold certainties. But, it created a spur.

Hem had kept three security people on his payroll. Ian was now downstairs and Phil had taken the evening off. Dennis was an assumed name for the third. He was part time and no strings were attached. The project was simple enough. All he needed was some luck. He called out to Ian, who was in the down stairs kitchen and said that they had a meeting at seven. Then, he opened his wardrobe and proceeded to change dress. He always felt better in a darker looking suit. The three-piece attire gave him more gravity. Gravity earned you respect. So, he picked one off the rail: it made him feel dominant and more manly. He looked at himself, in the wall mirror. He was captivated by the deep imagination of what he thought he looked like. That way, his mind never saw what his eyes were picking up. A fat man, in a slightly under tailored suit, became a professionally mature figure in a beautifully carved garment.

Suitably dressed, these two personas set off together. It was six fifteen and

Dennis would be waiting for their arrival. Hem knew full well, that Den was never late.

As they left the driveway, it was just starting to rain. Ian was driving fast and there was precious little in the way of conversation. Hem simply told him where to go and he drove. They stopped at the cross roads and Dennis placed himself into the front passenger seat. By this time, it was pouring down and he was wet through. He turned around to talk to Hem. But, Hem put a finger across his lips and so, no words were excreted. They drove on in silence.

Sondra had driven a couple of miles. When she pulled off the road, turned off her halogen headlights and got out. She had parked under the shelter of some old trees. She opened the vehicle's extensive boot. Inside, were a single pair of ladies jeans, a thick T-shirt, a pair of extremely thin gloves (the sort you can still feel things through) and a thick, but very light, jacket. Warm, but not too heavy.

She stood in the outside air, behind the car, and placed a cheap door mat on the floor. Then, under what remained of the leaf cover, she stepped out of her shoes, took off her tights, pulled on some warm socks and stepped into her jeans. Looking around and then satisfied she was alone, she lifted the dress off, over her head, checked her bra straps and pulled the weighty T-shirt on; over her head. Finally, she put the jacket on top, zipped it up tight and slipped her feet back into some cheap trainers. Then, she placed all of her casual wear into a green bin bag. Threw it in the back, thumped the boot firmly shut and climbed back into the driving seat again. Calmly, she switched the heating on to full and pulled away.

She arrived at Jenny and Petula's shortly after six twenty. Petula answered the door with the question, "Are you sure you still want to do this?"

"Yes," said Sondra and stepped inside.

Before her, was agent Jenny: dressed in what can only be called a camouflaged outfit. She looked like a special forces heroine and next to her was operational assistant number two. Her other name being Petula.

"You kids are hot," said Sondra.

"You're looking quite cool yourself," said Petula. "Okay, are we all ready then?" Everyone nodded their heads.

Petula carried on, "I've got a car at the back. Let's go and take her for a spin."

With that, three surreal figures scurried through the empty hall way, down the passage and outside, into the back garden. Then, through a rusting old gate and into a space where a little blue car was parked, by the roadside. It still looked tired and Sondra did have her doubts, but Petula was most insistent that it would get them safely there and back.

The key went into the ignition and the engine fired up. Then, Sondra turned and said, "Here we go girls!" With that, the car pulled away in a purposeful direction.

Ian calmly pulled onto the chalet car park and proceeded to place the car, neatly in a parking space. He reversed in, so that it was facing towards the property. That way, you only had to walk a few paces to reach the room. As promised, the room lights were on. And, as he was staying in the car, he had clear sight of everything that appeared in his line of view. The aim was to move quickly, if the need arose. It also gave some distance, if any shots rang out.

Hem and Dennis left the car and goose stepped across the puddled surface towards Room 4. Dennis went first. At the front, there were a couple of little show piece wooden steps. He carefully placed his feet on them, so as not to make a sound. He thought that knocking would be the polite approach. But, he wasn't paid to be polite. So, he kicked the door. He'd expected it to cave in. But, it was much better constructed than he had imagined. As a result, he twisted his foot and that caused him to yelp out. After that, he twisted the handle and, to his surprise, discovered that it wasn't locked. The door simply swung open to reveal the room. Looking inside, he discovered that it wasn't occupied. He turned back to Hem and said, "He isn't here?"

Hem smiled, "Tactics, dear boy. Tactics. We have only been invited into his boudoir. The very least we can do is politely await his arrival: time?"

"Six fifty, as near as."

"Then we are early. Mr Wilbur is a very exacting enterprise. Punctilious to the utmost and he rarely makes mistakes. Why don't we just take a seat."

There was coffee and tea making facilities on show. All were neatly spread out on a small, round table. It was situated by an electrical socket and that was on the back wall. Hem wasn't interested and to begin with, neither was Dennis. There didn't appear to be any hot water available anyway.

Besides the necessities, few words were spoken. But, their ears ran at fever pitch. Paying particular attention to every passing sound. By seven thirty, the two men were feeling somewhat stiff, in their upright chairs. Hem was tempted to put the television on, but he knew that would not help their situation. Wilbur might use the sound to creep up behind them both. Hem had laid the brown case on the bed. It contained the money. That same bed was sitting away, just to his righthand side: against the wall. In front of him was the room's entrance. It was more or less straight in his line of site. The big front window was shoulder to shoulder with the same doorframe.

The room itself, didn't appear big enough for its contents. Nor was it especially warm. That didn't hamper his mood. In the coolness, he was pouring with an ocean of eager sweat. He was also churning things over. His eyes were scratching at everything in the constant search for answers. Seeking out any sign of their assailant. Only, no matter where he peered, there was none plain to see.

Wilbur had been enjoying a nap. He had also taken a decent meal, in a local restaurant and then he wended his way up to a bicycle shop. It was just before five p.m. and they were about to close. But, this looked like a serious customer and so they entertained his ambitions. By five thirty, Wilbur was the proud owner of a new carbon fibre cycle. Complete with powerful lights and some reflective sportswear. It went well, in the darkness.

Sixty minutes later, he parked the bike up against a hedge row and de-robed. He did this by delving into a pack, which he'd carried on his back. It was heavy and he knew why. A quarter of an hour later, he climbed a fence and walked his way down the driveway of Mister and Missus Strumshell's house. Where, he paused and cautiously looked around. Like a presence, he sensed something, but caution dictated that he ignore the emotion and continue. As he came nearer, he saw a musty blue van tucked behind the curve of a hedge. That meant, someone else was here.

He plied away, to the right and strayed into the gardens. There was some light rain falling, but the dim moon light was cutting through the thinning cloud. That helped. He really didn't want to switch on the unprotected glare of a torch. Carefully, he made his way to the back door and twirled the handle around.

Fortunately, it opened…

Sondra was driving with a purpose. She knew who Ian Carter was and what he thought about women. He'd only been working with Hem for a short while. But, he was a clever sod and when he correctly deduced their marital situation, he forcefully seduced her in a room. That room was next to Hem's and Hem was in it. She'd just come out of the shower in her dressing gown, when he was waiting for her. He looked at her and she felt a need. But, instead of being nice about it, he had treated her badly. He became extremely violent, even forceful and he hurt her. He repeatedly swore and beat her about. He was vile.

As a result, she was now covered in bruises and he clearly thought that is how women liked it. Once out of her bedroom, he became the perfect mask of respectability. After all, he wore the most expensive suits and, from the outside, he looked the epitome of a professional man. Only, he had a dreadfully uncontrollable violent streak and that was frightening to see.

On the other hand, Hem seemed to like him. So, that made him feel secure. That said, he wasn't attracted to this one and he'd never seen the alternative face of the coin. After the first event, he had repeatedly tried to force himself onto her. Sometimes, she could and, other times she couldn't get him off. He abused her and, as a result, she hated the man.

She didn't normally feel this much hatred towards someone, but right now, she was looking right at him and getting angry.

His eyes were transparently centred on a room: across the car park. Petula knocked on the driver's window.

Sondra wheeled it down.

"He's in the room with the lights on," Petula hushed.

Sondra looked at her and then made a move.

Ian Carter was looking to his right. In the dim light of the car park, he made out the shape of two women moving to the rear of a car. It was parked a couple of spaces away from him. Annoyingly, the white vehicle, next to his, was in the way and he couldn't really see what they were doing. He didn't feel under any threat, but he was curious.

Petula opened the boot. Inside was the thick zip bag, which she had placed there. Inside that was the marksman's rifle that Sondra had retrieved from Ian's car. There were plenty of bullets. Sondra picked it up, with her gloves on and slung it over her shoulder. Then, she turned and dropped down to into the undergrowth. In the darkness, she ran. With the light rain on her face, she scrambled across the terrain; until the ground rose sufficiently. Whereupon, she stopped to catch her breath and take account of what lay in front of her.

Wilbur stepped onto a tiled floor, with wet shoes. He proceeded to walk along the corridor, passed the kitchen, and came to the staircase. As he turned left, to climb them, his foot squeaked and it sang out like a mouse with a microphone. He stopped still. But, no one made a sound. He looked around again and then continued his journey to the first-floor study.

As he came up, he heard someone moving about. Stooping down, he watched out. It was a young male. Dressed in a dim grey-coloured overall. He seemed to have come out of a bedroom and he was heading towards Wilbur and the staircase. As he approached, Wilbur took something out of his pocket and waited. Moments later, Brian came towards the stairs and found himself being hit with something spiky.

This made his consciousness fade away.

Wilbur, simply picked the defused figure up and carried it back into the bedroom which, he discovered, had been daubed with crimson paint and the most obscene language. Looking at it appalled him. Reading what was written, brought tears to Wilbur's eyes. It was shocking. Then, he looked at the quiet figure, whom he had just laid on the bed. Looking with unbegotten hatred. He shouted, "You don't ever do that to anyone! No matter what they have done to you! You don't do that to no one! Do you hear me?"

The man in question never moved. Wilbur breathed in, through his teeth and pulled out a lengthy black cable tie. He bound the man's wrists to such a degree that, if he moved at all, it would cut his flesh to the bone. Wilbur was furious.

A few parked cars away, Ian was aware that something was going on. But, he couldn't see clearly enough. His line of sight was perfect for Room 4. But, useless for seeing anything else. He was frustrated with his poor choice. He wanted to move the car. But, then that would defeat the object of the whole plan. So, he bit his lip and sat tight.

Inside the room, Hem wasn't feeling any the better. The atmosphere was getting to feel like a chilled cabinet. It was now close to eight o'clock and there was clearly no sign of Wilbur. Dennis was getting agitated, but at least they had found a kettle and he decided to make a hot drink. It was cheering to hear the kettle warming up. At which point, they heard an all mighty 'crack'. It came from the room next door. Dennis threw himself on the floor. Whilst Hem leaned his back into the wall. The kettle was full and boiling water then started to run all over the table top. In the mock silence, all you could hear was hot water; dribbling off the table and onto the carpet.

After a few minutes Dennis said that he would take a look around outside. He then appeared at the open door and was hit with a single bullet. The force sent him backwards; several feet, into the room.

Relieved of his hand, the door caught the breeze and banged shut. Hem threw himself onto the floor. At the same time, four more shots were fired from the room, next door. Holes appeared in the walls; as bullets rained out across the place. From outside, he heard a large car pull up and a door opening. It was Ian. He opened the door and told Hem to run outside. Which he did. As the car pulled away, another high-powered shot reared out and hit the bonnet of the Mercedes. It then ricocheted off into the field beyond.

Then there was silence.

Ian turned the engine over and pumped the accelerator. The car suddenly roared back to life and he hit the floor: hard. As he did so, the Mercedes responded with speed. They tore off along the road and plummeted along the wet surface. As he drove, he could see the engine's temperature gauge rising. He guessed that the bullet must have hit the radiator. He didn't know how long it would run, but with aggressive faith, he headed straight for home.

Wilbur was still angry. Why on earth would anyone write that kind of filth? It was beyond comprehension. He knew such words existed. But, they belonged in another place and that place was far removed from here. Whatever, she'd done to him, this was not the way to deal with it.

Then he paused. It was happening again. He was getting upset. "Emotions," he said. It was annoying though. Just because someone else saw fit to be a git didn't

171

mean he had to get involved. He had a job to do and, with that little pep talk complete, he closed the door and freed his mind.

Walking along, Wilbur thought that this was actually quite an interesting house. Not many houses had balconies or a study. It was stylish, but it also had a faint smell of staleness too. It was an emotive aroma. But, wherever it came from, he didn't like it. He stopped, at the top of the stairs and looked. The whole building was too old for its time and it definitely needed updating. That's what was wrong. New carpets, new wall paper and much lighter colours throughout. That's what was needed. It would lift the atmosphere appreciably.

Petula, went to the room and eased the door ajar. On the bed was the unprotected suitcase, so she reached in and picked it up, with her gloved hands. Meanwhile, Sondra positively sprinted across the wet ground. She had left the gun in situ and went to the back of room three. Where, Jenny was desperately trying to unsnag the buttocks of her of stretchy leggings. Somehow, they had attached themselves to a splinter on the edge of a wooden drawer. Sondra came up and unhooked her. Jenny turned around, looking all girl like. They then came around to the front.

In the momentary still, two ladies were viewed calmly walking and talking their way across the car park, until they reached the white car that had been parked next to Ian Carter's. Meanwhile, Sondra had walked by the old blue car. Into which, she struck a match and lit something sparkly. Then, she came over to the girls. They all got in and she quietly drove away. Leaving, behind them, an unattended blue car which spontaneously burst into flames. A few moments after that, a number of flashing blue lights flew passed them. They were travelling in the other direction and at speed.

"You hit his shoulder," said Petula.

"As long as I didn't kill him," said Sondra.

"I don't think you did. He was still moving when I looked. Oh, and there was a hand gun on the floor too." She looked over to Sondra, but Sondra was keeping her eyes firmly on the road ahead. They came to a tight roundabout and went down a mushy looking lane, which led into a decrepit outbuilding. A dark one with a leaky open-air roof. Inside, was an old fire place that had been freshly stocked with some fresh straw and a packet of fire-lighters. Next to that were some plastic bags. Inside those, were some clean, dry clothes. The three assailants then changed form and rematerialized as three mature ladies again. Jenny then struck a match and they watched on, as all their evening's misdoings went up the chimney in the flame and form of smoke.

***

Chapter 33
Go with the Flow

Wilbur heard the car. It excitedly raced up the driveway and travelled at far too much speed. It then had to make a sharp swerve which led onto a screeching halt. The car doors made a sound and then banged shut. Next, the house front door flew open and in they came.

"What the hell do we do now?" said Hem. He was fidgety as hell.

"Call Phil!" said Ian.

"Why?" Hem shouted, "That son of a bitch has tried to kill me! What the hell can Phil do about it?" He looked at Ian and said, "Is Dennis dead?"

"I can't say, sir."

Hem, didn't like it. "Okay, let's calm down. We need to calm down and I need a strong drink." He wanted to go upstairs, but that wasn't how it played out. Instead, he started stomping around. His arms were flying; everywhere. He was desperately trying to de-stress himself. But, something was on his mind and then it suddenly hit him, "Oh my God!" he shouted.

"What is it, sir?"

"The bloody money! All that bloody money!" He turned to Ian. "We've left all the sodding money behind." he went bright red and started shouting, "BLOODY HELL! SODDIN' HELL! FUCKING HELL!" he screamed and screamed. Then, he stopped and said, "Bloody, fucking hell!"

Upstairs, some of the sound seemed to have permeated Brian's brain. His eye lids briefly moved and he was suddenly half awake. But, he didn't really know where he was; what he was seeing or why. He felt so completely relaxed that he really didn't care. So, he calmly closed his eyes again and went back into a comatose dreamworld.

Sondra had now taken to the helm again. She was backing out of the muddy track. Fortunately, it was really raining now and she knew that any tyre marks would soon wash away. She turned the car back onto the main road and headed for home. Next to her lap, was an old and worn hand bag. For some reason, it was also remarkably heavy.

"What did you say?"

Ian said, "We've got to call the police."

Hem lit up. "Why in hell's name did you say that?"

Ian stood his ground. "Because, sir, they will soon be all over the chalet site and remove your finger prints. They will also want to know how the money got there."

Hem went for him. He leaned into Ian's face and screamed, "Are you some kind of fucking therapist? I don't pay you for counselling sessions! I pay you to help me."

"That is what I am trying to do, sir. You must call the police."

"Sod off." He started to walk away and then he came straight back and stood right in front of Ian's face, "If you betray me then I'll boil your fucking balls; whilst your still wearing 'em." He pointed a hand at his chin. "I'll even do it with my own bear hands." Hem was livid. "You're not here to be a fucking professor. You're here to look after me. And that means you kill anyone who I tell you to kill. Even the police! Don't you ever stray beyond your measure boy! Do you understand?"

"Yes, sir."

Having cleared the air, Hem began to tuck himself in. "Right, I'm going up to the study and I need a bloody good drink." As he paced away, on the stairs he said, "And where the hell is Sondra?"

Outside the white Vauxhall pulled onto the drive way and stopped in front of the gates. Petula and Jenny put on their dark green rain coats and got out. They immediately spilt up, but kept walking towards the house. Sondra flicked her remote control, opened the new gates and then drove through them. Her heart was pounding like a base drum.

She came up to the front and stopped; climbed out of the car and slammed the door. Then, she set off with the aim of invading the show.

She walked onto the tiled floor space and saw Ian materialize with a cocked gun in his hand. He instantly apologized. But, he was still wearing those deeply despising eyes. He replaced the weapon into his shoulder holster.

"Where is he?" she said.

"He's upstairs, Ma'am… in the study." Ian pointed.

Sondra, opened her bag and removed the folded A4 envelope, from inside. Then, she walked towards the staircase and began her assent. She started calling out for Hem.

Hem stepped out and looked at her from the balcony top. "What the fuck do you want?" he forcefully said.

"I want a divorce: from you."

"I've already told you, fuck tart! You're mine and I'm not letting you go!"

"Why? You haven't been a husband to me for years. Why, won't you just end it and let me have a life?"

"You what! You little cow! You've been screwing anything which arrived in trousers for years. Any man who comes here is in danger. Who's the latest one…?" He repeatedly clicked his fingers. "…don't tell me… I know… Yes, I do; it's that fucking little boiler man. Isn't it?"

"Plumber darling, that fucking little plumber man."

"Well I'm so very pleased you remember. Why don't you go back and screw his dick some more!"

"Herbert Strumshell, you are the filthiest man I have ever known! And, let me tell you something: the only reason I had to sleep with anyone is because you wouldn't fuck me yourself. Even when I was desperate for it, you still went off screwing the arse holes of other fucking men. The scent of their buttocks did more for you the lure of my fanny."

She spat at him and pointed a straight finger. "And talking about male members, the stale smell of their dicks were all over your body. EVERY TIME you climbed back into our bed. Think of what that did for me sailor!"

Hem didn't think. He swung his oat fisted hand in a direct collision with her right eye. She took a full force blow; which travelled her body through the air and across the landing. As she flew, she rotated. Then, her face and chest collided with the

174

wooden balcony. She hit it with such a force that it winded her. Next thing, she fell helplessly backwards and, then down onto her knees. Looking at the floor, she convulsed, with a mouth full of her own blood. Spitting some of it onto the cream coloured carpet. She was visibly gasping for air and it was really hurting her to breathe.

Her hand bag was laid a few inches away and, as she tried to reach out for it, Hem kicked her arm away. He stood on her arm, pointed at the carpet and shouted, "Now, clean that fucking mess up! And then get your tarty arse out of my sight: for good!"

She was still moving around, with her knees under her, on the floor. Desperately trying get some air into her lungs. He saw his chance and was about to kick her again; when, something else caught his eye. That was when he stopped what he was doing and looked.

It was the study door; it was standing wide open. He was sure that he'd closed it, earlier on. He nervously ran his hand across his perspiring chin and poised himself. He had a nasty feeling about this. So, he stood to attention and decided to look inside.

The study itself was completely dark. When Hem first walked in, the lights of the landing were still in his eyes, so he couldn't see anything at all. He had to stop and take things in, for a while. He waved an arm, like he was feeling for something. He really wanted to turn the lights on. But, something was holding him back. That something was his own curiosity.

He knew that the study had a broad exterior wall. It had two bay windows on it and they were good at catching hold of any available day light. Only, there was none, at this hour. In the darkness, he desperately tried to make-out the shapes of things. His eyes ran around the room. Searching for every familiar shape.

To his right; he knew there should be a small rack of books. They were housed on several, solid looking, book shelves. He thought that he could just about make them out. To his left; there should have been a computer desk and that should have a drinks trolley by its side. He couldn't see those.

The middle was taken up with the large study table. A broad round looking affair. It was made from an old-fashioned solid oak. Over the years it had gathered a few extra features; which included several wear marks and some noticeable scratches. Hem used it for informal meetings. It was seated opposite one of the windows. And there, in the shadows, was one Wilbur Mortanant.

As his eyes adjusted to the darkness, Hem had seen him move. He looked comfortable. As though he were posing for an occasion. What had given him away, was the half-light, which was harshly pressing on through, from the landing. As Hem peered into the blackness, Wilbur wasn't about to surrender to his employer's ambitions and, with good reason. So, he waited.

In the quiet, Hem began to feel more confident about the situation and started to move again. That was when the lights suddenly came fully on. Hem cried out, in pain and screwed his eyes up. Rubbing both of his eye-lids vividly did not help; so, he said, "What the hell are YOU doing here?"

The usual calm voice gave its peaceful response, "Yes…" He paused and allowed the sound to find a home in Hem's mind. Then, slowly he went on, "…I felt it would be more appropriate to discuss our little defray within the warmth of your home." He slid an unfolded slip of paper across the table. "Much more respectful. Don't you think?"

Hem saw the edge of the document. It was the contract and Bailey's signature was clearly scribbled upon it. Suddenly, he forgot about the embarrassing circumstances and lurched forwards. He reached out and took hold of the paperwork. Lifting it up, he could see that it was the real thing. He sighed and looked down at Wilbur. He was calm and smiled. "Can I offer you a drink?" he said.

"Neat scotch, please."

Hem put the contract back down: on his side of the table. Wandered over to the drinks trolley and poured out; two large single malts. They arrived into their respective crystal glasses. Then, he came over and sat himself opposite Wilbur, at the table. The table was not clear and, leaning his elbows onto the leftovers of Sunday's old newspaper. He spoke, "You've got it then?"

"Of course… You employ me to do a job and I use all of my personal resources to complete it. That's what I get paid for. Isn't it?"

"What the hell was all that chalet crap about?"

Wilbur sighed and then uttered, "You mean you don't know?" He looked irritated and, on the table surface, he twirled the fingers of his right hand around in a big circle.

"You disappoint me, Hem. Don't you recall your own actions, in all of this? You've been trying to kill me for months and you are trying to kill me now: aren't you?"

Hem looked uneasy, "I wasn't going to kill you at all. You turned on me: and you killed Sudo; didn't you?"

"That bastard sent an assassin for me. The same one who tried to kill me before."

Hem frowned, "What say?"

Wilbur's fingers began to scratch at the unprotected surface, "He was a loose cannon. Even worse, he was a fornicator and he liked to sleep with his employers. I think, one of them actually loved him." He shook his head. "The thing was he didn't love them. Did he?".

Hem didn't respond.

"He simply betrayed them: I saved you from that.

"There was a time when he used to be in my team and he had enough problems then. The main one being, he couldn't keep his hands off. He always adored the affection of young men's flesh. He wouldn't behave. So, they threw him out. Only, that wasn't enough to make him disinherit his desires. I hear, he went private. He was a good shooter. Only, he became a joke."

"Meaning what?" Hem was becoming aware of something.

"If you live, then seek some medical assistance Mr Strumshell and don't wait too long."

Hem's facial colour faded. He blanched white. Momentarily, he was beaten. The message was clear. But then, he grimaced and as the anger flowed back into his features; he spat out the words, "You liar! Sandy was a top man. He had a perfect body and he never harmed a fold of my skin. He was a truly beautiful person. Adorable. A male of utter beauty. Something you can never be. He loved me with all his heart and I don't believe one fucking word from you. Ever…!"

"Tell me; is faith born of belief? Or is belief the courier of faith?" Wilbur waited. Then, he wafted his hand away, "It matters not, your belief, is your own affair. I simply tell you what I know."

Outside the room, there was a muffled sound. Hem turned to see what it was, but Wilbur carried on unabated, "I have complied with every demand that you have ever placed on me. You now possess your contract from Anthony Bailey and everyone is dead except you and I. So, there are no martyrs worthy of being resurrected. Simply, pay me my money and I will depart in peace. Cross me again and I shall end it all for you. The choice is yours." The room absorbed the sincerity of his malice.

After a moment, Hem started to laugh and he leaned back. As he did so, Ian raced straight into the room with a fully exposed hand gun. He levelled it at Wilbur's face. Only, at that precise moment something else caught Wilbur's eye. He didn't move a muscle, he just watched as a blood splattered Sondra Strumshell came in and shot him straight in the back of his head. The pressure of the discharge caused her to fall over, backwards. Ian simply went face down into the carpet. Hitting the floor like a bag of cement. His skull even made a quaint 'crack' as it imbedded itself into the red and gold patterning.

In that moment, Sondra managed to pick herself up again. She attempted to recover some of her posture and was soon standing under the full-length beams of the ceiling lamps. It created a sheen on her hair, like the glow of a silky mane. Wilbur was astonished. He instantly knew who she was and her eyes widened as she came into the full line of his sight.

Despite everything which had happened. Seeing him properly made her heart race and she drew her lower lip in, under her tongue. This was the man she had dreamt of and, it was true; he was real. Thing was, he was sitting opposite her oaf of a husband and they were surely talking about death and money. Hem immediately picked up on their eye contact. He started to giggle. Then, came the laughter, which quickly became more and more hysterical. Finally, he seemed to realize something. He quietened down and continued to sip at his whiskey, with a stray hand. *This could be entertaining,* he thought and gave them the space to make their sounds.

She came closer to the table. More or less in a trance. She could still see Hem. He was chuckling and drinking more of his scotch, but the man in front of her wasn't touching anything. He was wearing deep eyes which were solely focused on her. She felt that. She also knew she wanted him and, as she approached, her feelings rose with a surge of desire. And yet, she wasn't sure. She still didn't know anything about him or what on earth to say. They'd never really spoken a word.

Wilbur felt he had a dry throat, but he persisted to try and locate some words. In a bewildered tone, he uttered, "Who are you?"

Sondra searched out all of his features with her eyes. She listened to every aspect, of every tone of every word spoken. As though she wanted to be absolutely sure that he was real, before she spent any expensive energy in trying to speak. She had doubt and was about to tell herself off. But, then she gave in and said, "I'm Sondra Strumshell. Who are you?"

"I'm the man you met in the car," he said.

Hem was still sipping his malt.

"I know," she said.

"How did you do that?" Wilbur still looked fascinated that she was real.

"I'm not sure," she said. She looked apprehensively at him. Completely lost in a whirl.

Wilbur went on, "I've dreamt about you. Over and over again. You keep coming into my head and I don't understand it."

Hem chuckled and took an even larger mouth full of his weakness.

"I've felt it too. How do you do that? And, who are you? I've never wanted anyone so much in my life." She paused and then came back with, "How is it that you are here?"

Wilbur looked down and said, "I'm only here so that I can go. Hem, is paying me for the work I have completed and then I am going abroad to live.

"Would you like to come with me?"

Sondra's jaw moved sideways, her eyes went to the table top and she pointed at the contract. "What's that?" she said.

"It's my sodding business. That's what it is," said a heavily enumerated Hem. His words were pouring out, but all wrong.

Wilbur reached forward and pushed it towards the remarkable lady. The one, who was wearing a tight cream-and-black dress. He could easily make her figure out. She was slim, but definitely not thin and she had a firm shape, with a smooth looking muscle tone. From that, he knew, she would have her opinions. She was strikingly beautiful and impeccable with it. Every move was coordinated. He was captivated by what he saw.

She removed her gloves. Her hands glided over the paperwork and she leafed through the documents. They were only three pages long and just one had the message she needed. Upon reading the text, her hand came up to her mouth and a tear ran down her face.

Wilbur came over and pulled out a handkerchief. He carefully daubed her cheek.

"Are you all right?" he said.

Sondra looked at him and then at Hem, who had begun giggling, at both of them. He was behaving like a child. After a moment or two, he hiccupped and fell over. He proceeded to land on the carpet. Where, he began to snore.

Wilbur quietly said, "He's had a lot to drink."

"He always does."

"It will take a few hours for him to recover."

"He is a real bastard, you know."

"Yes, I do," he said.

Sondra looked deeply into his eyes and then her fingers hungrily felt the pastels of his face. She looked up and said, "Please hold me." Wilbur put his arms around her and carefully pulled her into his body. He could smell the fragrance of her hair, as she held him. "I've wanted this, since the first time we met," he said.

And Sondra wept as she said, "I didn't know we had."

Petula appeared at the door and both sets of eyes looked around. Wilbur squeezed Sondra's shoulder and said, "It must be time to go." Then, he looked up with a question mark expression.

With her usual style, Petula said, "And what?"

"And there is a prat next door," he said, "who has sprayed some kind of obscene remarks about Sondra. It's all over the bedroom walls and the furnishings."

"What?" said Sondra. "Who the hell is he?"

"I'm afraid I don't know."

Sondra eagerly stomped off and then gave a shriek. Her head reappeared, "It's disgusting. What he's written. Why the hell did he do that?"

"Stay focused," said Petula. "Or we will all be in serious trouble."

"Do you have the money?" Wilbur asked.

"Yes," said Petula. "Why?"

"Because if I can carry him to his van, then, when he comes round, he can drive it home."

"And the money?" Petula scowled; her eyes were angrily burning into him.

"Well, it's supposed to be mine. So, I can give it away. Can't I?"

The two girls' eyebrows rose and they stared at one another, "Meaning?"

"Look, we need to get out of here before furnace brain wakes up." He looked at Sondra. "Do you have those papers I brought here?"

She smiled back and said, "Yes, I do."

Wilbur looked things over. "Then, let's leave your divorce stuff on the desk. This side…" he pointed, "…and then get the finger prints off your gun," which was laying by the open door.

Sondra said, "I have gloves on!".

"Is it yours?"

"Well, not exactly.".

"Ok. So, let's get all the prints off it." Wilbur pulled on some cotton inner gloves. He simply picked up the gun, cleaned it off and wrapped it firmly into Hem's right hand. Suddenly, things were beginning to size up.

Then, Wilbur went next door and hauled the semiconscious Brian outside. He carried him over to his van. The keys were in his pocket. So, Petula opened the door and they placed the money case, on the passenger seat. Next to his knees.

Petula had walked behind Wilber in silence: whilst he was carrying Brian. But now, her curiosity began to sprout shoots. "Are you a killer, Mr Wilbur?"

"Not really," he replied.

"What exactly does that mean, son?"

"It means, I don't go around just killing people. I have to have a very good reason."

"And why did you kill Bailey?"

"Bailey? Kill Bailey? You're mad. Hem wanted me to kill Bailey, but I never found him. He led me on several blind trails, but I never got them concluded. I know he's alive, only, I don't know where he's living."

"You're joking?"

"No, I'm not."

They were walking back up the driveway now and Wilbur could see the vehicle they had driven to get there. "Is that kind of thing still allowed on the road?"

"Look you…" Petula prodded his side, "…we've been fighting a losing battle with you for months. "As a result, we've had to develop our own unique style of expertise. This is just a prime example."

"A vintage one, at that," said Wilbur.

Back inside, everything was in place. The house was alarmed to the high heavens and the feeling was, that a small fire should create the required attention. Petula opened the car boot and they carried some brown looking blocks into the down stairs living room.

The cool air was playing on Sondra's injuries. She was also bruising up and breathing still hurt. Although, in pain, she kept smiling at Wilbur, all the time. At that moment, he had absolutely no idea why.

They laid the material, on a cooking tray: below a smoke sensor and set the little bundle alight. It instantly went up in flames and large quantities of smoke began to pour out. The girls ran out and seconds later the water sprinkler kicked in. As did the alarms.

Everyone crammed into the white Vauxhall. As he was getting inside, Wilbur was sure he could see a gap through the sill. Petula put the car in first gear and pulled away. Only, he couldn't help himself, "Don't anyone sneeze, otherwise it might fall

179

apart." Everyone gave him a look and then they began to laugh.

Petula was managing the old car surprisingly well. She came over to the unoccupied disposal site and it gave a hefty creak or two. But, she still parked it in the pre-arranged position. Everyone had got out beforehand and, looking at her parking skills, no faults were found. They looked across at a solid stack of tired old cars, which were now in a neat line. Then, everyone helped their slimming mate climb out from the back end of the hatch-back. One which was now neatly sat in the middle of all the other wrecks.

They walked a little way over to their respective vehicle. "I'm knackered," said Jenny. Everyone looked at her. She did look dreadful. Petula came to her aid, "I've never heard you speak like that before, Jen. Are you all right?"

"Of course, I am. We just need to get back before breakfast starts. That's all."

Sondra climbed into the driving seat. Her Mercedes was big enough for everyone. She insisted that Wilbur sit in the front passenger seat because, "…I want to keep my eye on you." Then, they set off for home and the peace of the 'Ormregana Guest House'.

When they arrived, Jenny gave Sondra an on-street parking permit. She said that one of the top rooms was hers and gave her the keys. She was about to hand a set to Wilbur. But, he never got the chance to take them. Because, Sondra pulled him, by the hand, and took him away for safe keeping.

***

180

Chapter 34
Oh, What a Mess

Hem came around on the floor. Someone was shining one hell of light into his face and saying something. At first, he didn't recognize a word of it. Then, suddenly: wham! He was back and understood every syllable.

"Are you all right?" the man said.

"Yes," said Hem. Even though he didn't really know. He looked around. The lights were still on. He also had one hell of a headache, but otherwise seemed okay.

Then, he noticed that everyone looked like a policeman. One was looking right at him, from across the room. He tried to sit upright. As he did so, he caught sight of Ian Carter's body on the floor. That was when he remembered what had taken place and felt the intense urge to say nothing to anybody.

"I think he needs to see a doctor," someone said.

Those words came from a woman in a green suit. Hem tried to focus on her and then he thought she must be a paramedic or some such thing. He had been laid out on his chesterfield sofa. For some reason, he was soaking wet. Yet, by gathering his strength together, he had managed to sit upright and that made the room move around him a bit. He proceeded to lean on one arm and watched as the paintings changed their shape on the walls: all by themselves.

Someone asked for his name. He gave it, but couldn't be sure that it was right. Someone else started rubbing his hands with something cold and wet. He hadn't realized that they were dirty. But, he did say, "Thank you."

After a little while the green lady asked him, "Can you walk, Mr Strumshell?" He looked at her and broadly grinned. Then he said, "Of course I can," and passed out.

"Funny business, this," said the detective. "I mean, why shoot someone, who you employ and then sit there and drug yourself up; in the same room as you committed the crime?

"Oh, and then, whilst you're unconscious, you decide to go down stairs and set light to some smoke packs which will set off the fire alarms?"

The sergeant looked equally blank, "And get this; although his finger prints are all over the gun, he has no gun shot residue on his hands."

"Where is he now?"

"He's being detoxified at the hospital. The doctor sounds encouraging. Said, he should be up and around in a couple of days."

"The wife?"

"Don't know at the moment. He was saying something about her being with her friends. But, he didn't make enough sense for us to follow it up with anything."

Sondra was wide awake and totally oblivious to her aches and pains. She was caressing her man and he was softly breathing; nice and slow. She didn't want to wake him.

Instead, her thoughts were making words, *So, you are real.* She was letting her mind wander rather than speak out loud. *You are as real as me.* She stroked his bare chest. He took such large and slow breaths. She was studying him and she liked what she saw.

He had been very tender with her. There wasn't any angst with this man. He wasn't motivated with anger or selfishness. He felt her movements, listened to her needs and responded to her desires. Both verbal and physical. She'd never experienced this before and it was new. To her; this is what a man should be like.

She placed her head on his chest and that woke him up. His hand came over and his fingers stroked her neck. She came up and kissed him good morning. He peered into the depth of her eyes and realized that she was going to be the love, whom he had needed, for all of his life.

Down the stairs, Petula was in the kitchen washing up. If she didn't do that then she would fall fast asleep. Speaking of which, Jenny was out for the count on the dining room table top. 'Hermit' was after her attention and wasn't getting any, so he became disgruntled and marched into the kitchen to give Petula one of his 'needy' looks. "It's no good you being like that with me, young cat!" Petula pointed out. Hermit licked his lips, yawned and stretched out. His full length was on display and right in front of her. At this stage, his patience was far greater than hers.

It was ten fifty and the sky was beginning to lighten from the gloominess of a cloud, which had been spitting and spotting droplets on the windows. With bright eyes, Sondra's face appeared in the dining room doorway. There was Jenny, fast asleep and there, in the kitchen was Petula, almost asleep. She ran straight over to her.

"He's lovely," she said.

Petula dropped a cup, which Sondra caught on the way down and said, "Ta-ra!" She curtsied too.

Petula looked at her friend and just nodded.

"You look knackered," said Sondra.

"So, do you. Only, I feel even worse, believe me." Petula leaned on the work surface. "Tell me, how is wonder boy?"

"He's all mine and I love him. So, keep your hands off," she said.

"That's not what I meant. Do you want something to eat?"

"That would be really nice. Only, wouldn't you like a rest first?"

"I would, but Jenny is right. We need to do as normal a day as possible so that no one can see anything as being out of place." She sounded hoarse and her tone was dreadful.

"Listen, if you two don't get some rest, then you may fall asleep in someone's soup." The words came out all right. Only, poor Petula was so tired that they didn't make any sense.

Sondra took her slowly down to the front lounge; put a cushion under her head and then placed a shawl over her shoulders. Two seconds later, Petula was out for the count.

Sondra then walked up the stairs again and stopped in the doorway, wearing a frown. She was happy. Upstairs, was her man and she could go up and wrap herself in his arms any time she wanted. Innocent stuff really. But, that is how we are made. So, with no breakfast, she ran up the stairways and sprang back into bed.

Hem finally regained his meagre existence; just as the sun poked its face from behind the clouds. The light stung his eyes. But, at least the worst was over. What the hell Wilbur had given him, he didn't know. But, it was like trying to think inside a sand storm.

It looked like he was in a hospital. For some reason, he could see that he was in a private room. He guessed that, as soon as they diagnosed that he was okay, then they would escort him into police custody. So, he had to get away. He looked around the room. There was precious little to see, in the place. He tried to open a side cabinet, but his cannula pulled taught and he yelped: he hadn't noticed that.

Conscious that he had cried out, he quickly closed his eyes, but no one came in. So, he used the other hand and then saw that the little unit was completely empty. So, where were his clothes? He sat back and tried to recall how he had come here. Only, there was nothing to remember. He couldn't even recall passing out. Though, he was sure that he must have. And then there was that blurry woman in green. Who she was? He didn't know. He didn't want to know, either.

How was he going to get out? That was the thing.

The door suddenly opened. Hem jumped and in came a young female nurse. She introduced herself as 'Mary' and proceeded to check his pulse and take his blood pressure. Then, she tested his eye movement and commented, "You're on the mend, Mr Strumshell. I'll have a word with the doctor and get you something to eat." Then, she was gone.

Hem flung the bedsheet off and looked again at the cannula. He knew these things could hurt, but he spoke, "Here goes!" With that, he pulled it out and wrapped his hand in a paper tissue. He looked around the room and managed to find his clothes. They were in a black plastic bag, which had been thrown onto a low chair; at the end of the bed.

Ten minutes later, Hem casually strolled out of the hospital entrance and onto the car park, where he called a passing taxi. He asked to be driven straight into town.

Depending what you are up to, it is fair to say, that some days can seem far longer than others. For Jenny and Petula, they spent most of theirs trying to vainly come alive. For Sondra and Wilbur, they were constantly preoccupied with each other. For the police, they were totally mystified and, for Hem, he was verging on being terrified.

Everywhere he went, the police appeared to be waiting. All he wanted to do was go home. But, he knew they'd be there. If he went to the office then, he knew, they would appear. If he wandered around the town then they'd probably see him and then he'd be taken into custody. His world was rapidly crimping him in and he just didn't know where to turn. Then, in mid-flight, he suddenly stopped and looked at himself reflected in a shop window. He was completely drawn. His cheeks appeared hollow and he could really do with a damn good shave. That said, he realized that the panic attacks he had been suffering were probably because he hadn't eaten anything for hours. God knows what was in the drugs he'd swallowed, last night. But, even in the warm sunlight, his hands were still freezing cold and his body was chilled right through to the core. He also felt empty inside. So, he ventured over to the 'Castle Hotel' and ordered something to eat.

He was soon sitting in a sunny and warm window seat. He took a fresh coffee, and was waiting for a piping hot breakfast of fried sausages, hash browns and beans. Whilst he was there, Tim Bradshaw saw him through the glass, and knocked, twice. Hem waved back. Tim then turned tail and came in to see him. "Where've you been

Hem? I haven't seen you in weeks."

"Oh, I've been… busy. Family and things. You know."

"Yeh, I heard about the things." He also noticed that Hem looked drum-dreadful. Still, he wasn't there to sympathize, "What's with that new docks contract you were bidding for?"

"Mellows…? Oh, that went sideways. Shortly after they shelved the offshore wind-farm project. I suppose it could rear its head again, but only if they can rummage up some new funding."

"I know someone who's interested."

Hem's cooked breakfast arrived and as he tucked in, a sense of optimism began to rise again. He ate and Bradshaw kept entertaining him. He was constantly spieling out all the gossip about a wharf contract he was getting into. He was selling the idea of what a fantastic opportunity it was going to be. Only, he needed some help with getting the finance sorted.

Hem kept nodding. He couldn't care less really, but he appreciated the bull-nosed company. It frightened other more sensitive vultures away. When he was done, he then excused himself for a moment. After which, he walked straight out of the back door and across the rear car park. All, whilst calling a number on his mobile. He called his secretary, Ruth. She was suddenly wrapped up in telling him about everything that had been going on at her end. Apparently, the police did want to see him, but he was not a suspect. However, no one could find Sondra and everyone was afraid that the business may have to close.

Hem stopped walking, in the middle of the street. He ran his tongue around his unbrushed teeth, "Look Ruth, I think we need to settle a few nerves. And I mean, right now! Please arrange a press statement to be given. I'll organize the exact wording and you can even invite some of those journalistic wretches around to hear it. Let's say one p.m., in my office and tell everyone not to worry. Business is good, we have a full order book, good prospects and I am going to quickly get things back on the road." With that, he terminated the call and reached his hand out towards a passing taxi.

Brian had woken up with a jolt. It was light and he was sitting in his van; with a large suitcase on the passenger seat. He knew he was awake and was about to cruise his thoughts for how he got there, when he started to remember.

Someone had struck him with something. He rubbed his skin and, sure enough, his neck was stinging. He touched it again. It had a sore lump and it hurt. There wasn't any blood though.

He recalled spraying paint in the slut's bedroom. He actually enjoyed doing that. It liberated his feelings. She would have to pay for the clean-up and he wasn't going anywhere near the place ever again.

Then, he turned his aching head and looked at the mysterious suitcase. He had no idea what it was or why it was there. Reaching out he noticed that his wrists were badly inflamed. There were thin burn marks all around the skin. Something sharp must have been tied across them. He had no idea what it had been, but they were really sore.

One thing he did know was that this suitcase wasn't his. The van was and he didn't want someone else's belongings inside his vehicle. So, he unclipped the seat belt and got out of the driver's side. He walked around, opened the passenger door and reached inside for the case. Clasping it, he completely misjudged the weight. It fell straight out of his hands and hit the wet floor. As it did so, one of the clips came loose and it half opened.

He could instantly see something sticking out. Brian thought he recognized it. But, he wasn't sure, so he stooped down and freed the second lock. Then, the entire lid sprung up and he fell onto his bum. He was now sitting in the wet mud. As the wetness soaked into his underpants, he stared at the open case, in total disbelief. Seeing what he saw gave him a seriously worried face. And, all he could think to say was, "What the hell do I do now?"

***

Chapter 35
To Rouse the Troupes

Hem stepped into his office at ten thirty-eight. The place was alive with excitement. People were scurrying around; everywhere. Hem came in and spoke to Ruth. He asked for everyone to come into the boardroom at eleven o'clock. He wanted to address them all, directly. He also wanted some food and drinks to be made available. Then, he disappeared into his private office. His voice could be clearly heard on the phone. He was arguing with someone or other. But, the words he spoke were completely lost in the malaise outside.

As the boardroom clock began striking the hour, a fully suited Hem raced inside. The room was packed. Some people were standing. Whilst others sat. Some on chairs, some on the edge of the oval table, others leaned against the outer walls. It was clear that they were all uncomfortable. So, he motioned for everyone to bear with him. He was standing across the breadth of the wooden table. Facing his close knit and attentive audience.

He began with the words, "I want to personally thank you all for coming here. I really appreciate what you've all been going through, over these last few hours.

"I want to stress, that you are not alone. I know that we have been receiving a lot of bad press recently. Some people seem to have a personal vendetta against this company and specifically the man who happens to run it. And I want to assure you that—they— are—wrong!

"We all suffer things. Particularly when it comes to personal crises and I am no exception. But, I love this business through and through and that means each and every one of you too! No one has the right to destroy our livelihoods. And I promise that I will do all that I can to make sure that it never happens.

"Now, I want to steady the ship. I also want you know just where we are and where we are going. I want you to be aware that we have a full order book…" his hands waved as he said, "…We have no problems attracting new business and we are receiving phenomenal growth in our public sector contracts. It is all looking really good. NOT just good. REALLY, REALLY GOOD!

"I have secured all the short-term financing which we need. The contracts we are running are sound and that means, that your jobs are one hundred percent safe. You have absolutely nothing to worry about and, as part of my personal appreciation for your commitment and support, I have just confirmed a five percent pay rise for every single member of staff.

"Stay with us and be with us because we are going all the way to the top!"

Next, he banged his hands on the table top. At the same time, his employees richly applauded and cheered him on.

With that done, he left the boardroom like a talent show host and walked straight into the sight of two waiting police officers. Apparently, they had some questions which needed his attention. He waved at them, in a sideways motion, and ushered them into his office. Where he then politely closed the glossy oak door.

Sitting in the cold mud, Brian had suddenly been hit with something. He realized, that the money in front of him would sort out the rest of his life. He didn't know how much there was, but there was plenty. Thousands. Maybe, tens of thousands. Maybe even hundreds of thousands.

With his soggy underwear in place he climbed back into the van and drove home to Linda. In his heart, he wanted to keep the money. But, his head was saying that this could prove to be trouble and he knew trouble well enough to stay clear. So, what he needed was a sound level head. Linda would know what to do. Only, when he got there, she looked dreadful. Her mother had just been rushed into hospital again and she was on her way there to find out what was going on. Clearly, the last thing she needed was him asking her silly questions about money. She quickly drove off. Leaving him standing there, in clothes, which the air was now drying off, into a series of trendy white tide marks.

He stood there for a while, in a trance, and then decided to go to his job. He was still working on the Pride Road housing estate. Then, he remembered, Allan was on that site too. Maybe, he should ask him what to do? After all, he would know. Wouldn't he?

"Are you rich?" she said

The question caught Wilbur out. "Meaning?"

"Well, you've been in the execution club for quite a while now. Haven't you?" Sondra was stroking the individual hairs on his chest. "How many years?" Her face came up to look at his.

"I don't really know," he said.

"You must be sitting on a fortune. How much do you charge?"

"It's not like that." Wilbur sat up and placed a pillow behind his back, "This kind of work comes through contacts. Different specialties require different approaches.

"I know one guy called 'Phil'. His speciality is driving trucks through walls. He's good at it. But, not skilled at much else."

"Where is he now?"

"I think he's in prison."

"And you?"

"Me? Well, I always took the road as a journey and not a final destination. I never saw this kind of work as a profession. But, that is what it turned out to be. You can't survive unless you have an edge. I used to think that whoever employed you would always be completely trustworthy. For a while, it appeared they were. But recently, things have changed and so I have made plans to get out."

"Am I in your plans?"

"You are now. But, only if you want to. You see, a few days ago, I was aiming to get away from everything. But now, you seem to have changed all of that. I want to be with you and I want you near me."

She smiled and said, "You make me happy."

"Likewise. You are certainly something special to me." Wilbur carefully touched one of her ribs and she jumped. "May I ask, how did you get all those awful bruises?" He pointed, at the rest, but did not go near.

"That's a long story. But, you know something?"

"What?"

"Bruises heal themselves. Especially, when you're in a warm and loving relationship." She was grinning.

"Then, get used to it my love. Because this one is set to last." He reached out, pulled her close, and this rekindled the warmth of some passionate kissing.

As evenings approach into view, evening meals need to be cooked. They also need coaxing into a presentable form and serving to the guests. There weren't many, but it still had to be done.

Wilbur and Sondra worked in the kitchen, whilst a slightly brighter Jenny undertook to serving. By seven p.m., it had actually gone quite well and they all sat themselves down to eat the remnants. It came as a saucy bolognaise dish, which Sondra had concocted from her cookery days at school. It was quite nice.

"So, what do we do next?" said Petula.

"Well, we have to sort things out. Don't we?" said Sondra.

Jenny didn't say a thing. She was still trying to get over living, what was to her, three days' labour on just one night's sleep.

Wilbur asked, "What's the issue?"

Sondra looked at him and firmly took his hand. "We think that my dad may still be alive?"

"What's his name?"

"Bailey, darling. Why?" Wilbur's face churned on what he had just heard and it betrayed something which Sondra saw immediately. "What is it?" she asked.

"Well, it didn't make any sense at the time. But, now you mention it. I might have come across a clue."

Sondra turned her head and with half a smile she said, "Do you know him?"

"No. At least, not that I'm aware of. But, I do have something which may help us all." He rummaged through his pockets: it wasn't there. So, he had to think of the last time he had held it and what he was doing. Then, he recalled where it was. "It's in my room upstairs," he said. Sondra gave him a look. Running up the stairs, he called back, "I was already staying here, before we ever met."

He nipped off and then came hurtling back with a bundle of papers. "Hem had me looking for those documents from Anthony Bailey. But, the old man was cleverer than both of us. I came across something which led me to an empty property and a locked safe, inside which were those documents that you have already seen and these… which you haven't."

Everyone looked. There were some photographs and then came an envelope with the words 'For Sondra' on the front.

"I didn't look inside. I considered it private. Only, for some reason, I couldn't leave it behind. I haven't looked at it. Honest."

The envelope was neatly folded over, like legal envelopes used to be. Across the join was a deep, blood-red embossed wax seal. Something was written into the face of the stamp mark. It was in Latin and read, 'persona iuris'.

Sondra ran her finger along the course of the envelope's fold and all around the outside. As though she were feeling the extremities whilst pondering on the contents inside. For a moment, she paused. Then she breathed in, ran her fingers to the ridge of the seam and broke the seal through.

Inside were two pieces of paper. They were intertwined by an artful and unusual fold. It was as strong as a staple. But, neither sheet was pierced. She opened them out. The top one was a letter. The first line captivated her and she began to read,

To my dear Sondra,

I am sorry that we haven't been able to keep in touch. I wish I could. Only, it just wasn't possible.

I hear that some good changes are taking place for you. I hope this continues. I always had mixed feelings about Hem. But, it encourages me to hear that your life is on the mend. However, I also need to take my share of the blame:

Before you married Hem, I did some work for a man called Sudo Kingsley. Ironically, I introduced them to one-another. To begin with, my role was very rewarding. Sudo was involved in some high-stakes business adventures. There was lots of money floating around. He knew plenty of influential people and meeting them proved very useful. Unfortunately, that was when I found out he had other seedier interests too.

When I confronted him: he threatened to kill me. So, I had to find a way out. At the same time, I had my doubts about Hem. So, I set up a trust-fund for you. On the basis that you could access it, but only if you divorced him or died. That way, I tried to protect you and your boys.

As far as Sudo was concerned, he gave me the run around. He sent a guy called Al Bailey (no relation) after me. When I met him, we talked and that was when I made a deal. Al set Sudo up, but it didn't quite work-out. Then, he tried to get away. A man called Jeff got hold of him, but he wouldn't talk. Then, they went after his brother in-law: Max Oakley. Only, he didn't know anything. So, they dressed him up, in Al's old raincoat, drugged him up and let him go. The last I heard, he was still living on the street.

Fortunately, I managed to get out alive. Though, Sudo said he would never forgive me. So, I had to be careful. I also had to set a trap.

Your new boyfriend seems very capable. I believe that he has a very keen eye and I would certainly like to talk things over with him.

On a personal note, your mother and I have settled our differences. We are now living in Jersey and we would love for you and your boyfriend to visit.

I also understand that Hem is proving a little difficult, coming to terms with your need for a divorce. These things can often become too complicated. May I suggest contacting an expert: Mr Edvard Soames-Smith of Montrose House, in Felders street, Eastbourne. He is an acquired taste, but very thorough and I have already covered your fees.

Finally, if you are wondering how we know so much, this is because Surely called in, and brought us up to date on events.

With all our love

Franklin (& Charlotte) Bailey

Everyone in the room was trying to follow her eyes. As though, without reading the paper, they might deduce the text of its contents. When she had finished; Sondra looked up, put her elbows down and smiled. "It's from my dad."

Petula said, "And?"

"And I think he's up to something."

Petula said, "And?"

"He wants me to divorce Hem: which I sort of get. He also knew about my attempts to divorce Hem: which I don't really get. Except, he did mention Surely?" she looked across at Petula, "Then, he said that he wants Wilbur and me to see some special divorce solicitor, in Eastbourne?

"At least, I think that's what it said."

At this point, everyone should have been serious. After all, Sondra had just received the first word from her father in years. And the message was like a spooky ghost in the room. It was also quite painful. But, the heart is often more compliant than the mind. The effects were soon whirling around the room. Everyone read the letter. Wilbur was the one who gained the most. It answered quite a few of his questions.

The girls seemed far more at ease. Smiles began to appear and once that happened, then the wine bottle popped open. They drank a toast to long life and Petula asked, "What did he say about him?" She was pointing at Wilbur.

Sondra was filling up with emotion. She gave a nervous laugh. She tried to speak, but the words came out of context and in a series of half broken dribbles, "If I read it right…I am supposed… to bring… my new boyfriend… with me… to see my parents." She couldn't help herself and was almost in tears and that was because she was choking with laughter.

That started Jenny off and then the whole room began to glow. Soon it was filled with a wonderful release of tension. Laughter came forth and it performed as a gracious dose of therapy for all.

After a while, everyone took a sample of their time to reread the letter. Whilst the girls read it one way, Wilbur was more absorbed with something else. He looked at the second sheet which had been tethered to the back. It was a certified copy of a blank sheet of paper. He held it up to the electric light, but there was nothing visible on its surfaces. He looked confused, "He's got me with that one," he said and handed it back to Sondra.

Sondra didn't care. All she knew was that the light had come on. The biggest light ever: in the whole of her previously dark world and she was feeling happy.

***

Chapter 36
Hem or Not?

People are often found as types. They portray their wares, in public, and seldom change their ways, in private. They have ridden their ludicrous path through the majesty of life; by being just what they are. Nudging against the angst and doing precisely what they want to: when they want to. Even at extreme personal cost and, often to the detriment of everyone else around them. Some persons are so incredibly driven. That they are able to put up with every single kind of obstacle and still steer themselves straight through to the journey's end. They do this, by keeping to their own principles. Like a lone sprinter on a permanent run.

Hem was furious. He'd spent the best part of two hours with the police and their stupid questions. They did say that their investigation was more attuned to finding out what had actually taken place. Rather than pointing any fingers. That didn't console him very much. But, it did wake him up to the fact that he had to do something about Wilbur and Sondra. Whilst their relationship had been an hilarious joke, at the beginning. Things had now changed. This was getting serious again and he desperately needed a clean break. Either she complied or she had to go. And divorce was not the method which was formulating in his mind. He wanted her to pay for this.

He had spent all of his life building a business up. He had sacrificed all of his free will and his precious family life. Just, so that she could sit there coated in his wealth and screw any male prancer she fancied in boxer shorts. He hated that, now, and he knew, he didn't need her anymore.

Yes, she had helped him with some of the start-up capital and she had come up with a few good ideas. But, they soon dried up and it was only his hard work and competent decision making, that made his business thrive. Bailey had financed some of it and Sudo had organized one or two of the larger contracts. Yet, it was him who had sweated and toiled throughout it all. He, who had brought the business to where it was today and the last thing he was going to allow; was for her to take half of his wealth, just to have sex with a former janitorial employee. One who had one hell of a grudge. No! It was all going one step too far.

In such a mood, Hem flung himself along the corridor. His feet thumped past Ruth and took him straight into his office. He slammed the wooden door shut, with such force that it danced on its hinges. He plonked his behind onto his grey leather seat and reached for the desk telephone. Moments later, he was talking to Trevor Sibley. Hem told him to get to his office by two p.m. and slammed the phone down.

After that, he irritatingly rapped his fingers on his desk top and then chewed on his tongue until he calmed down. After which, he stood up, smoothly walked over to the office door and made his way towards Ruth.

Ruth, eyed him up and wondered what was coming. She paused her telephone conversation, smiled at him and said, "Good afternoon, sir." Her hand was covering the receiver.

Hem showed no interest. He totally ignored her greeting. Instead, he was wearing his own facial ignorance and his first grunted words were, "I want Samtells." His pitch went up. "What's her first name?"

"Jaine?"

"That's the one… Jaine! Well, I want her here to go over those bridge plans with me. Now!" He stood there, staring down at her. Ruth still had her hand over the phone. She abruptly put it down and then called the lady in question.

Hem was still hovering around. Ruth was getting nervy and beginning to feel the strength of it. Finally, someone picked up the call. At that moment, Hem's direct line rang in the background, and he headed off, to pick it up. Ruth then found out that Jaine had called in sick and would not be available until further notice.

As she put her hand set down, she could hear Hem shouting. He was screaming at someone about a cost overrun, on a project.

She knew her employer well. To her, Hem was a totally selfish and self-conceited man. She knew, that providing she did her job well, then he would never even notice her existence. At this particular moment though, he was flowing at full pelt and that meant, that she had to put on her best aplomb. All, so that she could calmly break the news that Jaine was not going to be available for this impromptu meeting. As she stood up, she conscientiously tried to pace her footsteps evenly across the worn carpet. Even so, the prospect of what she was about to face was making her legs begin to wobble. She hated this side of the man. At times, he was highly abusive and he could even turn violent. As she approached, Hem was suddenly alight with zeal. He looked up, saw her coming, and spat out the words, "What the hell do you want?" At which point, Ruth stopped in her tracks. She breathed in and was hit with a horrible wall of doubt. At that moment, she turned around, receded away and then politely closed the office door behind herself.

Once outside, she stopped, for a little while. Her eyes looked at the office desk. The place where she worked such long hours and then she slowly walked across to the ladies' toilet. Once behind the closed door, she stood in front of the wide wall mirror and began to cry.

At two p.m., Bee and Pete strolled into the office suite of Strumshell's business. A phone was loudly ringing, but the place was barren of all human life. They didn't care. They walked straight past the empty secretary's seat and went into Hem's private office. Hem was busy, staring at a gold carriage clock and checking the accuracy of its time. Then, he saw them approaching. He leapt immediately up and came straight over to greet them, "It's good to see you, boys: how are you?"

Bee looked blankly at him and licked his lips. Pete just stared him in the eye. Bee spoke first, "We ain't here for your grace and we don't want none of your monies. We want him that that did it. You understand?"

They both sat down and stared at him.

Hem smiled with appreciation, "Yeh, I understand." Not that he did. He was actively trying to work out, how the hell they'd got out of Jeff's place alive. But, he could see that they had. So, he lightened up. After all, Hem was always one to relish the charm of an opportunity. "I understand what's happened boys and I want to help. I also know that unless you listen to me real good, then you'll go the same way as Jeff."

They both looked at him.

"This guy is serious, Bee, and he won't stop at nothing."

Pete spoke up, "I guess he's right, cousin. The old man never hurt a fly unless they deserved it and this sod deserves it all right."

There was some left-over food on a tray. Pete stood up and began to pick and choose from the cold scraps. Despite the smell, they tasted surprising good.

Hem was sweating. "He's living with someone."

Bee jumped up. "Who?"

"Sondra."

Bee grinned. "What, your wife's getting fucked by that bastard? Ha! That's a bloody laugh an' a half. What's she screwing him for? Ain't your dick worth the effort?" He saw that Pete was eating and went over to choose from the available selection.

Hem could feel their sickening lack of respect. They were taunting him and he liked it. That, and the fact that the room was filling with their anger. *Uncut stones,* he thought. *Uncut stones.* But, he needed to sharpen them up a little and use their vibrant skills. So, he played them along, "I know where they're at. Would you like to know the details?"

Bee was swigging from an uncorked wine bottle. He stood his ground, turned and spat some at Hem. It missed. He pointed his finger down an elongated straight arm and spouted the words, "Don't you fuck with us, pratster. We ain't got the time for your sodding delicacies. We want him dead and we will fucking fry his balls in beetroot fat and smash his face in, to do it."

Hem was suddenly dumbstruck. He couldn't ever recall beetroot having any kind of fat in it? He speedily looked around and reached out for a small peppered advert. It was a worn and discoloured looking brochure. It read about the warm and cozy comforts available at the 'Omregana Guest House'. "They're there," he said. "Wilbur's room is somewhere at the top. Faces out and onto the main road, I think."

Bee snatched it away. "And what about your whore of a wife?" He spat again. A minor puddle of red spittle appeared on the light coloured carpet.

"Treat her with all the respect she deserves. You can even screw her, if you like," said Hem.

Bee showed down a smile and suddenly warmed towards him. He came over and excessively shook his hand, "You can rest assured. We'll burn every ounce of hair off her fucking skin: whilst she's still crawling around inside it. Then, we'll feed their remains to the fucking dogs. They ain't got no work anymore and they've been so hungry since Uncle Jeff went away."

He looked around, content with himself and what he'd seen. Then, he clicked his fingers. With that, Pete joined him and they both walked out. Meanwhile, a whiter looking Hem, teased the lid off an alcoholic beverage. The contents were soon pouring out into a crystal-like container. In one gulp, it went straight down the hatch and he let his breath out. Then, he reached out again. This time, for the phone.

Sondra asked Petula to accompany her to the new divorce solicitor. It was quite a drive and she was adamant that Wilbur stay at the guest house with Jenny. She did not want any sort of distraction. However lovingly nice that may prove to be. She also knew the feelings which Wilbur evoked in her and she needed a clear head, right now. So, he had to stay behind.

They set off in Petula's reconditioned car. It took well over four hours to get there. Eastbourne, itself, looked assaulted by the wintery season. Tired and mulish in the weakness of the winter sunshine. But, neither Sondra nor Petula were too worried about that. Sondra had telephoned and arranged an appointment with Mr Soames-Smith for two fifty p.m. It was now two fifteen and they were looking up at a very strange looking brass statue of a reindeer. One which had parked itself outside the solicitor's front door. It was very lifelike, but huge and its legs looked way too thick. In fact, they dominated the poor thing and that meant, it just didn't look right.

"Yes. Funny old thing, he's been there for years. We call him Henry," said Mr Soames-Smith; as he walked away.

Despite his age, this fellow espoused himself as a painfully thin and spritely figure. Wearing a rustic, mud brown, three-piece suit and a cardboard stiff, double cuff shirt. Somehow, it shaded itself into the withering shallows that resembled a dead tone of cream. The kind of colour which remained, once the washing suds had faded away. He also wore, a deceased form of bronze tie. One which speared his plumage, for a purely professional effect.

He took them on a mild saunter through a weave of tired old corridors. For some reason, they smelled of camphor oil. He was seemingly on a mission and it was hard work keeping up with him. Yet, suddenly, he would just stop and then change direction. At one such moment, he clicked his fingers, whistled and then took both guests into a vacant side office. "One of our more contrite units," he announced and then placed his hands in an outward semblance for them to be seated.

"Now, what precisely can one do for you ladies on this day?"

Sondra looked at Petula and raised her eyebrows. Petula wore a stayed expression which meant it was all up to Sondra now.

"I've come to get a divorce," she said.

Edvard waved his hand from side to side, at the two ladies and said, "Are you two married?"

"Yes," said Sondra.

"No," said Petula.

"I see. Err, well… whom are you desiring to dispose of, Miss?"

"Mrs Strumshell," said Sondra.

"Ah, so there is another lady involved."

Sondra looked at Petula, and Petula was having a problem looking back. The main issue being, she was starting to find it funny. So, she sucked the air out of her cheeks and that made her face appear unusually thin.

"Mr Soames-Smith…" said Sondra, "…I am here to employ your devout expertise in my divorcing an animal of a man called Herbert Peter Strumshell. Can you help?"

From the moment those words ceased, the room went dead pan silent and Edvard visibly faded away. He looked every bit like he had just been transported into oblivion. He sat motionless for, what seemed, a good two and a half minutes. The two girls didn't know what to do and, when he finally moved again, both Sondra and Petula jumped. That also caused Petula to lose control. Her cheeks refilled with air and that made an unpleasant rasping sound.

"No need to apologize," said Mr Soames-Smith. "Now, will you please meld me with the specifics of the details.

"I mean, how long have you been cordially married and exactly why have you suddenly decided to chase yourself into the coarseness of such an action?"

Petula was hopeless now. She was silently rocking, back and forth on the chair and desperately trying to hold it in. Any further comment could release the most stifled and strained morsel of a giggle.

Meanwhile, Sondra was picking up on the immoral support of her friend. The same one who was clearly suffering considerable difficulties in keeping a straight face.

She purposefully spun around and looked away from Petula. Slowly breathed in, cleared her throat and said, "I have been married to Strumshell for twenty-two and a half years. We have two grown-up children, who now live independently abroad. He has been sleeping with other men for years and I can't take it anymore. So, I want a divorce. Is that clear enough?" Sondra was pleased with herself and let her shoulders fall. She also breathed out and realized that she had finally regained her composure.

But then, Edvard dared to open his mouth, "Do we know why he has been sleeping with other men? I mean, not to put it too delicately, does he feel the cold very badly?"

Sondra's eyes glazed over but then, realizing where this was going, she came right back, "What are you on about? He screws them. He pulls his pants down and leaps into a bed, where he bangs away for hours on end with any agreeable male he can find. It has nothing to do with his body temperature. Or any lack of humidity. He flirts with his men friends. Sees a new one and takes them to bed." Her nose went up. "The smell is awful and I thank God, that he totally refuses to oblige his wife."

"Ah, he refuses natural contact. Yes, I can see this being a very simple case. Do you have any substantiated marital disloyalty as proof?"

"What did you say?"

Petula collapsed, broke wind and began laughing out loud.

Over the laughter, Edvard was clearly seen to be struggling. Nonetheless, the long endearment of his considerable experience saw him begin to repose himself. "I simply enquire as to whether you have any evidence of these misguided misdoings. Do you ever?"

Sondra stood up, walked over to Petula, gave her a scowl and whipped the surveillance documents, straight out of her hand. Turning about, she bit her lip; forcefully slammed them onto the table and allowed Edvard Soames-Smith to re-enter his trance like state, for what seemed like an hour and fourteen minutes.

Being familiar with the scene, no one dared move during this delicate time of deliberation. And, sure enough, at the end of it, Edvard started to breathe once again. He twitched a bit at first, but then his face came back on line with a wide and charming smile. "I didn't realize that your father had sent you. If only you had mentioned this, at the beginning. Then, I would have known what to do straight away." He picked up something, from a pot. It looked like a quill and wrote a note on the outside of the envelope. Then, he looked up. "I have some papers, already prepared, for you. Just serve them on Mr Strumshell and I will take care of everything else."

"Is that it?" asked Sondra and sat bolt upright.

"Almost," he replied. Then, he flummoxed with his hands to pick up an old-fashioned dial telephone. It came out of a squeaky wooden drawer. Mr Soames-Smith presently, rotated the zero hole around its face. As it travelled, it made a series of mechanical clicks. "Ah, Stephanie, would you be so kind as to release those reluctant documentations; the ones which we were speaking of this very morning. Do retrieve them, from the closet file, and place them into the fair hand of young Mrs Strumshell."

A faint 'yes' could be heard through the telephone receiving device.

Mr Edvard Soames-Smith then said, "I foresee very little to interfere with this conclusion. Please see Stephanie, and hand the prepared documents to the Hem."

Firm eye contact was made.

Edvard gave a rich and warming smile and then said, "Your father gave me his name. Mrs Strumshell, please be assured, I always keep my promises."

Sondra's face swung around, "How long do you see this taking?"

Edvard replied, "Very little time, my child. You see, this case is so highly straight forward.

"Do have a safe return journey. Won't you?" With that, he walked them into the corridor of corridors and stumbled them back to the distant reception area. Where an old queen was sat knitting a white shawl: one, with spotty red flecks in the middle. Next to her, sat another waiting lady who was busy rubbing a shiny harmonica on her woolly knees. Neither of them looked up.

Once outside, the two girls stopped, opposite the brass reindeer, hugged one another and then burst out into completely uncontrollable laughter. All of this, in the full view of a bemused autumnal general public.

Inside the guest house, Jenny was preparing for tea. Petula had gone away with Sondra, but Wil was still about. Jenny was thinking that, if it worked out, then they would all be going to Jersey for a few days. She was really looking forward to that. She had never been to the Channel Islands before and it would be nice to get away from the daily hustle and bustle of guest house routine. Not that there was much going on, at the moment.

She was feeling much better about things now and, in Petula's absence, she had spent most of the morning cleaning the kitchen. It was absolutely spotless.

Due to the lack of guests, at this time of year, she had decided to sparkle and clean every single surface she could find. She switched off one of the freezers and a large looking refrigerator. So, there they stood; empty and clean. The doors were propped wide open, so that the air could dry them off. One door swung open to the left. Whilst the chest freezer stood open mouthed, like a hungry ottoman. The dripping white shelving units were arranged on the sink drainer.

Today's menu was going to be extremely simple. With no guests remaining, she was making some sausage rolls and was going to serve them with a small array of vegetables. All wrapped up, in a rich gravy sauce. That way, if Petula and Sondra got back late, then she could quickly warm them up and make a pleasant bite to eat. She was busily making the flaky pastry and repeatedly rolling it out, on a sheet of tin foil: when she heard a strange sound from outside. It was just as though someone were at the door. Yet, there was no doorbell sound.

She stopped her work and leant forward. Wiping some of the condensation away from the window, she peered down, at the street. It was grimy grey outside, but she could see a man walking towards her front door, with what looked like a cannon in his arms. Jenny wasn't a weapons expert, but she knew trouble at first sight. In a second, she had picked everything up, wrapped it inside the tin foil and disappeared into the recess of the empty kitchen. Beyond which, stood two available options, the refrigerator; or the open recess of the chest freezer.

Downstairs: there came a huge 'bang'! The front door flew straight off its hinges and collided with the radiator, on the wall. Yellowy coloured water began to trickle onto the dry carpet. Bee stepped right through it and headed for the stairs. He ran up to the first floor, turned right; pointed his gun and looked at the empty dining room. It was all in complete darkness, but he was sure he could smell something. It was just like some kind of raw cheese. He didn't care, though.

Seconds later, Pete pounced up behind him and nodded. They both moved off, up the stairs. The next level saw three rooms, on a single landing. All the doors were closed and Bee felt the need to express his true feelings about this place. So, he pulled the trigger. Incendiary bullets proceeded to fly everywhere. Big round holes appeared in everything. Like molten rain, combined with the rock and roll thudding of a roaring muzzle. Holes appeared in the walls, the doors, the floor and lightening sparks flew around, as the windows were shot to pieces. He even hit the grandfather clock and it chimed a strange sound before toppling over. Bee was thoroughly enjoying himself and he was proudly wearing a big grin.

After a few more seconds; happy that he'd done so much damage, Bee relaxed his grip and stopped firing.

Pete lifted his foot and kicked in, what remained of the doors. He shone a portable flood light inside each of them. Only, to find that no one was there. "He ain't here, Bee. He ain't in these bodes."

Bee nodded, then grinned all the more, "Let's go up bro!" he shouted.

The upstairs landing was wrapped inside a serene darkness. Because of the lack of guests, no one had been there to turn the lights on. Half way up the flight of stairs, Bee stopped and, for the first time, used his brain. "I dun't think they're 'ere," he said. "'Fact, I dun't think anyone's here. What do you say?" He turned to his cousin.

Pete was scratching his hand. "I wish you'd let me turn the door handle before you blew it off. If it was locked, then we'd know no one was 'ere."

"Okay smart arse. What do we do now?"

"Get out before the police turn up."

"And?"

"An' what?"

Bee looked angry. "What the hell is wrong with you? Do you seriously think that I'm just gonna drive back home and forget what he did to Uncle Jeff? 'Cos if you are, then I'll fucking kill you right now!"

Pete looked at Bee in complete admiration. Somehow, he always knew how to handle a situation and he was doing really well right now. "Why don't we go back to Hem? He told us Wilbur would be here. He ain't, so let's kill him."

Bee seemed to summon a new sense of awareness. He majestically nodded his head and then he said, "You're on! Let's go." At which point, the two men clomped their way down the empty flights of stairs. Now, freshly cajoled into shape. Missing whole sections of balustrade and wearing plenty of round holes in the flooring.

On their way out, they jumped onto the toppled front door and scratched its face, as they walked over it. Meanwhile, up the stairs, the door of a first-floor freezer unit gingerly opened and a sweaty little red face appeared, above its unlit rim. Jenny didn't mind hiding, but a woman of her size had limited options and this one was getting far too warm for comfort. She was sweating profusely. As a result, she was soaking wet and her bra straps were beginning to itch. So, she levered the door further upwards and listened to the peace. Then, she cautiously reached out for the mature resources of the light switch.

***

Chapter 37
Violence Becomes Violence

Sondra and Petula had made good speed. They set off at three p.m. and made it back to town around six thirty. Petula said she needed a drink, so they called into her bungalow and shared a bespoke hot chocolate. Content with its effects they set off for their main task. It was just gone seven p.m. when they arrived at Strumshells head office. It was dead to the world. But, the front door was open and so they ventured in.

Moments later, Hem was bubbling up, into another fresh frenzy. Of all the people in the world: who he did not want to see! Yet, in his eye sight, there stood some fat looking tart and the ultra-slim Sondra. Who was also holding an A4 envelope. One that she readily plonked on his desk. He looked at it and then back at her. He was wearing an expression, as though the remains of the 'Titanic' had just sailed quietly into his wharf.

"What the hell is this?" he asked, stabbing the envelope with the prod of an overweight finger.

"Those are your divorce papers, darling."

"What? You think I'm going to divorce you? No sodding' way!" His hand waggled as he went on. "I don't care if you screw the entire judiciary on the cleanliness of my office rug. Or, fuck every shitting lawyer on earth! The answer is piss off! You aren't getting a bloody thing. AND: I won't let you go!" He smashed his hand on the table top.

Sondra had expected this behaviour and came back with. "You know what you are?"

Hem sat back, with the readiness of distilled anger still darting across his face. He politely replied, "No, tell me, my sweetness. I hold my breath in anticipation."

Sondra was yearning to let rip and soon her arm was pointing straight at him. "You are a fucking leech. That's what you are. You don't love anyone except yourself. All because you can't. It's totally beyond you. All you can do is suck every bloody ounce of flesh from those around you. You don't want me. You never wanted me and now you can never have me. So, you're bloody jealous. Jealous of me! And that's not all!

"It's pert of you to parade my little form in front of your ogling friends. To put me on show, inside your social do's and to ingratiate your professional functions. You even encouraged them to slap their hands on my arse!

"I will say this, though. At least, some of your male friends do try to get their hands where yours should have been all along. Maybe you should get one of your lovers to try on a sexy skirt and stockings! Or would the prospect of them appearing as they truly are be too much for your fucking ego to handle?"

At that moment, Sondra deliberately slowed her pace down. She was livid with him and that wasn't good. Her tone was getting too fractious and she wanted the meaning to clearly cut through. "You are getting a divorce and I am having one with you. I want you to fully enjoy the deep and penetrating relationship of sharing something special and unique. A final climax, with your long-lost love. Or, to put it another way: take this fucking offer now, because you'll never get such a bloody good deal with me, ever again!"

Hem scrunched up the envelope and forcefully threw it at her. It hit her chest and bounced onto the floor. Sondra was about to take the bait and unwrap the full force of her temper. That was when Petula felt the urge to tap on her shoulder. Sondra stalled and looked around with a look of fire on her face, "What?" She snapped.

"I think it's time to go, honey. Don't you? After all, Mr Strumshell has his legal papers served, in front of a witness and we do have a million and one other things to do before tea. So, let's go. Shall we?"

Sondra pursed her lips and turned back towards Hem. She shook her head and raised a smile. "Doesn't it help to have such good friends? They save so much unpleasantness. Don't you think?" Then, she dropped herself into the force of a stare and viewed him through utterly hateful eyes.

Hem just shook his head and reached for his phone. He was disappointed: the bitch wouldn't even argue with him anymore.

As they were going, Hem paused for consciousness sake. His thoughts were recognizing something. Slowly, at first, but it was beginning to dawn on him. The way things were going could mean that he may well be in serious trouble. At that point, the two women left the room and the word, "Hello," began echoing from his ear piece.

As the two girls left Hem's office. They came down in a shoddy looking yellow lift. It was a solid, metallic, clunker of thing; which had clanked its way through several years of service. Sondra had always thought it should have been firmly parked on a suitable waste tip and not left inside the company's headquarters.

As they exited and approached the main entrance, they saw two burly looking men, in scruffy clothes, heading their way. They had appeared out of nowhere and were walking at quite a speed. They also looked totally out of place. Petula instantly picked up, on their mood, and nudged both Sondra and herself, behind the tall standing foyer plants. The figures stomped straight past them and headed for a door.

Petula murmured, "They look like trouble." as they went by.

In a low voice, Sondra responded, "I agree, but they seem to know their way around." Sondra had said that, because instead of accepting the well-lit lift entrance; they had purposefully turned to the left, where there was a darkly glazed stair way. Only the staff knew about its existence. Petula and Sondra watched them striding up the stairs. You could see them, through the darkened glazing. Two steps at a time, they went. Seeing this, Sondra suddenly shivered. Petula took her arm, so that they could quickly move away from the place and thence, to safety: outside.

Bee was absolutely fuming. "How the hell we gonna get 'em in an empty house? Total fucking waste time!"

Pete was trudging behind and saying very little. But, he was with Bee, one hundred percent, "Foolin' around!" he said.

"Yeh, and the fucking rest."

"We gonna kill him?"

"Don't know… But, he is gonna pay!"

At that point, they reached the top landing and barged straight through the twin doors. Only to find that the place was deserted again. No one was about.

"Where the fucking hell is he?" asked Bee.

Pete looked suspiciously around. He saw that Hem's office door was wide open and he went inside. Meanwhile, Bee was sure he could hear a woman sobbing. He couldn't see one and other than that, the place was empty.

He crunched in through the semi-open doorway and looked Pete in the eye. "Found him?"

"Yeh, he's here." He was pointing down onto the floor space behind the desk.

There, behind the wooden desktop, and on his knees, was the large, uplifting rear-end of Hem. Elbows out; one to each side, he had started to read the crumpled paperwork from his divorcing wife. He had been hit with the sudden need to open it out properly. Which meant retreating onto the floor. The papers, he soon realized, were written in some kind of bluish ink. It looked wet, but did not smudge, to the touch. The pages looked as though a fluffy squirrel had stood in an ink pot and, then taken an unescorted walk across the paper.

The words were all there. Only, they didn't seem right. They were written in a total abstract of the English language. There were various terms which he failed to understand. Numerous nuances about his personal behaviour, which he enjoyed reading, and something about his '...parsimonious expletives which were endeavoured towards his beloved partner of twenty-two-and-a-half vertiginous years...'

What he read made no sense in terms of divorce proceedings, but the artwork of the sprawling pages, were testament to a balmy nut cracker without any evidence of his own kernels or shells. Turning the pages, he reached the final demand for him to forfeit his wife in return for a set sum of money.

It seemed to come down to the basics that all she wanted was fifty thousand pounds and her belongings. In other words, 'Hey presto'. He was free.

He lifted his head up and smiled. He couldn't really believe it! He could actually get rid of the tart for next to nothing. Cheap at half the price and that would be perfect! It was so very appealing and the thoughts of being able to keep everything he wanted was actually beginning to turn him on. He pulled out his pen and signed it. Ruth could post it tomorrow. After all, if he changed his mind overnight, then he could shred it; first thing, in the morning. Couldn't he?

At that stage, his heart was racing and a surreal sense of sunlight seemed to have risen into his soul. That was when he suddenly heard the realistic 'click' of a hand gun and, then he felt the coolness of its chamber; touching his forehead.

Without a word, his eyes shifted sideways. His head was also drawn in symmetry with his vision. Behold: he was now staring straight into the vexed expression of a sour looking Bee. Unperturbed, Hem asked, "What's the problem?"

"They ain't fucking there and that's your problem!"

Hem gave a verbal sigh. And so it was, that just as heaven had shone a brief redeeming light into his murky little existence. Suddenly, it also revealed that a whole dirty avalanche of sludge had just been flushed down the mountainside. And, it was heading straight for his face.

As they drove off, Sondra was looking increasingly worried and she turned to Petula, "I'm frightened. I think we've got to get out of here and fast."

Petula wasn't at all keen, "And then what? Do we put on men's trousers, wear false beards and live life like two forgotten cross-dressers? I'm not one for being a fool. We've got far too much to lose here and, even if we gave them everything we own, then I'm quite sure that those two would still be chasing after our blood."

Sondra stopped her. "Do you feel anything?"

"Such as?"

"I don't know." She gave an angelic frown and went on, "I can sense something. Only, I can't put a finger on it." Sondra went quiet and began to twirl the ends of her hair through her fingers. The car crisply pulled up outside the guest house. Where Petula and Sondra shut the car doors and plied their way in: over the wreckage of a front door. Petula's jaw dropped in shock; as she saw the mess.

"What on earth has happened here?" Petula said and then she shrieked out, "Jenny!"

From the top of the staircase came the calm words, "Jenny's okay."

As they came up, Wilbur carried on talking, "Two angry men decided to try and terminate our existence. Only, we were not here to receive their advances. So, Jenny and I are fine."

Sondra ran and gave him a huge embrace. Then, she pulled straight back and peered down onto the carpet beneath her feet. Wilbur, held her waist and drew her towards himself. Leaning forward, he kissed her head and breathed in her aroma. "There's nothing to worry about, my love. Let's go and see Jenny. She's cooked some hot tea for us. She also has the makings of a really good plan."

Bee physically dragged Hem out of his office. He held him by the collar of his shirt and pushed the lift button. Hem had just spilled the beans. Apparently, Wilbur had been tipped off, so they had all run for cover. Only, once Bee and Pete had done their business then, Wilbur and Sondra thought they could sneak back into their new home.

Bee didn't really know whether to believe him or not. To him, Hem was a bastard and he could still be lying. But, at this range, it was worth a punt. So, he grabbed Hem, shoved him into the lift and they were off to do a swift revisit, with their podgy new friend.

Pete was eyeing Hem closely and he was thinking that Hem was looking far too smug. He wasn't the least bit afraid and he figured that he should be. He wasn't arguing either. Pete thought something was wrong.

The lift calmly descended and landed at floor zero. The doors mechanically slid open and instantly, Trevor Sibley lobbed a smoke grenade into the lift compartment. Nobody knew what was going on. But, it quickly filled with smoke and Hem ran out for cover. As Bee came out too, Trevor thumped him, hard, in his lower chest. That completely winded him. Then, he took Pete's right arm for a crunch test against the closing lift doors. With both men incapacitated and on their knees, he took Hem and they scurried away from the scene. Bee, belatedly tried to stand up, but a considerable stabbing pain caused him to fall over again. Pete just sat there and stared it out.

After a while, they regained their composure and went back up to the office suite. They looked the place over. There wasn't much of any interest. Pete noticed some names on a sheet of paper. He recognized two of them. Only, they weren't the right people for this particular occasion.

Jenny was still wearing the same flowery overall she had adorned, during her cleaning spree. Things had changed a little since then, though. The bent sausage rolls were steadily cooking away in the oven and her face was straight as a ramrod. The table cloth was now at an angle and covered in a variety of hot drinks. Around those, were gathered a small number of new arrivals. They were all displaying their merits; engaging in an open and frank discussion.

Jenny explained what had taken place, "I was busy cleaning the kitchen and emptying the freezers. All of the 'out of date' stuff is now thrown away and the remaining food is in the main freezer, over by the wall. Then, I defrosted the other one and cleaned it out.

"I was just going to dry the shelves and place them back into the fridge unit when there was a bang: it was horrible. Sounded like an elephant had farted. It was completely out of place, so I knew I was in trouble Then, I turned off the lights and climbed into the chest freezer.

"Whilst I was in there, I could hear gun shots going off: they've blown half of the house away, you know!

"Anyway, I stayed in there..." She pointed to the chest freezer, "They didn't look inside and I heard them walk back down the stairs. So, I opened the lid a little bit and heard them say they were going to see Hem. And that was it.

"Oh, and I was so sweaty being in there. Freezers are really warm places to hide in, you know."

"So, that's what they did," said Petula. "And what do we do now?"

"The odds are, that they went to see Hem," said Wilbur. "And that means they will be back again; to get what they wanted, first time around."

"Which is?" asked Sondra.

"If I'm right, they probably want you and me. No disrespect to Petula and Jenny. Oh, and they probably want the five hundred thousand pounds we left with that abusive kid too. Anyone see it any other way?"

No one said a word.

It was just gone eight p.m. and having calmed himself down, Bee was now just in a foul mood. He was still furious that they had been sent to an empty house, with no prospects of finding Wilbur the 'fucker'. They had effectively driven countless miles, visited Hem, been tossed around and wasted the whole day for nothing. As a result, they were now sitting a short distance from Hem's house and he wanted revenge. Only, what did they find? The whole place was sealed off with some kind of police tape. Something must have happened, but he didn't care what it was.

They got out of the four by four and strayed onto the grounds. Except for some brief glimpses of moon light, it was completely pitch dark and they had to be careful not to trip up on anything. Half way over the lawn, Bee stubbed his toe on the corner of a stone plinth. It hurt, but he didn't make a sound.

As they approached the front of the building both Pete and Bee saw some movement. They paused, to see what it was.

Bee whispered, "It's a cop."

Pete tapped him on the shoulder and whispered his reply, "Let's go that way," and pointed.

"Okay."

They silently scurried off and headed around to the other side of the house. No one was about and Bee said that they'd better be quiet or the copper would hear them.

The house was clearly no longer a home. All the curtains were open and it was possible to peer in through the clear glass. Pete did exactly that and he saw a light in the background. Someone was in there. So, he levered the window apart and broke the lock. Seconds later, they were inside what appeared to be, a ground floor spare bedroom. Only, there wasn't a bed in there.

"Come on," said Bee and they moved over to the door frame. Around which, was an electric light glow. Bee cautiously opened it and saw that the place was empty. He listened for a what seemed like an eternity and then he turned back to Pete and waved him through.

They were now at the bottom of the stairs. There wasn't a sound: anywhere. So, they carefully turned right, walked up the staircase and arrived in Hem's study. The lights were on and there was a strange acidic smell in the air. Like a faint whiff of cream soda. Bee went over to the desk. It was unlocked. He began rifling through the contents. Pete stood guard at the door.

Pete knew that Bee was looking for something. But, he also knew that if he asked what it was, then he'd get his head bitten off. So, he kept quiet and played along.

It was unusual for Bee to be this calm and it showed a side of his character that few had ever seen. Unlike his cousin, he was highly educated. He had actually passed an O level. To Pete, that meant he knew what he was talking about and you never argued with that level of a man. Did you?

Bee gave a sigh, "It's not here," he said.

"What?"

"The old man always said that Hem had a contract. He borrowed something like half a mil' from Sudo. That's how he started up. If we can get hold of it, then we can get the old prat to sign his business over to us."

"Why?"

Bee's voice began to rise, "Why? You stupid or something? He killed Jeff. We ain't got no income anymore. Meanwhile, he's off doing what he sodding likes."

Pete nonchalantly nodded. It sounded right. So, that's what this was all about. He opened up, "My guess is anything like that would be with his solicitor."

"You cretin! How the bloody hell could he have a dodgy loan placed with them? It's got to be in here. Somewhere. Has to be!"

"How about that wall safe?" Pete pointed and Bee blushed bright red. "We need the code. Can't blow it; with a bobby downstairs. Can we?"

Bee was angry again and he was having considerable problems coping with the size of this dilemma. As often happens, when you can't cope, emotions bubble to the surface.

On the floor and around the desk, there were any number of screwed up papers. None of which met his needs, but in his pocket was a packet of matches. And in a moment of unreserved zeal, Bee struck one and lit the edges of the amassed sheets. It began to flame up, nicely.

Whilst this was going on, their voices had been steadily rising and the officer outside the front door began to pick up that something might be taking place inside. He radioed his observations and, in the peace of the night, a small entourage of quiet police vehicles cozied up to the property. They disembarked their contents and headed for the front door.

Pete heard them coming and said, "Run!"

They both headed for the room's bay windows. Bee looked out of one and waved Pete over. Next, they opened it wide. Below them was the raised glass structure of a swimming pool roof. It kept the pool area warm in the winter months. But, in the summer, it could be pulled back towards the house: leaving an exposed pool below. At that moment the frame was tucked back, against the brickwork. So, the end of the pool was open to the fresh air.

Bee could see, that providing you were careful, it should be possible to pace your way along its outer metal edges. Where there were some steel supports.

Bee and Pete rapidly shimmied down the brick work and began walking along it; until they reached the end. Then, they jumped and plopped themselves into the deep end of the water. A few minutes later, they climbed out and ran off into the darkness.

Inside, the police entered an empty room, which was alight with flames. They quickly took to using a dry powder fire extinguisher. It instantly killed the fire. But, the assailants had reaped their opportunity and succeeded in getting away.

***

Chapter 38
Steady as You Go

Jenny was trying to stay calm. She seemed to have been through such a lot in such a short-tempered time frame and she was beginning to lose her self-confidence. She felt both tormented and lost. All these emotions and all the commotion of numerous conversations were still echoing around inside her head: and that didn't help. She felt that she should say something. But, what she was thinking truly appalled her. Even so, as the discussion waned from one poor strategy to another, she finally looked up and spoke out. It came straight from the heart. "Why don't we kill them?"

Everyone completely shut up and looked at her. She suddenly felt like an empty gold fish bowl on display.

"What did you say?" Petula quietly asked.

"Well, I was thinking. If they come back to kill us again, and I know they will; then we have to call the police. But, they will arrest Wilbur. So, the only other way is to shoot them to death, isn't it?"

Someone coughed and everyone changed their position to look at Wilbur. "That's not a good idea, Jenny," he said. "These two are stupid human beings and you need to be clever. Otherwise, they win. They also have friends. Friends who we have never seen before. They have contacts and those contacts can send other people, in their place. People, like me; to do their dirty work for them.

"They pay well and so they have little difficulty in buying what they want. They don't pay to negotiate. All they want is what you can give and you must provide precisely what they demand; or you are dead.

"My life has been one long journey of dealing with people like these. If you are good enough, then you live, but only as far as the next contract. My contract is over, but to some, it's incomplete.

"One thing is for sure; there is money here. Vast amounts of money and most of it is illegally obtained. These two men are the rough end of the stick. But, I don't presume they matter. If we blow them up, others will appear and they will continue to appear until we deal with the apex."

"Meaning what?" said Sondra.

"Sudo was the lynch pin and Hem was his strumming guitar. I never listened properly. I didn't pay attention. I had no cause to. Only, now, I realize that I should. Sudo had far more money than he should have and Hem always needed ready amounts of cash. Some of it to inflate his legitimate business. But, once he got it, he was happy. He really didn't care where it came from or what Sudo did, to get it. At least, as long as he wasn't personally involved.

"The thing is, life is rarely that simple. Put another way, he is involved and the only way to deal with this situation is to stand up to his mysterious masters and show them what they have created."

"Do you think that these two are running their own show?" said Petula.

"I'm not really sure. It could be that they are just out for the revenge of old man

Jeffrey. It's that, or they have been sent to see us off and collect a cash reward from some mystery leader."

Petula said, "I never saw any mysterious characters. Hem always lived his life locally. Few people ventured in."

Sondra chipped in, "He used to visit Sudo and Sudo used to see him. At least, they did, from time to time. They liked spending time on that golf course. Sudo didn't really speak to me and I always felt that their relationship was plutonic. No sparks there."

"Except, the money," said Wilbur.

"Perhaps," said Sondra. "Either way, I think these two sparrows are well outside of their nest and they're gunning for you. We are not really all that important. Even Hem has no need to shoot me. Least of all, now he knows that I don't want anything."

Wilbur and Petula nodded. "Point taken," he said. "Coming back to our problem then. It seems that I need to reorganize things a little.

"I'm sure they will come back and most probably tonight. So, I think it's better, if you all go." He looked across the table. "Petula, can they stay at your home?"

"Of course. But, does Hem know about it?"

"I wouldn't worry," said Wilbur, "If he does, he won't say much. Simply because he will just be a part of their cargo. I can't see them harming him, unless they have to and I can't see him telling them any more than he has to. Call it mutual disrespect."

With that, the girls all packed their over-night things and, one hour later, 52 Mount Terrace decanted itself into the serenity of complete quietness.

Once they had left the office, Trevor drove away. But, Hem made him stop and asked to be taken home. Trev wasn't sure that was a good idea. But, Hem insisted. He said that he wanted to pick up his BMW. It was parked near the garages. It would also be a good pretext to see if the police would let him in.

Hem thought that Bee and Pete would be far too preoccupied with Wilbur to bother about him anymore. So, they drove around and then came up to the house. The gate had been pinned open and the driveway was clear. But, as they came along its length, they could see several police cars. They could also see several officers running around in the grounds. Something must be going off.

Trevor said, "I think we need to abort this one, guv."

Hem tapped him on the shoulder. The car stopped and the next thing, he got out. Then, he told Trevor to go and waved him off. If all went well, he would catch up with him later on. With all the commotion going off, he calmly walked over to his prize car, got in and drove away.

Meanwhile, Bee and Pete had been sprinting for all they were worth. They had covered the grounds, at break-neck speed, and were just a few yards from their truck. That was when they saw Hem coming out of the drive-way in his BMW. Bee saw him first. He fired a shot which glanced off the windscreen and Hem threw his foot to the floor. Bee called to Pete and they hurried straight over to their truck.

Hem was now driving away, at break neck speed and making good progress. He was thrilled to bits with Trevor's help. He had been brilliant. They had actually got out safely and in one piece. The car was moving fast and he was set to get well out of harm's way.

At the same time Bee was riding high and Pete was thoroughly enjoying the experience. The truck had some punch to it and Bee was soon spoon feeding it to nearly ninety mph, on the speedo. It took just a few minutes for Bee's headlights to line up on Hem's blue car. "Clip his wings," he shouted to Pete.

Pete reached behind the seat and pulled out a small firearm. He pressed the button and lowered the electric side window. Then, he calmly took several ill aimed pot shots. The first of which spun off the rear window.

Inside, Hem knew exactly what was going on and who it was. He also knew that being scared had its advantages. Because, although he really wanted to drive away, he knew that they would not stop until he was dead. So, at eighty-four miles per hour, he decided a new approach and firmly hit the brakes.

Bee was generally a good driver. Anyone he hit was totally intentional and rather than demean himself with unnecessary insurance matters, he generally killed the other party at the scene. This time however, he was caught out.

The four by four was doing ninety-two miles per hour and coming up again on Hem's BMW, when he braked with such a force that the truck went straight into the back of the car. The impact was so powerful that Pete sailed straight out of the open-window. The truck lost its grip and toppled clean over. It repeatedly topped and tailed over and over; until it stopped, at the bottom of the road embankment. Then, it sank into a ditch. The lights went out and all that could be heard were the fresh screeches of car tyres, as the wounded BMW tore away for cover.

Hem was now in charge again. He was feeling a rush of positive vibes feeding into his rampantly ascending soul. He came around a blind bend at ninety miles per hour and then flew though the village of Beede. All, via the empty ring road. Where he headed out again, straight for 52 Mount Terrace and the Omregana Guest House. It took all of fifteen minutes to get there and he was pleased to see that the street was practically clear of traffic. He pulled onto a metered lay by and quietly exited his dented car.

Bee was still conscious. Although, there was some bloody snot running from his nose. He could also hear Pete calling out.

"Are you okay?"

He shouted back, "I feel like I broke my arm. But, it still moves."

Pete stuck his head in through the window and said, "Really? Are you okay?"

Bee asked, "How the hell did you survive?"

"I fell into something wet. It stinks like horse shit. Only it isn't."

Behind them was a huge brown cesspit; filled with liquid chicken excrement. In the background, there were security lights on and the smell was holistically toxic: it reeked.

Bee laughed and Pete came up with a smelly grin on his face.

"Are we gonna live through this, bro?"

"You bet!"

The truck was all bent up, but despite its forceful tumble, it was still upright. Amazingly, Bee was able to restart the engine and drive it back onto the road. Pete got out and checked the lights. In an astonished high-pitched voice, he said, "They're all working!"

Bee then said, "Let's fuck off then," and he put the scarred truck into first gear. With that, it coolly pulled away into the pitch darkness.

The Ormregana Guest House was in a quiet street and during the off season it was not unusual to find workmen doing a variety of structural repairs. 52 Mount Terrace being the latest to open itself up for prospective invitations. A passing police car noted that the usually bright shiny door was now missing. There were bits and pieces of material in the entranceway. Not all that unusual so, it calmly carried on its way. Inside however, the mess was a little more apparent.

In his recklessness, Bee had shot at everything he could. Walls were strewn with enormous round bullet holes and the first flight of stairs had lost most of their balustrade. The bullets had chopped them off like a pair of sharp scissors. That level of force meant, all that remained were a line of spiky balustrade posts. Sharp, thin pieces of wood were sticking up, all over the exposed edge of the staircase. The carpet was also torn away, leaving an uneven serrated edge.

For some reason, the stair frame looked significantly less secure than when Jenny, Sondra and Petula had walked down it. After they had gone, it seemed to have degenerated. Developing a severe list, from the wall. It must have loosened itself from the wall fixings. It also wobbled, when you walked on it.

As you went up, doors had been shot off their hinges and visible holes could be made out through the balcony landings. A great deal of work would now be required to make the building safe and respectable again. Even the lights didn't work properly anymore.

Wilbur had reasoned that the two men would be likely to want his blood. After all, he had killed their uncle. Knowing what they were, meant that vengeance potently drove every sinew of their beings. They couldn't exist unless they had appeased the cause of their pain. They would kill every one, in their way, just to get at him. No one was safe and there was no doubt about it.

Wilbur was content to believe that. He had also prepared himself accordingly. But, what he didn't expect was to hear Hem, ambling across the dismantled door. He was still wearing his slidy leather shoes and crying out, as he slipped himself into the hallway. All of this at eleven thirty in the evening. Even if he had, he would never have imagined that he'd be calling out to Sondra, like a possessed wimp. Something was clearly wrong.

Wilbur was purposefully quiet and sitting upstairs in the total darkness. His back was resting against the deceased grandfather clock. This had allowed his eyes the precious time to attune themselves to his surroundings. Although he couldn't see everything, he could see clearly enough to spot any sudden movements. What was intensely annoying was the current behaviour of the character in his sights.

Hem was repeatedly shouting, "Sondra! Sondra! Sondra!". All; at the top of his voice. He was also gingerly climbing the creaky staircase and panting like he was about to explode. By the time he'd reached the first-floor landing, he noticed that the balustrade was completely broken away. So, he walked away from the open edge and rubbed his shoulder against the wall. All of this, whilst he was still calling, "Sondra! Sondra!"

This was beginning to irritate Wilbur. Not least, because he needed to hear when the two main culprits arrived and not five minutes after they had stormed their way into this shell of a home.

All things being reasoned, he waited for a break in Hem's repeated words and then leapt in with the eternal phrase, "What the hell to do you want?"

Hem instantly stopped and shut up. He turned his head along the dark stairway. "Is that you," he said.

Wilbur was now angry, "That depends... which 'you'. You are talking about?"

Hem went silent and then, in his more normal down beat voice, he said, "Wilbur... I thought it was you."

"And?"

"You'd better be prepared for this."

"What?"

"Those two bastards are coming to kill you and Sondra."

"I know."

That confused Hem for a moment. But then, he remembered who he was talking to and carried on, "How do you know?"

"It's my job to know and I feel that we have adequately covered this richly fertile ground before. What, exactly are you doing here? Do you want a room?"

Hem wasn't finding this easy. But, he was resolved not to piss his pants again, so he tried a new approach. "Those two sods have just tried to take me captive, bring me here and then kill all of us. They blame me for killing Jeff and they want you, because you pulled the trigger."

"Why do they want Sondra?"

"Because she's mine, I guess."

Wilbur stood up and began strolling down the stairs. As he walked, he said, "That's not true."

"I know." Hem was aware that their voices were getting closer.

Wilbur went on, "So why are you talking to me?"

"Because you're here."

Wilbur sighed. He'd more or less had enough of this conversation by now, "Will you please ingratiate me with something interesting or I'm strongly tempted to do their job for them."

A frightened Hem replied, "Look, I know we have had our differences and I appreciate what I've put you through. But, we've got to get out of this alive."

"We do?"

"Yes, of course we bloody do! They won't stop until we're all dead. And I don't see anything in that for either of us. So, for God's sake do something!"

At that point, Wilbur heard a screech and some kind of a heavy car door slam shut. He tapped Hem on the shoulder and quietly whispered, "They're here. So, Keep your mouth deadly shut or I'll make it a permanent arrangement. Understood?"

In the shay of the darkness, Hem simply nodded his head. And they both retreated up a few of the carpeted stairs.

Bee was full of himself. Striding out like a midpoint marathon-man. He came at the door like a bull in a ring and proceeded to clip his toe again. This time, right on the edge of his shoe. As a result, he went face over tit and slid along the shiny door surface. As he went down, so did Pete, and the two men began to quarrel.

Once the pain had subsided, Pete was able to stand up again and Bee grunted himself back onto his feet. He felt along the wall and flicked the light switch up. Nothing happened. Then came the quality words, "What the fuck!"

Pete said, "What?"

"The bloody lights is what."

"What?"

Bee spun around to his fellow mate. "Listen prat face, the fucking lights don't work. Got it!"

"Maybe we should have waited."

"Great words of fucking wisdom from wigwam Pete!"

"So what do we do?"

"Well, I can't see fuck at all. Is there a light in the cab?"

"Dunno."

"Well go and take a fucking look!"

Pete did exactly that.

Moments later he came back with a bruised light which shone a weak and very yellow beam into the solid darkness.

Bee said, "Is that the best you can do?"

"It's this or nothin'. The other one's bust."

Bee sighed and took the light. Which he forcefully banged against the wall. After that, it glowed a little brighter. Then dimmed down again. He began to mutter, as he walked away up the stairs. "I'm gonna kill these fuckers. I really am. Every fucking one of them. Not one bastard is going breathe for another fucking day.

"I want that fucking Wilbur and that cow of Hem's."

"Sondra?" said Pete.

"You fucking know who I'm fucking on about."

They climbed the first staircase and were half way up the second flight, when Pete became aware that they were bouncing around.

Bee suddenly stopped and asked, "Are you limping?"

"Yup! After all the excitement, my leg is cramping up."

"Well, we'll go an' get some grub when this is done."

"Don't think that will help now."

"What will?"

"Good soak in a bath of hot…?"

They were now close to the top of the second stairway and Pete had just seen something. He didn't know what it was, but it stopped him speaking. Bee turned, with what remained of the light and pointed it in his face to ask a question. "What's up?"

That was when, there came a colossal 'thump!'.

Under their feet, an entire section of stairway fell completely away from the wall. Throwing them out and into the open air. They drifted, effortlessly, right across to the centre of the vacant hallway. With nothing to hold or take grasp of, they fell. They fell thirty feet, straight down the middle of the opening until they landed on the sharply exposed balustrade posts; on the lower staircase.

Both men fell and both men landed on target. Behind them, came a wimpish torchlight which shattered on the open floor space and became one of a million separate pieces.

Up and on the third-floor landing Hem let his breath out and said, "I assume I can talk now."

Wilbur said, "I'd strongly advise you to listen first."

At twelve fifteen a.m., the two men calmly made their way down a steel ladder railing. It was there, in case of a fire and ran down the entire exterior of the building. It took them down, into the small back garden of the broken Omregana Guest House. Once there, they casually walked through an unlocked swing gate and over to a conveniently parked vehicle. One, which appeared to have been deliberately parked there.

Wilbur took to the driver's seat and started the engine. As they drove, he let the air settle between himself and Hem. The journey proceeded in silence and so it was Hem who broke the ice first.

"Where are we going?"

"Somewhere safe."

"That being where, exactly?"

"That being wherever you need it to be. Are you staying in a hotel?"

"I was. But, if you drive me there, then they'll hear the car."

Wilbur shook his head.

"What?"

"You've done so very little in this miserable world. I'm surprised you're still alive."

At that moment the car glided to a halt at the cross roads between 'Street Green' and 'Hambeltons Way'. Wilbur turned to face his guest. He offered a half full bottle of whiskey. "When you get out, swill some of this around your mouth. Wander into the reception area, but don't stop unless someone is there. If they are, go over and be sure to breathe on them. Make a civil comment and then go quietly to your room.

"Do not make any unnecessary noise. Oh, and do take the advantage of a good night's rest. It may be the last you get for a while."

Hem suddenly looked spooked.

"What is it?"

"I've been having nightmares," he said.

"Then drink the drink and wash them away."

The passenger door swung out and then clunked shut again. Wilbur wasn't in the least bit interested: he just drove away.

Hem found himself on the empty roadside. He made steady progress to the hotel. But, his eyes were constantly darting about everywhere. Not that he was bothered about the hotel staff. He was far more concerned that, that bloody woman: Surely, might pop out of the undergrowth again and go, "Boo!"

Wilbur discreetly lodged the old car next to Petula's little Peugeot. He dimmed the yellow headlights, swung the tired door open and placed the sole of his clad foot onto the pavement, then something stopped him. He felt it. So, he purposefully paused to listen and was reassured to find that it was remarkably quiet. Everything was wrapped up in the mystic charcoal of an earthly darkness. No lights were visible at this depth. Happy with the scene, he turned to pick one sweetie out of his liquorice packet and there she was again. Glowing, as real as life.

"Hello Surely. I was wondering when we'd meet again."

"Good evening, Mr M, how are you?"

Despite only wearing his tired incarnation, he watched her with a warm sense of sincerity. She was even more striking, than before. Her dark, glossy hair was ribband and spilling down over her shoulders. She shook her head and, once again, it swept back into a seamlessly perfect form. It was hypnotizing. Yet, Wilbur was now aware of the feelings which she raised and so he tempered his emotions carefully, "A little better than at our previous meeting. Remarkably, I now have a beautiful woman of my own to love."

She warmly smiled, "That's good and it pleases me. I was very concerned about your loneliness. No one should ever be alone in this world. It's so cold here." She visibly quivered.

"Why have you come, at this hour?"

"Strangely enough…" her hand became real and it began to stroke his arm, "…I needed to find you… alone."

"Because?"

With a deep, longing sigh, she murmured, "Because I have something to say, my love and you know how I adore telling you things."

Wilbur was aware that this female was enjoying every moment of her show. Illusive she may be, but alluring too and sensual with it. Her actions were definitely affecting him.

"Where do you come from?" he asked.

She gave an alluring look and smiled, "Why, you should already know."

"And why should that be?"

"Well, my darling, you created me."

Wilbur gazed at her and revealed an open mouth. He quickly racked his senses and then reasoned, that her words did, in a way, make some kind of sense. Only, he couldn't recall attending any formal lessons.

Surely was clearly enjoying his movements and she went on, "I bear your image. The one you wanted me to have. Only, as with all created beings, I have become me and you have lost the control. I live where I do and I do as I do. Strictly, because of my needs and your imagination. But, it is you who makes me real."

Wilbur listened and said, "How could I possibly have made you? You are your own. You come and go as you please." His back was starting to ache and he turned slightly, to ease his seating position. "And I have heard others speak about seeing you. How do you explain this?"

"You are the one who created me. No one else sees me as I am. How can they? They do not know me like you do. Only you...."

"Please, go on..."

She changed her tone, "You seem to have garnered a new friend?"

"Sorry?"

"Hem: he seems to be developing a conciliatory tone towards you. Do you like that?" Her eyes lit up.

Wilbur was sedated with her words. They made little in the way of sense. So, he stopped asking and looked into her and she allowed it. He really wondered where it was, she came from. Then, he recomposed himself and aimed his best shot of a reply, "I believe Hem is an utterly repulsive man. I don't know why I am saying that. But, he is. He will corrupt and manipulate everyone he can. Simply, to meet his own ends. At the moment, Sondra hasn't asked for much. So, he is balmy about the situation. I don't believe it will last. It can't. The man is soleless. Is that what you are looking for?"

She shook her head again and her hair settled into a newly sweeping genre. "I'm so pleased that you have listened. Don't trust him, for he will turn on you. Such is his kind. If it were possible; he would turn on everyone. Even if there were no need on earth to do so.

"He is inarticulate and he heavily preys on the weak. He can't help it and he won't restrain himself on any account."

"Meaning, he'll try to kill me."

"I think you already know the answer to that question."

"And Sondra?"

"He really hates his spouse with an uncalled for intensity. Partly, because he never loved her to begin with. He is full of nothing, but jealousies. So, his heart isn't interested. He feels betrayed. Especially, when he doesn't get what he wants. He also feels that being a man, he should be attracted to her. But he isn't, so it is convenient;

if it is all her fault.

"It's a wonderfully convenient flaw. If he confided in her and confronted his own ghosts, then he would find the happiness he craves. Instead, he seeks the blinds and shutters which may betray his soul. He is miserable. Therefore, he hates to see other people who are happy.

"Don't let him dent you. Money is his weakness. He wants it. Even though he has excess and it gives him no pleasure in return. If you give him the promise of money, then he will always leave you alone."

"And me?"

Surely, tilted her head a little and her face looked deeply touched by his question. It was her mark of respect. The respect of two people who know one another well. It was also open and the strength of it saw her appearance change. Like a queen adorning her regalia, inside the formalities of a robe. She became even more alive. Radiating with the vibrancy of colour and a deep sense of presence. "You, my love, have a very special place before me and it pleases me that you occupy it.

"I am not the one for you. You know that now. But, all I will say is; love her with all your heart and let her love you with all of hers. That way, no one can separate you. The rest of the feast will take care of itself." She looked sad, for a moment and said, "You know that I love you. I always did, from the very beginning. Know it and feel it, for all of your days."

There was a fraction of a second when he thought he had heard something. Her expression had changed. So, she must have heard it too. He turned to the right and there was Sondra, at the garden gate. He came out of the car, stood up and as he turned to close the door, he caught a whiff of something deeply aromatic. A fragrance, all alone, in the night air.

Sondra came over, "Were you speaking to someone?" she said.

"If I were, where are they?"

She looked inside the vacant vehicle. Then, she turned and gave him a longing deep kiss.

***

Chapter 39
And Life Carries On

Hem was chuffed with himself. After a few days, his home was released by the police and he was allowed to return to his house. His house it was and his house it was going to remain. Everything in it belonged to him and he spent a small fortune on buying another new security system. He also signed the new divorce papers and Sondra's solicitors set keenly to work on the process.

He felt that he had finally turned a corner. With Wilbur and Sondra out of the way he would be free to take up the reigns of his business again.

Sudo, it appeared, had a clause in his will which allowed Hem to gain full control of his business. He was absolutely over the moon.

Wilbur decided it was time to adopt a new name and that was when Tony Peterson made an appearance. When the police called to Jenny's guest house, they insisted on interviewing everyone. The fact that they had all been at Petula's ruled them out of the events and it seemed that the stair way, on which the two deceased men had been walking, was structurally insecure.

In the newspapers, it seemed that there were no unusual finger prints at the scene, and no one was in the house when it happened.

Jenny, took the bait and decided to use the winter months to completely refit the whole property. With some insurance money, she rebuilt the interior and, by the new holiday year, things were well on the way to completion. By late spring, it would all be completely done.

As promised, Petula bought Jenny an engagement ring. Everything was in place for their marriage. Only, they still couldn't make their mind up about when that would be. Petula wanted it to be in the spring, whereas Jenny desired the warmth of a late summer month.

One vexation in their relationship was Jenny's desire to see Petula's mother. Petula defiantly didn't want her to go. Yet, despite her protestations, her mum and Jenny did want to meet up. She was still deeply uncertain as to what would happen. Especially, if her mother's tide came up too fast for Jenny's shoreline to cope with. Still, she had to concede that they would all meet up on the wedding day. So, maybe, she just had to let it happen and see what developed.

Sondra and Tony Peterson flew to the airport in Jersey, where her mother and father had them collected. The spring was yet to arrive, but the weather there was remarkably kind. The sun shone with all of its early seasonal warmth.

The divorce papers came through in the summer and they married in the autumn.

By that stage, Hem was again involved in another conspiracy. The fullness of his face was cast across almost all of the tabloid headlines. He had acquired another construction company and borrowed heavily to fund it. As a consequence, he was out to cut costs and somehow or other, he now appeared as the man who had defrauded his shareholders. Something about him buying their shares ex-dividend, but they hadn't received a dividend in the first place. He argued that a loss-making company didn't have any provisions to make the payments. This was a legal technicality and firmly a lawyer's tasty issue.

That aside, all was going extremely well and things were evening out nicely. Hem was well and he even had a new boyfriend.

Suddenly, it was seven p.m. on a mid-August evening and the doorbell was ringing again. No one was in the house at this hour. So, Hem discretely went down the stairs to see who it was. When he opened the newly alarmed door; there stood Brian and Adrian. In front of them both was a dirty, beaten-up suitcase and it was full of someone's money…

***